The
ADAT

By

George Donald

SIX WEEKS PREVIOUSLY

Jumah prayers had been over for almost an hour when they met within the crowded rear stockroom of the small corner grocery shop in Handford Road in Ipswich.

A ripple of anticipation run through four of the five men and the air was charged with fervour.

Fadi Hussain, at just nineteen and the youngest of the five men, was excited at being included in the meeting and scratching at the soft hair on his chin, his knees jerked rhythmically underneath the wide table. Upon the table lay a plate of dry crusty bread, a collection of chipped mugs and two jugs of water. At the head of the table sat Rahib Chowdhury, ten years Fadi's senior and leader of the group who despite his youthful age the group acknowledged as their Sheikh.

"We need to do something, show them that we mean business, that they can't just ignore us!" The fair haired speaker, at thirty-three years of age the oldest of the group, banged a fist down onto the table. Unlike the other members of the group, he had not been born into Islam but converted four years previously when he changed his name from Joseph Crocker to Abdul-salam Nasher.

"And just what do you propose?" asked the heavy set man sitting opposite who stared curiously at Nasher. Aarif Sidiq had celebrated his twenty-fifth birthday just two days previously, but already wore the hung dog expression of a man in his fifties.

"What I propose," Nasher snarled at the smaller man before turning his glance to Rahib, "is that we take executive action; find somewhere, do something that the kafir will not expect. Something that…"

"Enough!" they turned to see that Rahib had raised his hand for silence and held their breath, for the four men realised the moment had now arrived and they stared keenly at the slim man.

"For too long, my brothers, we have met and sat and discussed this issue. For too long," he stared at each of them in turn, "we have trained and promised ourselves that we would strike, that we would inflict upon the kafir the hurt and pain that they daily inflict upon our brothers and sisters and our children in the holy lands. For too long," his voice softened, "we have sat and enjoyed the tales of daring of our brothers who carry and continue to carry the fight to the kafir in those lands. For too long we have sworn to undertake to bring the fight to the kafir in his homeland. While others suffer and sacrifice," he reached forward and disdainfully struck with the back of his hand at the plate of crusty bread, causing the bread to scatter upon the old, wooden table, "we sit in comfort in the land of the kafir and do nothing!"

He paused to let his words sink in, then with a sigh, continued. "We have trained and dry practised in the hills of Wales and now," he paused for effect, "now we are ready."

He slowly turned his gaze upon the man seated to his left, his eyes narrowing as he stared at the scars upon the face of Abdul-hameed Muhammad, scars received when the former al-Qaeda fighter had the misfortune to be caught standing near a Toyota Land Cruiser that was ferrying his Emir when it was targeted by a British military drone strike in the Helmand province of Afghanistan.

Rahib hesitated, for he knew of Muhammad's constant fear of electronic surveillance by the dreaded MI5, but reasoned that prior to the arrival of the others, the scarred man would have painstakingly searched the room to ensure it was clear of bugs.

At last Muhammad asked, "The equipment, my brother; you are certain the equipment will be available to us?"

"It is as you asked, mukāfiḥ (fighter)," answered Rahib. "The long arms and the tight sweaters," he grinned at the toothless Muhammad whose gums also bore scars where his teeth had once been, but removed some years earlier during a four-month interrogation by Pakistan's security service, the ISI.

"My contact has affirmed the delivery will occur in one week," Rahib smiled and with a soft bow, he addressed all and added, "I do not wish to offend you, my brothers, but perhaps you will understand when I say the time, date and location of the delivery and place to store the equipment is best left to me."

"Hamdullah. As it should be," Muhammad interjected.

"How will you decide where we must strike, my brother?" asked Abdul-saleem Nasher, his eyes shining brightly and his question indicating how eager he was that after so many years, he might at last strike a blow for Allah and prove his loyalty to his Faith.

Rahib's brow furrowed and he reached forward and lifting a piece of bread from the table, dipped it into his glass of water before placing it in his mouth. Thoughtfully chewing at the bread, he swallowed before answering, "After the delivery, there will be another day of training in the hills of Wales. Once we are satisfied that the weapons are suitable and you are all proficient in their use, we will set a date. However," he sighed as though in pain, "it is no secret, my brothers, that the police in the major English cities, London, Birmingham, Manchester and their dogs of their secret service constantly watch our people; watching and spying upon us even as we pray."

There was a mumble of consent and nodding of anger.

"It pains me to admit that even among us," he turned to again stare at each individual, "there are those the kafir have turned and bought with their gold to betray us, vile dogs that they are," he spat on the wooden floor, spraying little pieces of bread mixed with his saliva. He licked at his lips and continued, "I studied and considered for a long time where we might inflict the maximum damage with the minimum of resistance. Some place where the kafir will not guard or protect as well as the English cities. A place that will attract worldwide attention. A place where many kafir throughout the western world will call home, either truly or ancestral."

He paused for breath, seeing he had their complete attention and smiling, continued. "During my study, my research if you will, I read an old book, a kafir book," he explained, his hands extended as though in apology, "that boasted of the invincibility of the British Empire. A book that recounts the glory of the second city of the British Empire."

"The city that I have chosen we strike," he paused and grimly smiled, "is the former second city of the kafir Empire. Glasgow."

CHAPTER ONE

The dismal fall of rain saw the midday pedestrians scurry back and forth, most being office workers who had risked the light downpour to visit the numerous snack bars and takeaways that flourished in the heart of the city centre.

Limping along West George Street, the hood of his anorak pulled tightly down over his neatly trimmed hair, he cursed his stupidity. Another job down the drain because he couldn't keep his mouth shut and shaking his head, continued towards the Employment Agency premises in Albion Street.

For the first few days it had seemed that he might settle into the call centre job in Bothwell Street, dealing with the in-coming insurance queries. Nothing that he couldn't cope with, he had thought. But then again he hadn't bargained for some of the demanding and occasional foul mouthed customers he had to deal with nor remembered that his calls were being monitored by the supervisory staff.

Supervisory staff?

He shook his head and sighed. Kids. Young men and women in their early twenties who because they could work a bloody computer thought they were the bees' knees.

Bollocks, he was better out of there before he did one of them some damage.

Not that he'd hit a woman, not even the young lassie who instructed him to turn off his computer and come to the quiet room for a chat.

A chat? More like a bollocking, he grinned at the memory.

"Now, we can't speak to customers like that, can we?" she had begun, using the royal 'we'.

"She called me a useless shit because I wasn't fast enough attending to her complaint," he had reminded the young woman.

"Well, that was no reason to tell her to eff off," she had sweetly replied with a fixed smile.

He hadn't intended reducing the young woman to tears and felt bad when he saw her lip trembling, but stupidly had lost it and his temper got the better of him when he told her where to stick her job.

Ah well, he thought, no point in writing to them for a reference then.

He glanced up at the cloud filled sky and sighed again.

He had lasted just five weeks and four of those weeks had been spent training for the job.

It had been long in the planning and now, this wet, miserable and damp Tuesday, it was time.

The journey north in convoy had been long and boring with just three comfort stops at motorway service stations.

None of the five men had even been north of Birmingham and crossing the border into Scotland, cheered each other that at last they were nearing their goal.

Travelling in the stolen, blue coloured Skoda Octavia ahead of the white Transit van, Aarif Sidiq drove as Rahib Chowdhury dozed in the front passenger seat while Fadi Hussain curled up in the rear seat, fitfully slept.

Driving the Transit van a quarter of a mile behind the Octavia, Abdul-hameed Muhammad grinned at Abdul-salam Nasher and said, "Tell me truthfully, brother, were you surprised that I am so proficient with the weapons and the explosives? Did you doubt me, wondering if I spoke boastfully? I will not be offended."

Hasher's eyes narrowed and he considered his reply. "I must say, brother that you did surprise me. When you spoke of your ability with the rifles and the vests…" he grinned, "the long arms and tight sweaters, I thought is this truly happening? Are we at last to strike at the kafir?" He shrugged and nodding forward through the windscreen, continued. "I did not doubt Rahib's passion or his commitment to the Jihad, but I confess to doubts that his rhetoric would come to this day." He slapped his hand at his chest and slightly bowing his head, added, "For that I utter my apology to Allah, praise His name, to you and my brothers. I am unworthy to accompany you on this quest."

"Do not worry, my brother," Muhammad favoured Nasher with a toothless smile. "Your effort and mine this day will make up for any doubts that lingered with you," then suddenly raising his head, shouted, "Allāhu Akbar!"

Grinning, Nasher punched at the roof with a fist and loudly repeated, "Allāhu Akbar!"

In the Octavia, Rahib Chowdhury shook his head as though to clear it and reached to the floor and lifted the two-way radio.

"My brother," he spoke into the microphone.

"Brother," Nasher in the Transit van replied.

"We are approaching a service station at the place called Hamilton. We will meet there for a last minute briefing. You are satisfied you have not grown a tail?"

Unconsciously, Nasher turned his head to peer at the passenger wing mirror and replied, "Nothing that I can see, brother."

"We will park at the furthest corner of the service station and watch for you entering. The same routine. Drive slowly twice round the car park and we will watch for a tail. If we fail to flash you an all clear signal, you abort and take the first opportunity to return south. If the kafir try to stop you, you have the…means. Understood?"

"Understood."

He glanced at his watch and remembered he had left his lunchbox in the refreshment room fridge.

Bugger it, he shook his head. No way was he going back for a plastic box and the corn beef sandwiches it contained. He stopped at the junction of Wellington Street and West George Street and reaching into his pocket, checked what change he had in his pocket. He knew there was a ten and a five pound notes in his wallet, the money that would have to suffice till his pension hit his account on Friday. Sweeping the hood from his head, he fetched his dark coloured plaid cap from his pocket and pulling it tightly down onto his head against the drizzling rain thought at least there's enough for a newspaper and a pint in the Counting House and continued walking eastwards towards George Square.

Satisfied they had not been followed, the Transit van pulled in alongside the Octavia and stopped. Rahib and Fadi Hussain got out of the car and into the van by the back doors while Sidiq remained in the car to act as lookout for the cursed kafir police.

In the rear of the van Rahib squatted with the other three men and said, "Once more, my brothers, I stress upon you this is not a suicide mission. Allah has other uses for you and you *will* survive today." He stared meaningfully at Muhammad and Nasher in turn and forcefully told them, "You have chosen to wear the vests, my brothers, but hear me. You will not use the vests unless there is no other option. The virgins are there for you, I swear, but *not* today. Now," his voice grew softer, "let us go through the plan one more time."

He withdrew a sheet of paper from an inside pocket of his jacket and holding it open for them all to see, snapped his head around and said, "Fadi. Your position?"

Fadi gulped as though with the thought that this is real, this is actually happening and replied, "After we exit the van and the brothers go forward, I cover their rear. I wait beside the back of this building," he used a bony forefinger to point on the map, "and when they call me, I move forward to here."

"Mukāfiḥ?"

Muhammad manically grinned at being called 'fighter' and replied, "I take the lead and advance along the street, here," he pointed to the map. "I execute any kafir who dare oppose us and continue along this route, here. I continue to lead through this area and rendeavous with you at this point here."

"Good. Abdul-salam?"

"With Aarif Sidiq as my wingman, I follow Mukāfiḥ's lead and take down…" he saw Rahib grimace and his face flushed, said instead, "execute any kafir who get in the way. About this point here," he pointed to the hand drawn map, "Aarif and me collect what prisoners we have taken, order them to kneel with their hands on their heads and execute them."

Rahib stared hard at him before reminding him, "Your prisoners will likely include women and kafir children. Can you do this, brother? *Can* you send the devils to their God? I know you have never before…"

"I can do it, brother," Nasher hastily interrupted, his teeth gritted. "I have trained for this and yes, I will follow Mukāfiḥ's example. I will make you proud."

"It is not I who you should make proud," Rahib leaned forward to awkwardly place a hand on Nasher's shoulder. "It is Allah, praise his name, whose pride you seek."

"Praise his name," the others echoed.

A grave silence fell upon the four men, broken when Rahib said, "Get ready."

He limped through the stationary traffic to cross the road and entered the Wetherspoons with the intention of having a pint, but instead ordered a coffee and picked up a 'Metro' newspaper lying on the bar.

Taking the coffee and newspaper to an empty table, he sat down and began to read. It was the appeal on the inside page that caught his eye and he smiled.

It had been a long time since he had donated.

Rahib cast an eye over the three men, now similarly dressed in black cargo trousers, heavy Doc Martin boots and faded military jackets, purchased from several secondhand militaria stores throughout the greater London area to dispel suspicion. Muhammad and the six foot Nasher seemed particularly bulkier than the slightly built Fadi because of the bomb vests they both wore.

Each man clutched an assault weapon and wore extra magazines in military webbing pouches slung about their body.

"Good," Rahib smiled, a lump of pride in his throat. "You have your masks?"

They each held up black coloured ski masks.

"I will send Aarif to get dressed. When you are ready, use the radio and then follow me, remembering to keep your distance."

He took a deep breath and said, "You have planned for this, my brothers. You are the spear of Allah," his voice rose, "You are the curse of the infidel! You are the killer of kafirs! Make me proud! Allāhu Akbar!"

"Allāhu Akbar!" they loudly responded.

He left via the rear door and glanced about the car park before opening the driver's door of the Octavia, then told Sidiq, "The brothers await you, Aarif."

As Sidiq climbed out of the car, Rahib took his arm and quietly said, "Take care of Fadi, my brother. He is…" he paused and licked at his lips. "He is young and impetuous. He might…"

"Do not worry, Rahib," Sidiq grinned at his lifelong friend. "Fadi will not…*none* of us will fail you. Assalamu alaikum wa rahmatullah."

"And peace be upon you, my brother," Rahib hugged the smaller man to him.

He supped the last of the coffee and folding the 'Metro' slipped it into his anorak pocket. At the door, he glanced upwards and saw the drizzle had for the time being stopped and stepped out into the rain sodden pavement. Not one to trust the Glasgow weather, he returned his cap to his head and continued to walk eastwards again, crossing West Nile Street at the green light and turning into Nelson Mandela Place where he stopped at the junction. Smiling at his decision, he turned left and strode towards the Blood Donor Centre, passing the advertising billboard outside the ornate entrance before making his way inside.

Rahib glanced in the rearview mirror and saw the white Transit van some distance behind. He carefully observed the speed limit and glancing up, saw the signs that indicated the M73 and the M74 motorway that led to Glasgow.

He startled, realising the M74 motorway sign that indicated the route to Glasgow might be confusing for the brothers. He turned left onto the slip road that led to the M73 and unconsciously slowed, incurring the wrath of a truck driver behind and quickly glanced into the rearview mirror. His blood chilled. Did the brothers see him take the slip road?

He exhaled with relief when he saw the nearside indicator of the Transit van flashing as the van turned onto the slip road.

He pushed open the door of the brightly lit large room where he saw the beds arranged throughout the room. A reception desk was to his left and making his way there, he was greeted by an attractive redheaded woman in her late forties who startled when she saw him, then smiled and said, "Can I help you?"

He was used to people being surprised at his appearance and no longer took any offence, accepting that it was just the way things were.

"Ah, it's been a while since I donated and I was thinking, I've got time to kill, so…"

"You've donated before then?"

"Eh, yes. But not for some time."

"Right," she turned to her desktop computer, "can we start with your name and date of birth, please?"

"Ian Macleod," he replied and gave his date of birth.

"So, that makes you forty-one, Mister Macleod."

"Aye, that's right."

Her brow furrowed. "I'm sorry, I can't seem to find your record on the computer. Was it here at this centre where you last donated?"

"No, I was in the military when I made my donations. I take it your system isn't linked?"

"No," she smiled and reached for a clipboard, "but what I'll do is get you to fill out this form and the nurse will have a word with you, if that's okay."

"Sure, that's fine," he smiled back at her and took a seat opposite her desk.

His mobile phone lying on the passenger seat beside him, chirped in the robotic male voice and directed him off the M8 motorway down a slip road past a large hospital to his left. The Satnav in the Transit van would direct the others off the M8 Motorway at a place called Charing Cross and then through the north of the city towards the road where they would first set the explosive charge then abandon the van before beginning their assault.

In the front passenger seat of the van, Nasher could almost feel his heart beating faster than he had ever known and sneaking a glance at Muhammad who was driving, wondered at the coolness of the former al-Qaeda fighter.

"After 100 meters, take the right hand off ramp to Charing Cross," said the monotone voice of the Satnav.

"Right hand off-ramp?" repeated Muhammad, shaking his head. "Where else in this forsaken country of the kafir is an *off* ramp on the right hand side!" he spat in disgust.

In the rear of the van, Fadi giggled, though Sidiq suspected the younger man's laughter was down to nerves rather than humour.

"Mister Macleod?" the smiling nurse stared down at him, but he saw her eyes betrayed her curiosity at his scarred face. "If you'd like to follow me, please."

She walked off without waiting and he limped after her towards a small corner of the room that was screened off with three, five feet high room dividing walls, creating a private cubicle.

"Please, take a seat," she gestured towards a plastic chair and sat behind a small, metal desk and took the clipboard with the form from him. "Now, Lizanne at reception said you have donated before, but not for some time. How many years ago, can you recall?"

He blew through pursed lips and replied, "I'm guessing about five, maybe six years."

"And that was where?"

"A base hospital. Camp Bastion in Afghanistan."

"Ah, right," she stared with narrowed eyes and said, "Forgive me for asking. Can I take it you have been through surgery yourself?"

He unconsciously reached a hand towards the left side of his face and grinned, "What gave it away?"

The nurse blushed and pretending to read his completed form, asked, "When was your surgery, Mister Macleod?"

"Just over three years ago. Surgery to repair damage to my face, the left side of my head," he patted at his damaged half ear, "and to my left leg, hence the limp."

"Did you or do you know if you were transfused during the surgery?"

"I received emergency surgery in the field, nurse. I understand I was given a number of units of plasma."

"Oh. I'm not certain if…"

"Don't know if it helps," he interrupted with a shrug, "but I've donated blood since that time."

"Really? Where?"

"I wasn't immediately retired from the military. A few weeks after I was wounded and when I was medically stabilised, I was repatriated to a rehabilitation wing of a hospital down in England. During that time while I was in physio rehab I donated down there."

"Oh, well…"

He could see she was uncertain, confirmed when she said "Can you give me a minute, please?" and left him alone.

He arrived at the rendeavous point and for a moment, panicked for he stupidly passed by the exit door, but did not immediately see the entrance to the car park. Driving round the block and back on himself, he sighed with relief then pulled the car into the covered car park in Montrose Street. Switching off the engine he sat for a moment to calm himself, then made his way to a coin machine to purchase a parking ticket. Returning to the car he fetched the second parking ticket from his inside jacket pocket and stared at it.

He had not told the others, preferring to keep the information to himself that one week previously he had driven to Glasgow in a hired Transit van. He had used this very car park to leave the hired van while he reconnoitered the area, familiarising himself with the streets and roads and detailing the information that his team would use during their assault upon the city centre; an assault he had been told was assessed to take no more than five or six minutes, but would inflict substantial damage to the kafir and the public's confidence in their police as well as the British Governments promise that they were safe from Islamic terrorism.

He had also been told that the Scottish police's armed reaction to the assault would take longer than the few minutes his team needed to complete their mission; a straight forward run through from point A where they debussed to point B, the pick-up point and during that run the team would inflict as many casualties as possible in the given time.

Once his previous weeks reconnaissance was completed he had driven the hired van to Edinburgh and left the van in a long stay car park at Waverly station before catching the train and returning south. It was his decision not to inform the others of their escape route for the simple reason that in the unlikely event if one or more were taken alive and confessed the route home to the kafir police, they would assume that route would be via the M74 and not as he had planned, through Edinburgh to the east coast route and the A1 south. He smirked at his own cleverness, for the short distance from the Montrose Street car park to the M8 motorway was but a few minutes and once on the motorway, while the kafir were hunting his team, they would be long gone and en route to Edinburgh and towards the second van. Even if by chance the kafir had identified the registration number of the Octavia, they hunt for the car travelling south on the M74 and not east towards the kafir capital city.

He smiled and squirmed into his seat.

He had planned everything to perfection.

Nothing could or would go wrong; of that he was convinced.

CHAPTER TWO

The sergeant strolled through the corridor to the refreshment room and pushing open the door, poked his head into the room and said, "Daisy, have you finished your break yet? That's another complaint about the woman begging down in Buchanan Street. Get yourself down there and either tell her to give it up or give her the jail. Your choice, hen."

"Right, Sarge," she nodded and lifting her chipped white enamel mug, slurped the last of her tea. Lifting the mug, she swirled it round in clean water at the sink and set it down onto the draining board to dry.

"Needing a neighbor, hen?" asked the old cop sat at the table.

Turning, she smiled at William Murphy, known throughout the Central Division as Spud and shook her head. "No, you're all right, Spud. She's just a bloody nuisance, nothing to suggest she'll give me any trouble. But thanks anyway."

"No bother, hen; you know where I am if you need me," he nodded.

Aye, in the back staff room of the Pavilion Theatre playing pontoon with the doormen, she inwardly thought.

Grabbing at her utility belt, cap and fluorescent jacket, she made her way to the door and prepared herself to hoof it down to the Buchanan Street precinct.

He had been watching the blonde haired Mary Forbes since she started at the firm almost three months previously and sought any excuse to speak with her, but never had the opportunity to exchange more than a few words. Now, holding his breath, he approached her desk with his new phone.

"Ah, Mary, I was wondering," he nervously began. "Do you know anything about mobile phones? I mean, the camera bit of it?"

She smiled up at him and his heart almost melted. "Why, is there a problem with it? Just take it back to the dealer," she suggested.

"No, it's not a problem," he shrugged and added, "I'm just not great with mobiles, that's all."

"Right," she held out her hand, "let me see it here."

Sandy handed her the phone and watched as she slid out from her desk and stood up, turning towards the panoramic window of the office that looked out from the first floor of the building onto Nelson Mandela Place below.

He stood behind her, staring at her slim neck and sighed, watching as she operated the phone and turned it to camera mode.

"Here, look," she handed him the phone. "It's dead easy, Sandy. Just turn it to the camera arrow, point and shoot. If you want to record, it's this button here," she took his hand and gently placed his finger upon the button.

"Now," she guided him towards the window. "Have a look through the viewfinder. See what I mean? It's got great pixels this camera. My sister's got one."

He pretended to look through the small viewfinder and grinned. "Yes, I can see what you mean. Thanks, it got me a wee bit confused."

"Did it?" she smiled knowingly at him and to his surprise, winked before settling herself back down at her desk.

The nurse returned to the small cubicle and smiling, said, "Is it okay for you to wait another few minutes, Mister Macleod? The doctor will have a word, but she's just speaking to another donor at the minute?"

"Aye, I've nowhere to be anyway," he replied.

"Brother, are you there?" the hand held set crackled.

Rahib snatched at the radio and taking a deep breath, replied, "Go ahead, brother."

"We have arrived at the departure point."

Rahib had thought long and hard where they would abandon the Transit van, finally settling upon the roadway on West Nile Street, outside a cinema that was no more than two hundred yards from the target area. He had calculated when the Transit van exploded it would impact upon the kafir who were at that time in attendance at the cinema and with luck, blow down the exterior walls and cause multiple casualties inside the building.

The short run down West Nile Street would then bring the four brothers to the start of their target area where the slaughter would commence.

"Prepare yourselves, my brothers," he eagerly cried into the microphone.

It was fortunate the divisional van was passing when Daisy exited Stewart Street office.

"Give you a lift, copperhead?" cried out Mickey Allison from the driver's seat.

Daisy grinned when she saw his tutor cop, Joan Crawford reach across from the passenger seat to slap the back of her neighbor's head.

Climbing into the van through the side door, Daisy was still grinning when she heard the matronly, grey haired Joan muttering, "Insolent bloody pup. No wonder you don't have a girlfriend, you obnoxious wee shite."

"Aw, come on mammy, I was only kidding," whined Mickey and turning, cheekily winked at Daisy.

Known throughout the Division as 'Mammy Crawford', the policewoman who was a little over a year away from retirement, boasted that he had shagged more senior management than any other woman in the Force and nobody could touch her because she knew all their secrets.

Daisy felt privileged to count Joan as a close friend.

"Where you off to, hen?" Joan turned in her seat.

"Just down to Buchanan Street. I've a complaint …well, actually, it's a repeat call. Some lassie at the begging. Apparently she didn't take the warning the first time I spoke with her."

"What, begging in Glasgow? Never heard the likes of it," snarled Joan, giving her unsaid opinion of what her city was coming to.

"If I let you out in Nelson Mandela Place, Daisy, will that do you?" Mickey said, but before she could respond, Joan asked, "Do you need a neighbor in case you lift this lassie, hen?"

"No, you're all right, Joan. If I need you I'll call in and thanks for the lift."

"Right, watch yourself," the older woman warned, as the van drew to a halt at the junction of Buchanan Street precinct.

Watching her stroll off, Mickey turned to Joan and with a smile, said, "She's a right looker, is Daisy. How come she doesn't have a man in tow?"

Joan, not one to gossip about friends though everyone else was fair game, thoughtfully replied, "There was a guy, but I thought him a bit of a prat, to be honest. I tried to tell her, but she didn't see it, not until she came to her senses and that's when it finished."

"Nobody since?"

"No," Joan shook her head and with a wry grin, said, "Why? You fancy her yourself, wee man?"

"There'd be something wrong with me if I didn't fancy Daisy

Cooper," he replied, then with his own grin, the twenty-three year old turned to face his neighbour before cheekily adding, "But I've always fancied an older woman, Joan, and I'm up for a bit of experience, so how's about it then?"
That comment earned him another slap on the back of the head.

"Well, the thing is Mister Macleod," said the youthful doctor, "with respect to your generous offer to make a donation, if you have received any kind of transfusion then it negates our opportunity to take advantage of your kind offer. Unfortunately," she tapped lightly at his completed form, "the rules have become so tight these days that since nineteen-eighty, we don't accept donations from patients who have themselves been transfused. I'm sorry, so you'll understand why we can't on this occasion take your donation."
He smiled and shook his head. "It's no problem, doctor. I just thought as I was passing I'd pop in and make the offer."
"Well," she stood and smiled, though he could see he was eager to get away, but told him, "even if we can't take your donation, Mister Macleod, don't forget to have a cup of tea or a juice before you go."
He watched her stride off towards a donor lying upon a bed nearby and thought, I can't even give my blood away and shaking his head at his shitty day, stood up and cap in hand buttoned his jacket as he prepared to leave.

With bated breath the others watched Muhammad carefully connect the detonator to the battery and just as he had been taught in the dusty hills of Helmand, hooked the trip wire to the inside handle of the rear door of the Transit van; the trip wire connected to the two beer keg bombs that lay hidden underneath the tarpaulin at the rear of the van. With a relieved sigh, he turned and grinned at the others and said, "That's it, my brothers. When the kafir come to check upon this old van, they will stupidly open the door and," to their surprise, shouted, "BOOM!"
Fadi almost fell back and the other two laughed nervously at his shocked face.

"Aarif," Muhammad turned towards the portly and heavily bearded man, "do not forget to take this," and shoved the two-way radio at him. He watched as Sidiq forced the radio into a breast pocket of his camouflage jacket.

"Now," Muhammad stared at them in turn and grinning wildly, pulled on his ski mask, "perhaps we should get out of the van through the front door, eh?"

Daisy Cooper, strolling along in the drizzling rain, wondered when the bloody weather would make its mind up. That's when she saw the young woman sat forty yards into the precinct with her back against the window of the fashion shop, an old scarf covering her head and a blanket wrapped around her shoulders. Her legs were drawn up as she huddled against the cold and she saw that the woman had placed a cardboard coffee cup at her feet in the vain hope of soliciting change from passersby.

Daisy had been a police officer for almost twelve years, mostly on the beat but with stints in the female and child protection units as well as a year-long secondment in plain clothes. During her service she had dealt with all types of individuals, but was embarrassed to admit she still had a soft spot for the homeless. It irked her that the council's policy of moving them on and away from the city centre was a priority for the police and she had often argued, to where? Cutbacks in the council's social departments had taken their toll and the charities were hard pressed to keep up with the increasing number of young people now living on the back streets and alleyways of Glasgow city centre.

Still, she had a job to do and hitching up her utility belt, began to walk towards the young woman.

Sandy Nichol stood up from his desk and arching his back, pretended that he was examining his new phone and moved towards the window where Mary's desk was.

Stood at the window, he slid the phone to camera and practiced taking some photographs of people in the street below, some with umbrellas held aloft as they hurried through the drizzling rain.

Ian Macleod courteously nodded to the receptionist Lizanne before limping to the door of the donor centre and towards the stairs that led down to the main entrance and into the street.

The four men, wearing their ski masks and carrying their assault rifles, burst out of the front doors of the van and began to loudly shout, "Allāhu Akbar!"
An elderly woman, standing across the road stared openmouthed at the men, then shaking their head at their nonsense, muttered, "Silly buggers," before she carried on shuffling up the street, dragging her shopping trolley behind her.

Oops, thought Ian Macleod, and awkwardly stooped just inside the entrance doors to tie his loosened shoelace.

Still stood at the window, Sandy Nichol sneaked a glance at Mary Forbes, but she turned quickly and catching him staring at her, she smiled at him and his face flushed with embarrassment.

"Look, hen, I sympathise with your predicament, I really do," Daisy stood with her hands upon her hips, staring down at the shivering young woman who she guessed was no older than late teens or twenty-something, "but you can't be sitting here in the rain, begging. Have you nowhere to go?"
The woman, wearing an ankle length deep brown coloured loose fitting skirt, brown leather sandals, a man's black coloured reefer jacket and her long jet black hair covered by a tight, brightly coloured headscarf and her arms wrapped about her, shivered with cold and shook her head, afraid to look up. A worn backpack that seemed stuffed was by her side with a strap looped around her foot, apparently for fear it might be snatched from her.
Daisy reached down and lifting the sodden coffee cup, rattled the change inside.
"Do you have any money at all other than what's in here?"
The young woman did not answer, but slowly shook her head.

With a sigh and compassion, Daisy reached into her trouser pocket and withdrew a crumpled five-pound note. "Here," she stuffed it into the coffee cup. "See that you get over to that Greggs down the road and get yourself something hot to eat. Mind," she wagged an admonishing finger to the startled woman, "Don't be spending it on anything else, do you hear?"

The woman, a girl really thought Daisy when she saw her smile, nodded.

"Aye, so you do understand English, then," Daisy grinned at her and from a pouch in her utility belt withdrew her notebook. From the inside cover, she fetched out a small business card and bending to hand it to the young woman, said, "Here, take this. This is the address of a charity drop-in centre down in Argyle Street, near to the M8 motorway overpass. Its run by a woman called Aileen Dee. Now, if she's not there, one of her staff should be able to help you out."

Hesitantly, the woman took the card and staring up at Daisy, didn't speak, but swallowed and simply nodded her thanks.

"Here, let me give you a hand up," began Daisy and reached for her, but stopped dead, for that's when she heard the rattle of gunfire.

Sandy Nichol turned sharply towards Mary and eyes widening, said, "Did you hear that?"

His lace tied, Ian Macleod stood upright and was putting his cap on his head when he froze. There was no mistake. He knew that sound better than most, a sound he had not heard for several years; the rattling sound of a 7.62mm semi-automatic Kalashnikov assault rifle, used by communist armies and terrorists alike and better known to the common man as the AK47.

In a loose diamond formation with Abdul-hameed Muhammad at the point, Aarif Sidiq and Abdul-salam Nasher behind him on either side of the road and Fadi Hussain twenty yards from him at the back, covering the rear just as they had practised in the hills of Wales, Muhammad moved forward, sending another burst of three rounds into the air as he strode fearlessly into Nelson Mandela Place, his rifle at the ready.

A bus driver turned to stare with horror at Muhammad who sent a burst of bullets towards the bus, watching as the windows shattered and the broken glass crashed down onto the terrified passengers who instinctively ducked, but not quickly enough for one young pregnant woman whose head exploded in a bright crimson spray of blood as she fell into the passageway. The driver slammed his foot down onto the accelerator and fought to steer the bus as it careered through the bend in Nelson Mandela Place and continued at speed away from the madman with the rifle. Muhammed fired more rounds at the fleeing vehicle, seeing them strike the rear engine casing, but the bus did not stop. He glanced at his watch, seeing that just a minute had passed since they exited the Transit van and they had at best five minutes before the kafir reacted to their assault.

Behind him, Nasher and Sidiq watched as pedestrians turned towards the sound of the gunfire then ran for the lives, seeking shelter in shops and doorways.

Grinning beneath his mask, Sidiq saw dozens of people running for safety away from the gunmen and fired a burst of five rounds down West Nile Street, watching as the bullets first ricocheted off a wall before striking a young man in the legs who fell badly wounded to the ground.

At the rear, an enthusiastic Fadi Hussain hysterically screamed, "Allāhu Akbar!" and then grinned when he heard the cry loudly repeated by his comrades.

Time to begin collecting the kafir for execution, Muhammad thought then saw an elderly couple tightly holding onto each other as they fearfully crouched against a wall to his right.

"Take them," he pointed and shouted at Nasher who moving towards the pair, hustled then from the wall then roughly pushed the old couple along in front of him, recalling from Rahib's detailed map there was a pedestrian precinct close by and just up ahead.

A woman with two small children stepped out in front of Muhammad, who pointed his rifle at them and screamed, "Get over there!" pointing with the barrel of the weapon towards the nearby wall.

Terrified, the woman dropped her shopping bag to the ground and clutching the wide-eyed children to her, did as she was ordered and was joined by the elderly couple.

"Kneel!" Sidiq screamed at the prisoners then indicated they place their hands on their heads.

Fifteen feet above street level, Sandy Nichol stared in amazement at what he was seeing, aware that Mary Forbes was at his side and with her hand to her mouth.

Ian Macleod hurried down the marble stairs to the entrance and standing to one side, saw a bus career at speed through Nelson Mandela Place closely followed by a man dressed in camouflage who entered the Place from West George Street and quickly walk towards Buchanan Street precinct. The man was holding at the ready an assault rifle that Ian saw to be an AK47.

He startled when he saw a second then a third man enter the Place, the third man pushing an elderly couple in front of him.

He heard a man cry out "Allāhu Akbar!" and the cry repeated by at least two perhaps three others.

"Fuck!" was all he could say.

"Use your phone…the camera," hissed Mary.

"What? Oh, yeah, of course," replied Sandy and switched it to record mode.

The two men walking up the stairs from the Buchanan Street Underground had not heard the gunfire and each carrying umbrellas against the drizzling rain, were laughing at one's joke when to their surprise they saw people running past them. Turning their heads to stare at the fleeing pedestrians, they hesitated before crossing the road towards the south side of the precinct.

They had no chance of survival when seeing them stood there, Sidiq lowered his rifle to his waist and cut loose with a vicious volley of a dozen rounds of copper jacketed lead bullets that cut through the men's bodies like a hot knife through butter and splatter shattered glass from the overhead canopy down onto their riddled bodies. Beneath his ski mask, Sidiq grinned as the kafirs bodies jerked like marionette puppets before they fell dead to the pavement.

Just as he had been taught, Fadi Hussain walked backwards into Nelson Mandela Place, his rifle swinging back and forth in an arc and his eyes staring through the slits of the ski mask as he watched the rear for any sign of the armed kafir police. Backing against the metal fencing that surrounded the rear of the building in the centre of the Place, he stopped and listened for the sound of his brothers executing the kafir prisoners, the signal that he was to continue moving east.

Presumably because of the inclement weather, it was fortunate that the normally busy precinct was quieter than usual that day, however, a number of people were still moving about and presented Muhammad with an opportunity for some target practise. He lifted his rifle to his shoulder and fired a burst through a large, plate glass shop window and it was then that he saw the kafir, the policewoman in the precinct with another woman and screamed at them, "Over here! To me, now!"

The homeless woman panicked and getting to her feet tried to run, but her leg became tangled in the strap of her bag and she got no further than a few yards before Muhammad shot her several times and watched her dance a jig as the bullets struck her. The woman fell face down to lie in a pool of blood that seeped from beneath her punctured body to spread in a wide arc among the rain sodden pavement.

Daisy, shocked and bewildered at the sight of the dead woman, turned her head to see a masked man pointing a rifle at her and beckoning her to him. Fearing she would be shot, she raised her hands and slowly began to walk towards him.

Two middle-aged woman, confused by the gunfire and carrying numerous shopping bags, exited the store at the corner of Nelson Mandela Place and Buchanan Street and walked into the horror of the two men being gunned down. Screaming, they turned to walk back into the store, but were prevented from doing so by Nasher who used the butt of his weapon to smash one woman in the face, breaking her cheekbone and knocking her into her friend and watching as both fell to the ground

"Over there, with the others," he screamed at them.

Weeping loudly, the uninjured woman stared in terror at the masked man and with difficulty, dragged her dazed friend to sit against the wall.

"On your knees, bitches!" Nasher hissed at them then as if to reinforce his threat or his own bravado, tilted the barrel of his rifle upwards and fired a burst of rounds into the air.

The sudden noise brought the women to almost hysteria, but staring at the wild-eyed Nasher, both complied.

Backed against the wall just inside the entrance to the building, Ian Macleod experienced a helplessness that he had not felt before. Sneaking a glance out of the door, he saw one of the men, the tail end charlie he guessed, standing with his back to the metal railings that surrounded St George's Tron Church, his body facing the road entrance to Nelson Mandela Place, but his head alternatively watching his front or turning to his left and away from Ian as the gunman sneaked a glance towards his comrades round the corner and out of Ian's sight.

He knew there was nothing he could, nothing that he could use as a weapon, yet his training, his very instinct told him to do something!

The emergency nine-nine-nine operators were overwhelmed as callers phoned in, screaming, "They've got guns! They're shooting everybody!!

"For fucks sake, get somebody down to Buchanan Street now!"

"They've shot and killed people!"

"There's lots of them!"

Or simply, "For God's sake! Help us! Help us!"

Muhammad reached forward and knocking Daisy's cap from her head, grabbed her by the hair, his fingers painfully twisting into her chestnut locks, deciding that for now he would keep her alive; a hostage in the event the kafir police arrived sooner than expected. Already he could hear the distant sound of sirens. She reached up to ease the pain, but he screamed at her, "Hands up above your head, kafir bitch!" and dragged her to one side of the precinct.
The policewoman grabbed at his hands with both of hers to ease the pain of his grip upon her hair, but he savagely shook her head to keep her hands away and again screamed at her, "I told you, hands up above your head, bitch!"
His breath was coming in spurts and he reckoned that two minutes had now passed, assessing they had just four minutes at most to cross over the area known as George Square.
He had a mental image of the map drawn by Rahib and knew they must hurry and make their way to meet with the Sheikh in the escape car parked in the in the car park on the other side of the Square.
He turned to shout at Sidiq and Nasher, but frowned, for they had not yet turned the corner.
Instead he loudly screamed, "Kill the prisoners!"

In the first floor office, Sandy Nichol, his body shaking, continued to use his phone camera to film the two gunmen who were forcing the people to kneel against the shop front window with their hands on their heads while Mary Forbes was filming the armed man standing just below the office window with his back to the metal fence. It was then from the corner of her eye she saw another man moving quickly from the entrance of the building where the Blood Donor Centre was towards the gunman and…her brow furrowed; what the hell was he carrying?

It was all he could find.
Taking a deep breath, his stomach knotting and silently praying his bum leg wouldn't let him down, Ian lifted the CO_2 fire extinguisher

from its wall mounted bracket and knocking out the safety pin, held the handle in his left hand and the hose in his right. With a final glance at the gunman, he saw his head was again turned away from Ian.

Moving from the main entrance door as quickly as his left leg would permit and keeping close to the wrought iron fencing surrounding the Church, he closed the gap on the gunman. Almost panicking, he saw the man's head begin to turn back.

Fadi Hussain's balaclava mask was annoyingly ill-fitting and kept slipping on his face, upsetting his concentration to recognise any threat that might appear in front of him. Peering ahead through the road junction, his peripheral vision caught movement to his right. He was in the act of turning his head to face this potential threat when Ian depressed the handle of the fire extinguisher, sending a stream of concentrated foam at the younger man's face.

Instinctively, Fadi raised both hands that held his rifle to cover his face, screaming in surprise when the white foam splattered against him and soaking the ski mask and the eye slits.

Without stopping, Ian swung the heavy metal extinguisher at the gunman's head, hearing it clatter off the stock of the rifle and striking the gunman's fingers that held the weapon as well as continuing to send a spray of foam everywhere.

Fadi fell back against the railing, screaming in pain from the blow that broke his fingers and eyes stinging from the foam as he tried desperately to bring his rifle around to bear on this madman who had attacked him, but Ian wasn't finished.

The impetus of the swing bounced the extinguisher back towards him and grabbing the handle with both hands, swung it against the gunman's head.

With a crack, Fadi's head was knocked backwards against the railing, cracking his skull and splitting the skin. He could feel the warm blood running down the nape of his neck. His knees were buckling as slowly, too slowly, he tried to lift the rifle again, but once more Ian swung the metal extinguisher and caught the gunman full in the face, breaking his nose and jaw.

Fadi's legs felt weak and he could no longer stand and was sliding to the ground when for a third time, Ian swung the extinguisher above his head and brought the base of it down with a soft thud onto Fadi's skull, causing slivers of bone to be broken off by the blow that pierced Fadi's brain, killing the gunman.

Ian stared down at the dead man, his body shaking with adrenalin, but then his military training kicked in and reaching down, he lifted the assault rifle from the broken fingers and tore at the bandolier on Fadi's shoulder, spilling out two full magazines that he stuffed into the side pockets of his jacket.

CHAPTER THREE

Muhammad, continuing to pull the terrified Daisy by the hair, one-handed fired a burst of rounds at a nearby shop window then heard the click as the magazine was expended.

Without warning he released Daisy's hair and as she stumbled, he grabbed the stock of the AK47 with his freed hand and used the butt of the rifle to strike her to the left side of her head, knocking her to the ground where she lay stunned, a trickle of blood seeping from her wound that dripped down her cheek to her chin.

While she was on the ground he quickly changed the empty magazine for a full one of thirty bullets and shoving the empty magazine into his bandolier, reached down and again grabbing the young police officer by the hair, pulled her to her feet.

"I told you already, you kafir bitch," he hissed at her, "hands held up high!"

Stunned, she lurched on legs like jelly and did as she was told, conscious that her radio was broadcasting reports of gunfire in the Buchanan Street area and her heart sank when she heard that all units were to standby from the area till armed response units arrived, estimating the first of those units to be five minutes away.

"So, bitch," Muhammad taunted her, "where are your crusader cavalry when you need them, eh?"

Grinning widely, Muhammad knew then that with the armed kafir five minutes or more away they would escape to the getaway car without meeting any armed opposition, then turned to stare at the corner, wondered why Sidiq and Nasher had not yet executed the kafir prisoners.

"Sandy," she whispered as though fearing the gunmen at the corner might hear her. "That man, that man down there; I think he's killed one of them and now he's got a gun! Sandy!"
"Wait, Mary," he firmly replied, concentrating on filming the two gunmen with the people kneeling before them. "Oh God, oh my God! Holy shit! I think they're going to shoot those people!"

The driver of the shot-up bus turned into High Street before he risked stopping and rushing from his cab, his eyes widened when he saw that some of the lower deck passengers had been shot. Making his way through the groaning and stricken passengers, he stepped gingerly through the broken glass to find the young pregnant woman, her hijab stained with her blood and her head cradled in the lap of an elderly man who himself was sporting a bloody facial gash and sitting with the other passengers in the passageway. With a tear stained face he looked up at the driver and softly said, "She's dead. The poor wee soul, she's dead."

Throughout the city, armed response vehicles, each two-man car crewed with officers wearing Glock pistols on their hip and carrying Heckler Koch semi-automatic weapons in locked cases in the boot of the vehicles, sirens sounding and lights flashing as they raced to the city centre while the reports of the gunfire continued to be broadcast. Many of those officers, male and female, licked at their dry lips and wondered; this is what I've trained for.
How will I react?
Will I do my job?

Ian cocked the rifle and saw that there was a round in the breech and let the cocking handle return, then risked a glance round the corner. He stared at his hands, surprised to see they were shaking.

Lifting his head, he could see that about thirty yards away two gunmen stood with a number of people…people? My God, there's kids there!

The gunman had forced their prisoners to kneel with their hands on their heads and had their weapons pointed at them.

"I will give you the honour, my brother Abdul," Aarif told him, glancing about him, but confident that there was no immediate threat near.

Nasher licked at his lips, his hands shaking as he stared down at the kafir.

This wasn't going to be as easy as he had thought. His throat was dry and he could feel his chest tight as his heart battered against his ribs. The old man and old woman stared up at him and his eyes narrowed for while the woman looked scared, the man looked…peaceful.

"Please," the woman with the children hugged them to her, terror in her eyes and bemusement in her children's eyes as she begged, "Please, don't shoot the weans! Not my weans! Please!"

He lifted his rifle and perspiring so heavily under his ski mask that he wanted to rip the fucking thing off, then pointed the barrel at the wailing women and the distraught mother.

An inexplicable anger overtook him and he thought, fuck the kids! They're all kaffirs anyway!

Taking a deep breath, his hands sweaty, he prepared himself to squeeze the trigger.

Ian Macleod, now thirty yards away, the Kalashnikov butted firmly against his right shoulder and his left eye closed, peered down the iron sights as he advanced towards the enemy just like he had been trained, knowing that these bastards would not surrender and forcing his body to stop shaking, exhaled and took aim against the taller of the two gunmen as he gently squeezed the trigger.

Though still tightly held by her hair, Daisy Cooper's terror had turned to anger and already accepting that she was going to die, gritted her teeth and prepared to have a go at the mocking bastard!

The two rounds, the double-tap fired by Ian in rapid succession, struck the tall gunman in the right side, the first bullet piercing his right arm then entering his lower chest and lodging in his right lung, but it was the second bullet that did most damage. The bullet entered his upper chest then deflected by a rib, tore through Nasher's heart. The very impact caused the tall Abdul-salam Nasher's body to spasmodically jerk as did his hands that released their hold on his rifle that as he died, fell with him to the ground.

Caught out that a threat had presented itself from where Fadi was supposed to be covering their rear, Aarif Sidiq turned and was raising his rifle to defend himself, but seeing the man already closing the gap with his own rifle pointed at Sidiq, realised with a sudden fatalness he was already too late.

Ian stopped and breathlessly adjusting his aim, fired two rounds at the second gunman, seeing the bullets strike the stocky gunman in the chest and watching as he fell backwards, his rifle bouncing onto the ground beside him.

Slowly continuing his advance towards the fallen gunmen, Ian shouted at the kneeling prisoners, "Get up! Run behind me! Find some shelter! Go! Go! Go!"

He did not take his eyes from the fallen gunmen, but was peripherally aware that the old man and the women were struggling to assist each other and the children to their feet. Still, as he advanced, he kept his eyes upon the two fallen gunmen his eyes widening when he noticed one of the gunmen's torso was bulky under the camouflage jacket he wore.

Now just a few yards from them, he fired again, one shot into each of the gunmen's head to ensure that they no longer presented a threat against him, watching their bodies jerk as the rounds hit home and tore their skulls apart.

Searching about him for further threat he saw the two business suited bodies lying ten yards away, both riddled and still.

And that's when he heard the scream from the precinct around the corner.

"Fuck you!" she grabbed at the hand that held her by the hair and lashing out with the toe of her Doc Marten shoe, felt her foot strike his shin with a satisfying crunch.

Taken unaware, Muhammad stumbled back and snarling with rage, released his hold on the policewoman who stepped awkwardly backwards, but somehow managed to stay on her feet. Cursing, he raised his rifle to shoot the troublesome bitch.

A mere five feet from the gunman, Daisy jumped at him, her chestnut hair falling about her face and mingling with the flow of blood from her head wound, but he skilfully used his rifle to sideswipe at her and watched as she fell heavily on to her face.

Turning, her teeth gritted, she stared defiantly up at him.

Sneering down at her, he raised the rifle to his shoulder and pointing the barrel at her, pulled the trigger,

Daisy flinched at the expectant impact of the bullet, but heard only a click.

Confused for a second, Muhammad realised when he had changed magazines, he had forgotten to cock the weapon and there was no bullet in the chamber.

Had Mohammad been British infantry trained and made that schoolboy error it would have cost him at least fifty press-ups or more likely a boot in the testicles from his instructor, however, he had been taught the use of the AK47 in a dusty valley in the north of Pakistan near to the Afghanistan border where weapon drill was not so strict.

The mistake not only cost Muhammad valuable seconds, but saved the young policewoman's life.

With a mocking grin, he reached for the rifle's cocking handle, but then felt a powerful thud in his back that knocked him down onto his knees, unaware the jacketed bullet that struck him had severed his spine. In shock he stared down to see blood oozing from a hole in his chest.

Astonished, he tried to turn his head, his arms already feeling weak and saw a man in a dark jacket walking slowly towards him. Sheer will forced his body round to see the man with the rifle fire again and shoot Muhammad twice in the body, the impact of the 7.62mm

copper-jacketed bullets spinning him around. He knew he was
falling and with a thud landed on his back, his rifle falling from his
unresponsive hands. With difficulty he raised his head and saw that
the man, now just yards away was again pointing his rifle.

He didn't hear the fourth report of the Kalashnikov nor felt the bullet
that tore into his head and splattered his brains across the wet
ground.

Stepping astride Muhammad, Ian stared curiously down at him and
seeing the girth of the fallen man's torso, with sudden realisation
muttered, "Oh, holy shit!"

Seated in the driver's seat of the Octavia with the window fully
open, Rahib Chowdhury could hear the distant crackle of the high
velocity rifles and grinned. The plan was working. The kafir were
being taught that they could not with impunity rape the lands of the
Prophet, praise be to his name, without paying the consequence in
their own city.

More importantly, he was carrying out the plan as he had been
instructed.

Anxiously he turned in his seat towards the pedestrian entrance to
the car park and switching on the car engine, watched for the arrival
of his fighters.

Ian Macleod had seen and dealt with four gunmen, but that didn't
mean there wasn't more about.

His head swivelling on his shoulders, the rifle held at the ready, he
softly said to the police woman on the ground, "Are you hurt?" and
reached down for her hand, though his eyes continued to sweep the
area about them.

"Listen to me! Can you get up?" he snapped at her,

"Yes," she breathlessly replied and though still dazed, took his hand
and scrambling to her feet, stared down at the dead gunman and
fought the nausea that threatened to overwhelm her.

"Can you make it to the side of the building," he asked her, his eyes
everywhere, seeking a new threat.

"Eh, okay, yes, I think so."

"Good, get over there and squat against the building. If we've got that at our back, then it will be a one-hundred and eighty degree arc and easier to watch for any more of them," he said, bewildered when he saw her waver from the path he indicated, then almost laughed when she stooped to recover her fallen cap.

Together they shuffled across the precinct, Ian walking carefully backwards and sweeping the rifle back and forth, listening for any further gunfire, but all he could hear now was sirens that were getting louder by the second. Crouching down beside her, he stared at her wound and reaching into his pocket, wordlessly handed her a clean, folded white handkerchief that she dabbed at her head.

"Who are you?"

"Me?" he grinned. "Just a guy that was passing by."

He saw the young woman lying face down on the ground twenty yards away. "That lassie over there. Is she…"

"Yes, I think so," Daisy replied and added, "but I'd better check." She almost made it to her feet, but Ian firmly grabbed at her arm and told her, "No, I can't be sure that there aren't any more of these guys about. Help must be on its way, so for now stay behind me, Constable."

"Daisy, my name's Daisy," she sighed, her lips trembling as she fought at the tears that now threatened to spill from her.

"Daisy," he repeated with a nod. "I'm Ian."

Her radio was still broadcasting, requesting that any unit in the area provide a situation report, a sit-rep.

"Alpha three-six-four," he heard her respond. "I'm in Buchanan Street precinct with a…" she stared curiously at him. "Who or what are you, Ian?"

"I told you, Constable Daisy, just a guy passing by. Here," he held out a hand for her radio, "Can I use that? I might have a better idea of what's happening."

Without protest, she handed him the radio and he said, "Control, I'm with Constable Daisy in Buchanan Street near to the junction with Nelson Mandela Place. Please take a note. There were at least four tangoes, all armed with high velocity rifles; so far?"

The controller wisely didn't ask Ian to identify himself, but took the view that information from any source was more urgent than protocol and agreed he understood by answering, "So far."

"No indication where, but every likelihood there might be further tangoes, not yet seen or identified. So far?"

"So far," repeated the controller, hurriedly scribbling upon his notepad

"At this time," Ian continued, "four tangoes down and slotted; so far?"

There was a definite pause before the controller responded, "So far."

"At least one of the downed tangoes possibly wearing an IED vest, so suggest EOD. So far?"

He could feel Daisy staring curiously at him and eyes still sweeping the precinct, grinned and quickly explained, "IED is the acronym for improvised explosive device, Constable Daisy. The EOD are the bomb squad, the Explosive Ordinance Detachment. Usually they're based through in Redford Barracks, in Edinburgh."

"What, they've got fucking *bombs* on them!" she stared, shocked, her eyes turning fearfully towards the dead gunman.

"Aye, well that one probably has," he nodded to where she was staring.

"So far," said the controller.

Ian raised the radio to his mouth and continued, "One confirmed friendly probably KIA in Buchanan Street precinct, two probable friendlies down and likely KIA near to Buchannan Street subway, so far?"

Again, the response, "So far."

Daisy didn't need an explanation for KIA; killed in action.

His head jerked up as a marked police car screamed to a halt in the road twenty yards away and he and Daisy watched as two police officers, both wearing bullet proof vests and carrying semi-automatic weapons, alighted from the vehicle and took up a position behind the vehicle, their heads swivelling as they secured the immediate area.

It seemed to them both the arriving officers had not yet spotted them. Blowing through pursed lips, Ian grinned and laying his rifle and the spare magazines from his pockets down onto the ground, said, "I don't think there's any need for me to use this now, Constable Daisy. I'm guessing you might want it for evidence."

"Wait here," she snapped and setting her cap upon her head, wincing as she did when the rim rubbed against her wound, she pushed herself to her feet and with her hands raised high walked towards the officers who beckoned her forward then pulled her down behind the car and out of Ian's sight.

He watched as a second and then a third police car screamed with screeching tyres into the precinct and discharged armed cops who began to spread out. Suddenly the police cars were joined by ambulances and there was a cacophony of noise of sirens, shouted orders and the wailing and screams of distraught civilians. It seemed to Ian that suddenly there were armed police and medical personnel everywhere and with the presence of the armed cops, dozens of people who had taken shelter in the nearby buildings began to emerge, standing in groups or being shepherded by police officers away from the location of the bodies on the ground.

He stood and decide to step away from the Kalashnikov, worried that some overzealous police officer might mistake him for one of the gunmen.

His body had stopped shaking, though he could still feel the adrenalin coursing through his body.

God, I couldn't half murder a pint, he inwardly sighed, still trying to come to terms with what he had done. He watched as officers, both armed and unarmed, fanned out and began to stretch blue and white police tape across the pedestrian precinct, tying it to door and lampposts.

A tall, young police officer with a roll of police tape in his hand approached and eyes narrowed, stared curiously at Ian's scarred face before asking, "Are you okay, sir?"

"Yes," Ian smiled. "I'm fine, thank you. I'm just waiting…"

"Aye," the officer cut him short. "Well, just wait down there, eh," he indicated with his hand towards the south side of the precinct where the civilians were being directed.

"Sorry, I don't think you understand…" Ian began, but the officer held up a hand to stop Ian speaking and interrupting him, said, "Oh, I understand just fine, pal, but this isn't the time for hanging around, so get your arse out of here or I'll take the time to arrest you. We're far too busy for rubberneckers, okay?"

Ian stared at him, but saw the young officer wasn't for arguing, so shrugging, replied, "Okay. If that's what you telling me, then I've no choice, have I?"

Turning he walked off and thought, *now* I'll find a pub.

Within twenty minutes Nelson Mandela Place and much of Buchanan Street precinct was cordoned off and cleared of just the essential personnel required to guard the area as the police awaited the arrival of the EOD to deal with the suspected bombs that were worn by the deceased gunmen.

Assuring the armed cops that really, she was fine, Daisy Cooper made her way back to where she had left the tall man, only to find he had gone with a young officer standing guard by the discarded rifle and magazines. She glanced up and down the precinct, but there was no sign of the man who called himself Ian.

"Taken a right dull one there, Daisy," the officer grinned at her, pointing to her head that was now wrapped in a makeshift bandage. "Where did he go?"

The cop's eyes narrowed, his face a blank. "Where did who go?"

"The guy that was here. The tall guy with the scars on his face," she indicated on the left side of her own face.

"Eh, what about him?" he nervously replied.

"Tommy!" she gritted her teeth, "*Where* is the guy that was standing here?"

He shrugged and realising that something was amiss, asked, "Was he important or something?"

Her nostrils flared and staring angrily at him, she demanded again, "Just answer me! Where is he?"

"Honest Daisy, I thought he was just a punter and that was hanging around to see what was happening, so I told him to fuck off."

Her mouth fell open. "You told him what!"

"Told who what?" asked the voice behind her.

She turned to see a balding, middle-aged man wearing a dark coloured raincoat standing listening, a pipe hanging out of the right side of his mouth. Beside him was a young woman about her own height and age who wore a pale blue coloured business suit and stood under a telescopic umbrella, staring curiously at Daisy.

"Sorry sir, but you are?" she asked, but already guessing he was some sort of boss.

"My name's John Glennie, Constable Cooper," he flashed a warrant card at her. "I'm a Detective Superintendent with the Counter Terrorism Unit out at Gartcosh Crime Campus." He turned to the woman and added, "This is Maureen McInnes, my Detective Sergeant," then he smiled as he added, "I like to call her Mo. Now, I'm told that you, young lady," he pointed the stem of the pipe at Daisy, "were in the thick of this debacle, so I'll ask you again; told who what?"

Daisy glanced at the red-faced Tommy and taking a deep breath calmly said, "We seem to have lost a witness, sir."

Glennie didn't immediately respond, but again using his pipe pointed at her bandaged head and slowly nodding, replied, "I think it best that Mo and I take you up to the casualty at the Royal Infirmary, Constable Cooper," then took her aback when he flashed a broad smile and asked, "Can I call you Daisy?"

She nodded as he continued, "And when you're getting that split head stitched you can tell us all about your missing witness, eh?"

He had waited almost ten minutes past the agreed time, but still they had not arrived.

Drumming his fingers uneasily on the steering wheel, he knew now that something terrible had happened, that the operation had gone wrong.

The sound of sirens continued to echo throughout the area.

He could wait no longer, deciding it would be catastrophic if the kafir police arrived and arrested him too.

But why would they, he reasoned. They could not know about him sitting here in the car in this large car park.

Not unless…

He glanced at the two-way radio on the seat beside him, tempted to go against his own instruction and call Aarif Sidiq.

His brow knitted. There had been no sound of any explosions.

If they had been in danger of arrest, why then had Abdul-hameed Muhammad and Abdul-salam Nasher not activated their vests?

There could only be one answer and his blood run cold.

They must be dead or so badly injured they were unable to activate the vests. Worse still, he inwardly shivered; they might be arrested. Better they are dead, he thought, than give the kafir the opportunity to interrogate them.

Unlike his team Rahib had formally dressed in a business suit, shirt and tie, reasoning that if there were any reason he was stopped and the police questioned him, a respectably dressed man would be considered less of a threat than one wearing a camouflaged jacket. Indecision coursed through him and his brow knitted for he was tempted to leave the car and walk towards the place called George Square and see what was occurring.

Still the sirens sounded loudly.

Now panic was beginning to set in and overtake him and decided then that if any of the team had been captured alive it was possible they had given him up.

It was as well, he sighed that he had not told them of the alternative escape route through Edinburgh and tyres squealing, hastily drove towards the car park exit.

Ian Macleod followed the police instructions to leave the precinct where it met Argyle Street and made his way through the curiously silent crowds and the media vans that were beginning to arrive and assemble at the hastily erected barriers. Knowing there was no likelihood of getting to the Counting House just off George Square, he instead turned left and hunched down against the drizzling rain, made his way to Sloans pub on Argyle Street.

Settling himself on a stool at the near empty bar, the pretty young waitress who drew his pint took great pains not to stare at his scarred face and conversationally asked if he knew what was going on in Buchanan Street.

"No," he shook his head and glibly lied, "I was just passing and saw the crowd. Probably just another one of these demonstrations against something or other."

"Aye," she agreed with a shake of her head, "and if people aren't careful, one of these days somebody is going to get themselves hurt."

CHAPTER FOUR

All the UK, European and most of the American television news channels interrupted their programming to report on the information that a terrorist attack had occurred in the Scottish city of Glasgow, one American channel embarrassingly informing its viewers that Glasgow was a major town located in northern England.

Details of casualties was at first sketchy with on-site reporters scrambling to interview anyone they could find who had a clue what had occurred.

In their office in Nelson Mandela Place, Sandy Nichol and Mary Forbes stood with their colleagues watching the situation unfold on the wide screen television in the refreshment room.

"Mary," Sandy whispered to her and with a nod, indicated she follow him out of the room.

In the narrow corridor outside, he glanced about to ensure they were not overheard and in a low voice, held up his mobile phone and said, "How much do you think the news channels would pay for exclusive footage of what we recorded?"

He knew right away he had made a mistake when he saw her face flush and her eyes narrow as she replied, "You want to make money out of what we saw? Jesus, Sandy! People got killed out there! What kind of arse are you?" and turning away, returned to her office to fetch her own mobile phone.

Quickly she scrolled through Google till she found the phone number for Police Scotland and called the number on her screen.

"Police?" she breathlessly began, seeing Sandy entering the office and staring contritely at her. "My name's Mary Forbes. It's about the incident in Nelson Mandela Square. Yes, that's right, I work here just above where it happened. Look, I've got some footage I took on my mobile phone. Who do I send it to?"

DS McInnes smoothly brought the CID car to a halt in a bay outside the casualty department at the Royal Infirmary.

Seated in the rear seat, Daisy Cooper was stunned to see three ambulances unloading injured and wounded people and a large number of nurses and doctors scurrying about as they accompanied the ambulance crews wheeling the patients in through the double doors.

Detective Superintendent Glennie turned from the front passenger seat and said, "Most of those people are off a bus one of the gunmen shot at. Killed a young woman, I'm told and wounded quite a few others."

He paused as the significance of what happened suddenly hit her and seeing her eyes widen, said, "Right then, Daisy, let's get you in there and fixed up, eh?" then without waiting for a reply, stepped out of the car and turning, courteously held open her door.

"Are you feeling okay there or do you need a wee hand," he smiled at her.

"I'm fine, sir, really," she returned his smile, but he could see her face was as a white as a sheet.

"No, Daisy, you're not fine," he replied and subtly nodded to McInnes.

Her legs now shaking, she stepped from the car and with him on one side holding her arm and McInnes supporting her on the other side, the three slowly made their way to the entrance doors.

He finished his pint and taking a deep breath, nodded his thanks to the young barmaid before leaving the pub.

Even though almost an hour had passed since he saw the first gunman, Ian Macleod's body was still shaking and he assumed that it was the adrenalin kicking in.

At least the rains off, he thought and shoving his cap onto his head, thrust his hands into his pockets. Deciding to walk off the shakes, he turned west onto Argyle Street and began the long walk home to his flat in the city's Anderston area.

Seated behind his massive desk in his office at the temporary headquarters of Police Scotland located in the Fife village of Tulliallan, Martin Cairney, the ex-rugby playing six foot five inch Chief Constable, stared at his newly promoted and recently appointed Head of Counter Terrorism, Detective Chief Superintendent Cathy Mulgrew.

"I have a briefing meeting in two hours at Bute House with the First Minister and the Justice Minister, Cathy. So, what can you tell me?" he asked.

She leaned forward from her chair and spread an enlarged map before him that displayed the immediate area in Glasgow city centre surrounding Nelson Mandela Place.

"This is the crime scene that we're dealing with, sir," she began, pointing with a manicured finger at a rough circle encompassing the streets about Nelson Mandela Place.

"Bloody hell, Cathy," he leaned forward to stare down at the map. "*All* this area is now cordoned off?"

"Yes, sir," she slowly nodded. "As you can imagine, it requires a large number of resources and I'm pulling in officers from all the suburban divisions to assist the City Centre Division with guarding the area. I've appointed Detective Superintendent John Glennie as the hands on Senior Investigating Officer, though of course I will have a watching brief and it will be me who'll accompany you to any press briefing. John's team will include detectives from both the Counter Terrorism Unit and the Major Incident Unit, roughly totalling fifty plus officers and will include HOLMES and clerical staff. On that issue, I'd be grateful if you will consider speaking with the Justice Minister for extra funding to pay for the extra officers whose rest days I'm going to have to cancel."

"Right, well, I don't see any option on that score. Now, the bad news. What's the casualty figures?"

She paused before replying, "Aside from the four gunmen that have been accounted for, we have six civilians confirmed dead. Two men shot and killed as they left the Buchanan Street subway. A young homeless woman who is still to be identified, killed in Buchanan Street precinct, a young Somalian woman travelling on a bus who…" she paused again and rapidly blinked. "The woman was pregnant, sir. Thirty-two weeks. An asylum seeker who had apparently fled the violence in her own country."

"That's four," he gruffly replied, aware that his own voice sounded shaky.

"An elderly woman on the same bus," continued Mulgrew, "who suffered a fatal heart attack that the doctors are initially attributing to extreme shock, but the post mortem will likely confirm that. The sixth death was a middle-aged male shop assistant who was caught in the gunfire when one of the attackers fired through a shop window on Buchanan Street."

"And the wounded?"

She glanced at her notebook before replying, "Two critically, one from the bus where the women died and one young man who was walking in West Nile Street who suffered leg wounds. It's the loss of blood that's concerning the doctors and if he survives, there is the likelihood he might lose one leg."

"And?"

"A number of others wounded, twenty-four at the last count. The injuries range from minor cuts inflicted when the gunmen shout out the plate glass windows of some stores to injuries sustained when people were running away in West Nile Street, several of whom were hit by metal fragments from bullets that struck the walls of the buildings before imbedding as shrapnel into the victims. One young police officer…" she glanced at her notebook, "Constable Daisy Cooper of the City Centre Division who was briefly taken hostage by one of the gunman. She suffered a head wound and shock. The head wound was treated with three butterfly stitches, so she'll be fine. Her shift Inspector has signed her off as injured on duty."

"Thank God she's okay," Cairney sighed. "What about notification of the deceased to their next of kin?"

"Once identification has been confirmed, I've family liaison officers stood by to make those visits. The only hiccup is the homeless woman, but as we speak, inquiry is ongoing to identify her by fingerprint or DNA."

"Good," he made notes on a pad in front of him. "Now, tell me about the bomb vests these gunmen were wearing."

"Well, fortunately we got a heads up about those from our mystery hero, but I'll speak more of him in a minute. As for the bomb vests, the army's EOD unit successfully defused the vests on two of the gunmen and the Captain in charge reported that both vests were viable IED's with pockets filled with steel ball-bearings, screws, small nuts and bolts. Had they been activated the consequence of their detonations might have caused multiple casualties to any persons stood within a thirty to forty metre radius."

"And this Transit van that has been discovered?"

Mulgrew allowed herself a quiet smile and said, "We had a wee bit of good luck there, sir. That's down to a wee nosy Glasgow woman who lives in the flats at Cowcaddens. When she heard about the incident on the radio, she phoned in to say she saw four men she had thought were students messing about, running out of a white coloured van in West Nile Street behind the cinema there. As soon as the control room received the information, they sent a unit to have a look. Fortunately one of the cops was immediately suspicious because the registration plates were for a different type of Transit van. The cop then called the EOD team to the van and the soldiers discovered it was booby-trapped. Apparently it was quite a basic detonating device, but any police officer examining the Transit van would have exploded the bomb in the back. My information is that the bomb was destructive enough to bring down the adjacent cinema building and likely killing everyone inside."

"Jesus H Christ," he shook his head. "These four men. What do we know about them?"

"Nothing so far, sir. They weren't carrying any identification, all were similarly dressed in combat camouflage jackets, black coloured cargo pant trousers, Doc Marten boots and all carrying AK47 semi-automatic weapons with spare magazines. As you know, two were also wearing bomb vests. One of the four is a white man while the three others seem to be of Pakistani or Arab origin. All were bearded and a rough guess at ages is anything between late teen for the youngest and early to late thirties for the oldest. Constable Cooper, the injured officer, is certain the man who held her hostage spoke with accented English. It might also be significant that a number of witnesses heard the gunmen shouting 'Allāhu Akbar' or something similar."

"Allāhu Akbar. Isn't that…"

"Roughly translated it's Arabic for 'God is Great' and that particular phrase has been heard shouted in previous acts of Jihadist terrorism."

"Where is she now, Constable Cooper I mean?"

"She was interviewed by John Glennie, who after getting her wound treated at the Royal Infirmary had her dropped home."

"Good. I'll make the time to pop in and visit her. See that my secretary has the lassie's address, Cathy."

"Sir," she acknowledged with a nod.

"Now, what about this man who killed the gunmen. What do we know about him?"

"Well, sir, we'd know more if some bloody cop hadn't told him to, and if you pardon my French, fuck off from the location. According to John Glennie, that's a direct quote."

"Tell me more," sighed Cairney.

"According to the witnesses who had been herded by the gunmen against a wall and who were quite certain the gunmen were about to shoot them, this unknown man appeared with a rifle that we assess he took from one of the gunman that he killed with a fire extinguisher."

Cairney, almost in disbelief, slowly shook his head. "A fire extinguisher you say?"

"Yes sir," nodded Mulgrew. "We discovered one gunman had been battered to death with a fire extinguisher. We believe that's where our mystery man obtained the rifle he shot the two gunmen with; the gunmen who were about to kill their hostages, then used the same rifle to shoot the man who was about to kill Constable Cooper."

"God, you couldn't make this up," muttered Cairney, who added, "So, this man accounted for all four gunmen?"

"Yes, sir."

"And after saving a number of hostages, one of my officers told him to *fuck off*!"

Mulgrew, recognising Cairney's rising anger, swallowed and replied, "Yes, sir. Apparently."

"And we do not know who this man is?"

"No, sir, at this time, we don't."

He drummed his fingers against the desktop and slowly exhaling, asked, "Do we know *anything* about him?"

"Well, we know his forename is Ian," she licked at her dry lips and added, "that's what he told Constable Cooper; that his name is Ian. She gave John Glennie a very good description, describing the man as being badly scarred on his left side and some of his left ear missing. He apparently also walks with a limp. Glennie run the description through the police PNC, but no hits, I'm afraid. The fact that he took down four gunmen would seem to suggest he is familiar with weapons and from what the controller who spoke with him has told Glennie, this man Ian used Constable Cooper's radio to inform the controller what was happening and used what can only be described as proper radio procedure and the controller said he sounded military. The man Ian apparently recognised that at least one gunman was wearing an IED vest and actually used that acronym, then cautioned the controller about officers touching the bodies. He also suggested the EOD, another acronym he used, be sent for. Apparently he told Cooper that the EOD were based in Redford Barracks in Edinburgh; I would suspect that's not commonly known."

"There's one other thing, sir," she added.

He sensed her hesitation and his stomach tightening, asked, "What?"

"After shooting the gunmen, witnesses and I include Constable Cooper, say this man Ian finished them off with a bullet to the head to each of the three gunmen he had shot."

"Do we know if they were alive or dead before this head shot?"

"No, sir, we don't."

"Oh, dear. When this ghastly business settles down, that *could* prove to be awkward," he exhaled.

The door knocked and without waiting for a response, Cairney's prim, middle-aged secretary poked her head into the room and said, "Sorry, Mister Cairney, but that's an urgent call for Miss Mulgrew," she turned her head towards Cathy and added, "It's a Chief Inspector Downes from the Media Department, Ma'am. I can transfer the call to Mister Cairney's desk for you?"

Cathy turned towards him as he replied to the secretary, "Yes, please do so," and pushed the phone towards her.

"Harry, you're on speaker and I'm with the Chief Constable."

"Oh, right, Ma'am. Good afternoon, Mister Cairney, sir," Downes formally replied.

"Good afternoon, Chief Inspector," Cairney replied, then added, "but let's dispense with pleasantries, Harry. What do you have for us?"

"I've just learned from an idiot on my staff that over an hour ago, a young woman contacted the Media Department to inform us that she has footage of the incident in Nelson Mandela Place. I regret my staff member didn't think to inform me right away and for that I unreservedly apologise."

Cathy suspected from her terse comment that Harriet Downes, known throughout the Force as Harry, was not best pleased at her staff's lack of urgency.

"Have you seen the footage, Harry?" asked Mulgrew. "Is it relevant?" then immediately kicked herself, knowing Downes would not have contacted her if it were not.

"Very relevant, Ma'am. In fact, the young woman, ah…" Cathy suspected Downes was checking her notes, "a Mary Forbes sent two footage items that were taken by her and a colleague. Both work in an office one floor up in a building located in and overlooking Nelson Mandela Place."

"Through the wizardry of technology, Harry," interrupted Cairney, "can you send that footage to my desk top computer?"

"Give me five minutes, sir, and it will be with you," then added, "I'll send the footage to Miss Mulgrew's police e-mail account."

"Thank you, Harry," he smiled at Cathy and ended the call.

"Time then for a coffee I think," and pressed the button to summon his secretary.

Ian Macleod arrived at his one bedroom first floor flat in Corruna Street thirty minutes after setting out from the pub.

The walk from the pub had given him time to reflect on what had happened; a three or four minute madness that saw him kill four men.

He thought again of his shock at hearing the familiar crack of an AK47 and swallowed hard remembering his indecision, whether to hide and ignore the gunfire or act as he did, as his training had taught him.

He hadn't fired a weapon for a number of years yet surprised himself how quickly it had all come back to him.

The first man he killed.

Man?

Though he had worn a ski mask, Ian suspected from his slight build the gunman was probably a teenager, but shaking his head reminded himself that teenager or not, he had been prepared to use his AK47 to gun down Ian.

The shooting of the second and the third man; those he had no choice for he knew, just knew, they were about to kill those people kneeling in front of them.

His teeth gritted when he recalled shooting the gunmen again as they lay wounded or dead. He had no regrets about the head shots, recalling Angus McCready from all those years before.

The likeable corporal had been a section commander in Ian's platoon; a young man with a bright future ahead of him in the Regiment. Or at least he had been till one fateful day after a vicious gunfight in an Afghanistan village, in a fit of compassion McCready went to tend to a wounded al-Qaeda fighter and kneeling beside the stricken man had been blown to bits when the fighter detonated a bomb-vest. Since that time, the standing order in the Regiment had been to dispatch wounded enemy combatants who continued to present a viable threat.

Locking the door behind him, he entered the neat and tidy, if slightly Spartan lounge and switched on the television, choosing the BBC twenty-four hour news channel.

As he thought, the gunmen's assault in the city centre was the main news with the ribbon at the bottom scrolling forward and disclosing the number of dead and injured.

He walked into the kitchen and switching on the kettle, made himself a coffee before returning to slump down onto the couch and settled down to watch the news.

An enterprising reporter and his cameraman had somehow gained access to a second floor window in a building overlooking the junction of Buchanan Street and Nelson Mandela Place and softly reported what the camera was seeing; a large number of uniformed police officers, some armed and white boiler suited personnel from the Scene of Crime Departments carrying out Forensic examinations. Two white tents had been erected over the bodies that lay in the precinct, though the reporter could not know these were the bodies of one of the gunmen and the innocent young woman that the policewoman had been so intent on helping.

Just across the road to the north of the precinct a third tent hid the bodies of the two men who had been murdered by Aarif Sidiq.

As Ian watched almost in disbelief, the ribbon at the bottom of the screen changed to report that a further, critically injured victim who was not named, had died of injuries received.

"Bloody hell," he angrily muttered, "that's seven people those bastards murdered!"

While the reporter in the building continued to comment on the police activity, a small box appeared in the top corner of the screen with the face of the anchor-woman who asked,

"Has there been any comment by the police on this attack, Peter? Is it as we suspect, terrorist related?"

"There has been nothing yet from the police, but I believe that the Police Scotland Media Department will be issuing a press bulletin sometime within the next hour, Fiona. All I can tell you is that I have learned from a source there were four gunmen involved in this shocking city centre incident and this source told me none of the gunmen survived."

"Peter, we're getting reports of a man who apparently tackled these gunmen and is responsible for saving a number of lives. Have you any information about this man?"

"Again, all I can tell you, Fiona," replied the reporter in a hushed voice that caused Ian to suspect Peter had no permission to be where he was, "is that some witnesses to this on-going tragedy told me earlier that a man armed with a rifle is responsible for shooting dead the attackers. Who this man is, I have no information, but it was suggested he might be either part of an undercover police unit or indeed perhaps even a member of a covert Special Forces team who the Government have tasked to hunt down these terrorist cells. Whoever he or they are, there's a debt of gratitude owed to them by those whose lives they saved today."

Shit, thought Ian; now I'm either in the SAS or a cop and gently patting at his injured left leg, smiled humourlessly as he muttered, "Seems you have your uses after all, gimpy."

Sitting in the lounge of her lower cottage flat in Kingsheath Avenue in the Rutherglen area of the city, Daisy Cooper, her arms wrapped about her and knees tightly locked together, rocked back and forth, the vision of the young homeless woman being cut down in front of her playing over and over again in her mind.

After he cleaned her wound and applied butterfly stitches, the casualty doctor had suggested keeping Daisy in overnight in case she suffered some concussion, but she had argued she was fine and no, she had not at any time passed out.

The detectives had been kind; the Detective Superintendent at the hospital offering to contact Daisy's parents and have them return from their Spanish holiday, but she had argued that since her mother's operation, the stress and worry had taken such a toll on them both they needed the holiday and she did not want to worry them. No, she had also insisted, her two brothers were living in England and she'd contact them in her own time.

Then the Detective Sergeant who had run her home, Maureen something or other, had lifted the photograph of Daisy and Billy from the sideboard. "What about this young man. Your boyfriend or a pal perhaps?" she had asked.

"Former boyfriend!" Daisy had snapped, but had not meant to forcefully snatch the framed photograph from the woman's hand as she did, then found herself apologising.

"No need to apologise, Daisy," McInnes had sympathetically replied, then more softly said, "Look, I'm still working, but I'm certain the boss won't mind if I stay here for a while with you," and glancing at her Detective Constable neighbour, saw him nod his agreement.

"Thanks," Daisy had replied, "but honestly. Other than a sore head, I'm fine."

"Well, fine or not young lady," McInnes had surprised her by placing a comforting arm about her shoulders and pulling her close, "I'll leave my number and that will be for two reasons. If you recall anything that can help us, phone; if you need somebody to talk to, phone. I'm making that an order, Daisy. Understood?"

Her lips trembling at the Detective Sergeant's kindness, she smiled and barely managed to mumble, "Yes, Mo, understood."

That had been over an hour ago and now here she was, a blubbering wreck.

Then she heard the loud knocking and sighing, rose from the couch and rubbing with her sleeve at her eyes, made her way to the front door.

Opening the door she startled for there stood her pal, Joan Crawford who wearing a civilian jacket over her uniform, held a litre bottle of vodka in one hand and in the other hand, held a brown paper bag that smelled suspiciously like chip suppers.

"Jesus, Daisy! I leave you alone for five minutes?"

She shook her head then pushing her way past Daisy, added, "Chips first, hen, then we get pissed and you can tell your old mammy what the *fuck* happened today!"

He had abandoned the Octavia and now driving the hired Transit van, followed directions from his Satnav and was now almost clear of the Borders area and heading onto the A1 to England.

The bulletin on the van radio was worse that he had imagined.

If the reporter was to be believed they were all dead.

This was not the news he expected; in fact, if the reporter was to be believed, regardless of how many civilians the team had killed, neither the vests nor the Transit van had exploded.

Fuck!

The whole mission had been a disaster!

His face paled.

He shivered for he knew that when Rahib reported this news to him, the bastard kafir would not be pleased.

"Here, I'll let you operate this bloody machine," Martin Cairney stood and offered his chair to Cathy Mulgrew then standing behind her, leaned over her shoulder to watch the screen.

Tapping the keyboard she opened her police e-mail account and saw the latest message with attachments was from Harry Downes.

"Here we go," she muttered and double clicked on the first icon headed 'Sandy Nichol.'

It was immediately obvious that the camera phone was a little shaky, though neither doubted the man recording the incident must have been under some tremendous duress.

The scene opened with three gunmen walking away from the camera, one turning out of sight into Buchanan Street Precinct while the other two herded an elderly couple and a woman and two children against a wall and stopped to face them as though these pitiful individuals would present some kind of threat to two, well-armed men. Seconds later, two women who exited a shop doorway walked into the gunmen and they watched as one of the women was knocked to the ground with a rifle.

"Bastards!" Cairney unconsciously muttered behind her.

One of the gunmen then turned and fired across the street, but though they were now aware at whom he had shot, the two men he murdered were out of sight of the camera.

In the disturbing silence that was unique to the area for that time of the day, they listened and heard one man shout that Mulgrew, turning slightly to Cairney, asked, "Was that 'On your knees, bitches' or something like it?"

"That's what I think he said," agreed Cairney who added, "We should be able to get our Forensic technicians to clean this up, I suppose."

They faintly heard a voice scream, 'Kill the prisoners' and presumed it was the man who had disappeared from sight.

A young woman, from the nearness of her voice they guessed was stood beside the cameraman, was clearly heard to say, 'Sandy, that man down there. I think he's killed one of them and now he's got a gun,' then heard the man called Sandy who they assumed was filming the incident, replying, 'Wait Mary, oh God, oh God, I think they're going to shoot those people.'

Mulgrew felt her throat tightening.

Though they could not hear what was said, they watched as the people kneeling seemed to plead for their lives then both startled at the sudden loud crack of rifle fire and saw first one gunman fall to the ground and then the other also fall.

A man dressed in a dark coloured jacket and wearing a flat cap, limped towards the group and they heard him shout the group were to run for safety.

"That," Mulgrew said, "must be our mystery man, Ian."

Silently, they watched Ian deliberately shoot both fallen gunmen once each in the head before he turned out of sight into the precinct. A few seconds later they heard three further shots and then a fourth shot.

"My God," Cairney wiped a large hand across his face.

Mulgrew turned to loom up at him and said, "The second attachment, sir. Do you want to watch it?"

"Yes, Cathy. I believe we must."

She closed down the footage and double clicked on the second attachment titled 'Mary Forbes' and it became quickly obvious the footage was not as sharp as the first recording.

The footage opened with a masked gunman standing below the woman's office window, dressed as were the others and with his back against the railings of St George's Tron Church. The gunman seemed nervous and kept looking towards his comrades who were out of sight of the camera. It was as his head was turned away they saw the man in the dark jacket, the man they believed was called Ian, quickly limp towards the gunman who apparently realising his danger raised his rifle to protect his eyes as the man discharged the fire extinguisher at his face. They watched as the man then mercilessly beat the gunman with the extinguisher before lifting the metal container high and bringing it down with a crushing blow to the gunman's head.

"No prisoners, then," Cairney muttered just as the footage died.

"I suppose it begs the question, sir," she turned and stared blankly at him. "Did this man Ian act to save the people who were about to be killed or did he deliberately take the opportunity to murder the gunmen?"

"Here's a novel idea, Cathy," Cairney's brow furrowed as he stared at her. "Why don't you find him and ask him?"

The tall, handsome, middle-aged man with the full head of thick, grey hair was in the kitchen drying dishes and listening to the classical music on his radio when he heard the report of a terrorist attack in the British country of Scotland, in a city called Glasgow. His curiosity aroused, he made his way into the lounge and switched on the television, tuning the old set to the Al Jazeera news channel. As he suspected, the terrorist attack was the main item of news and he slumped down onto the couch to watch as the reporter described how a number of gunmen had indiscriminately fired automatic weapons in the city centre of Glasgow. The reporter continued that news was sketchy, but that a number of civilians were known to have been killed as were an unknown number of gunmen. The scene played out on the screen that seemed to be piggybacked from a British news programme, showed police officers and what looked like paramedics running back and forth through city streets. He reached for the control and killed the sound, but for a few moments continued to watch the screen.

He knew little of Glasgow and even less of Scotland; his knowledge of the country being little more than they produced fine whiskies and yet, his eyes narrowed, the name Glasgow rang a bell.

Standing up he made his way into her bedroom, hesitating at the door as though she were still there and petulantly annoyed that he was invading her privacy.

But, he sighed, she was not there and had not been there for some time.

He shook his head at his foolishness and pushed open the door, doing his best to ignore her love of the pop and travel posters on the four walls and believed that when he inhaled, he could still smell the fragrance of her scent.

He went to her dressing table that remained exactly as it was when she went away and began to sift through the books, lightly running his hand across the small, but beautifully bound Qur'an in the white leather dustcover she had left behind, until at last he found what he sought.

The paperback book lay under a number of others, an English language book called 'The Great Britain Travel Guide.' Opening the well-thumbed book he smiled at the coloured photographs that displayed the Underground map of London, red coloured buses, the Houses of Parliament, Buckingham Palace, large, bearded men wearing multi-coloured skirts called kilts and yes, his fingers danced across the pages with her scribbled notations; the city of Glasgow.

Curious that she left this behind too, he thought and wondered; was it deliberate? Did she leave the book and intend that he find it, that he follow her?

He had never understood her fascination with Britain or more correctly, with Scotland; involuntarily smiling when he recalled her eagerness to see the Loch Ness Monster and dance the Highland fling, whatever that was.

And now the city that Malika loved from afar had been the target of yet another Jihadist attack.

He scowled. Did these fools believe they were furthering the cause of Islam? Had they no sense? Could they not see the damage they were inflicting upon the Faith? Shaking his head he thought that

Allah, praise His name, will inevitably punish them for the dogs they are.

He turned to the window and drew back the curtains, looking out over the desolation of a once proud city; a city that had suffered so much, yet knew in his heart that with time Grozny would arise again for the Chechen people were, if nothing else, resilient.

CHAPTER FIVE

Detective Superintendent John Glennie and his team of fifty-five detectives, HOLMES and civilian clerical personnel, arrived piecemeal at Helen Street police office and took over the six large offices on the second floor designated as the CTU operational suite. Satisfied that the team were organised and that his second in command, DCI Louise 'Lou' Sheridan had things under control, he was making his way to the office designated for the SIO when his mobile phone rung. Fetching it from his coat pocket he glanced at the screen then pressing the green button, said, "Cathy. I've just arrived at Helen Street and we're setting up as I speak."

"Good," Mulgrew replied. "I'm in the car with the Chief Constable and we're en route to Bute House to brief the First Minister and the Justice Minister. Needless to say," he heard her sigh, "the press are all over us for a statement and already the headlines are describing it as a terrorist attack. So, anything further I should know?"

"You've seen the footage that Harry Downes sent over?"

"Yes," she glanced towards Cairney who was seated in the front seat of the speeding car, "the Chief also saw the footage, John. Anything on the mystery man Ian yet?"

"I've detailed some of my guys to track down the young couple that sent the footage and obtain their statements. The young woman Mary Forbes who took the footage of the man might be able to tell us more. The fire extinguisher he used to kill the first gunman is on its way to the Forensic Department at Gartcosh. If they can lift prints or even DNA from it they'll run them through the system to see if he's known to us. As soon as I get anything, I'll let you know."

"Thanks, John," she replied then ended the call with, "Keep in touch."

Glennie glanced up as the door opened to admit the small and demure, dark haired DCI Lou Sheridan who closed the door behind her.

"I've appointed Paul Cowan as the office manager, John. Since his promotion to DI he's fitted well into the Unit and I think he's ready for the responsibility."

"Agreed," he nodded his head.

"How do you want to run the post mortems on the victims?"

His face screwed as he considered her question then replied, "I've arranged that the duty pathologist and his number two and with the assistance of some of the county pathologists, conduct all the PM's tomorrow, commencing early doors. You and Paul divide the civilian deaths between you. Hopefully, as victims there shouldn't be any issues," and then paused. "Perhaps it would be better, Lou, if you dealt with the young Somalian woman who was killed and you might want to consider contacting the local Mosque. Find out what the religious protocol is for Muslims before you commence the PM."

"Good idea," she nodded.

"I'll deal with the PM's for the four gunmen," then asked, "Any word on the young unidentified female that was killed in the precinct?"

"Nothing yet," she shook her head, "but Mo McInnes is at the city mortuary. Do you want me to give her a call?"

"No, if there is anything Mo will let us know."

He had no sooner uttered those words when his mobile rung and glancing at the screen, to his surprise saw it was DS McInnes.

"Boss," McInnes began, "that young woman who was killed in the precinct?"

He glanced at the DCI and replied, "I'm with Lou Sheridan, Mo, and putting you on speaker. Go ahead."

"Curious thing, Boss. You recall the young cop that was injured, Constable Cooper. She told us that the woman she spoke with had an accent and was apparently living on the street, yeah?"

"That's what she said, Mo, yes."

"Well, I was with the attendant and signing the woman's body into the mortuary when it occurred to me that sometimes people living on the street hide their personal stuff, you know, like their DSS slips and suchlike, on their person. Look, I realise that we're not supposed to strip-search the body till the time of the PM, but I took it upon myself to conduct a wee search of her clothing."

"And?"

"Well, tucked into her bra I found a slip of paper with a handwritten word and a phone number. It looks like a mobile number, but it's definitely not local because it's got twelve digits."

"I'm no expert Mo," Sheridan interrupted, "but is that not a wee bit unusual? I mean, are you sure it's a mobile number?"

"Do you remember that gang who were trafficking the women into the country last year, Ma'am?"

"The gang from Eastern Europe; from Georgia, you mean?"

"Aye, well, I'm almost certain that mob were using mobile phones with twelve digit numbers."

Glennie glanced at Sheridan and asked, "What's the word on the paper?"

"I can't pronounce it, boss, because it looks like its Cyrillic."

"Cryllic," repeated Glennie, his eyes narrowing, "as in the Russian alphabet?"

"Aye, Boss, as in the Russian alphabet."

The detective interviewing the very nervous Mary Forbes, seated on the couch of her parents' home nodded that she was certain, that the man she saw wielding the fire extinguisher had come from the doorway of the Blood Donor Centre in Nelson Mandela Place.

The detective glanced towards his neighbour before asking Mary, "Is that the only premises in the building, do you know?"

"No," she shook her head, "I'm not certain, but I think there are other offices in that place too."

"But you *are* certain that's where the man ran from?"

"Oh aye, I'm certain, but" she frowned, "he didn't exactly run, kind of more limped or shuffled, if you know what I mean."

That was enough for the two detectives who finished obtaining the young woman's statement then made their way towards their car,

Their meeting over, Chief Constable Martin Cairney and his Detective Chief Superintendent Cathy Mulgrew were shown out of the door at Bute House and under an umbrella held by Cairney's Traffic Department driver, Matt Crosbie, a trusted constable who had served him for many years, they headed for their car parked outside.

Nodding his thanks to the driver, Cairney got into the rear of the vehicle with Mulgrew where he said, "Well, you have the First Minister's complete support and the extra funding, Cathy. Now, what's your next move?"

She glanced at her wristwatch and sighing, replied, "That phone call I was called away for during the meeting, sir. I didn't want to interrupt your brief to the First Minister, but it was John Glennie providing me with more information regarding the tactical side of our operation."

She rummaged in her handbag and fetch out her notepad.

"John reports that the incident room is already up and running at Helen Street office, sir. He's a good boss and knows how to manage his people, so I'm guessing that he'll likely wind up the inquiry operation for tonight and begin afresh tomorrow morning; undoubtedly commencing with the PM's. The Area Commander for the City Centre Division has the locus locked up tight, so the Scene of Crime can continue their examination tomorrow morning. Harry Downes has the press briefing being issued by the Justice Minister, but I assume that sometime tomorrow, you'll want to face the cameras yourself?"

His head wearily dipped as though the very thought of a press conference was exhausting and nodding, replied, "Have Harry set it up for the Dalmarnock office and of course, you'll attend too." He stared out into the darkness and the rain and quietly asked, "Now about those bastards that killed so many innocent people, Cathy. How far forward are we in identifying them?"

"From what John told me, I can confirm that their fingerprints and samples of their DNA, as well as post mortem facial photographs, have been sent to the Met's Counter Terrorism Unit and also to the Security Service at Thames House in London. If they are on anyone's radar, we should get a result sometime tomorrow. What I can confirm is that the only fingerprints and DNA found on the weapons belonged to our four suspects apart from one weapon that was used to kill the three gunmen. That weapon in addition had the DNA and fingerprints of one other individual; presumably our mystery man Ian and that DNA and prints are also being checked through the Met's CTU and the Security Service databases."

"Was Mister Glennie able to provide any information about the weapons they used?"

"He's had an initial report from our Forensic Ballistics Department at Gartcosh, so I can assure you that we've already got people working on that, sir. If the weapons have been used in previous attacks, they will be on a ballistics database somewhere. However, the initial report is that the serial numbers of the weapons, all four being AK47's, had been obliterated…" she paused, then added, "or rather an attempt had been made to destroy the serial numbers. Likely you're aware the Police Service of Northern Ireland have had great success in recent years recovering serial number on weapons where acid has been used on the metal, so if our guys have no luck I'll arrange to have the weapons sent to the PSNI Headquarters at Brooklyn House in Belfast. As for the explosives in the Transit van," she paused again, "John reports that according to the EOD people the bulk of it was homemade; fertiliser and diesel oil with a small amount of Semtex to initiate the bomb. Curious," her brow wrinkled, "that they should have resorted to an explosive mix that was popular with the IRA."

"Did the Semtex have a signature?" he asked.

"Too early to say, sir," then explained, "It's still being tested."

"Can I assume it was Semtex in the two bomb vests?"

"Yes sir, Semtex and hundreds of ball bearings, screws and other bits of metal."

"What about the detonators?"

"The EOD Captain told John Glennie that the detonators in the van and the bomb vests were commercial and of the type used by companies involved in demolition or in blasting rock. Apparently these type of detonators are a lot easier to obtain than you would think and the likelihood is that they were probably stolen from a quarry somewhere. The Captain said that when a theft of detonators occur, it's not always reported because it could mean the company losing its licence to use commercial explosives."

"And the van?"

"Stolen three weeks ago in London and fitted with false plates. The Met are following up the inquiry with the owner."

"Anything else I should know," he sighed.

"The woman who was killed in the precinct; the woman we haven't yet identified."

"What about her?"

"One of John's team discovered the woman had a scrap of paper hidden in her bra and..." Staring curiously at Mulgrew, he interrupted, "What the *hell* was he doing searching the woman's bra?"

"She, sir. A DS Maureen McInnes. Anyway, she found a scrap of paper in the woman's bra that had a handwritten word in Cryllic and what is possibly an East European phone number written on it."

"East European?" he turned to stare at Mulgrew. "The woman, she was homeless I think you told me earlier today. That operation last year, the illegal importation of those women; she wasn't one of these poor devils brought into the country, was she?"

"We don't yet know, sir," Mulgrew admitted. "John will arrange to have a Russian speaking interpreter call at Helen Street tomorrow and make the call to the number, then we might find out what details he can from whoever replies."

"Right, well," he rubbed a weary hand across his face. "We've done as much as we can for this evening, Cathy, so when we return to Tulliallan I think we'll call it a day."

The detectives who interviewed Mary Forbes called into Stewart Street police office and speaking with the duty officer, obtained the phone number of the factor's key holder for the building in Nelson Mandela Place where the Blood Donor Centre was located. Apologising for disturbing the man at home and explaining the urgency of their inquiry, but not the reason, the key holder agreed to meet with the detectives at the front entrance of the building and did so twenty-five minutes later.

After the key holder unlocked the front door and disabled the alarm system, it was immediately obvious to the detectives that the bracket on the wall by the main door was missing a fire extinguisher.

The senior of the two detectives, satisfied that at least he had a lead, realised there was little point in contacting the buildings eight business tenants and dragging them out at this time of night, that the inquiry to trace the scarred man called Ian would be better conducted the following morning.

In his flat, Ian Macleod was becoming frustratingly bored with the television coverage of the incident, for the TV broadcasters, with no live film of the shooting had resorted to re-running footage of the police response to the aftermath of the incident that the broadcasters now declared to be a terrorist attack. While reporters sought to track down witnesses to the incident, long range camerawork showed white suited Scene of Crime personnel walking between white tents erected in the precinct and armed police officers patrolling the area. The crowds at the manned barriers who now numbered several hundred, were over one hundred yards from the scene of the shootings. In the main the crowd stood quietly as they watched, eager to see the scene of the attack and apparently ignoring police warnings that there was the possibility of a further outrage. Mingling with the crowds, television and radio reporters endeavoured to find anyone who had been witness to or present at the time of the attack. Several people presented themselves for interview, most whom Ian thought seemed be under the influence of alcohol and keen to offer their opinion on what had occurred.

He listened as one woman spitefully used the opportunity to lambast 'all these bloody foreigners coming into the country' and wondered when the last time was that she had visited a hospital where a large number of 'all these bloody foreigners' nursed or doctored the ill and injured. Stupid bugger, he shook his head at the woman's racist rant. His eyes narrowed when the broadcast cut away to a second reporter who was speaking with an elderly man who informed the reporter that while walking in Buchanan Street precinct he had witnessed the shooting of the two men who had just exited the underground station. Trying to contain her excitement at discovering an eyewitness, the reporter pressed the elderly man for an account of what he had seen.

He had taken cover against a wall, he nervously related, hiding in the shadows for fear of being shot. While crouched there he had seen one of the gunman further down the precinct dragging a policewoman about by her hair. As he watched, he saw a man in a dark coloured jacket and wearing a bunnet as he described it, shoot the gunman with a rifle and seeing the gunman fall to the ground. The reporter, realising that she had discovered an actual eyewitness, hustled the man away from the crowd and into the comparative safety of two beefy men, security guards guessed Ian, who were accompanying the young reporter.

No, said the man who gave his name as Bobby Alexander, he was too far away to see much more and no, Mister Alexander couldn't say if the man in the dark jacket with the rifle was a police officer or a soldier, but didn't think the man was a soldier because he wasn't wearing a uniform.

"One thing though," the cameraman caught Mister Alexander frowning, "I think from the way the man was walking he had a limp. Aye, he was definitely limping."

He thought he was now about a hundred miles from Ipswich and his paranoia had settled a little, convinced that if the police had been surveilling him he would have been stopped and arrested long before now.

The mobile phone in his pocket chirruped and he startled. Only one person had the number and he decided not to respond, but the phone continued to ring.

Glancing in the rear view mirror, he indicated he was stopping and pulled the van over into the hard shoulder. With nervous fingers he fetched the phone from his trouser pocket and glanced at the screen. A cold shiver passed through him when he saw the name 'John.' Taking a deep breath he pressed the green button and apprehensively said, "Hello?"

"Bit of a fuck up, wouldn't you say," the man's cold voice replied. Before answering he closed his eyes tightly, for this man scared him shitless.

"I don't know what went wrong, I swear. I waited for them to return. I heard the shooting and…" but got no further when the man interrupted and instructed him, "You've not far to travel now; just over ninety-three miles, so go home old son and watch the news. I'll be in touch," before he abruptly ended the call.

Rahib, now close to tears, stared at the phone. The bastard knew exactly where he was and staring pointlessly at the dashboard, realised the van must be bugged.

He had little choice but to do as he was told and to return home, for there was nowhere safe, no place where the man could not find him. He took a deep breath, forcing himself to be calm and checking the road behind was clear, pulled out into the traffic.

CHAPTER SIX

The attack that had occurred the previous day in Glasgow city centre was confirmed to the media by Chief Inspector Harriet Downes, the official Police Scotland spokesperson, to be a terrorist attack and though Police Scotland did not at that time attribute the attack to any particular group of organisation, the media at large blamed fanatical Jihadists. The incident continued to be the main item reported by all the UK and European news channels as well as in the United States. Some of the news channels reported the Islamic State of Iraq and the Levant, the so called ISIL, were claiming responsibility and that the attack had been carried out by its soldiers, though none of these channels disclosed the source of this information.

During that morning the media presented interviews with UK Government ministers, leading figures in the Islamic community, self-professed experts in terrorism and local community leaders from areas with a high population of Muslim inhabitants. A number of former military strategists were among the usual faces rolled out by the television news broadcasters, who each offered their opinion as to why the attack occurred in Glasgow.

Newly showered and dressed and with a coffee in his hand, Ian Macleod was watching the television when a young man identified on the screen as Sandy Nichol, appeared on the BBC twenty-four hour news channel as a witness to the killing of two of the gunmen. There followed the phone camera footage Nichol had recorded that showed Ian shooting dead two of the gunman and rescuing the hostages the gunman had been about to murder; more worryingly for Ian, the footage also showed him shooting both gunmen in the head as they lay prone on the ground.

His coffee grew cold as he listened to a hesitant Nichol telling the anchor-woman that after providing the police with the footage, Nichol believed he had a public duty to bring the unknown man's heroism to the attention of the media.

Aye, and the fee that goes with selling the footage to the BBC, Ian wryly thought.

Shocked, he heard himself being described as a real hero by the anchor-woman who made an appeal for anyone who knew the mystery man to contact the BBC.

Ian stared at the phone number of the screen and shook his head for though Nichol's filming had been nervously shaking and mostly showed Ian's back and there seemed little chance he could be identified from the footage, he had family and some friends who might recognise the description of a military type individual that walked with a limp.

He realised he now had a decision to make; whether to contact the police and surrender himself or wait for that knock on the door that he knew would surely come.

On the south side of the city, Daisy Cooper suffered a sleepless night, though inwardly knew much of her wakefulness could be attributed to a generous helping of vodka.

Aware their daughter was a city centre police officer, her anxious parents had phoned her at one in the morning just after Daisy assisted a tipsy Joan Crawford into a private hire taxi.

Robert and Sharon Cooper had watched the news of the shooting in their hotel foyer and to their consternation, learned the police officer briefly held hostage by a gunman and slightly injured was their daughter, Daisy. Their call had been unexpected and speaking with them, Daisy found herself in a flood of tears while assuring her hapless parents that yes, she was fine and insisted no, she did not want them to return from holiday, but in the sure knowledge that her parents would ignore her plea and be on the first flight home later that morning.

Now, lying in bed, her mind was in a whirl as once more the gunman's face leered at her, recalling his nauseous smelling breath and maddened eyes as he pointed his rifle at Daisy and pulled the trigger.

Her head still ached where he had viciously dragged her by the hair and eyes widening, she thought of his hands touching her hair and suddenly jumped from bed, determined to wash his touch from her. Making her way to the bathroom, she stripped off her pyjamas and stepped into the shower where she vigorously soaped and shampooed herself, then stood for twenty minutes till her skin was red and wrinkling from the steam.

In the kitchen she prepared a light breakfast and though had put off the idea, decided to catch up on the news and the latest on the shootings.

Curled up on the couch in her dressing gown, her legs pinned beneath her and the bowl of cereal on her lap, she watched open-mouthed as the man she knew as Ian shot dead two gunmen before turning the corner to rescue Daisy.

"Oh my God," she whispered, a hand at her mouth, then listened with rising anger as the anchor-woman and a civil rights lawyer calmly discussed the legality of Ian's action in shooting both men in the head as they lay upon the ground.

But you weren't *there*, she furiously mouthed at the screen.

The mobile phone indicated a text message had been received. Turning in bed away from his snoring wife, a bleary-eyed Rahib Chowdhury lifted the phone from the bedside cabinet and stared at the message that simply read; *11am at number two in Leicester Square*

He dropped the phone back onto the bedside cabinet and turning onto his back, laid a hand across his brow as he stared at the ceiling. Number two, he thought; not in fact Leicester Square, but the quiet little restaurant facing the bank located in Panton Street, just off the Square. The false location another of John's deceits to thwart anyone intercepting and reading the text.

He turned to glance at the bedside clock and with a sigh, realised if he was to be on time and clean himself of any police tail he would need to get washed and dressed now. Swinging his legs from the bed, the movement caused his wife to awaken. As she turned towards him, he brusquely shook her and said, "I need to go out. Get up and get me some breakfast, now."

Detective Superintendent John Glennie, a cold and empty mug by his elbow, had already been in the Helen Street office for almost two hours and was preparing himself to attend the post mortems for the four gunmen when his desk phone rang.

"Heads up for you, sir," warned the civilian bar officer from downstairs, "that's the Chief Constable just entered the building." Thanking the man, Glennie straightened his tie and seated himself upright when the door knocked and was pushed open by Martin Cairney who was closely followed by Cathy Mulgrew.

Waving him back down into his chair, Cairney said, "Good morning, Mister Glennie. Miss Mulgrew and I thought we'd pop in and see how things are progressing," then courteously pulled a chair out for Mulgrew to sit and another for himself.

"The Scene of Crime personnel have completed as much as they can at the locus, sir," began Glennie, "so I'm confident that by midday both Nelson Mandela Place and the Buchanan Street precinct will again be open to the public. However, in accordance with your agreement and though it's unlikely there will be a repetition of the incident, I've authorised armed officers in the meantime to continue to patrol the area. In about," he glanced at his watch, "twenty minutes, I'm to attend at the Queen Elizabeth University Hospital mortuary in Govan for the post mortems on the four gunmen while my deputy SIO, DCI Louise Sheridan will show face at the PM's for the victims, each of who will have a dedicated officer attend each PM for evidential purposes. At midday, DCI Sheridan will return here to Helen Street and liaise with the Russian speaking interpreter we've engaged who will call the phone number that was discovered on the unidentified homeless woman."

"So you're satisfied it is a phone number?" Mulgrew asked.

"Seems to be, Ma'am," Glennie pursed his lips and sitting back in his chair, folded his arms. "If the call is answered, Lou has prepared a list of questions and will sit with the interpreter while he or she makes the call and talk the interpreter though what questions need to be asked and answered," he replied before continuing, "The next of kin for those identified victims who were killed have all been contacted. Family liaison officers will continue to maintain contact with the families."

He paused for breath. "As you are aware, Chief Inspector Downes presented the initial briefing to the media, however, I believe it would be appropriate…"

Cairney raised a hand to stop him and said, "The Justice Minister and I discussed the issue, John, and arrangements are in progress for us both to brief the media at a meeting later this afternoon at Dalmarnock police office. The First Minister is quite correctly outraged at this incident, however, we don't believe it to be appropriate for her to be present as for the time being this attack is being investigated as a criminal act. Now, tell me about the morale of your officers."

"Good, sir," Glennie nodded. "I'm pleased to report that the training and exercises we previously conducted for this type of terrorist incident is paying off and fingers crossed, so far there has been no issues that…"

The desk phone rang to interrupt him and glancing at Cairney, saw the Chief nod that he take the call.

They watched him lift the phone and say, "Detective Superintendent Glennie," then saw his eyes widen and take a deep breath before replying, "Excellent news. I'll have him met when he arrives." Replacing the handset he stared for a second at Cairney before telling them both, "That was the Duty Inspector at Stewart Street police office, sir. She reported that a man called Ian Macleod has just presented himself at the office there and told her he's the man who killed the gunmen; the man we're looking for. She's having him driven over here as we speak."

Cathy Mulgrew decided not to accompany Martin Cairney, who had a visit to make before travelling to Dalmarnock office for the briefing. Mulgrew instead remained at Helen Street, assuring John Glennie she was not there to interfere in his day to day running of the inquiry, but was keen to be present when the man Ian Macleod was interviewed.

"I was going to have my office manager, DI Paul Cowan and DS Mo McInnes interview him, but if you like, Cathy, you can sit in with Cowan instead."

She thought briefly about his offer and replied, "No, let McInnes do the interview. If you don't mind and if it's appropriate, I'll speak with Macleod when the interview is completed." He suspected there was something else on her mind and watched as she took a deep breath. "There is the issue of the footage the media has and witness statements, John, of this man Macleod shooting the gunmen in the head after they were incapacitated. I don't want to be the harbinger of doom, but if his actions should later prove to be criminal and he turns out to be some kind of suspect for murder…"

She left the rest unsaid.

Glennie stared at her and asked, "Are you suggesting that before they take his statement, Cowan and McInnes caution him?"

"I think it might be wise to do so," she replied.

"What if after being cautioned he senses he *is* a suspect and not a witness and refuses to provide a statement? What if he asks for a lawyer?"

"Then I suggest that you consider providing him with a lawyer, John," she sighed. "You must know that the media are already hailing him a hero on one hand and on the other hand querying his shooting the gunmen in the head. We can't afford to be taking a side; treating him as a hero then perhaps having to arrest him. We need to be seen to be objective and impartial."

"Fuck!" Glennie quietly responded.

"Indeed," Mulgrew agreed.

Seated in the rear of the police car, Ian Macleod reflected on his decision to come forward. Wearily he sighed, for really he had no choice.

The two police officers were gushing at his bravery, the younger officer, a man in his early twenties, Ian guessed, keen to hear a blow by blow account of the incident. He had forced a smile and suggested that perhaps he had better wait till he was formally interviewed by the officer's colleagues before making any comment. He could not guess how correct he was not to say a word.

Waving farewell to the bar officer, Cairney strode across the rear yard of Helen Street police office and with a smile and touch at his cap, acknowledged the formal salute of the two officers who passed him by.

He nodded to Matt Crosbie, his uniformed driver who held open the door for him and as though remembering, fetched a scrap of paper from his tunic pocket and handing the paper to Crosbie, told him, "We've almost an hour before I need to be at Dalmarnock, Matt. Can you find this address?"

"Aye," Crosbie nodded, "I know where that is, sir. I'll have you there in ten or fifteen minutes."

"Good man," Cairney replied and got into the front passenger seat.

The Glasgow Health Board pathologists, assisted by two colleagues drafted in from the Lanarkshire Health Board and one from the Lothian Health Board, had at last completed the post mortems on the six of the seven victims of the terrorist attack.

The senior of the two female pathologists now stood ready to examine the seventh victim while her colleagues between them would now proceed with the examinations of the four dead gunmen.

In the clerical office of the mortuary, DCI Lou Sheridan addressed the six detective officers who gathered about her.

"First, let me say that I'm grateful for what you guys did today. Attending any post mortem can be traumatic enough, but more so under the circumstances in which these poor unfortunates died. I regret to inform you that I need four of you to hang back for I have just been made aware Mister Glennie is now unable to attend the gunmen's PM's as he had expressly wished."

She paused and bit at her lower lip before continuing, "Once you've collected your evidence and you are satisfied that the pathology report is complete, make your way back to the incident room and lodge all your productions. Once that's done, guys, DI Cowan will issue you with new inquiries. Thanks again," she dismissed them with a smile.

As the officers filed out of the room, Sheridan followed them and made her way to a small, private room where she first knocked on the door before pushing it open and entering.

DS Mo McInnes, who was to be present at the post mortem of the seventh victim, occupied one of the armchairs and stood at Sheridan's entry while an elderly man and two young women occupied the other armchair and couch.

"Sheikh Abdul Muiz, As-salāmu ʿalaykum" Sheridan greeted the elderly man with a slight bow and smiled as he rose and courteously responding with his own bow, replied, "Waʿalaykumu s-salām."

"I trust that the arrangements that have been set in place for the post mortem examination are to your satisfaction, sir?"

The elderly Sheikh sadly smiled and opening his hands wide, replied, "The death of any person is by the wish of Allah, praise His name, however, I am certain that even Allah will grieve the passing of Erina Mahdavi, a woman in the first flush of youth and who herself bore life within her womb."

Almost apologetically, Sheridan told him, "With respect to your customs, Sheikh, I have arranged for a female Scene of Crime photographer and a female pathologist to carry out the examination. DS McInnes and I will also be present. The examination, as undoubtedly you are aware, is necessary to determine many factors and is compulsory under Scottish Law. I hope you understand."

He paused and opening his hands closed his eyes as for a brief moment, he prayed, then said, "I and the family of our dear departed sister Erina Mahdavi are grateful for the concern you have shown regarding our death rites, Miss Sheridan."

He smiled and continued as if in explanation, "The Prophet said, the key to Paradise is salah (prayer), and the key to salah is cleanliness." He took a deep breath and gently waving a hand at the two women, continued, "After the examination the sisters will wash the body and, as is our custom, they will shroud the body. I speak for our sister's husband and family when I offer gratitude for the opportunity to conduct our ritual."

His face hardened when he added, "And I also speak for the family when I say that those men who killed our sister were not truly of the Faith, for we are a religion of peace and violence has no place in Islam, not in our hearts and certainly not in our society."

Sheridan glanced at McInnes and saw in her face a reflection of her own thoughts; for both women had little doubt that what the Sheikh said was true.

After landing at Glasgow Airport, Robert Cooper and his tearful wife Sharon collected their luggage and made their way to the long stay car park to recover their car. Less than thirty minutes later they were knocking upon their daughter Daisy's door and when she opened it Sharon burst into tears and hugged her daughter to her. Manfully trying to keep calm, Robert failed miserably and bursting into tears, enveloped both women in his arms.

"This is silly," Daisy sniffed, "the three of us standing here on the doorstep crying like weans. Come in, come in," she ushered her parents through the door.

The next five minutes was spent assuring them she was okay while fobbing off questions from her anxious parents. It was almost a relief when the door knocked and suspicious that some reporter might have tracked her down, Daisy peeked through the spyhole in the door. To her surprise, it was a large man wearing police uniform. Opening the door, she was even more surprised to find the Chief Constable stood upon her doorstep.

"Constable Cooper," his deep voice boomed, "I trust I haven't caught you at a bad time, my dear?"

Daisy, suddenly conscious she was wearing her dressing robe, could only stare then remembering her manners, stuttered, "Ah, no, sir. Of course not. Please, come in."

Removing his cap, Cairney closed the door behind him and followed Daisy through to the lounge, unaware she was silently giving thanks that the room for once was neat and tidy.

He smiled at the suntanned couple seated on the couch and as they arose, extended his hand to each of them and correctly guessed, "You must by the proud parents."

Robert Cooper glanced at his daughter, suddenly beaming at the praise from her boss.

"May I?" Cairney indicated the armchair and at Daisy's nod, slumped down into the chair.

"I won't stay long and before you ask," he grinned at Daisy, "I've not time for tea or coffee. Now," his face turned solemn, "I'm only here Constable Cooper…can I call you Daisy?"

"Yes, sir," she smiled a little uncertainly at him.

"Well, Daisy, I've just popped by to find out how you are. That was quite a traumatic experience you had yesterday and," turning to her parents as he nodded, continued, "can I just say how proud of your daughter we all are."

"So, Daisy," he smiled at her, "how are you today?"

"I'm okay, sir, really. My head hurt a little from where he…the gunman I mean, pulled me about, but I've taken a couple of paracetamol and I'm fine."

"Good," Cairney slapped at his knee and said, "Well, fine or not, I have it from your Area Commander himself that you are not expected to return to work for at least a week."

"Really, sir, I…" she began, but stopped when he raised his hand and pretending to frown, said, "Questioning your Chief Constable are you?"

"No, sir," she blushed.

"Well, that's settled then, Daisy. Take a week to come to terms with what happened. I know that sometime today you might be contacted by one of Detective Superintendent Glennie's team to note your statement, but I believe they will attend here at your home so there's no need for you to travel to the Helen Street office."

He pushed to his feet and with a farewell handshake with her parents, followed Daisy to the front door. Replacing his cap, Cairney raised a forefinger to his lips to warn her not repeat what he said.

"The man who saved you, Daisy. He's surrendered himself at Stewart Street and as far as I'm aware, is en route to Helen Street to be interviewed. Just thought I'd let you know," he winked at her and strode off down the garden path.

Closing the door, her brow furrowed as she thought that was an odd turn of phrase the Chief used; surrendered himself.

To Daisy, it seemed the word surrendered seemed to imply he had done something wrong.

Dressed in a shirt and tie and suit and carrying a leather briefcase, he looked every inch the young businessman. He had had first taken the train from Ipswich into the heart of London, transferred to the Underground and changed at two different tube stations to clean himself of any tail.

Satisfied that he was not being followed, Rahib Chowdhury made his way to the small restaurant in Panton Street. Pushing open the door, he saw the man he knew as John sitting with his back to the wall at a table to the rear of the restaurant that was empty other than John and two men.

The two strongly built, middle-aged men dressed in loose-fitting suits, sat together at a table near the door and each with a coffee in front of them, stared at him as he entered. Otherwise the restaurant was empty.

Rahib recognised the two middle-aged men for what they were; bodyguards.

He could not know that the suit jackets worn by Ernie, the former Royal Marine nor Ernie's colleague Taff, formerly of the Airborne Division, were tailored to hide the shoulder holsters that carried the Glock 17, 9mm semi-automatic pistols.

He moved down through the tables and sat opposite John who he saw was halfway through a bowl of chilli.

"It really is delicious," John waved a spoon at the bowl, then pleasantly asked, "Can I order you something?"

Rahib hadn't noticed the waiter hovering at his elbow and snapped, "Just coffee."

John stared curiously at Rahib and quietly said, "You seem a little tense, my dear fellow. Anything to do with that complete fuck-up in Glasgow?"

Rahib's blood turned cold.

John pretended to seem puzzled by Rahib's silence and continued, "Well, am I to guess what went wrong?"

"I don't know what went wrong," Rahib quietly replied. "The plan was…" he stopped speaking as the waiter laid the coffee down in front of him and when the young man walked off towards the door that led to the kitchen, continued in a low voice. "The plan was perfect. The response times for the police was as you said. The weapons and the explosives," he shook his head, "they were all in working order. The tests and exercises we did in the Welsh mountains proved the weapons worked." Then almost in disbelief, he added, "Nothing *should* have gone wrong."

"But it did," John sighed. "Some individual you did not factor into your plan interfered and disposed of your four associates, Rahib. Four associates whom during the last year you nurtured and finally persuaded to carry out the plan. Four associates you radicalised for the very purpose of carrying *out* the plan!" he added with a shake of his head.

Rahib swallowed with difficulty and almost shrunk into his seat. This man, this John, had him by the balls. His life was in this *bastards* hands and there was not a damn thing he could do about it. "So," he shrugged, "I did what you instructed. I did all that you asked of me, it wasn't my fault it did not go according to plan. I'm finished," he crossly waved his hands in front of John. "I've done enough for you."

"You think so?" John seemed amused by Rahib's attempt to quit and sitting back in his padded chair, laid his spoon down into the nearly empty bowl. He sighed and as though speaking with an errant child, softly continued. "Have you no idea what this operation cost me? The time and effort identifying the four subjects, checking their backgrounds and their suitability for this operation? The manoeuvring I had to do to obtain the equipment and the financial cost of supplying your people? Even the time and energy I expended recruiting you?"

He paused then said, "You forget, my dear Rahib, what got you into this business in the first place," and leaning menacingly across the table, stared into Rahib's fearful eyes as he snarled, "Your…what shall we call it? Your indulgence for young boys, your predilection for primary school children; that's why you are tied to me Rahib and you will be until such fucking times I tell you otherwise!"

He stared threateningly at the pale faced man, "Do not forget who saved you from the court, Rahib. Do not forget it was *me,*" he thrust his thumb at his own chest, "who saved you from the ridicule, the shame, the punishment and your undoubted expulsion from your society."

He leaned forward and in a lower voice, added, "Do *not* forget who is pulling your strings!"

He slowly shook his head as though deliberating then calmer now, he glanced at his watch and continued, "I have to be somewhere for this afternoon."

Rising from his seat, he buttoned his suit jacket and staring down at the wretched Rahib, added, "Keep the phone on you at all times. Rest assured, I will be calling."

As the man called John turned away, he stopped and turning back, smiled at Rahib and said, "By the way, your tradecraft needs some work. My people outside picked you up when you arrived at Liverpool Street station. Keep practising, there's a good lad," and nodding, waved a hand farewell as he said, "Ma'a as-salaama."

CHAPTER SEVEN

The two uniformed police officers who had driven Ian Macleod to Helen Street police office were met in the rear yard by two detectives who were to escort Ian to an interview room.

To his surprise, before he turned away with the detectives, the younger of the two constables ignored the detectives and insisting that he shake his hand, quietly muttered, "My name's Mickey Allison, sir. Daisy Cooper, the cop you saved; she's a pal of mine, so thanks for what you did."

Taken aback, Ian could only nod and let himself be led by the detectives through the rear door of the office and up two flights of stairs to the second floor.

Acutely embarrassed he quickly realised that several people, whether police officers or civilians he wasn't certain, all seemed to be in the corridor to get a glimpse of him before he was directed into a windowless interview room that contained just a wooden table and three wooden chairs. Bolted to the table was a tape recording device and glancing up, he saw a small CCTV camera bolted to the ceiling in a corner of the room.

"Please take a seat," one of the detectives told him, then as he sat facing the door asked if Ian wanted tea, coffee or water, but he declined. The men left with the assurance that someone would be with him in a few minutes.

Idly, he tapped his fingers on the desktop then almost five minutes later he glanced up as the door opened to admit two grim-faced detectives, one who carried a file and each who took a seat. The male detective opened with, "Mister Macleod, my name is DI Paul Cowan and this is DS Maureen McInnes. Before we begin, I am instructed to ask if you might require the service of a lawyer."

Ian felt his blood run cold. He had not known what to expect at this interview, but from the attitude of the two detectives who received him in the rear yard outside, albeit they had been civil enough, had guessed it was not to congratulate him in killing the four gunmen. Before he could respond, Cowan almost conspiratorially, leaned forward and in a low voice, said, "Mister Macleod, I am also instructed that before my colleague and I interview you, we are to caution you." He licked at his lips and staring at Ian, continued, "I *urge* you to consider getting a lawyer, sir."

Ian glanced briefly at McInnes and saw the almost imperceptible nod as Cowan added, "Look, before you speak with us, before you tell us anything and definitely before I switch that on," he pointed to the tape machine, "you have to know there is a lot of sympathy for what you did. Shit, I even *admire* you for what you did; but that doesn't detract from what I have to do and what the law says about shooting those fuckers in the head. Mister Macleod, *please*; consider a lawyer."

Ian stared back, his mind in a whirl. Yes, he had shot three of the gunmen in the head and from what he had seen on the television news broadcasts, most of the UK as well as the rest of the world, had seen him shoot two of them in the head. He lowered his head as he considered Cowan's suggestion and sighed. What he had done was exactly as he had been trained, but realised that his training might completely differ from Scottish Law.

Raising his head, he slowly nodded and asked, "How would I go about contacting a lawyer?"

Lou Sheridan had returned from the PM's to Helen Street twenty minutes late and glancing at her watch, asked the civilian HOLMES operator, "When exactly did this guy say he would arrive?"

The man glanced up and told Sheridan, "The interpreter said he would be here at midday, Ma'am."

"Well," she moodily glanced at her watch, "the bugger's late."

The door to the general office opened to admit a civilian bar officer from downstairs who was followed by a long haired, scruffily dressed man in his late fifties who wore a wrinkled shirt, bright red tie, sports jacket, crumpled brown corduroy trousers and carried a leather briefcase.

"DCI Sheridan," said the bar officer, this is Mister…" but was interrupted by the man who introduced himself as, "Fedor Drugov, Miss Sheridan."

Drugov extended his hand with a smile and added in heavily accented English, "I am the senior lecturer in Slavonic Studies at Glasgow University. How can I assist?"

The twice married Sheridan resisted smiling at the slightly built and head shorter, bearded and bespectacled Drugov and ushering him to the office she shared with DI Paul Cowan, sat him down at her desk. Settling herself down opposite him, she explained that a phone number discovered upon the body of a young, female and so far unidentified victim of the city centre shooting was possibly of east European origin.

"What I'd like, Mister Drugov…"

"Please," he smiled charmingly at her, "Call me Fedor."

"Fedor," she force d a smile. "What I'd like is that you call this number and if the call is answered, I will feed you a number of questions. What I hope to gain from the call is the identity of this young woman and if possible, details of a next of kin."

"This young woman, Miss Sheridan…can I call you Louise?"

"If you prefer," she replied with the thought that Drugov was an unlikely charmer, but that didn't stop him trying.

"Louise," he rolled her name about his tongue, "This young woman, do you believe her to be a Russian speaker?"

"We have nothing, Fedor; nothing other than the phone number. No information whatsoever, other than a word written beside the number," and showed him the word she had copied onto her notepad.

He peered at the pad and muttered, "Father. The word is Russian for father."

"Father," Sheridan repeated.

"Ah, so, shall we proceed with the call?"

"Yes, please," she smiled and handed him her mobile phone.

He took a deep breath and slipped on reading glasses, then took from her the notepad upon which she had written the phone number.

She watched as he carefully dialled the number and hurriedly whispered that he press the loudspeaker button, but seeing his confusion, hastily reached across her desk to press the button for him. It didn't escape her attention that by doing so it gave the aging lothario the opportunity to glance down her ample cleavage.

Settling herself back down at her desk, she resisted grinning and both listed as the call rang.

A few seconds later, a man's voice softly replied, "Dah?"

Sheridan listened as Drugov read from the prepared script, his first sentence began by introducing himself; that he was calling on behalf of the police in Glasgow, Scotland, that he was requested by the police who were with him to ask certain questions and would the receiver of the call be happy to answer those questions?

There was a definite pause while the man seemed to consider what he was being asked them Sheridan heard his curt reply, "Dah," that she knew meant yes.

Drugov's finger followed the page to the next question, but before he began, the man softly and clearly said, "I speak English."

Surprised, Drugov was about to continue, but Sheridan snapped her fingers and reaching across the desk, took the phone from him. "Good afternoon, sir," she slowly began. "I am Detective Chief Inspector Louise Sheridan of Police Scotland. I apologise for surprising you with this phone call," she said. "If you have any difficulty with my accent, please inform me."

"I understand you perfectly," the man replied.

"Please sir, can I ask what you name is?"

"I would prefer if first you inform me why you have called me, detective," he slowly replied.

Realising that to argue for his name was at that time pointless, she moved on and glancing at Drugov, dragged the pad across the desk and readied her pen to take notes. "I regret that yesterday here in the city of Glasgow in Scotland, there was a terrorist attack that killed a number of people."

"I am aware of the attack from CNN. What is that to do with this call?"

"One of the victims of the attack was a young woman who we cannot identify. However, the young woman had this phone number that you answered on her, when we found her. We are very anxious to identify her and believe she might not be from Scotland, but visiting this country. We are anxious to contact her next of kin to inform them of her death. Can you help us, please?"

Again there was an almost lengthy pause and for a second, Sheridan thought the line had been broke, but then the man replied, "What do you need from me?"

"If I describe this young woman, perhaps sir, you might know who this unfortunate woman is?"

"Go ahead give me your, your…описание…I do not know the word."

"Description," whispered Drugov. "He's asking for the description." Sheridan nodded and said, "The young woman is about twenty years of age to twenty-five years of age. She had dark coloured shoulder length hair, with slim build and what seemed to be scarring on her left arm as though she had perhaps been badly burned at one time, perhaps when she was young."

"Burned arm? The left arm?" asked Drugov.

"Yes, burned on the left arm," repeated Sheridan, her eyes narrowing at the interpreters curiosity, before repeating into the phone, "The young woman had been burned on the left arm, sir."

Again the frustrating pause then the man slowly and very deliberately said, "You are certain it is the left arm, Madam?"

"Certain, sir," she glanced for confirmation at her notes.

"Then, you are describing my daughter, Malika. Malika was twenty-three years of age. She…" he paused and Sheridan thought she heard a sob. "I did not see Malika nearly two years now since...since she left home."

"Sir, I am so sorry to break this news," Sheridan continued to speak slowly. "Can I again ask with whom I am speaking?"

"You speak with Malika's father, Eldar. My name…my name is Eldar Umarov."

She was about to respond, but glancing at Drugov, was surprised to see his face turn pale and his eyes open wide.

"Mister Umarov," she began, but almost immediately frowned for the line seemed to be disconnected.

"What?" she stared curiously at Drugov's suddenly, pale face.

"Elder Umarov," he faintly whispered and then, his hands palm upwards as though to emphasis his explanation, said, "Miss Sheridan, that was Eldar Umarov!"

"Who?"

His hands reached to his head that he slowly shook then through gritted teeth, repeated, "Eldar Umarov. He is a very, *very* bad man!"

Kind though their offer was, Daisy Cooper declined to spend some time at her parents' house and waved goodbye to them, reminding them that the Chief Constable had told her the inquiry team would be contacting her at her home for her formal statement.

Her father raised his eyebrows, knowing that was a fib, that she could just as easily have phoned them to provide her parents address for the interview, but realising that his daughter wanted some time alone ushered his wife to their car.

Closing the door, it occurred to Daisy she hadn't eaten since the previous evening and went into the small, neat and tidy galley kitchen to prepare herself some lunch.

She turned the kitchen radio on and caught the one o'clock news that continued to report of the previous day's outrage in the city centre, then to her surprise reported that police had tracked down and were interviewing the mysterious man who had saved the hostages and killed the gunmen.

Daisy shook her head while wondering what bugger had tipped the wink to the radio station for she correctly believed that the police would not issue such a statement and certainly not while the man called Ian was being interviewed.

She was halfway through slicing the brown loaf, but stopped and thought of him, the scarred man. God, she had been so frightened, so scared and when the gunman had pointed his rifle and pulled the trigger; she involuntarily shuddered at the memory.

Then he had shot the gunman and helped her to her feet.

She had been amazed at how calm he had been while she…she blushed at the memory, thought she was about to pee herself.

Squatting there against the wall beside him, he had taken control while Daisy, the trained police officer, had simply shivered in fright.

Some bloody police officer I am, she angrily shook her head; one upsetting incident and I go to pieces!

Ian, the man who…her eyes narrowed and she softly smiled. What was it he said again, "I'm just a guy passing by" or something like that and she smiled.

Not just a guy, but the man who had saved her life.

She leaned on the worktop, all thought of lunch gone.

She had to thank him. No matter what else happened, she would find him and thank him; thank him for her life.

Detective Superintendent John Glennie called, "Come in," and raising his head, watched as DI Paul Cowan came through the door. "He wants lawyered up, Boss," Cowan told him and sunk into the chair opposite Glennie's desk.

"Has he said anything? Anything at all?"

Cowan shook his head before answering, "I think that he would likely have given us the full story, but when Mo McInnes and me cautioned him, well," he spread his hands, "he obviously decided that if he said anything then it might come back and bite him on the arse. For what it's worth, I think he's right."

Glennie stared at the DI then slowly nodding, replied, "And for what it's worth, I agree. But the law's the law, Paul and like it or not we need to follow the rules."

He slumped back into his chair and with both hands, rubbed at his face.

"Where is he now?"

"Well, he's not a flight risk," Cowan smiled, "because he came to us, so until the duty brief arrives I put him into one of the side rooms that at least has a window and gave him a couple of newspapers. One of the civvies has popped out to ASDA across the road to get him a sandwich and I've given him a coffee. My treat," Cowan grinned.

"Other than your hero worship," Glennie grinned, "what's your opinion?"

Cowan shrugged and said, "He seems a decent enough guy. He's kind of cooperated and provided us with his full details and as we suspected, he's former military. Mo McInnes is in the general office to phone the Military Police unit at Edinburgh castle. Macleod has given us his army number and former unit, so the MP's should be able to give us a backdrop of his service record, though how long that will take I really don't know."

"I've had dealings with the MP's at Edinburgh. They're usually on the ball when we make a request of them. His face and the limp," Glennie narrowed his eyes. "That anything to do with his military service?"

"Well, he elected not to say anything to us until a lawyer arrives, but I suspect that it is."

"What about the PNC? Is he known to us?"

"I've had him checked out on the PNC with the details he has provided, but nothing came back. When his mug is collected for a refill, it'll be replaced with a clean mug and the one he's using I'll arrange to be sent to the Forensics for fingerprint and DNA analysis."

"Smart work," Glennie nodded.

The door knocked and McInnes stuck her head in to say, "That's the MP's at Edinburgh informed, Boss. The woman I spoke with says she should get back to us within the hour."

"Within the hour? My, that's quick," smiled Cowan. "Right, thanks, Mo."

Turning to Glennie he said, "What about the phone call, Boss. Any word from Ma'am about that?"

"Ma'am is here behind you," said the voice and turning, Cowan stood when he saw DCI Sheridan and a scruffy older man entering Glennie's office.

"Paul, can you grab another chair," asked Sheridan, "I think you should sit in on what Mister Drugov has to tell us."

Ian Macleod had no complaints about the way the police were treating him. If anything, he was grateful that the skinny, fair-haired Detective Inspector had quietly forewarned him not to say too much, that though his actions the previous day had undoubtedly saved lives, shooting the gunmen in the head might later create difficulties for the former soldier.

Cowan had further explained to Ian that while the detective had to work within the rules of interrogation while the interview was being recorded, anything they said out with the recorded interview could be denied and would be open to credibility.

He had acknowledged the fairness of the two officers and was happy to give his name and address details and yes, admitted he was former military. He was surprised when Cowan raised a hand and insisted Ian say no more that he wait for the duty lawyer to attend and thereafter take the lawyer's advice what he could or should not admit to.

Glancing at his watch he was surprised to see it was now approaching two in the afternoon.

He turned when a pretty, young woman in a white blouse and tight, grey coloured skirt nervously entered the office and smiling, handed him a pack of sandwiches.

"Can I get you anything else, anything at all," she gushed.

He softly smiled and though he had no appetite, shook his head and replied, "No, this is great," but stopped and said, "Perhaps another coffee if it's not too much trouble."

"No bother at all," she smiled broadly and lifting his mug by the handle, left the room where in the corridor outside, she carefully slipped the mug into a paper bag and handed it to a detective.

The Duty Controller at Edinburgh Airport Air Traffic Control tower was curious.

It wasn't too often the Royal Air Force dropped one of their Sea King helicopters into the airfield and lifting the powerful binoculars from the ledge beneath the large, panoramic window, focused them onto the outer edge of the airfield and watched as the rotor blades slowed. The side door of the aircraft opened and man in a dark coloured suit and carrying an overcoat in one hand and a briefcase in the other, alighted from the aircraft and dropped lightly to the tarmac. As the controller watched, he saw the man, his head lowered against the backwash of the blades, met by a black coloured salon car whose driver held open the rear door.

Odd, vehicles coming onto airside should be cleared by us, he thought, then took a deep breath.

He switched his gaze to the aircrafts recognition numbers on the fuselage and slowly nodding in recognition, sighed.

He was a former RAF air traffic controller and recalled the same chopper previously dropping in, remembering the furore that arose when one of his colleagues had questioned its arrival.

It was a spooks aircraft; a military chopper used by the Government to covertly ferry its security personnel about the country.

He turned the binoculars onto the car, but by now the passenger was in the vehicle and heading for the exit gate.

CHAPTER EIGHT

Introducing Fedor Drugov and explaining his status at the Glasgow University to her colleagues, DCI Lou Sheridan turned to the spritely fifty-something and said, "Go ahead, Fedor, tell them what you told me."

"Let me start by saying that what I tell you is probably new to you and I will assume that you do not know of or have knowledge about the Chechen struggle against the might of Mother Russia."

He paused and awaited the shakes of heads before continuing.

"Historically, the Chechen people have long struggled for autonomy from Russia and this struggle has resulted in a number of wars dating back hundreds of years." He smiled and added, "We have long memories of past slights in the Slavonic countries."

"The first Chechen war was fought between the Russian Federation and the Chechen people and commenced in December 1994. The fighting ended when Boris Yeltsin's government declared a ceasefire in August 1996. That period has been well documented and," waving a hand in dismissal, continued, "can be argued at length about the rights and the wrongs of what occurred and who was to blame. What *cannot* be argued was the large number of deaths on both sides, both civilian and military and is estimated to be in excess of one hundred and twenty-thousand people; men, women and of course as occurs in these battles, children. Not to mention the enormous damage to the Chechen economy and infrastructure that also occurred."

Glennie turned to stare curiously at Sheridan, wondering where this was going and how it were connected to a young woman lying in the city mortuary.

She caught his eye and her glance said, patience.

"However, the struggle I wish to discuss or rather, inform you of occurred between October 1999 and 2000 in the capital city that came to be known as the Battle of Grozny; a siege that not only inflicted numerous casualties among the civilian population, but also came close to completely destroying the city, so much so the United Nations termed Grozny as the most destroyed city on earth. In fact," he smiled, warming to his story, "the Russians infamously set a deadline that declared if the residents of Grozny did not evacuate the city, then any persons who stayed in the city would be considered terrorists and bandits and would be destroyed by artillery and aviation strikes. The warning was clear; get out or die."

He paused to stare at each of his audience and again sadly smiled. "The dead young woman who we now know to be Malika Umarov. If what you suspect, she being in her early twenties, she would have been a very young child during the first Chechen war and not much older during the second war. Now," he rubbed at his jaw, "what I am about to relate is from the little I know of her father, Eldar Umarov and the reputation he gained during the siege of Grozny."

He took a deep breath and began, "It is commonly known that Umarov was gifted lecturer in languages at the Chechen State University in Grozny; of course the University was partially destroyed in both wars, but I understand is now rebuilt and today is a teaching campus. Educated at Moscow State University, Umarov graduated high in his year then was drafted into the then Russian Federation army and achieved the rank of First Lieutenant. Of course, he never actually served *in* the army for almost immediately his language skills attracted the attention of the Federal Security Service of the Russian Federation, the infamous FSB who of course you will be aware are the successors of the former KGB. As a Chechen and particularly as a Muslim who daily lived and practised his faith, Umarov was never trusted to serve abroad and so his service in Moscow was confined to translation duties. I cannot imagine how boring it must have been for a man whose linguistic skills were incredible. It was during this period that he married a Muscovite, a local Muslim woman whose name regretfully I do not recall. However, I am aware that from this union, three children were born with this woman. A boy and two daughters, one of whom was undoubtedly your victim, Malika."

"This is all very well and interesting though your tale undoubtedly is, Mister Drugov," interrupted Glennie, "how exactly does this affect our inquiry? I mean, we've identified the victim and the killers are dead. Really, what does this have to do with our inquiry?"

Drugov glanced briefly at Sheridan who politely said, "Bear with him, John. Fedor?"

Nodding that he understood he could continue, Drugov went on, "Now, his service completed, Umarov returned to his native Grozny in," his eyes narrowed as he tried to recall, "I think it was the early nineties and certainly before the first war. Anyway," he waved a hand, "when the first war commenced, Umarov was then lecturing at the University and making no secret of his view that he favored secession from the Russian Federation; of course that view brought him to the attention of his former masters, the FSB who had him arrested. If believed, the story is that he was brutally tortured before being released several months later with the threat if he continued his separatist activities, his family would suffer."

He sighed deeply and shaking his head, added, "But they did suffer."

"When the first war broke out, Umarov, with his particular knowledge of the workings of the FSB, was drafted into the Chechen irregulars as an intelligence officer. It was during this war his wife, among many thousands of others, was killed in an air raid. When the ceasefire was at last implemented, Umarov resumed his duties at the University, but now working and burdened with the responsibility of caring for three young children. I have no information about what happened to him during this relatively peaceful time. However, during the second Chechen war that involved the siege of the city, it once more embroiled Umarov in the conflict. Sadly his son, a mere youth and teenage volunteer in the Chechen irregular forces and also the younger of his daughters were both killed during this time, though I have no knowledge of how they met their deaths. The story goes that these deaths almost drove Umarov to the edge of insanity and no longer an intelligence officer, he joined the Arab Mujahedeen League in Chechnya that was led by Abdulla Kurd, the Kurdish Islamist, and that he took charge of a company of guerillas.

As their commander, Umarov quickly gained a reputation as a ferocious and daring leader whose company of troops took no prisoners or…" he hesitated as though the memory pained him, "those prisoners they did capture were subjected to the most horrific torture. In short, Umarov became a legend among his people, but a war criminal to the Russian Federation."

"And this is the man that you spoke with on the phone today?" Glennie glanced towards Sheridan.

"According to Fedor, it would seem so," she nodded.

"But how can you be sure?"

"I tried to call back several times," she replied, "but the line was dead. I suspect the phone has been destroyed."

"And for good reason," interjected Drugov. "If Umarov suspects that he can be traced, the FSB will stop at nothing to find him."

"But as I asked, how can we be *certain* it was this man Umarov?" Glennie directed his question to the interpreter.

Drugov reached into his briefcase and withdrew an IPad that he switched on before he replied, "I am certain, Mister Glennie and I know of this because the daughter who survived the siege of Grozny was injured. Here, look at this," and reached across the desk to hand the IPad to Glennie. "This is a much publicised photograph of Umarov holding his child; a photograph that can easily be found on the Internet that," his eyes narrowed, "I think was taken by a Swedish war correspondent. A photograph that shows Umarov weeping as he holds his child in his arms for she had been splashed by napalm from a bomb blast and her left arm was badly burned."

Glennie stared wordlessly at the stark black and white photograph, at the horror of war etched onto the man and the child's face and inwardly shuddered at the horrific burn wound on the girls arm; her left arm.

A silence descended upon the room, broken when Paul Cowan asked, "Mister Drugov, I still don't understand how this information will affect our inquiry?"

Drugov stared at the younger man as though about to lecture a child and replied, "And now we come to it. Chechnya, young man, is the only region in the Russian Federation where the ancient custom of Adat is still continued and functional. It is an old customary tribal law still practiced by the tariqahs and clans of Chechnya. Long held customs that were practised, just like your Scottish ancestors practised when they fought each other over trivial matters, yes?"

Cowan didn't think it necessary to point out that all over Glasgow on a Saturday night, drunken or drugged gangs still 'practised.'

"One of the customs of Adat," Drugov continued, "is the blood revenge. If a homicide occurs the kin of the wronged will customarily seek vengeance upon the wrongdoer and if not the wrongdoer, then the wrongdoers family. Of course," he spread his hands, "the clan elders can often intervene in a time of conflict, but let me ask you this. Eldar Umarov is likely to be completely ostracised from his family, his clan as it were, because of the FSB's hunt for him. He will have no one to turn to other than himself and besides, his daughter was murdered here, in Scotland. She is the last of his family and I suspect," he slowly shook his head, "he will no longer have anything to lose. Yes, the men who murdered his daughter are dead, but their deaths do not excuse their families." He turned towards Glennie and said, "I regret, Mister Glennie, that there is a strong possibility and if he so wishes, Eldar Umarov just might try to seek his revenge on the families of the dead and if he chooses to do so," he shrugged, "then, sir, you have a real problem on your hands."

The Chief Constable of Police Scotland, Martin Cairney was dropped by his driver at the front door of Dalmarnock police office and pulling his tunic sharply down, set his cap upon his head. The six feet five inch police officer looked every inch the leader when he strolled through the glass doors, but instantly smiled at the young officer who sharply stood to attention and saluted. Gracious as always, he smiled and shook the astounded constable's hand, courteously asked his name and where he served before waving cheerio and heading for the lift that would take him to the Media Department on the first floor.
He was met at the lift doors by Chief Inspector Harriet 'Harry' Downes who had been forewarned by the buildings commissionaire. Grinning, Cairney said, "So, the jungle drums work here too, Harry?"
She returned his grin and said, "The Justice Minister arrived ten minutes ago, sir. He's in my office having coffee. Can I…?"
"Yes, please," Cairney interrupted and added, "Are we ready to go?"

"Yes, sir, but I should say that there's gentleman asked to speak with you," she lowered her voice, "and says he's here from London and that it's urgent. I *think* he might be some sort of Government representative."

Cairney's eyes narrowed. "Where is he now?"

"I've asked him to wait in a side office. He said to give you his card," and handed Cairney a business card.

He glanced down at the card and glancing at the stamped gold coloured portcullis in the top corner, read, *'Barry Ashford'* and printed underneath the name, *'Her Majesty's Revenue & Customs.'* Raising his head to stare at Downes, he said, "I don't know where she is, Missus Downes, but contact DCS Mulgrew and if it means she has to hijack a traffic car, she is to get here as soon as possible. Tell her an old problem has decided to visit us and his name is trouble. In the meantime," he growled, "Mister Ashford can sit and wait. I've a press conference to deal with."

The young, pretty, dark haired and very junior solicitor who was next on the police 'Duty Lawyer Call-out' roster arrived at Helen Street police office with no idea that the man she was to advise was the media's hero of the Buchanan Street shooting and immediately felt slightly overwhelmed.

Sitting in the office with Ian Macleod she introduced herself as Louise Hall and immediately dropped her briefcase, spilling its contents across the floor. Stooping to help her recover the paperwork and pens, Ian smiled at the blushing young woman and said, "Look, Miss Hall, I understand that this might be a bit of a shock, so let me make it very easy for you. For a start, I didn't do anything that I wasn't trained for. I understand the police have a job to do and I suspect that the two detectives who spoke to me..."

"DI Cowan and his neighbour?"

"His neighbour?"

"His partner, I mean," and she blushed again.

"Yes," he smiled at her. "Well, as I was saying, I think they aren't too happy about what they have to do, so can I make a suggestion?"

"Yes, of course," she stared a little uncertainly at him.

"I didn't really intend spending so much time here today and while I realise that the police need a statement from me, I don't relish the thought of becoming a suspect for the killing of those gunmen. Look," he breathed deeply and slowly exhaled, "I don't think the police know whether or not to treat me as a suspect or a witness. Do you think that you might be able to persuade them that I'm not going anywhere and I'll attend any interview they might wish to set up, but at a later date? As far as I am aware, I am not under arrest and certainly wasn't expecting to be cautioned today and I really need to get my head around that."

She stared at him then slowly nodded. "I see what you mean. You believe that you are in a sort of limbo situation, Mister Macleod. Neither suspect nor witness." Growing a little more confident, she continued, "As the law stands or my interpretation of it anyway, shooting those men down you acted in defence of others who were at the material time in danger of being murdered, yes?"

"Yes," he slowly drawled.

"Thereafter, while the alleged criminal act of shooting those men in the head *does* constitute homicide or if you prefer, murder, but the police would have to determine that after being shot in the bodies, those men were still alive before you shot them in the head. Hmmm," she grimaced and asked, "I gather the post mortems have been carried out on the four men?"

"I'm not sure. The detectives didn't say."

"Well, if the PM's can determine the men survived the bullets you fired into their bodies…" He smiled when she involuntarily shivered and said, "Sorry. It's the thought of it. Anyway, if the PM's determine the men *were* alive, then we likely might be facing a charge of murder."

He almost smiled again at the royal 'we.'

"Right, if you wait here I'll go and speak with Mister Cowan and see if I can find out what the police plan for you."

He watched her now with a firm purpose leave the room and sighing, turned back to the newspaper crossword.

Rahib Chowdhury made his way to the Bond Street Mosque in Ipswich to offer prayers, intensely nervous that the brothers who were in attendance might ask after his friend Abdul-hameed Muhammad with whom Rahib was known to closely associate. Abdul-hameed Muhammad, he bitterly thought, who with his three fellow gunmen now lay dead in some mortuary in that God-forsaken, freezing shithole called Scotland.

Nodding to the brothers who, due to the rise in right-wing activities in the area, were on duty standing watch at the doors of the Mosque to prevent any direct threat by the local fascist thugs.

In the vestibule of the Mosque, Rahib removed his footwear that he placed on the shoe shelf and was about to make his way to the ablutions room, but startled when a hand was gently laid upon his shoulder. Turning he saw Sheikh Marzook Hussain, the white bearded elderly Sheikh of the Mosque who carrying his white stick and now almost completely blind, smiled and greeted him with, "As-salāmu ʿalaykum" and reached for his hand.

Returning the handshake, Rahib replied, "Waʿalaykumu s-salām, Sheikh."

"Is your friend Abdul-hameed Muhammad not attending salah today, brother?"

"Eh, no, not that I know of, Sheikh," he replied, surprised that the old man, blind or not had picked up on Muhammed's absence. "As a matter of fact, I haven't seen him for a few days now."

The elderly Sheikh stared at Rahib and blind though he might almost be, had not lost the use of his other senses. Acutely aware of Rahib's nervousness, he suspected there must be a good reason for the lie, for almost the whole of the last year the two men had been almost inseparable.

"Ah well, you are here and that's what counts," the old and venerable man chuckled. Offering his arm that the younger man might lead him, he said, "Now, my son, let us go and give praise to Allah, praise His name that He might consider our prayers and offerings worthy."

As they walked slowly together into the main payer room, the elderly man could almost feel the tension in Rahib and wondered exactly what was troubling him; troubling him so much that he would lie to a holy man.

The call from Harry Downes had surprised Cathy Mulgrew who driving her own car raced from her visit at Baird Street office towards the Dalmarnock office.

Ignoring the waved fists and angry car horns blasted at her she finally arrived a little breathless at Dalmarnock and hurried through the front door, nodding a greeting at the cheery young commissionaire who cast an appraising eye at the glamorous Ms Mulgrew as she passed by and entered the lift.

Exiting at the first floor, she made her way to Harry Downes office just as the Chief Constable, Downes and the Justice Minister were arriving there after the media briefing.

Downes, an armful of paperwork, stood politely to one side as Cairney with a smile, said, "Harry, can you give us the room, please?"

"Sir," Downes nodded as he closed the door behind her.

Sitting down on the couch, the Justice Minister waited till both Cairney and Mulgrew had settled themselves before asking, "So, Martin, who is this man Ashford?"

Cairney took a deep breath and began, "Barry Ashford is, regardless of what his business card might say, a member of Her Majesty's Security Service, Minister; MI5 if you prefer. He is a man with whom both Miss Mulgrew and I have had previous dealings."

His eyes narrowed as he continued, "You might recall a number of years ago an incident in Glasgow's east end when a car blew up, killing a prominent Glasgow based member of the Irish republican movement. The media suggested it was a bomb, though the official story was a petrol leak."

"Yes," the Minister's brow furrowed, "that seems to ring a bell." He stared incredulously at Cairney. "You're not suggesting it actually *was* a bomb? In Glasgow?"

"Whether or not it was a bomb is now irrelevant. What matters is that this man Ashford, this slimy, lying…"

"I believe what the Chief Constable is trying to suggest, Minister," Mulgrew hurriedly interjected, "is that before we speak with Ashford, you consider that anything he tells you to be a lie. If you work from that point, you won't go wrong."

"Exactly," agreed Cairney who red-faced, added, "Thank you, Cathy."

"You think his visit is related to the terrorist attack in Buchanan Street?"

"Undoubtedly," sighed Cairney, "and that is why I have requested Miss Mulgrew sit in on our discussion when I invite him through."

"Well," the Minister shrugged, "let's have him in, then."

The mobile phone chirruped while Daisy was having a shower and dripping wet, reached cautiously for it from the small stand beside the sink. Glancing at the screen she smiled when she saw her friend Joan Crawford's name.

"Hello, missus," she quipped and stepping over the rim of the bath, awkwardly wrapped a towel about her. "How's your head this morning?"

"Don't ask," Crawford groaned then said, "Are you alone?"

"I bloody hope so. I'm in the shower."

"I tried the landline a few times, but it was constantly engaged."

"It's off the hook. I've been inundated with calls all day from family and friends and though I know people are being kind or just a bit nosey, to be honest, Joan, it was getting to be a bit wearing."

"Is it okay to speak? Are you needing some time to yourself, hen?"

"No, you're okay so go ahead; cheer me up."

"Well, sorry about disturbing you and that," Crawford replied with not an ounce of remorse, then in a low voice, continued, "but I thought you might like to know. Your man, the guy who saved you; he was in here this morning, in the office."

"Yes," I heard," Daisy sighed. "Believe it or not, the Chief Constable popped by while my folks were in, to see if I was okay."

"The Chief? Well, bugger me with a hot poker," replied Crawford. "Your folks? I thought they were in Spain?"

"Long story, but the Chief told me before he left that the guy Ian had surrendered himself, whatever that's supposed to mean."

"Ian Macleod is his name. I read it on the Duty Officer's notepad, but don't say I told you. His address was there as well, just in case you need it, hen," Crawford coyly added.

"Oh, why would I want that?"

"Well, I was thinking you might want to send a thank you card for fucking saving your life, you stupid bugger!"

"Oh, yes, of course. Well, I suppose I *could* send a card," then a little guiltily recalled she had not even thanked the man who saved her. "I'll text you the name and address and again…"

"Don't say where I got it, I know."

She sat on the edge of the bath and asked, "Is he still at Stewart Street?"

"No, the Counter Terrorism people wanted to interview him so he was driven over to Helen Street by Mickey Allison and one of the community cops. Mickey's bragging he shook Macleod's hand for saving his wee pal…and that'll be you, hen."

"Oh, he is, is he?" Daisy grinned, then startled when her front door knocked.

"Look, that's somebody at the door, Joan. I'll give you a call later.

"Okay, honey, see you," Crawford ended the call.

Grabbing her robe from behind the door, Daisy slipped it on and wrapping the towel about her head, made her way to the door that was again loudly knocked. Peering through the spyhole she draw a man and a woman stood there, the woman holding up a police warrant card.

Opening the door, Daisy saw the woman smile and tell her, "Daisy? You might remember, I'm DS Mo McInnes. We met yesterday at the Royal."

"Yes, of course," Daisy nodded, then smiling added, "You and your neighbour; you brought me home and I was rude to you. Sorry about that."

"After what you had been through, don't worry your head about it," McInnes grinned at her, before adding, "This is DC Eric Chalmers;

we did phone, but couldn't get through on your landline. We're here to note your statement."

Daisy invited them in, telling them, "The kitchen is through there if you want to put the kettle on while I dress," and made her way to her bedroom.

The crossword completed, Ian Macleod stood up from his chair and slowly walked around the room to stretch his aching left leg. It was when he was staring from the window into the car park below the room door opened to admit his lawyer, Louise Hall, the detective called Cowan and an older, grey-haired man who did not shake his hand, but introduced himself as Detective Superintendent John Glennie.

Inviting the three of them to take a seat, Glennie turned towards Ian and said, "Mister Macleod. I am the Senior Investigating Officer for the incident that occurred in the city centre and as such it will be my responsibility to report the facts to Crown Office at their base in Gartcosh Crime Campus. If you will allow me to finish what I have to say, you may ask of me any question that your counsel," he turned courteously towards Hall and nodded, "may permit you to ask."

"Yes, sir, I understand," Ian nodded.

"Then let me continue. As you will likely realise the report will be lengthy for it will include the murder of seven citizens and the deaths of four men who we believe to be responsible for those murders. I say deaths," he paused, "because while I accept the men died and apparently at your hand, the circumstances of their deaths are a little," he hesitated, "I believe obscure is probably the correct word. You must know from media coverage that you are generally being hailed a hero for your part in saving a number of individuals who were at risk of being killed by the four men who allegedly carried out the murders. I use the word allegedly, simply because until such time a court decrees otherwise they are not yet proven to be guilty. Is that clear to you?"

"Yes, sir."

"Now, while some sections of the media describe your actions as heroic, other and admittedly some of the more acerbic sections of the press question your shooting of the fallen gunmen in the head."

He held up a hand and continued, "While you might believe you had good reason for that action, you must be informed that such actions could be construed as unnecessarily violent and fatal, given that the men had already been…" he paused, his eyes narrowing, "how can I put it; neutralised?"

He took a deep breath and continued, "Anyway, even as the SIO I am not in any position to judge you or decide if your actions yesterday were criminal or heroic. All I can do, Mister Macleod, is report the circumstances as it is Crown Office who will decide whether or not to proceed with any complaint against you. In consultation with Miss Hall, I contacted Crown Office prior to meeting with you and I have to inform you that like me, at this time they are not yet in any position to make a judgement. What they *have* instructed is that with your agreement and that of Miss Hall, I am prepared to allow you to leave the office without either providing me with a witness statement or continuing with any detention. That is of course if you give me your word you won't attempt to flee the country or anything?"

"I've nowhere to go, Mister Glennie and besides," Ian smiled, "I didn't realise I was being detained."

Glennie returned his smile and replied, "Not formally, of course, but if you'd tried to leave," he held out his hands, "I think we might have had to prevent that."

"Okay, I understand and you have my word, sir."

"Thank you. Now, one further thing that I should tell you is that as part of the inquiry into the incident, I have caused a background check to be made with the military regarding your former experience. Had I the opportunity to interview you for a witness statement, that would not have been necessary, however, as things stand…"

"Yes sir, I understand sir," Ian nodded.

"Now, have you any questions for me, Mister Macleod?"

Ian's brow furrowed, then he asked, "Is there some sort of time frame before Crown Office make their decision about my status as witness or accused?"

"That's a questions I *can't* answer for their decision is out of my hands, but needless to say as soon as I hear anything, I will arrange to have Miss Hall contacted…" he paused and added, "that is if you continue to seek her counsel?"

"I don't see why not," Ian replied.

"Good, then after Miss Hall is contacted, it will be up to her to inform you. Miss Hall?" he turned towards the young woman.

"Yes, Mister Glennie, Thank you."

"Anything else?" he asked Ian.

"No," he was about to shake his head, but stopped and drawled, "Yes, there is one thing. The young police officer. She told me her number was Alpha three-six-four and her name was Daisy. For what it's worth, I'd like to…"

"Mister Macleod," Hall interrupted him, but he raised a hand to quiet her and smiled.

"Nothing incriminating, Miss Hall," and turned back towards Glennie. "The policewoman. She had balls, if you excuse the pun. Even though she might have been scared witless, she went for the bastard that had held her hostage, I saw that. He used his rifle to knock her down, but she was defiant and gutsy. Anyway, I'd just like you to know, sir, that the lassie was brave and I think it should be brought to your attention."

Visibly taken aback, Glennie turned to the DI and nodding, with a soft smile said, "I think we should pass that on, Mister Cowan."

Turning back towards Ian, he said, "At this time, Mister Macleod, it is my job to remain completely impartial and I must not be swayed by what I hear or read in the media. However, I will say that I sincerely hope that when I report the circumstances to Crown Office they take cognisance of what I advise."

He stood, causing the other three to also stand and turning towards Cowan said, "Please show Miss Hall and her client out of the office, Paul."

Harry Downes ushered Barry Ashford through the door and was about to close it when with a charming smile, he turned to her and asked, "Couldn't find me a coffee, could you my dear? The stuff the RAF provide is quite ghastly."

Downes face turned white with fury, but at a nod from Martin Cairney, she hissed, "I'll see what I can do," and closed the door. Ashford turned and extending his hand to Cairney, said, "Martin, how good to see you again after all these years and belated congrats on your promotion to Chief Constable." Turning, he stared quizzically at Mulgrew and with a soft smile, was about to extend his hand and said, "And if I recall correctly, this is the charming Sergeant Mulgrew?"

"Detective Chief Superintendent Mulgrew," she quite deliberately placed both hands behind her back.

"Indeed," he smiled at the obvious rudeness before turning to the Justice Minister and again extending his hand, said, "And you, sir, of course need no introduction. I was only saying just yesterday to the Home Secretary what a marvelous job you are doing up here with your," he paused, "*provincial* Government."

The Minister bristled at Ashford's rudeness, but before he could respond they watched as Ashford reached into a suit pocket and withdrew a pack of French cigarettes and a gold plated lighter from another pocket. About to flip open the lid of the cigarette pack, Cairney forestalled him by raising his hand and telling him, "We have a no smoking policy in our buildings, Mister Ashford, so please observe our rules."

"Oh, my dear chap," he looked crestfallen. "Surely you can overlook my little bad habit on this one occasion?"

"Regretfully, no," Cairney firmly told him.

With a deep sigh, he returned the pack to his pocket as Cairney continued, "Why don't we all have seat and you can tell us, Mister Ashford, exactly what brings you to Scotland."

The four soft chairs had been placed around coffee table in preparation for their discussion. Seating themselves with Mulgrew opposite Ashford, it didn't escape her notice that he quite deliberately glanced across at her legs. Angry with herself that she had forgotten what a lecher the man is, she sat stiffly back into the chair and pulled down at the hem of her skirt.

"What brings me here?" Ashford repeated and stared at Cairney as though the questions was foolish, "Why, Chief Constable, I thought that must be blatantly obvious; the Islamic terrorist attack in your city, of course."

"You have some information as to who was responsible?" interrupted the Minister.

Ashford turned towards him and slowly replied, "Not as such, Minister, though I do believe that among many such groups, our Middle East friends from ISIL are claiming responsibility, are they not? However, regardless of who orchestrated the attack I am here at the instruction of the Director General and of course with the full knowledge of the Home Secretary and on behalf of Her Majesty's Government. My purpose is to offer any assistance or resources that your local people might request. After all, we *are* a United Kingdom under one rule, that of the Westminster Government. Is that not so?"

The Minister dearly wished to retort, 'for the time being', but instead turned towards Cairney and eyes narrowing, asked, "Do we immediately require any assistance from our southern neighbours, Chief Constable?"

"Miss Mulgrew?" Cairney turned towards her then as if in explanation, added, "Miss Mulgrew is our Head of Counter Terrorism here in Scotland."

"As I am already aware, Chief Constable, and I'm certain your little department will be in good hands," Ashford smoothly replied and then added with a sly smile, "So, what can we in the Central Government do to assist you in the wilds of the northern region?"

She felt her heart beat against her chest and refusing to be provoked, forced herself to be calm before replying, "You can start by explaining to us with all your resources that include two and a half thousand intelligence personnel, the vast interception facilities at your disposal at GCHQ and the immense budget you have access to, why you had no prior information about the attack launched yesterday in Glasgow. Nor why, with those resources at your disposal, you are unable to identify the photographs, fingerprints or

DNA samples of the four dead gunmen that yesterday evening were forward by courier to both Thames House and Scotland Yard Counter Terrorism Unit."

"What?" he pretended surprise, "you haven't had any response yet? Why, Miss Mulgrew, that *does* surprise me. Let me assure you when I return to the capital of our great nation, I *will* get onto that right away."

It didn't escape her notice he failed to answer the question about the prior information of the attack and ignoring the inference that was London the centre of the universe, she continued. "You might also wish to explain, Mister Ashford, why the four weapons and multiple ammunition that we recovered do not seem to be listed on any ballistic list, anywhere in the civilised world."

"My dear Miss Mulgrew," his cultured voice oozed scorn, "You must realise that the number of AK47's manufactured throughout the years now number in the millions. We at Thames House can't *possibly* keep track of them all."

"Agreed," she slowly nodded, her eyes narrowing as though deep in thought and staring at him, said, "but when did it become common practise for terrorists to use acid to remove or score the serial numbers from their weapons? My information is that there has never been a case where seized terrorist munitions have had their serial numbers removed and besides, why would they bother if their intention was to re-use those weapons?"

She stared intently at him and continued, "The removal of the serial numbers, Mister Ashford, suggest to me the weapons the gunmen used had likely previously been seized and if the gunmen's mission went ape shit, as it so drastically did, without the serial numbers there would be no link to the origin of the AK47's and therefore the supplier of the weapons."

"I would agree with your assessment," Ashford continued, his smile frozen to his face, "but what has that to do with Her Majesty's Security Service? We do *not* provide weapons to terrorists," he scoffed at the very notion.

Mulgrew didn't respond, but she could feel her heart beating rapidly.

Ashford's surprising defence of the Security Service seemed to imply that he was thinking on his feet. Closely watched by both Cairney and the Justice Minister, she decided to continue the verbal sparring and inhaling, then slowly exhaling, simply replied, "Moving on. I now refer to the Czechoslovakian manufactured Semtex that was discovered in the terrorists van that was to be used as the initiator for the home made explosive. The Semtex was from the same batch as that discovered in the bomb vests worn by two of the gunmen."

She smiled as though about to divulge a great secret and continued, "My Forensic scientists, in collaboration with their PSNI and Garda Síochána colleagues, inform me that the signature of the Semtex matches that of a large shipment of Semtex and munitions recovered by the Irish Navy when in 1984, they intercepted an IRA gunrunning ship, the Marita Ann." Her eyes narrowed. "Coincidentally, there was also a large number of AK47's recovered, many of which according to the Garda Síochána, were delivered to both the then RUC and British intelligence who had brokered a deal so that those weapons and others previously seized might be examined for the purpose of conducting ballistic checks against Irish republican attacks, both in Northern Ireland and the UK mainland. Also, interestingly enough, within the last hour while I was visiting our office in Baird Street, I learned from our Forensic people that when they conducted a test, they discovered the Semtex seized from the bomb vests also had the same signature as fragments that were recovered after a device that exploded a number of years ago in Glasgow; a device that was used to destroy a car that at the time was being driven by a Scottish supporter of the Irish republican movement. You might recall that incident, Mister Ashford?"

Almost in unison, Cairney and the Justice Minister's heads snapped round to stare at him.

A tense silence fell in the room, broken when the pale faced Ashford calmly asked, "Might one inquire where this conversation is leading, Miss Mulgrew?"

"Just asking, Mister Ashford and after all," she shrugged and smiled humorlessly at him, "it's simply conjecture on my part, though," her eyes narrowed again as she stared intently at him, "I *am* curious to know how four Islamic terrorist could possibly lay hands upon an explosive that would seem at one time to have either been in the control of the Garda Síochána or the RUC *or* Her Majesty's Security Service. The same Semtex that was also used by the people who killed the man in Glasgow all those years ago. Let me think," she theatrically placed a forefinger against her lips then pointed it directly at him. "You must recall the incident for I'm certain you were in the city at the time, visiting our offices in Pitt Street."

Before he could respond, the door knocked and was pushed open by Harry Downes to permit her secretary to pass her by and who carried a tray upon which rested a silver coffee pot, four cups and saucers, sugar bowl and milk jug.

Shit, Mulgrew inwardly thought, just when she had him on the ropes. The untimely delivery of the coffee inadvertently gave Ashford time to compose himself.

"Sorry, sir," Downes stared at Cairney and in a monotone voice, said, "We're out of them, eh, what do you call them? Those fancy English muffins."

Repressing a smile at the innuendo, Cairney nodded and replied, "The coffee will be fine, Chief Inspector," and smiled his thanks at the nervous secretary.

When the door was again closed, Ashford turned to Mulgrew and with an icy stare, asked, "Shall I be mum or would you…." he narrowed his eyes and continued, "Of course. Sorry, Miss Mulgrew, I forgot. Here, let me."

She turned pale and her body tensely shook at the inferred reference to her homosexuality, but inwardly determined that she would not be provoked.

They watched as he poured coffee into the four cups, milk into one and then lifting the milked cup, sat back and crossed his legs in his perfectly creased trousers.

None of the other three moved to take theirs.

"Regarding the nonsense you just suggested, Miss Mulgrew, I have no knowledge of such a thing," he evenly replied.

"No, of course you haven't," she smiled humourlessly at him.

Ashford turned to address the Minister and said, "Now that Miss Mulgrew's fantasy seems to have ebbed, my dear sir, I reiterate I am authourised to extend to you every assistance that you may require to ensure that this outrage against your city does not occur again."

"My city?" the Minister stared curiously at him as he experienced a peculiar revulsion for the man. "Strange words indeed, Mister Ashford, for that is the second time you have referred to Glasgow as 'your city'. It's almost," he half smiled, "as though you are keen to remind the three of us that we are *not* after all a United Kingdom. Now, you could not possibly be inferring that yesterday's attack in the largest city in Scotland was intended to remind the people of Scotland that we need the protection of the Westminster Government; that the Scottish Government is unable to provide protection for its citizens *without* the aid of the UK Government."

"Indeed I am not suggesting anything or the sort, Minister," Ashford returned his smile. "Why, after all we are *all* British, Minister, are we not."

He made a point of glancing at his watch and supping the remains of his coffee, got to his feet and smiling, said, "I am so sorry to cut this short, but the Director General has insisted that I return to Thames House with an update of our meeting prior to his bridge night."

Cairney also rose to his feet and with a smirk, replied, "Aye, we wouldn't want him to miss his bridge night, would we?"

"Well, you have our offer," he pointedly remarked, then turning, added, "Miss Mulgrew, as always, a great pleasure."

"Indeed," she could not help herself as she hissed a snapped response.

"So," Ashford smiled down at the seated Minister, "if there is anything that you would require of my Service, please do not hesitate to contact us, sir." he nodded a farewell and with a forced smile, left the room.

The Justice Minister, still seated, glanced up at Cairney and with a deep sigh, said, "Why do I get the feeling I need to wash my hands?"

They sat for another fifteen minutes, the Justice Minister shaking his head throughout, still shocked that Cathy Mulgrew had challenged the Security Service man in such a manner; her submission, tentative though it might be, that MI5 might not only have been aware of the attack but actively provided the equipment to the four gunmen. It seemed somehow…ridiculous!

"I gathered from what you said, Miss Mulgrew, that you infer the Security Service are hindering your inquiries attempt to identify these four gunmen?"

"They have tremendous resources available to them, sir. If the four gunmen are on any kind of watch list, we would have had an almost immediate response, but only if the Service play ball. Yes," she slowly nodded, "I suspect they are hindering our inquiry, but why I'm not yet certain."

"And you believe they might have had some knowledge of this attack on Glasgow?"

"It's open to speculation, but the Security Service are no strangers to deception or deceit. That's the very nature of their trade."

"But why? Why would they involve themselves in such a dastardly affair?" he stared at Cairney. "It just seems so incredible!"

He stared at them both in turn and settling his gaze upon Mulgrew, added, "Surely what you related is purely circumstantial, that there is nothing whatsoever to believe or even suspect the UK Government would have knowledge or even condone such an affair."

Mulgrew shrugged and replied, "Politics isn't my forte, Minister, but you and your Government have clearly indicated your desire to split from the Union. Now, this you must understand is an opinion only, but consider this; what if some element within the UK Government believe that the Scottish people needed reminding that as part of the United Kingdom, there is safety in numbers, as it were."

"And," the Ministers eyes narrowed, caught up in Mulgrew's suspicion, "by launching such attack against innocent members of the public, this is their way, this unnamed group of individuals I mean; their way of reminding us that we require the protection of the Union?"

Cairney again shrugged and said, "Not everyone who works for the Government in London acts in the interests of the people, Minister.

You surely cannot believe that we in Scotland represent a majority vote in Westminster, sir?"

"No, of course not," the Minister surly replied, then added, "I'm sorry, Chief Constable, I'm being rude. It's just that I'm still trying to get my head around what that man said."

He glanced over to Mulgrew. "You seem very sure of your facts regarding the weapons and explosives these terrorists used, Miss Mulgrew. However, regarding your opinion about the Security Service having some knowledge of the attack, will you ever be able to substantiate any of it?"

"The problem with Intelligence matters, Minister, is that much of what we know or learn is based on assumption; on the few facts that we can glean. Consider it to be like a jigsaw. We learn of this or that and employ professional analysts to put two and two together, though we don't always come up with four. However," she sighed, "you saw as I did Ashford's reaction to my questions so while you might interpret his response differently, I am of the opinion that what he told us was simply what he believed we wanted to hear. It's what he *didn't* tell us that interest me more. I reiterate that I am almost certain that in today's age of instant communication the request we made for identification of the four gunmen is being deliberately delayed, though why I am uncertain."

"I think it's a power play by Ashford," interjected Cairney. "He's letting us know that when he's ready, he'll pass the information when it suits him."

"Can't you speak with the Metropolitan Police Commissioner? Surely as one Chief Constable to another, he would be only too happy to assist us?"

"He seems to be a good man, Minister and I've no doubt he would," Cairney replied, "but I suspect that the Commissioner is also subject to the Home Secretary's instructions and she will be receiving her information from the Security Service."

"What a bloody system," the Minister shook his head. "Well," he wearily pulled himself to his feet, "it's been a bit of an eye-opener meeting that man, so if you would excuse me, Chief Constable, Miss Mulgrew," he nodded to them in turn, "I'll head back to Edinburgh and update the First Minister with what I heard here today. Don't be surprised if you both receive a summons to Bute House for a meeting about all of this," and with that, led them from the room.

He had made his decision.

There was nobody and nothing left for him here anyway and so in the kitchen, he knelt and carefully prised up the floorboard then reaching underneath for the diary, dragged out the dusty, heavy leather bag of gold coins.

Returning to the front room, he sat at the old table and poured himself a vodka. Raising the glass to his lips, his eyes narrowed and deep in thought, he stopped and stared at it.

This was not the time for drink, not if he was to accomplish what needed to be done. No, better to stay off alcohol until the job was done.

With a sigh he returned the glass to the table and flicked through the diary pages until he found the phone number that he needed.

He placed the glass onto the diary to keep the pages apart and opened the box with the new mobile phone inside, then burst the blister pack that contained the SIM card.

Inserting the card into the phone he removed his wristwatch then laid it onto the tale, face up and glancing at the diary, carefully dialed the phone number.

The call was almost immediately answered and taking a deep breath he said, "As-salāmu ʿalaykum, Akhmad Soslanbek; it is me. I estimate four minutes for a trace then I'm hanging up and destroying the SIM."

He inhaled and continued, "I need to call in that favour. Yes," he hurriedly nodded at the phone, "a passport, travel clothes, credit cards, some Euro's and a personal history that will endure an immigration computer check. Also, a contact over there from whom I can collect a weapon; a hand gun with a shoulder holster and sufficient ammo."

Soslanbek suggested three different weapons to which he replied, "Yes, the 9mm Berretta will do just fine."

He listened intently as the man called Soslanbek spoke then answered, "I know it is very short notice, Akhmad, but I would like everything to be in place by tomorrow morning and yes, I am prepared to pay extra. Payment will be," he glanced at the dusty bag and smiled, "in gold coin. Yes," he smiled with a nod, "gold coin. The Roman Antiquity Department at the University had no further use for their prize collection of Aureus of Trajan coins."

Soslanbek spoke again and he replied, "Where? To Britain, yes," then agreed that a flight to Heathrow Airport in England would be suitable and requested transport be arranged to carry him to where he wished to go.

As soon as the call ended he popped the SIM card from the phone and snapped it in half.

His wristwatch indicated the call had lasted less than three minutes.

The phone he would dispose of later when he went downstairs to speak with the trusted woman who cleaned and purchased groceries for him.

Between now and leaving for England, he had a lot to do and thoughtfully rubbed at his unshaven face and lengthy, unkempt hair.

He stared at the broken SIM card and his brow furrowed, his thoughts turning again to the attack that had killed his Malika.

The gunmen might be dead, but his experience in the wars taught him that they were but foot soldiers; the real mastermind behind the attack would not be anywhere near the fighting.

That was the man or woman he had to find.

That was the individual he was bound by blood to kill.

CHAPTER NINE

When she drove off after dropping him outside his close in Corruna Street, Ian Macleod turned to wave his thanks at Louise Hall.

He unlocked the close door and almost at once, Missus McPhail, the elderly spinster who policed the close like a Scots Guardsman, peeked her head from her front door and said, "Oh, it's yourself, Mister Macleod. Been out, have you?"

He almost replied that seeing as how he was entering the close of course he had been out, but had learned in the early days that nobody joked with Miss McPhail. Instead he grinned and told the old woman, "Just for a wee walk, Missus McPhail. I like to keep this exercised," and patted at his left leg as he walked toward the stairs.

"Aye, and so you should," she muttered in reply, then before closing her door, added, "Don't forget it's the recycle bin that's going out tomorrow."

"No problem," he cheerfully called out at her reminder of his weekly favour to her as he limped up the stairs.

He first switched on the kettle for a brew and then with a cuppa in his hand, settled himself into the comfortable couch in the front room that overlooked Corruna Street.

Sipping at the tea, he smiled almost in irritation, thinking to himself here I am, unemployed, unmarried, no girlfriend, most of my friends away serving with the Regiment and now I'm possibly facing a murder charge for killing three of the four guys that definitely deserved to be slotted.

He thought again of the man Glennie, the man in charge who seemed to Ian to be fair and who would be reporting Ian's action at the incident to the people at the top; the Crown Office people Glennie had called them.

If he was honest it angered him that he might have to wait for news and according to his new lawyer, Miss Hall, it might be at best weeks or at worst months before a decision was reached.

He softly exhaled and arched his back.

His leg ached, but what was new there. In time, the surgeon had told him, the ache would disappear, but not the limp; that was there to stay.

He sat for another ten minutes, his eyes closed and relaxing against the tide of frustration that sometimes threatened to overwhelm him. Opening his eyes, he reached to the side table for his IPad and logged into his bank account to check his finances.

The sacking today and loss of a salary wouldn't immediately impact upon him for he realised that if he was frugal, he still had the wound compensation money to tide him over for a couple of months. He owned the flat outright and other than rates and factor fees, that wasn't an issue. Though he held a driving license, he didn't own a car and most days walked both to save fares and exercise his leg. However, he did need to find a job and with a smile, opened a search engine to find vacancies where a gimpy, former soldier with a scarred face might just be employable.

Lost in thought at his desk in the room he used as an office, Rahib Chowdhury idly tapped a pencil against his white teeth.

The door was timidly knocked and his teenage wife of two years, her face shadowed by her hijab and her head politely bowed as she entered the room.

"Do you wish to eat here, my husband or at the table."

"How many times, Rabia, must I tell you? *I* will decide when I eat. Now, I am busy. Get out!"

She hastily closed the door with a soft thud.

He closed his eyes against the drum that suddenly began to beat a tattoo in his head.

He had been weak; weak and foolish and his weakness had left him exposed to the manipulation of the man called John.

No longer could he access the web sites for to do so would again bring him to the attention of the kafir police and ultimately, to that bastard John who promised so little, but demanded so much of him.

His life was a mess and it worried him that in the Mosque today, the elderly Sheikh Marzook Hussain had noticed the absence of Abdul-hameed Muhammad. The devout and truthful old man was as sharp as a tack and would not forget Rahib's association with Muhammad and particularity, not if he was asked.

His eyes narrowed as he wondered; but who would ask the Sheikh?

A cold fear enveloped him as the thought leapt into his head; a thought so dreadful that even thinking it frightened him.

To save himself and to prevent the old man relating his suspicions about Muhammad's absence, would it be necessary to dispose of Sheikh Marzook Hussain?

He shuddered and shook his head to rid himself of the dreadful image of him killing the old, blind Sheikh.

He needed a release, something to take his mind off his fear.

He turned quickly towards the door and knew that he was safe, that Rabia would not again enter without him calling for her and certainly not without knocking.

Licking at his suddenly dry lips, he reached down and pulled open the lower drawer in the desk and from beneath a pile of papers, lifted out the glossy magazine.

With trembling fingers, he flicked through the pages of the magazine and stared at the photographs within; images of prepubescent children being subjected to the most vile, sexual practices.

Staring intently at the photographs, his breathing became labored and he reached for his groin.

They made their official farewell to the Justice Minster at the front door of Dalmarnock office, conscious that some reporters and cameramen had hung about in the front foyer to record the three of them leaving the building and watched as the Government car bore the Minister rapidly away before returning upstairs to again occupy Harry Downes office.

Seated with a fresh cup of coffee, Martin Cairney stared keenly and suspiciously at Cathy Mulgrew.

"So, tell me about this information you received from the Forensic people when you were at Baird Street, *Miss* Mulgrew. This information that the Semtex in the Glasgow east end explosion all those years ago that had the same signature as the Semtex recovered yesterday."

"Ah, well, there might have been a wee white lie there, Chief Constable," she formally replied, a mischievous smile playing about her lips.

"You devious bugger," he grinned at her. "Well, if nothing else, it bloody threw him anyway. Did you see his face?" he smiled at her then became a more serious when he asked, "That story you related about the Semtex and weapons from the ship that was stopped by the Irish navy and the weapons we recovered. All true?"

"Yes, sir. All true," she confirmed with a nod.

"You realise, Cathy, that you all but accused Ashford and his mob of being complicit in yesterday's atrocity?"

"All I did was present some facts, sir. How he construes those facts is his business though I did find it interesting that he denied the Security Service *were* involved. Guilty conscience, do you think?"

"Well, you certainly gave him some food for thought and not just Ashford for I believe that the Justice Minister will be in the back of that car putting everything he heard today down onto paper before he meets with our First Minister. Believe me when I tell you, she is one smart lady and if there is even the *hint* of the Westminster Government being aware of or God forbid, complicit in yesterday's attack," he didn't finish, but simply shook his head and shrugged when he added, "Like the Minister told us, I expect we'll likely get a phone call tomorrow inviting us for a wee chat, so keep your diary free."

"What about Ashford, sir. What position does he hold now in the Security Service?"

"I'm not certain, Cathy, but he must be up there near the top of the tree if he is here representing the Director General and of course, those snide references to having wee chats with the Home Secretary. You know as well as I do what these buggers are like. Everything about them and their shenanigans in Whitehall and Westminster is all posturing, namedropping and political one-upmanship."

He paused and smiled at her.

"Seeing him today brought back a memory. It was after I was accepted for the Senior Command Course at Bramshill Police College down in Hampshire, just when I was promoted out of the Special Branch. One of my fellow students was a Superintendent in the former RUC and we got to talking about intelligence issues. Curiously, Barry Ashford's name cropped up and quite frankly my colleague had nothing good to say about him. He knew Ashford when they were both members of a covert team trying to sign on informers to act against the IRA and," Cairney smiled, "told me that Ashford's nickname among the team was Corkscrew."

"Corkscrew?"

"Aye, apparently the rest of the team called him Corkscrew because he was the most twisted bastard in the unit and he warned me that Ashford was most definitely not to be trusted."

Mulgrew's mobile phone indicated an incoming call and glancing at it, said. "Excuse me, sir. It's John Glennie."

"John," she answered the call and Cairney watched as her brow furrowed. "Yes, thank you," she said and ending the call turned to him to say, "Glennie's team just received a package couriered to Helen Street by a Military Police motorcyclist. The package contains names and details of the four gunmen. With your permission, Glennie requested I attend there now, sir."

Cairney grinned and said, "Seems that little chat with Ashford paid off then. Keep me apprised, Cathy and even if it's late, you can contact me at home. You have my number."

He sat alone in the body of the Sea King as it flew across the border and onwards towards London City Airport where a car would be waiting to convey him to Thames House.

Bloody woman, he continued to fume!

Fucking queer bitch!

Talking to him as though he were some sort of subversive!

His eyes narrowed at the mention of the Semtex being from the same batch as that used all those years ago to kill that Irish republican sympathiser, Frank Brogan.

If ever a man deserved to die it was that fucking IRA loving, child rapist.

Still, his eyes narrowed, the reference had thrown him and grudgingly admitted, well played Miss Mulgrew.

Her information about the AK47's serial numbers had also been spot on as was that about the Semtex. He assumed that she had lied when she said it was a collusion between the Forensic scientists of those police services that provided her with the information.

No, he wryly grinned; that was a poor lie. Those Forensic people never divulged anything to each other, not unless they were ordered to.

Her lie suggested to him that it was Mulgrew herself who had discovered that information and inferred she had excellent sources among both the PSNI and the Garda Síochána. Sources that he would ferret out and turn to his own advantage.

His phone call to release and deliver the information about the four gunmen had been timed just as he was being driven from the Dalmarnock office. The timing would demonstrate to those parochial Jock *bastards* who sought to divide the Realm that they were at the London Governments beck and call, that they could not conduct their inquiries without the authority of either Scotland Yard, who in turn were themselves subject to the say-so of the Security Service. The Jocks, just like their Mick counterparts in Northern Ireland, constantly needed reminding that there was a pecking order and at the top of that ladder was Her Majesty's Government at Whitehall.

His thoughts turned to the Justice Minister; a skinny, bespectacled bastard who believed because he had a fancy title that it gave him some sort of autonomy in his little, backward country.

The man had been totally out of his depth, sitting listening to the verbal sparring he had conducted with Mulgrew.

Wanker, he dismissed him from his thoughts.

He glanced at the RAF crewman who with his radio link trailing behind him like an umbilical cord, left his seat for a moment to enter the cabin of the aircraft, then returned and made his way towards Ashford.

The crewman tapped at the side of his helmet to indicate Ashford plug his own helmet lead into the communication socket behind him.

"Yes?" he snapped at the crewman.

"Pilot says to inform you, sir, that we land in forty minutes and message is you are to proceed with due haste to Thames House for debrief."

It didn't help Ashford's mood the crewman had a soft, Scottish burr to his voice.

Surly nodding his acknowledgment, he jerked his lead from the socket, unaware that as the crewman turned away he thought the suited spook to be a right miserable arse.

He lowered his head, his brow furrowed as he considered the message.

Of course when he landed it was already his intention that return to Thames House.

But the message; proceed with due haste?

No, that was not a request.

His mouth tightened.

It was a summons.

The media continued to lead their news broadcasts with the shooting incident and though Buchanan Street was now open and no longer being treated as a crime scene, visibly armed officers patrolled the area while unarmed officers, notable in their yellow fluorescent jackets, stood monitoring the rain soaked crowds who for their own reasons continued to flock to the location.

The sites where the two men and the young homeless woman had been brutally gunned down were now awash with flowers, candles and messages of sympathy as was the pavement beside the shattered shop window in Buchanan Street where the middle-aged shop assistant had been gunned down when the store was sprayed with bullets.

Taking advantage of the large crowds, a number of enterprising buskers who were now working among the crowds in the precinct. Several hundred yards away at the place in the High Street where the bus that had been riddled with gunfire stopped, even more flowers were laid in tribute to the young pregnant Somalian woman and the elderly lady who suffered the heart attack, though the street was free of crowds.

At intervals in the television broadcasts, reporters sought the views of experts or those individuals who believed themselves to be experts, on either the root cause of the attack or the so far unnamed individuals who committed the atrocity or what should be done to prevent a similar tragedy.

Much discussed was the unnamed individual who had thwarted the gunmen's murder of a number of hostages with some experts calling him a hero while a minority continued to question his shooting three of the gunmen in the head.

The word 'execution' was also bandied about.

One issue that infuriated the media bosses was that no matter how many witnesses their reporters spoke with, none gave the same description of the man who was being dubbed by the popular press as the 'Flat Cap Hero.'

While some witnesses were certain the man walked with a limp, others were not so sure; a small number of witnesses thought he might have had a facial scar or scars, yet none recalled nor mentioned his deformed ear. Most admitted that while in close proximity to the gunmen who held them hostage or from whom they ran, they were so terrified that if they did see the man who the media sought, so traumatised were they that they took little notice of anything other than that he carried a rifle. What the more certain witnesses were sure of was the man wore a dark coloured jacket and a hat of some sort.

Unable to track down the 'Flat Cap Hero', the media turned their frustrated attention to lambasting the police and the apparent lack of armed officers who were in the city centre at the material time of the attack, with broadcasters continuing to remind viewers that the Police Scotland official statement declared they would not discuss or disclose operational matters. Needless to say, this statement was heavily criticised by the armchair warriors.

However, fairer inclined reporters did remind their viewers that the Police Scotland officers, like their English and Welsh colleagues, were not routinely armed and thus most of those officers in close proximity to the incident would not have been able to resist an armed attack anyway.

Another consequence of the attack in Glasgow city centre was an upsurge of religious and racial tension that swept across not just Glasgow, but the United Kingdom as a whole and even as far afield as the European continent, where right wing groups made much of the murders.

The media also seized upon reports of Muslim men and women being verbally abused in the streets of Glasgow and sensationalised one disturbing incident, a Muslim grandmother who was escorting her two grandchildren being threatened with violence by a drunken man.

What the news channel failed to add in the report was the intervention by two passers-by, Christian women who set about the thug with their rolled up umbrellas as well as the crowd that gathered to harangue the drunk who upon the arrival of the police, was thereafter taken into custody for his own safety.

Another incident that the media either failed to report or considered of little interest was the packet of pork link sausages thrown at the door of a Mosque in the Pollokshields area of the city. The two Muslim women who volunteered to remove the offending missile fell about laughing when they saw the sausages were still tightly packaged in their cellophane wrapper, one of whom took them home for her pensioner neighbour with the comment, "Wee Andy in the flat below is on his own since his wife died, so these will do fine for his dinner."

The statement had taken just over two hours to note and by the time DS McInnes and her neighbour DC Chalmers were satisfied that Daisy could tell them no more, she was both mentally and physically shattered.

Seeing them to the door, she turned and with a smile accepted their thanks for the coffee and sandwiches.

She was about to turn away when she remembered and said, "Sergeant…Mo. One more thing. The young lassie, the homeless girl. Have you identified her or managed to trace any relatives?"

McInnes bit at her lower lip and made the decision that it was not in the young constable's interest to be informed as to the real identity of Malika Umarov. At least not yet and not until she run it past the boss.

Staring Daisy in the eye, she replied, "No, no one. I don't think we'll trace a next of kin, Daisy. Sorry."

Daisy slowly nodded and taking a deep breath said, "When it's done, the PM I mean. She'll likely be buried here if you can't trace any relatives. I know that's it's not really any of my business," she choked back a sob, "but it just doesn't seem right she gets buried with nobody there. Could you…I mean, can I go; attend the ceremony?" She paused to catch her breath then added, "To the funeral, I mean. I was the last person she spoke with and, well, anyway…"

She could feel herself welling up and fought back the tears. McInnes reached across to rub comfortingly at her arm and with a sigh, replied, "I can't see anyone objecting to that, Daisy. I'll run it by my boss and I've no doubt he'll probably agree. One thing, though; you're on sick leave as of now, so if you *do* decide to attend, don't wear your uniform. Go in civvies because I've no doubt the press will be there too and you don't need the hassle of them interviewing you, okay?"

"Okay, and thanks."

"Right then, I'll give you a phone call when the funeral time and date is set. Bye for now."

It was when she closed and locked the door behind them, she slid down to the floor with her back to the door, her knees tightly together and wrapping her arms about her legs, uncontrollably wept. Time passed and she thought she had been sat there for anything between five and fifteen minutes before she forced herself to her feet and wiping her eyes and her nose on the sleeve of her sweatshirt, steadied herself against the wall for her legs felt shaky.

She took a deep breath and stumbled into the lounge, groping her way towards the couch where she flopped down, her head suddenly pounding.

Get a grip of yourself, you stupid woman, she inwardly hissed and rising to her feet, made her way to the bathroom to wash her face. Stood at the wash hand basin, she filled the glass tumbler with water and took deep gulps, gasping as the cold water hit the back of her throat and spilling some of the water onto the front of the sweatshirt. Wiping at her mouth with her sleeve, she stared into the mirror and considered that maybe her parents had been correct; maybe she needed some time with them, being cared for and fussed over.

She continued to stare into her eyes, now red and bloodshot from weeping and made her decision.

Before she did anything else, she had something to do. Something she had to attend to before it was too late; something important to her.

Cathy Mulgrew identified herself on the intercom set into the concrete post by the entrance gate and watched the heavy metal bollards recess into the ground. It was standard practise when a terrorist related incident was ongoing that Helen Street police office operated the bollards to prevent unauthorised vehicles trying to access the rear yard.

Parking as close as she could get, she covered her head with her handbag against the rain and made a dash for the rear door. It was by good fortune the door was opened by two officers who were leaving the office as she arrived, one of whom recognised her and smiled. Dashing past them, she shook the raindrops from her handbag and made her way via the rear stairs to the suite being occupied the Counter Terrorism Unit inquiry team.

John Glennie was standing in the corridor with one of his junior officers when he saw her and smiled, indicating with a nod they proceed to his office.

"Coffee?" he pulled out the chair from opposite his side of the desk.

"No, thanks. I had one before I left Dalmarnock. Two cups within an hour and I'm peeing for Scotland."

"Right," he grinned and settled himself into his chair. "We've had a result. The Military Police from Edinburgh brought through files on our four gunmen," and placed a hand upon a cardboard folder. "Do you want to review them or shall I give you a verbal briefing?"

"Verbal, please," she rubbed at her aching forehead. "Bloody weather always seems to bring on a headache."

He smiled and referring to his handwritten note on his pad, began. "Their names, though likely they won't mean anything to you, are as follows. Aarif Sidiq aged twenty-five, Abdul-hameed Muhammad also aged twenty-five, Abdul-salam Nasher who is thirty-three years of age and was formerly known as Joseph Crocker…"

"He's the white man?"

"That's him," Glennie nodded and continued, "and lastly, Fadi Hussain, who was the youngest at nineteen."

"Photographs?"

"There's a selection," replied Glennie who handed her a number of photographs across the desk. "As you can see, Cathy, the photographs are mainly surveillance photographs though the convert Crocker…"

"Revert," she interrupted.

He stared curiously at her.

"There is a belief in Islam we are all born Muslim, but some lose their faith and when they return to the faith, they revert back to Islam."

"Every day is a school day," he quipped. "Anyway, the photograph of Crocker was taken at his time of arrest by the Metropolitan Police when, wait for it, he was a neo-Nazi and arrested at a demonstration."

"Neo-Nazi? You're kidding!"

"Nope," he shook his head. "Apparently it's quite common for some of these…reverts, to change sides. Something to do with their need to belong as well as their need to be involved in violence."

"The fact that they were under surveillance," her brow furrowed. "Does that mean they were known as activists?"

"According to the reports I've read, they were all recorded as low risk followers of a couple of notorious rabble rousers in the London area. Recorded by the Met because of their attendance at demonstrations, that sort of thing."

Her eyes narrowed in suspicion. "So, these reports are all Metropolitan Police reports and photographs; nothing yet from the Security Service?"

"No, why?"

"It's just that I find it rather odd that four," she waggled her fingers in the air, "low risk types suddenly pick up rifles and explosives and conduct a synchronised, coordinated attack upon a major city centre. It doesn't take a genius, John, to realise that this operation that was conducted took planning, recruitment of these four individuals, timing, and the acquisition of resources that include stolen vehicles and…"

She stopped and stared at him.

His eyes narrowed as he asked, "What?"

"All along we've assumed that this was some sort of Jihadist suicide group acting like others have in Europe. A group prepared to die to send out a message that no matter where in the West we are, we're vulnerable anywhere. You would agree with that?"

"Yes," he slowly nodded.

"But what if we're wrong," her mind was racing now. "Why were they wearing masks?"

His eyes widened as he replied, "Not to terrorise their victims, but because they didn't want to be identified that in turn would suggest…"

"They didn't intend to die or be captured!"

She shook her head and continued, "I don't believe this was a suicide mission. The van they booby-trapped. They weren't going back to it, were they; so how the *fuck* did they intend to escape?"

"Shit!" he slapped a hand down onto the table and grabbed at the desk phone. Dialing an internal number, he snapped out, "Paul. Mister Glennie. Find Lou Sheridan and both of you get in here now."

They stared at each other, then Glennie closed his eyes and grimacing, slapped at his forehead with the palm of his hand and muttered, "That's why there was only one two-way radio recovered! The gateway driver had the other!"

A minute later Sheridan and Cowan hurried through the door. Before they could speak, Glennie looked from one to the other and said, "We missed something. This wasn't a group on a death mission like we thought. They intended to escape to a vehicle and it must have been parked close by."

He glanced at Mulgrew and said, "They were moving eastwards."

Turning to Cowan, he asked, "You served in the Central Division, Paul. What's eastwards of the incident location where a vehicle can be hidden out of sight? Somewhere not further than a four hundred metre walk or run?"

"Other than at a parking meter on the street…"

"Unlikely," interrupted Sheridan, her hands raised. "They wouldn't want to be spotted entering the vehicle if it was parked out in the open and risk some passer-by taking their registration number and vehicle type."

"Then if it's under cover, Boss, I'd say you're looking at the nearest car park which is," Cowan's eyes narrowed as he pondered, then snapping his fingers, said, "the Montrose Street NCP car park."

"Right," Glennie pointed at him, "get someone over there to seize all their CCTV recordings for the last week. Any argument, cite the Terrorism Act and scare them shitless. Once you've done that, get onto the Central Division at Stewart Street and ask for their CCTV coverage for that area. I know we've already asked a lot of them, but explain we're extending the search area. Got that?"

"Boss," Cowan nodded and headed out the door.

Glennie turned to Mulgrew and sighed, "Sorry, Ma'am. I've fucked up. I should have considered that."

"Well, John," she dryly replied, "if as you so succinctly put it, fucked up, then so did I. What was to stop me thinking about that too?"

His eyes darted between Mulgrew and Sheridan in turn, then he said, "The Military Police also brought this over, Ma'am," and handed Mulgrew an A4 sized envelope. "It's the service record for Ian Macleod. It makes interesting reading, too." He smiled and said, "Verbal or do you want to read it?"

She returned his smile and replied, "Maybe you can summarise it for me."

"Well," he pulled the paperwork from the envelope and passing her a photograph, said, "that's Macleod before he was facially injured." She glanced at the headshot of a solemn and to her surprise, handsome looking man who stared back at her.

"Twenty years ago he joined the Royal Highland Fusiliers, who are now part of the Royal Regiment of Scotland, and attained the rank of Colour Sergeant. Served in several theatres including Northern Ireland, Iraq, the Baltic States and Sierra Leone and was on his fourth tour of Afghanistan when he received life threatening injuries."

He paused and with a shrug, added, "It was there he was awarded the Conspicuous Gallantry Cross."

She frowned and said, "I don't know what that medal is."

"I had to look it up on the Internet," he admitted and continued. "It's awarded for bravery and is second only to the Victoria Cross."

"Bloody hell! What did he do to earn that?"

"There's the copy of a document called an Action Report in his file. According to what I read, he was leading a patrol in the Helmand Province when one of his men stepped onto a mine. Another soldier went to help and triggered a second mine. At that point the patrol came under fire and though both wounded men were lying in the open, Macleod ordered the rest of the patrol to get into cover while he went out into the open after the two soldiers. Though he was continuously under fire, he got one soldier back into safe cover. However, when he went back out after the other soldier the Taliban fired something called an RPG rocket at them and blew Macleod twenty feet away, causing massive wounds. That didn't stop him though because while still under fire he crawled back and brought the second soldier into cover. Unfortunately, the poor lad later died through blood loss and shock. Macleod and the other wounded soldier were evacuated to the base hospital at Camp Bastion and later transferred back to the UK."

"I assume that his injuries were the scarring and the limp in his left leg?"

"Yes. The military kept him on the payroll for almost three years during his rehabilitation period, but he was officially discharged several months ago. My understanding from what he informally told Paul Cowan is that he's finding it difficult to hold down a job and only yesterday, before the incident in Buchanan Street, had just walked out of a call centre job in Bothwell Street."

"You know, John," she thoughtfully stared at him, "this palaver that's going on about Macleod shooting those bastards in the head. I don't want to unduly influence you and I'm certain you will make up your own mind, but it might be worth considering letting the Crown Office know that if they do decide to bring charges against Macleod that they will be prosecuting a highly decorated and injured war hero."

He grinned at her and replied, "My thoughts exactly."

The man under discussion was dozing while he sat on his couch and wakened by the knocking on his door.

His worry was that the police might deliberately or inadvertently slip his name and address to the press and the last thing he needed right now were reporters hammering upon his door.

Preparing himself for an argument, he limped to the door and pulled it open, but to his surprise, the young woman with the chestnut coloured, shoulder length hair, her hands thrust deeply into the side pockets of a navy blue coloured windcheater and wearing blue denim jeans and hiking boots, seemed vaguely familiar.

She also seemed nervous and hesitantly, he asked, "Yes?"

"Mister Macleod…Ian. I'm Daisy. Daisy Cooper. From yesterday. The policewoman? Your downstairs neighbour let me in the front door."

His eyes opened in recognition and he stuttered, "I'm sorry. I didn't recognise you with your clothes on. Oh," he felt himself blush. "What I mean is…"

She grinned self-consciously before replying, "Without my uniform, you mean?"

"Yes," he returned her grin. "Without your uniform."

They stood for a few seconds staring at each other before he startled and said, "Oh, I'm sorry. What am I thinking? Please," and stepping to one side, invited her in.

Her hesitation was clear and she said, "Look, I'm sorry. I don't really mean to disturb you. It's just that I didn't get the opportunity yesterday to say thank you. For saving my life, I mean. I got your name, well, your surname I mean, and your address from the office. I work out of Stewart Street and you were in there this morning. I just wanted to visit you and, well, tell you how grateful I am."

"I can put the kettle on," he smiled at her and fibbed, "I was about to have a cuppa anyway."

He could tell she was still ill at ease and softly added, "I'm not really a threat to you, Constable."

"Please," she grinned at him, "Daisy."

He saw her inhale as though making her mind up and at last, she puffed then nodding, said, "Okay and only if I'm not disturbing you. A cup of tea would be lovely."

He led her through the hallway to the lounge and learning she took milk only, made his way through to the kitchen. Putting on the kettle it occurred to him he should have asked if she'd like a sandwich and returning to the lounge, paused at the door and stared.

Daisy, her hands demurely clasped in front of her, was standing by the window peering out to the street below.

As he watched her, Ian thought her not beautiful, but certainly attractive and experienced an odd lump in his throat.

Like most men of his age, he had previously experienced relationships with women and on one occasion when in his late twenties, was briefly engaged. However, in the recent years since his wounding he had shied away from female company, conscious of and embarrassed by his facial scarring and the obvious limp to his left leg that he knew was not the best aphrodisiac known to man. But staring at the younger Daisy he realised that he missed female companionship, though not for an instant believed such an attractive young woman would look twice at him now. Once maybe, he inwardly grinned.

Daisy caught his reflection in the window and turning, saw Ian staring and smiled.

It was an awkward few seconds before he stuttered, "I haven't eaten this evening and was wondering if you'd maybe like a sandwich or something with your tea?"

"You haven't eaten," her brow furrowed, then she said, "Well, neither have I and to be honest, I haven't had much of an appetite today. But," she licked at her lips and her eyes narrowed, "I worked the beat around this area when I did a stint at Cranstonhill office. How about as a thank you, you let me buy you dinner." She grinned and continued, "There's a cracking chippy on Argyle Street."

"Eh," he hesitated and shrugging, nodded and with a smile replied,

"That would be grand."

"Fish and chips?"

"Yes, please," he nodded again.

"Right, Ian, you set the table and pour the tea," she passed him by, her eyes shining bright, "and I'll be back in five minutes."

The grey haired and exquisitely groomed man who sat behind the solid oak desk in the large office lifted the desk phone and said, "Yes?"

"Sir," his secretary replied, "that's the Director of Operations just arrived."

"At last," he sighed. "Send him in, please."

A few seconds later the heavy door opened to admit a breathless Barry Ashford, who made his way to the chair in front of the desk and with a polite nod, sat down.

"Sorry I'm a little late, Director," he said. "Traffic from the City Airport is murder at this time of the day."

The Director General sat back and making an arch of his fingertips, thoughtfully stared at his protégé.

"How did the meeting go?"

"Perhaps not as well as expected, sir. As instructed, I attended at the office in Glasgow where the Justice Minister for their local Government," he almost smirked, "and the Chief Constable were having their media briefing. Sodding yokels kept me waiting for almost an hour," he spat out, "then when at last they did condescend to meet with me, invited the Head of their Counter Terrorism Unit to sit in too. A woman called Catherine Mulgrew; a bloody dyke," he slyly grinned, "though, to look at her one would never guess about her sexual preference."

"Stick to the point, please Barry, there's a good fellow."

"Sorry, yes. Well, it seems that Miss Mulgrew has already made her own inquiries about the weapons used by...the terrorists," his eyebrows raised, "and discovered the rifles serial numbers were scorched with acid. Regretfully that has caused her to suspect their origin..."

"I do hope you are *not* about to give me bad news, Barry" the DG interrupted.

Ashford raised a hand and replied, "No sir, not at all. There is no way that Mulgrew can trace the weapons to their origin, whatever that origin might be," he smirked again.

"What about the profiles for the four gunmen. Have they been dispatched to Scotland?"

"Yes, sir. Immediately I left the meeting I instructed the profiles to be released and conveyed by military courier from our satellite office at Edinburgh Castle to the office in Glasgow, from where the police are running their inquiry. The information contained within simply lists them on our Watch List as attendees at Islamic demonstrations here in the Greater London area."

The DG paused and inhaling, leaned forward and placing both chubby, but manicured hands flat upon the desk, asked, "Is there anything, my dear fellow, anything at all that might come back and bite the Service in the arse? Anything that might attract the unwanted curiosity of our esteemed Home Secretary? You do understand that I will not tolerate questions being asked of us."

Ashford stared thoughtfully at the Director General.

He would not admit that he believed Cathy Mulgrew to be a dangerous spanner in the work of his operation, a woman who surprised him by turning out to be far brighter and shrewder than he had anticipated. The strategy conceived by him to shock those Jock bastards and their republican notions of independence would undoubtedly have worked had it not been but for the intervention of the man in Glasgow, and so he glibly lied, "No, sir. There is nothing."

What he dare not disclose was the *one* little loose end that just might need tying up.

One loose tongue that could undo all that he had worked for.

One insignificant man who he was certain no one would ever really miss.

CHAPTER TEN

The red-eye Air France Bae 146 glided to a smooth landing at Heathrow Airport and ten minutes later, taxied to the Gate at Terminal Four where it discharged its cargo of early morning business passengers.

The tall, well-built man in his early fifties with the neatly cropped salt and pepper hair, trimmed beard, wearing the expensive Italian business suit, gold framed spectacles and carrying the leather briefcase and matching suit-carrier, joined the queue for European travellers who waited patiently to pass though the Border Control Desk. Upon being called forward, the man produced the French issued passport in the name Fernand Marchand and smiled engagingly at the large black man who with the fixed smile, waved the European passport holders through, already having decided the man did not merit more than a passing glance.

Once through the gate he unconsciously breathed a sigh of relief; the first hurdle past.

Making his way to the exit he followed the signs towards the car park and remembered his instructions to keep to the left of the large car park where he would find the car.

Less than five minutes later he came upon the two-year-old maroon coloured BMW coupe and matched the registration number with the information he had been provided; with a glance to ensure that no one was watching, he bent down to recover the key from behind the nearside rear wheel.

Unlocking the car, he first opened the boot and lifting the carpet saw the brown coloured, thick, bulky envelope and a black leather shoulder holster. Again ensuring he was not being watched, he tipped up and emptied the envelope onto the carpet and smiled. A Berretta semi-automatic handgun dropped out along with a loaded spare magazine and a box of nine millimetre ammunition. Lifting the Beretta he weighed it in his hand and pressing the release button, the magazine in the weapon sprung out and he saw it was already loaded.

He smiled with relief.

His old friend Akhmad Soslanbek, now a leading figure of the Chechen mafia, had been true to his word, albeit the equipment and everything else Soslanbek had provided had come at a high price; almost a quarter of the coins in the bag of ancient Roman gold. Still, he had no complaint so far and the preparation and all the materials had been provided both speedily and exactly as he required.

Replacing the weapon and the ammunition into the envelope, he returned it to its hiding place under the carpet and lifting the suit carrier and the briefcase, placed both items in the boot.

Removing his jacket he laid it onto the rear seat and getting into the driver's seat, adjusted the seat and the rear view mirror before removing the parking ticket from under the visor.

Within the glove box he found a clean phone and saw the Satnav had already been programmed for his trip to Glasgow.

Taking a deep breath, Eldar Umarov started the engine and smoothly drove out from the parking bay.

Daisy Cooper turned over and yawned before glancing at the digital clock on her bedside table. She closed her eyes and snuggled even deeper into the quilt cover, enjoying the warmth of the bed and reluctant to get up.

She had been late home, her visit to Ian Macleod lasting far longer than she anticipated.

What had been planned as a quick handshake and thank you for saving my life turned out to be a fish supper dinner and lengthy conversation that carried almost past midnight.

Her eyes closed, she smiled at the initial awkwardness of their talk and even in her own bed, blushed at the memory of Ian smiling and telling her, "You're curious about my face and my ear."

She couldn't reply, only nod and that's when he told he had been injured in an explosion while serving with the military in Afghanistan. He didn't go into details, but her feminine intuition told her there was a lot more to the story than the few details that he did give.

What he did disclose was his experience when he was evacuated to a hospital in England, the realisation that his military career was over and that he would be left with both permanent scarring and a limp, though undoubtedly grateful that he lived.

He had paused and she suspected though did not ask that there was another or others who did not survive the explosion that injured Ian. He told her of the rehabilitation, of experiencing posttraumatic stress disorder that he referred to as PTSD, of the months of counselling and with a wry smile, of getting used to seeing his new face each morning when he shaved.

It was during his rehabilitation that he discovered the joy of cooking, of bashfully telling Daisy of his experiments with food and they laughed when he recounted his first attempts at feeding his creations to his fellow wounded soldiers and finally after months and months of studying, trial and error, at last attaining his catering qualifications from the college that was located near to the convalescent hospital.

No, he had said, there was no wife or children though had once been engaged, but narrowly escaped marriage when he discovered that when serving abroad for months on end, his fiancée was not as faithful as he had hoped she might be.

Comfortably huddled on his couch, she confided she too had recently been engaged, but the relationship ended when her bricklayer fiancé Billy presented her with an ultimatum; him or her job.

She had thought he was merely worried about her safety and briefly considered resigning from the police, but then realised to do so would be giving in to him when what she thought what they had was a partnership. It was then she began to notice little things; other occasions when Billy would get his own way and for the sake of avoiding argument, she would give in to his demands. She had shaken her head and told Ian, "He was trying to control my life and I just couldn't marry a man who didn't see me as an equal."

Curiously, Ian had suppressed a laugh and when a Daisy had frowned, he quickly explained that if she believed Billy had been worried about her safety, what would he think now after her very public near death experience yesterday?

Curiously, after their admissions, they had chatted like old friends; she learning his mother had died when in his late teens and his father remarried and then immigrated to Australia with Ian's younger sister and their father's two new step-children. Though his father had been keen for Ian to also emigrate, he had instead enlisted in the army. Yes, he told her, he kept in touch with his father and sister, now married and yes, he had visited his family several times over the years.

A little embarrassed, he had admitted that his while hobby was cooking, his ambition was to open his own café. Nothing too large or too fancy, he smiled at her; just a drop in place where he would serve good, wholesome food then a little hesitantly confided that with the money he had left from his injury payout and his regular army pension, he was seriously considering doing just that.

She was impressed by his enthusiasm, then told him of her two brothers who were both married and lived in England. She began to laugh when she recounted opening the door yesterday to her parents who learning of the attack in Glasgow had cut short their holiday, but then when recounting the story, to her surprise and absolute mortification she had unaccountably burst into tears.

She had been inconsolable and Ian had quietly left the room, returning a few moments later with a glass of water he laid on the table and a clean handkerchief he wordlessly handed her; then again left the room to permit her time to compose herself.

Five minutes later, calmer and after a visit to his bathroom to wash her face, she had found him in the kitchen brewing a pot of tea.

He didn't refer to her tears, but stood with his arms folded, his back against the worktop and quietly told her, "Shock is a powerful force. It can creep up on you when you least expect it; minutes, days, sometimes months after an incident. Believe me, Daisy, as someone who has experienced PTSD, I'm no stranger to emotion. In time, though you will feel better and come to terms with what happened to you," then forcefully added, "but you must *not* bottle up your anger, your grief and even your pain at what happened. If you have a good friend, then share your experience, how you feel." He had smiled and added, "Believe me, talking about it *is* therapeutical."

When they had parted they did so like old friends and she surprised him when she tightly hugged him and told him that if he ever needed her help, he had simply to call.

She raised her head from the pillow and glanced across the room at her jeans that lay draped across the chair. His handkerchief was in the pocket and though they had exchanged phone numbers, but made no arrangement to meet again, she smiled for returning Ian's hankie provided her with the opportunity to phone him.

John Glennie was at his desk trying to commence the report that ultimately would wind its way through to Crown Office in Gartcosh when the door knock.

"Sorry, I know you're busy," said Lou Sheridan, "but that's the check addresses arrived from the Metropolitan Police regarding our four terrorists and all okay so far."

Glennie laid his pen down and indicating Sheridan sit, said, "Tell me."

She glanced at a notepad she carried in her hand and said, "The Met CTU called at the address of Aarif Sidiq, aged twenty-five years and spoke with his brother. Apparently the family are very decent and in shock, according to the Met and the brother had no idea that Sidiq was even out of England. He had told the family he was going on some kind of religious retreat with the local Mosque. The Met followed up the claim, but nobody at the Mosque had any idea or knowledge of a retreat and members of the Mosque the Met spoke with described Sidiq as quiet and often very reserved. The brother will make arrangements for family members to travel to Scotland to reclaim the body."

She flicked the notepad over to the next page and said, "Abdul-hameed Muhammad, he's the guy that tried to shoot Constable Cooper," she reminded Glennie, "was also aged twenty-five. Now," she grimaced, "this guy is a different kettle of fish, a real piece of work. The Met CTU did the door knocking and again, his family are reportedly to be a decent group of people who had no idea where he was. However," she almost grinned, "the family did say that over the last year he had been taking off at irregular periods doing what he told them was 'a little spot of training,' unquote. One of the Met detectives took it upon herself to do a little digging at Muhammad's local Mosque and spoke with the main man there," she glanced down at her notepad, "who she told me is an elderly man, a Sheikh Marzook Hussain. According to the detective I spoke with this guy Hussain was a mine of information and completely willing to assist the inquiry. What he told the detective down there is in complete contrast to the file we received from the Security Service."

"Oh?" Glennie leaned forward.

"Apparently Muhammad was a former al-Qaeda fighter and as a teenager fought with the Taliban in the Helmand Province in Afghanistan. Born in South London of Pakistani parents, he travelled on Jihad to Pakistan and was trained by al-Qaeda, then suffered injuries during a drone strike that killed his Emir; his leader," she explained. "Sheikh Hussain also told the Met detective that while in Pakistan, Muhammad came under the watchful eye of the Pakistani Security people and was tortured by them; however, upon his return to the UK he declared himself to be finished with violence and was a regular attender at the Bond Street Mosque in Ipswich."

She paused and said, "The Met guy I spoke with told me this Sheikh Hussain was extremely upset to learn of Muhammad's involvement in the Glasgow attack and said the old guy was completely distraught and blamed himself for not recognising the signs of radicalisation."

"Interesting that the Security Service seemed to have omitted that from the files they sent us, eh?"

"Omitted or just downright lied," Sheridan replied.

"Yes, well *I* favour a lie," said Glennie, his voice dripping with sarcasm.

"Regarding the other two addresses" she continued, "Abdul-salam Nasher, aka Joseph Crocker who we already know was the former Neo-Nazi, and Fadi Hussain, who was just nineteen; again both addresses for these two checked out and again neither family knew of their trip to Glasgow or any association with any group planning terrorist attacks. The Met boys that knocked on the family doors to

break the news said that Fadi Hussain's family were devastated and thought he was on a two day apprentice training trip to London."
She grinned.
"What?"
"When the Met CTU boys went to break the news to the Crocker family, they went team handed for apparently it turned into a full blown street fight and resulted in the mother, the father and a couple of Crocker's brothers all getting the jail. It seems the family are well known in the Southall area of London for thieving and violence and apart from their son Joseph or Abdul-salam as he liked to be known, none of the family have any connection to Islam."
"So for the moment we're at a dead end regarding a getaway driver. What about close associates for them, apart from each other, I mean?"
"One interesting fact that was disclosed by this old man in the Bond Street Mosque, Sheikh Hussain, is that Abdul-hameed Muhammad was a close almost inseparable friend of a regular attender at the Mosque, Rahib Chowdhury," she read the name from her notepad. "According to Hussain though, he spoke with Chowdhury just yesterday and when he asked him about Muhammad, Chowdhury claimed he had not seen him for a few days."
"Might be worth getting a statement from this guy… Chowdhury, did you say?"
"Rahib Chowdhury," she nodded and added, "I'll see it gets done. I'll contact the Met and inform them that we're sending a couple of people down to interview this guy Chowdhury; say tomorrow?"
"Yes, the sooner the better," replied Glennie, then asked, "What about the CCTV footage from the underground car park in Montrose Street and the surrounding street? Anything worthwhile from that?"
"The car park footage is crap quality," she sighed, "but I've sent it to the Forensic people at Gartcosh anyway. They've got the equipment for cleaning up the film. As for the street footage, I'm waiting on word back from Stewart Street. They've got a guy there working there, Mickey Hughes, a former Traffic cop who was injured in an accident and now works in the CCTV unit. If there is anything of value, Mickey will find it."

"Right, then," he reached for his pen and said, "keep me informed and I'll continue to try and get something down on paper."

His bladder told him it was time to stop for a comfort break and pulling off the M6 into a service station, he parked the BMW among the numerous vehicles already there. Getting out of the driver's seat he stretched and yawned, the early rise that morning now starting to overtake him. Collecting his jacket from the rear seat, he held it over his head against the fine drizzle of rain and hurriedly made his way to the cafeteria building.

After a visit to the toilet, he purchased a takeaway coffee and hot bagel and decided to make his way back to the car.

Now returned and in the driver's seat, he fetched the mobile phone from his jacket pocket and switching it on, flicked to the directory where only the one number had been added.

Pressing the green button, he heard the phone ringing and then a male voice answered in English, "Yes?"

He did not refer to Akhmad Soslanbek by name, but responding in English simply said, "A mutual friend told me you might have some information for me."

There was a few seconds pause before the voice, an accented English speaker, he now realised, abruptly replied, "Nothing yet. Tonight, six o'clock. Call again," then ended the call.

Refreshed and the contact made, he glanced at his watch and decided that an hours nap would benefit him if he was to continue driving. Tipping the driver's seat backwards, he closed his eyes and settled down to sleep.

The media were becoming almost frantic for nobody had yet learned the name of the mysterious man who had saved the hostages.

Not only in the United Kingdom, but across the western world there had been a upsurge of support for the heroic gunman who had killed the terrorists; however, there were those few in the media who continued to vociferously complain about the man shooting the terrorists in the head and who supported the campaign to have him, when identified, arraigned for murder.

Conspiracy theorists suggested or alleged that he was in fact a member a police or army undercover team and reminded the public of the ongoing debate about the so-called 'shoot to kill' policy that was disputed by the Westminster Government.

However, though reward money was offered and favours pulled in, still the man's name eluded them.

While he made his way through the corridors of the Glasgow City Chambers to the staff canteen and oblivious to the ongoing inquiry, the George Square beat man and recently divorced Constable William 'Spud' Murphy had absolutely no intention that day of divulging any of the details he had overheard about the man who saved young Daisy Cooper from being murdered.

No, Spud had his own set of values and besides, he really had no time for the media anyway, as he was fond of saying.

But like many of his colleagues, Spud liked his public to think that he had his finger on the pulse and was fond of tapping a forefinger against his broad nose, then smiling as though he was privy to many secrets.

It was unfortunate then that upon arriving at the staff canteen and after collecting his roll and sausage and mug of tea, he sat with his back to the table where one of the buildings cleaners, Winnie Munro sat alone, having her breakfast. It was commonly known among her cleaning staff colleagues that the nosy, gossiping and unpopular Munro could reputedly hear a safety pin drop onto a shag pile carpet at fifty feet.

Seated beside Spud was Marion Whyte, the newly recruited City Chambers female commissionaire; a woman in her early forties who had already given Spud the glad-eye and outrageously flirted with him.

After a few minutes, Spud and his prospective girlfriend's conversation turned to the Buchanan Street attack and with his habit of tapping at his nose, Spud told a blatant lie with the aim of impressing the wide-eyed Marion; he confided that the man Ian Macleod, who had saved the hostages, was well known to Spud and the two men regularly shared a few beers in Macleod's Corruna Street flat.

Enthralled, Marion was all ears as behind them, was Winnie too who halfway through her own roll and sausage, stopped chewing to intently listen.

Ten minutes later, Winnie was on the phone to the 'Glasgow News' news desk and whispering as she asked, just how much *was* on offer for the name and address of the man the paper was looking for?

CHAPTER ELEVEN

Detective Inspector Paul Cowan dialled the phone number for the Metropolitan Police Counter Terrorism Unit and when it was answered, identified himself and asked to speak with DI Aamira 'Mira' Khalifa.

When the call was passed through, Cowan smiled and said, "Hello again, Mira."

"How's my favourite kilt wearer," replied Khalifa. "Still chasing the women?"

On his side of the call, Cowan grinned for he could almost see the twinkle in Khalifa's eyes. The stunningly beautiful and glamourous Khalifa, who insisted on wearing fashionable silk, hijabs, had worked hard, particularly being Muslim, to rise through the ranks in the Met's traditionally Anglo, male dominated CTU and after spending two weeks with her as students on an anti-terrorism course at Scotland Yard, Cowan considered her to be one of the brightest and shrewdest women he had ever known.

"Mira," he began, "what's your current role within your CTU?"

"Well, recently I took over the department that deals with the radicalisation of young Muslim men and women. That and anything else related to Islam that the bosses throw at me," she sighed. "It's one of the problems being Muslim. The management believe I've a knowledge of everything going on in the Islamic world. They just can't get it into their heads that Islam is like Christianity; there are so many different sects and factions within the Faith."

"Well, Mira, if you can give me a little time from your oh so busy world," he replied, "I'm on for a favour. In furtherance of the excellent work your guys in the CTU did in checking the four addresses for us, one of your detectives took it a wee bit further and interviewed a man at the Bond Street Mosque in Ipswich, a…"

"Sheikh Hussain?" she interrupted.

"Aye, that's him. You know him then," and wasn't surprised by her answer when she replied, "I've had a few meetings in the past with him, yes. For all his age, his poor health and his near blindness, he's a wise old man and has his finger on the pulse of what's going on in his Mosque. As for the detective who spoke with him, that would be Clare Ball, she's one of my lot. A good worker and keen as mustard."

"Well, in light of what DC Ball discovered my boss Mister Glennie has instructed me to inform you that we intend sending down two of our people to interview a friend of one of the gunmen, a man called Rahib Chowdhury. According to Sheikh Hussain, Chowdhury was quite tight with Abdul-hameed Muhammad and so we'd like a statement from him. I was wondering if you could liaise with our guys and…"

"Wait," she slowly interrupted, "perhaps there's no need for your guys to come down here. Though I don't know Chowdhury, the dead guy Mohammad I certainly did know. His file has crossed my desk more than once, so what I'm suggesting, Paul, is there any need to send two people down here? I can arrange for Chowdhury to be interviewed. In fact," she rubbed at her forehead, "I'll go myself if you want," and scribbled Chowdhury's name on her desk pad.

He surprised her when he then asked, "Can you speak?"

She glanced about her, picking up on his terse question that what he was about to disclose was for her ears only.

"Yes, I can," she slowly replied.

There was the slightest of hesitation from Cowan, but he trusted Khalifa and so told her, "I'm not privy to all the politics of what's going on; that's a couple of pay grades above me, Mira, but I do know that there is some question in my bosses minds that the Security Service are not disclosing all the information they have on these four men who attacked Glasgow. I also know that the files they sent to the inquiry here didn't reflect their true profiles."

"Heavens, Paul, surely you have been dealing with Thames House long enough to realise that the Service will only tell you what they want you to know. After all, they operate on the basis that, what is it you Jocks call it; it's my ball and you're not playing."

He laughed at her understanding of the Scottish mentality and replied, "Bang on, Mira. Now, on the question of you interviewing this guy Chowdhury. It won't create a problem with your bosses, will it?"

"No, Paul, and if any of them question why I'm conducting the interview on behalf of Police Scotland, all I have to do is remind them that we're all fighting the same threat for after all, are we not?"

"Yes, Mira, we are."

"Good. Right," he could hear her shuffling some paper as she continued, "I'll clear my desk and I'll probably take young Clare Ball with me. Won't do any harm to continue her interview with the Sheikh because though he is almost blind and very devout, he's still got an eye for the ladies. Once we've got the lowdown and done our homework on Chowdhury, we'll interview him."

"Lucky man then, having you dropping in on him," Cowan replied.

"Why Paul," she almost drooled through the phone, "is that you making a pass at me?"

"If I didn't, I'd be off my head."

"Right," she grinned at her handset, "enough of this. I'll call you and summarise my meeting with the Sheikh then send the paperwork through to your e-mail address.

"Great," he said and ended the call.

Khalifa replaced the handset into the cradle and beckoning over one of the civilian analysts to her desk, said, "Jenny, can you make an entry in the office diary that I'm leaving the office with DC Ball to conduct an interview on behalf of Police Scotland."

"Yes, Ma'am. Where are you going?"

"Eh," Khalifa reached down to collect her handbag from the floor and standing up from her desk, continued, "we're off to Ipswich, the Mosque on Bond Street to speak with Sheikh Hussain. There shouldn't be anyone looking for me, but if the bosses ask…" she tightly smiled at the younger woman.

"You'll have your mobile phone with you, Ma'am?"

"Yes, of course," she stared curiously at the analyst. Since the quiet, almost shy Jennifer Fielding had joined the CTU some months previously she had kept herself to herself, seemingly reluctant to join any of the team for breaks or the occasional night out. However, competent at her job, Fielding had never given any rise for concern. She watched as Khalifa purposefully strode across the large room to Clare Ball's desk and speaking briefly with the DC, both women then left office, their overcoats draped across their arms.

As casually as she could, Fielding walked to the office front door and glancing out through the glass window in the door into the corridor, saw Khalifa and Ball enter the lift. Nervously inhaling a deep breath, she gathered some paperwork into her arms and casually made her way to Khalifa's desk where hovering over it, she glanced down at the notepad the DI had left open on the large, pseudo leather desk pad.

The name Rahib Chowdhury leapt out at her and she committed it to memory.

Her head down, she returned to the desk near to the office entrance door where the office diary was located and made the timed entry. Glancing about her saw that with nobody paying any particular attention and slipped out of the office, her handbag over her shoulder and to all intent and purpose heading for the loo.

In the empty corridor by the lift, Fielding pushed through the door that led to the stairwell and ensuring that nobody was using the stairs, fetched her mobile phone from her handbag. Her heart pounding and nerves stretched almost to breaking point, she hurriedly composed a text message and satisfied the message was sent, deleted it from her phone.

At the conclusion of the message, she fearfully glanced up and down the stairs, but there was no sound. Pushing back through the door, she quickly made her way to the female toilets.

In his claustrophobic cupboard of an office in Stewart Street, the former Traffic officer Mickey Hughes stretched his aching leg; the leg that he almost lost when he and his motorcycle came a cropper all those years before.

The request from the CTU team at Helen Street had been described as urgent.

"Everything is bloody urgent," he had grumbled when informed of the task by the Duty Officer, but glancing at the handwritten note saw the request had been made by Lou Sheridan and he grinned.

It would never be discussed or disclosed, but back in the day and before both were married to their respective partners, Mickey and the then svelte Lou had on more than one occasion privately partied at his one bedroom flat in Shawlands and for those memories, Lou's request jumped to the top of his never-ending list.

Now here he was, bored witless watching vehicles entering and departing the Montrose Street car park entrance/exit. He was about to wind the CCTV DVD on when a car caught his attention and hurriedly stopped the recording.

Winding back a few seconds, he leaned forward in his chair and watched a dark coloured saloon car exit the car park so fast the vehicle almost struck the opposite pavement as it turned right and speedily drove towards the lights at the junction of Montrose Street and Cathedral Street."

"Damn," Mickey muttered as the vehicle drove out of sight of the CCTV camera covering that stretch of the road.

Noting the time he searched through other recordings and finding the disc whose camera covered part of Cathedral Street, inserted it and wound it to the material time and date.

Slowly he wound the disc forward and smiled when the dark coloured car came into view.

To his surprise, he watched the car race towards and through a red light at the pedestrian crossing, causing two young women, students he guessed because of the proximity of Strathclyde University, leap back to avoid being struck by the speeding car.

Winding the tape back, he slowed it and enlarged the rear of the vehicle, seeing it to be a Skoda Octavia and in his opinion, dark blue in colour.

A further enlargement revealed the registration number of the car.

He checked the handwritten note again.

The start time of the attack in Buchanan Street and the time on his screen at the Montrose street car park were within thirteen minutes of each other. Allowing for the times to be approximate and for the CCTV recording to perhaps be a few minutes out, he reckoned the times were close enough and smiled.

There were no further CCTV cameras along that stretch of the road, but the very fact the car was heading east caused Mickey to guess it was making towards the M8 motorway. He checked the list of vehicles that had been stolen that day in the city centre, but none described a Skoda Octavia and he slowly nodded.

"Got you, ya bastard," he hissed.

A quick search using Google on his phone indicated where Malika Umarov would find a city centre hotel and calling the hotel as he drove northwards, booked a double room for three nights, albeit it was not his intention to stay there a for the full three nights.

Using the vehicles Satnav, Eldar Umarov arrived at the hotel's underground car park in the Anderston area of the city and registering at reception as Fernand Marchand, used his false credit cards to pay and the French issued passport as identification.

He didn't forget to register the car parked underneath for with the gun and ammunition still secreted within for he had no wish that the vehicle might attract undue attention from the hotel security staff.

The young receptionist was charmed by the handsome and grey haired, slightly accented Mister Marchand and after booking his table reservation for dinner, helpfully provided him with a street map of the city. At his request she agreed to have every local newspaper and UK publications delivered to his room.

Declining the service of a porter, he shouldered his own suit carrier and making his way to the fifth floor room that overlooked the motorway, decided to first have a shower.

Ensuring the room door was securely locked, he stripped off and carried the mobile phone into the bathroom with him where after making his toilet, he showered and changed into a fresh shirt and pair of chinos.

Refreshed, he opened his door and saw that as he had requested, the porter had delivered over a dozen newspapers that lay outside his door.

As he had suspected, the attack was still the number one news item and over the next hour he devoured every scrap of information about the attack, every article, though shook his head at some of the media's obsession with criticising the unknown man who had intervened.

One newspaper, the 'Glasgow News' had over eight inside pages an artist's description of the route that gunmen had apparently taken. Laying out the street map, he followed the newspaper's description on the map that included not only where the gunmen had been killed, but also the victims of the attack.

To his dismay, in the area known as Buchanan Street Precinct, his fingers unconsciously traced the silhouetted figure that was described underneath as the young unidentified, homeless woman; the homeless woman that he suspected to be his daughter Malika

He took a deep breath and slowly exhaled to calm himself. In his mind he followed the route taken by the gunmen, imagining their progress as they shot and killed their victims or took hostages before being themselves killed by the unknown man.

He was surprised the police had not yet traced this heroic man and that the description of him varied from article to article. The only thing the newspapers seemed to agree on was witnesses who apparently told reporters the man walked with a limp and wore a dark coloured jacket and some kind of flat cap.

He pored over the newspapers eyewitness accounts, those individuals the reporters had managed to track down. It seemed to him as he read that none of the eyewitnesses saw everything, but from their accounts he was able to piece together the story and paid particular interest to the account of a young man, Peter McCready, whose second floor optical business premises in the Precinct provided McCready with a birds eye view below.

McCready described opening the window of his workshop to permit the smoke of an illicit cigarette to escape and idly watched a policewoman in the Precinct below speaking with a homeless woman. He described how the officer bent to hand the woman what he thought might be money and was helping her to her feet when he heard what sounded like gunfire. McCready had craned his neck through the window and was looking to his left when an armed man wearing camouflage clothing appeared and without warning, shot down the homeless woman before taking the policewoman hostage. McCready went on to describe how the gunman had marched the policewoman by the hair then struck her to the head with the rifle, causing her to fall to the ground.

Umarov continued to read that the gunmen pulled the officer by the hair to her feet and it was then she attacked the gunman.

"Brave girl," he murmured.

However, the article continued, the gunman released his hold on the officer's hair and she fell backwards onto the ground. To his horror, McCready told the reporter, he thought the gunman looked like he was going to shoot the policewoman, but was himself shot by a man wearing a dark jacket and a flat cap; a bunnet, the man called it in the article, who also told the reporter this man walked with a limp. And there's that limp again, thought Umarov.

McCready had left the window to use his office phone to call the police, but all the lines were engaged and by the time he had returned to the window, sirens were sounding and armed officers were all over the Precinct.

He laid the newspaper down and his mind wandered to what he had to do that evening. Glancing at his watch, he reached for his jacket and decided he had better go now.

Ever conscious of his personal security, he closed and locked his room door then took the precaution of marking the door by spit-wetting a strand of his hair and placing it across the door jamb. Downstairs, he made inquiry at reception where he might find a large supermarket and was directed to an ASDA store in the west end.

Driving the short distance to the store, he parked up and at the phone counter flattered the matronly assistant who helpfully assisted him in his purchase of a clean pay-as-you-go mobile phone and second SIM card.

In the Men's Department of the large store he selected a number of items that he purchased.

Returning to the hotel some fifteen minutes later, he saw that he had some time before his six o'clock call and kneeling by the window, faced east and offered prayers.

Cathy Mulgrew decided that rather than phone she would visit John Glennie for an update on his team's inquiries.

Finding him in his office she waited while he fetched two coffees from the general office then watched as he prepared his notes.

"First things first, you were dead on. The file that the Security Service delivered was incomplete. No surprises there, I suppose you'll say and to be honest what they *did* give us was a right load of shite."

Mulgrew smiled for John Glennie was a man his officers were aware infrequently used any form of bad language.

In concise sentences, Glennie delivered a synopsis of the inquiry completed so far.

"The team obtaining witness statements are almost done, the Forensics and ballistic inquiries is concluded and we should be receiving the documentation within the next day or so, arrangements have been made to return the victims' bodies and those of the gunmen to their next of kin. That is, aside from the lassie we now know as Malika Umarov, but Lou Sheridan is making an arrangement to have her buried in a Muslim ceremony. Continuing," he breathed out, "outside Forces inquiries are likewise all returned bar those being conducted by our Met colleagues," and then recounted his conversation with Lou Sheridan who had received the Metropolitan Police results of the address checks for the four dead gunmen. "Lastly, I'm commencing my report to Crown Office and when it's finished, I would appreciate if before I submit it you might consider proofreading it for me."

"No trouble," she smiled and then continued, "This man who is alleged to be a friend of Abdul-hameed Muhammad, this…"

"Rahib Chowdhury," Glennie glanced down at his notes.

"Chowdhury. You intend interviewing him?"

"Oh, indeed I do," replied Glennie. "We're missing at least one of the team and if we're correct in our assumption that will be the getaway driver. I'm hoping that if the Met are correct and Chowdhury was a close friend of Muhammad, he might be able to give us some names that we can follow through with."

"Who do you intend sending down?"

"I *was* going to send two of my people, but Paul Cowan has persuaded a local DI to conduct the interview for us."

Her eyes narrowed as she said, "A local DI? From the Met CTU? You do realise they are extremely close with and often work hand in glove with the Security Service?"

Glennie inhaled and said, "I know what you're thinking, Cathy, but Cowan trusts this woman and I trust Cowan. If she doesn't come back with anything or does come back with something we're not happy with, *then* I'll send two of my guys down."

"Sorry, John. You're right, of course. It's your inquiry, your call," she shook her head. "Since that bastard Ashford showed up I'm seeing spooks everywhere."

He grinned and replied, "Anything further from the Scottish Government about your suspicions regarding the weapons and explosives?"

"No," she shook her head again and sighed. "The Chief Constable phoned me earlier to inform me that the First Minister is engaged in a Parliamentary debate for the day, but this evening she wants to meet with us both and that I'm to make myself available at short notice. What short notice is, I'm not certain, but I might have to order a Traffic car to blue light me through there. I'm definitely not speeding on the M8 in my own car."

He smiled at her and was about to comment when the door knocked and was opened by Lou Sheridan, her face flushed and smiling.

"Mickey Hughes, the CCTV man at Stewart Street. He's come up trumps."

It was just good fortune that he was standing at the window looking down into the street when the private hire taxi draw up outside the close. Watching with idle curiosity, he saw a man get out of the front passenger seat, but it was the man in the back who when he exited the taxi Ian saw was carrying the camera round his neck and who glanced up at the tenement building, causing Ian to step back out of sight behind the curtain.

As he watched, the taxi switched off the engine and he saw the driver lift a newspaper to read, apparently preparing himself to await the return of his passengers.

There was no doubt in his mind who the two men were; they were reporters.

They had found him at last.

He took a deep breath and made his decision not to confront them. Minutes later there was a pounding at the front door and his name was called loudly through the letterbox, but by then he had switched off the interior lights and closed the inner doors that led off the hallway.

In the kitchen, he waited them out and ignored the repeated hammering and their calls for him to open the door. His instinct was to pull the door open and throw them both down the stairs, but was acutely aware that these days his ability to physically defend himself were limited.

Sighing, he sipped at his coffee then an idea struck him.

Lifting his mobile phone he dialled the new number and when it was answered, nervously said, "Daisy? It's Ian Macleod. That offer you made of helping me," he licked at his lips. "I'm in a bit of a spot. The press have got my address and they're at the door now. I was wondering…"

She cut him off and replied, "I've a spare room and it's yours. Pack a bag and give me twenty, maybe thirty minutes to get over there and I'll phone you when I'm downstairs."

She abruptly ended the call and he stared at his mobile.

Was he being too forward, he wondered and if those two sods at his front door persisted in waiting him out, how the hell was he going to get past them?

The digital clock/radio by the bed read six o'clock.

Seated in the comfortable leather tub chair at the desk, Eldar Umarov, placed his watch on the desk and holding the pen in one hand and the hotel stationary ready before him, dialled the one number in the directory.

The same accented male voice, or so he believed, answered, "Yes."

"I will text a new number when this call ends. You have four minutes then I end the call."

Without preamble, the voice quickly said in English, "Our friend in Scotland Yard informs us that the Met police terrorist people will visit a Mosque in Bond Street in the town of Ipswich. There they will seek to speak with the Mosque Sheikh, a man called Hussain. The name Rahib Chowdhury might also be of interest to you. We do not know why they wish to speak with Hussain or their interest in these men or what if any, the connection either Hussain or Chowdhury has with the attack in Glasgow. We do not know anything further about Hussain or Chowdhury. Our friend will try to find out more, but nothing is guaranteed. Do you wish further inquiry be made?"

Umarov, hesitated. He had come all this way north, yet the police were speaking with men in the town of Ipswich that if he recalled correctly, was a town located close to the capital city of London. But why?

"If you learn anything else, I will call again at the same time, tomorrow. Agreed?"

"Agreed," the voice said then ended the call.

Almost immediately, Umarov glanced at the watch. The call had taken just over two minutes. Copying the phone number from the phone's directory onto the sheet of paper, he then opened the back of the mobile phone and removed the SIM card that he snapped it in half.

Placing both halves of the mobile phone on the tiled floor of the ensuite, he brought the heel of his shoe down sharply onto them in turn, breaking them and into smaller pieces.

That done he collected the pieces of the phone and broken SIM card and placed them into the ASDA plastic store bag. He would dispose of the bag in a bin in a lower floor hallway when he went to eat.

Carefully, he assembled the newly purchased pay-as-you-go mobile phone and added the phone number to the directory. That done, he texted his new number to the number he had saved.

Committing the information he had written to memory, he destroyed the sheet of stationary.

Glancing at the digital clock, he plucked another hair from his head and rising from the chair, decided to go to dinner.

With John Glennie and Cathy Mulgrew stooped over her, Lou Sheridan accessed her e-mails and opened the recently delivered attachments from Mickey Hughes.

The short films showed the Skoda Octavia departing the Montrose Street car park then almost running over the two young women in Cathedral Street.

They each read the information that Mickey attached to the files informing them that he had managed to obtain the registration number of the vehicle. Further, Mickey had checked the registration number of the Octavia on the PNC and discovered that the plates referred to a vehicle registered in the London area of Southall, but a note on the PNC indicated the plates from the vehicle had been stolen a week earlier. As a former Traffic officer, Mickey offered the opinion the Octavia on the screen was not the vehicle to which the plates had been issued, but possibly a stolen vehicle bearing the stolen plates. Thus if the vehicle was the subject to a casual check by the police, the plates would match that type and colour of vehicle and the officer conducting the check would be none the wiser.

"Smart buggers," muttered Glennie.

Mickey had also checked the PNC for any complaint made by the two young women, but had been unable to find one and regretted that the CCTV cameras showed the vehicle from the rear so there was little likelihood of obtaining a photograph of the driver from what he had to work with.

"That's good work," commented Mulgrew with a smile. "Lou, can you get that number broadcast as soon as, please?"

"Yes, Ma'am, on my way," Sheridan replied and left the room.

"What Mickey Hughes has given us is worth a definite pat on the back," Glennie told Mulgrew. "I'll give Hughes a phone call and thank him."

"So, if the vehicle is travelling east on Cathedral Street," mused Mulgrew, "it's possible the driver was heading for the motorway. What about CCTV cameras on the M8, John?"

"I'll have someone from my team contact the head office of Traffic Scotland and give them the registration number, see what they can offer in the way of traffic CCTV cameras…"

"Maybe ask about the overhead cameras on the M74 too, the average speed cameras that monitor the traffic in case the vehicle headed south."

"Good idea," he nodded.

The door opened to admit Lou Sheridan who breathlessly said, "Mickey Hughes had already put on a lookout for the Octavia onto the PNC with the incident room phone number," and smilingly, she continued. "I'd no sooner had our operator enter the details on the PNC when we got a hit. Twenty minutes ago a cop with the British Transport Police at Waverly station in Edinburgh checked the Skoda Octavia on the PNC. According to the officer I spoke with the driver had paid for four hours parking, but the vehicle has been there since the day of the attack. When the cop checked the parking ticket and saw it was out of date, he PNC'd the registration number with the intention of checking if the car was stolen or if not and contacting the registered keeper. That's when he read Mickey's entry and he phoned us. He told me the entry and exit for the car park is covered by CCTV and with my authority, he's arranging with his boss to have the DVD recording sent to us by a Traffic motorcyclist. I've arranged for the Traffic Department's flatbed truck to collect the Octavia from Waverly car park and take it directly for Forensic examination to Gartcosh. I've also instructed that the motorcyclist take the recording to Mickey Hughes at Stewart Street. I believe with his experience he's best suited to check the recording and knows what he's looking for."

Mulgrew's mobile phone indicated she was receiving a text and opening the phone, said, "That's me got a message that I've to make my way through to Bute House. I'll never get through the traffic in my own car," and turning to Sheridan, smiled and asked, "Can you sort out a Traffic vehicle for me, please Lou? Preferably *not* a motorcycle. I'm wearing my best skirt," she grinned, "and I have no desire to flash my pantyhose to passing motorists!"

He knew the reporter and his cameraman were either still in the close or interviewing his neighbours, for their vehicle remained parked outside. As he stared down at the parked taxi, his attention was drawn to a police car that drew up behind the taxi and watched as a tall and stocky built police woman and a young male colleague got out of the car. The woman spoke with the taxi driver and glancing up at the tenement building, both she and the male cop disappeared from Ian's sight, presumably into the close, he thought.
A few minutes passed then the cops reappeared, but while the cameraman was being pushed from the back by the male cop, the policewoman had the other man by the collar of his jacket and was forcibly propelling him in front of her.
That's when his mobile phone ran and the screen indicated it was Daisy.
"When those two are back in their taxi and gone," she said, "leave the close and turn left onto Argyle Street. I'm parked outside the pub, just past the corner."
He didn't get the opportunity to respond, for she ended the call and watching from his window, saw the two cops bundle the men into the rear of the taxi that almost immediately, drove off.
It took but a couple of minutes for Ian make his way down the stairs and out into the street where the two cops standing by their vehicle, grinned at him and waved.
Bemused, he waved back and the made his way round the corner into Argyle Street where he saw Daisy stood by the driver's door of a bright green coloured Fiat 500 and urging him to her with a wave. He hobbled to the passenger's door and getting in with his bag clutched to him, turned as she started the engine and grinned at him. Throwing his bag into the rear seat, he fumbled with the seat belt and managed to get it clicked into place just as Daisy raced off and he

said, "I'm guessing you arranged that wee diversion, Constable Daisy?"

She laughed and replied, "Aye, and you'll get to meet them two later on. They're coming round for a drink when they finish their shift at ten."

He stared straight ahead and taking a deep breath, said, "Thanks. For this, I mean."

She snatched a glance at him and replied, "It's the least I can do, Ian. I'm sorry that you found yourself in this position, but we both know if you remain in your flat, at least for the time being you'll be having reporters knocking on your door every two minutes."

She slowly shook her head and continued, "I think we both knew that at some point the press will track you down and want your side of the story; particularly in light of those idiots that are trying to accuse you of…"

She paused, but Ian finished for her and, his voice flat, said, "Accuse me of murder, you mean."

"Yes," she sighed and nodded before continuing, "This way you can keep your head down for a while until you're ready or your lawyer believes you to be ready to answer any questions." She turned quickly towards him and added, "But only if you want to answer their questions."

"Who do you think provided them with my name?"

Daisy shrugged and said, "It could have been any one of a hundred people; a neighbour in the close, cops who heard your name being discussed at Stewart Street after you attended there, someone who knows you and thinks you deserve recognition for what you did or even somebody who wanted to claim the reward money the newspapers are offering for information about you."

"They have my address, Daisy."

"And that's why I'm delighted to offer you sanctuary, Mister Macleod," she pompously grinned at him. Her brow furrowed as she added, "But don't think I'm an open house to any man who crosses my path."

He picked up on her attempt to humour him and smiled before replying, "Just so long as there is a lock on the spare bedroom door,

Constable Daisy. I don't want to have to defend my honour in the middle of the night."

She turned to stare at him and he thought for an instant he might have overstepped the mark, but she coyly smiled and replied, "It's not me you to have worry about, Ian. Wait till you meet my pal, Joan Crawford."

CHAPTER TWELVE

The two women, DI Aamira Khalifa wearing her hajib and DC Clare Ball's head now respectfully covered with one of the silk scarves that were made available for visitors to the Mosque, waited till the evening prayers had been completed.

"How long do the prayers last, Ma'am?" Ball whispered to her boss.

"Well, we Muslims pray five times a day, Clare," Khalifa softly replied. "Fajr is the pre-dawn prayer, Dhur is the midday prayer, Asr is the afternoon prayers, Maghrib is the sunset prayers that are being said now and Isha'a are the night prayers. Maghrib prayer begins when the sun is setting and should officially last till the red light has left the sky in the west. However, that's the official definition of the prayer time, but like everything else in life, people of all religions lead busy lives and not everyone is as devout as Sheikh Hussain, regardless of what deity they worship or pray to." She paused and smiled. "The young brother we spoke with when we arrived will likely inform the Sheikh that we need to speak with him, so I'm hoping that he might cut short his prayers to speak with us, then," she grinned, "we can get home for our dinner because frankly, I'm starving."

She stood patiently and quietly with the younger woman, ignoring the curious glances they attracted from the men and women who were arriving or departing the Mosque.

She liked Ball and taken to the fair-haired girl when five months earlier she joined the CTU from a police intelligence department. Not a rank conscious detective and as two of the few women in the CTU, she and Ball often took their breaks together and was considering inviting Ball and any partner she might have to dinner at her home with Khalifa and her husband, a paediatric surgeon.

Some ten minutes later, the brother returned leading the Sheikh, who held the young man's arm as the brother guided the partially sighted man towards the two detectives.

"These are the sisters who wish to speak with you, Sheikh," the brother politely nodded to the women.

"My eyes might be old and worn," the Sheikh said, his soft voice oozing charm, "but my nose tells me the rose scent I detect is worn by a lovely young woman called Aamira."

Khalifa smiled and responded, "And though your eyes might be old and worn, Sheikh, your words are as soft as the silk that covers my head."

The old man laughed and reaching for his arm to be taken by Khalifa, said, "Perhaps you and your colleague might guide me to my office, Aamira, and we can speak there."

He turned his head towards the young brother and courteously dismissed him with a nod and a smile.

With Ball by her side, Khalifa led the elderly Sheikh through the side corridor of the building towards his cluttered office where they both saw that he was obviously aware of the generously sized room's layout. Ignoring the desk that sat at the top of the room, he lifted two chairs that sat against the wall and one after the other placed the chairs beside a third chair that was at a small round coffee table and invited the women to sit.

"Rahib Chowdhury," began Khalifa. "Is he here, at Maghrib, Sheikh?"

"Rahib Chowdhury," he softly repeated, then continued, "No, not tonight, Aamira. I have no eyes, but there is nothing wrong with my hearing and listening to their voices, almost to a brother and sister I can tell who is in attendance at Maghrib. Brother Rahib did not attend tonight," he shook his head and his brow furrowed as he cocked his head slightly to one side. "You have questions for him?"

"The Scottish police wish more information, Sheikh. They do not suggest Rahib is in trouble, but wish me to speak with him. You told my colleague DC Ball that Rahib and the brother, Abdul-hameed Muhammad were close. How close?"

He raised and parted his hands and shrugging, replied, "They often attended salah…" he stopped and smiling at Ball, explained, "Prayers, dear child."

"If Rahib is not here then can you provide me with his address, please Sheikh?" asked Khalifa.

She saw the hesitation in his face before he replied, "I am sorry, but all information in the Mosque that we hold on brothers and sisters who are part of our community, is confidential. My hands are tied."

She did not immediately answer, but then as though with difficulty, replied, "I understand your reluctance, Sheikh, but Rahib Chowdhury is not a suspect in this inquiry. He is a possible witness who might be able to provide us with valuable information about the men who murdered seven innocent people." Her voice grew a little more forceful when she added, "I need not remind you, Sheikh, that one of those men was also a member of your community, Abdul-hameed Muhammad."

She could see the struggle in his face, but he sighed and with a shrug turned to DC Ball and said, "Sister, please fetch the plastic box from the top left hand drawer of my desk."

Ball arose and did as she was asked, lifting a large Tupperware tub from the drawer that she saw was neatly stacked with index cards. From her brief glimpse she also saw the cards were written in Arabic.

"Please hand the box to your colleague," said the Sheikh who asked, "You do speak and read the language of the Prophet, praise his name?"

"I do, Sheikh," replied Khalifa who saw the cards were in alphabetical order in Arabic and almost immediately fished out Rahib Chowdhury's details.

From her handbag she withdrew her notebook and wrote down his details.

Handing the tub back to Ball, with a nod she indicated it be replaced in the desk and said to Hussain, "Thank you, Sheikh. I will never misuse information that is not for the benefit of the community, no matter what faith or creed that community follow."

"And that, dear sister," he softly smiled, "is why I gave you brother Rahib's address."

It was when they returned to the car that she instructed DC Ball to check Rahib Chowdhury's details on the PNC, adding, "If the guy's got a record our come to our attention, Clare, I want to know about it."

The meal was excellent and dabbing lightly at his lips, Eldar Umarov smiled gallantly at the two ladies of mature years at the adjoining table who had been eyeballing the handsome foreign man from the moment he had sat down to dinner.

With a polite bow towards the two women, he arose and made his way to the restaurant door and turning into the large foyer area, glanced towards the bar to his left.

He smiled for though a devout follower of Islam, he sometimes gave in to temptation and broke the strict ban on alcohol and treated himself to a brandy.

But not tonight, for tonight he had a mission to accomplish.

As he made his way to the elevator, he glanced through the main doors and saw that again it was raining and already night had fallen. That was good for it suited him perfectly and riding the lift to the fifth floor, made his way to his room. The hair at the door jamb was in place and though he did not believe the Russian FSB were operating here in this city, he had survived for many years by remaining under their and other security services radar.

In the room, he locked the door behind him and from the ASDA plastic bag, changed into the black tee shirt, black coloured tracksuit top and leggings and navy blue training shoes. The black gloves he had brought with him in the suit carrier were stuffed into the pocket of the tracksuit top as was the black woollen ADIDAS hat and the brown paper bag.

Ready now, he once more checked the location of the city mortuary and entered the post code for the Queen Elizabeth University

Hospital into his new phone before with a grunt, jerking a hair from his head.

At this rate, he grimly thought as he left the room, I'll be bald in a month.

While Ian sat in the lounge watching the evening news broadcast, Daisy busied herself in the kitchen and conscious that having told her he enjoyed cooking, wondered if he might be a little critical of her efforts.

"No pressure, then," she muttered to herself as she rolled the pastry flat to cover the steak and sausage pie.

"Needing a hand at all?" she turned to see him leaning against the door frame, surprised that he seemed somehow…taller.

"Cutlery's in that drawer," she nodded to the unit, "if you'd like to set the table."

"Yes, Ma'am," he grinned at her and limped behind her.

"Your leg," she turned to stare at him. "Does it give you much bother?"

"Only when I'm nearing the end of the marathon's I run each week."

"Really," she stared fixedly at him, making it clear she was unimpressed by his humour and a lock of hair falling across her eyes that she blew away. "The press are hunting you, you're hiding out here at my good grace and you're giving me cheek?"

He smiled and replied, "I shouldn't be teasing a woman holding a rolling pin, should I?"

"No," and there was that blasted bit of hair again.

"Here, let me," he reached forward and gently manoeuvred the straggling hair into place beneath her hair clip. He was standing so close she could almost feel the warmth of his breath on her cheek.

"There, much better and for what it's worth, I *am* grateful that you're letting me kip here for a couple of nights."

"Well," she smiled bashfully, a little disconcerted at his nearness and his touch, "if you like you can make dinner one night to show me just how good a cook you are."

"It's a deal," he returned her smile. "Right then," he took a deep breath, "I'll get this table set then and if you need me…"

"I'll shout," she finished for him and returned to beating the pastry to death and wondered why her chest felt so tight.

The reporter and his cameraman who returned emptyhanded to the 'Glasgow News' were still irate at the attitude of the two officers who had chased them off from the close in Corruna Street.
Their editor was angry with them, but livid at the police.
Snatching at his phone, he dialled the number for the Media Department at Dalmarnock office and demanded to speak with Chief Inspector Downes.
The young civilian assistant who answered the call knocked nervously on Downes door and when told to enter, saw the older woman had changed into her overcoat and carrying her handbag, was about to depart for home.
Apologising for disturbing her, the young woman told Downes of the wrathful man who wished…no, demanded to speak with her.
"Put him through, hen," Downes tightly smiled and placing her handbag onto her desk, wearily sank back down into her chair. It had been an effing long day and some instinct told her it was going to *continue* to be an effing long day.
When the phone rang she lifted it and gritting her teeth, calmly answered, "Chief Inspector Downes. How might I be of service?"
"Aye, hello there. It's Larry McNaught, news desk editor at the 'Glasgow News.' I'm on to complain about two of your people who threatened my reporter and his cameraman when they were about to interview the man that killed those gunmen in the city centre attack. Your two sods chased my people off and I want something done about it!" he thundered at her.
"Two of my people? What, from the Media Department?"
There was a definite pause before he replied, "No, two polis in uniform. Two cops."
"Oh, then *not* two of my people," she said with a twinkle in her eye and added, "Do try to be a little more accurate, Mister McNaught. After all, you *did* say you are a newspaperman, did you not and we wouldn't want to get things wrong now, would we?"

He could tell she was fucking with him and angrily retorted, "Smart answers will get you nowhere, Chief Inspector, so you *will* get this attended to or I'll be doing something about it!"

"Now, that sounds like a threat and need I remind you, Mister McNaught; all calls to the police are recorded," she coolly responded.

"Threat? What threat? What the…what are you talking about?"

"Right, calm down now and tell me what the substance of your complaint is, Mister McNaught."

She could almost hear him take a deep breath as he replied, "We received information and paid out good money for that information and one of my reporters was following it up…"

"What information? About who?"

"The man who killed the gunman, like I told you," his voice began to rise again.

"And who is this man, what's his name?"

"What? You're the polis and you don't know?" he sneered.

"Well," she drawled, "I'm only asking because I might be able to confirm if your information is correct or incorrect."

She listened, but other than hear him breathing heavily, he didn't respond and she decided he was trying to assess if she was winding him up or not.

"You mean to tell me," McNaught slowly replied, "that you might confirm if the name we have is correct?"

"I might," she grinned at the phone.

"His name is Ian Macleod and he lives in a tenement flat in Corruna Street, just off the city centre. Right, I've given you the name, so what's the catch? What do you want in return? The complaint dropped, is that it?"

"No, Mister McNaught, not the complaint. What I want is for you to hold back on the story until I give you the thumbs up."

"Now wait a minute…"

"Listen to me," she hissed. "If you agree then here's what I'll do. I'll give you the heads up to release your story and possibly I might be able to arrange an interview with the man you're looking for, though I'm not confirming or denying you have the correct name. No promises though, but you have my word I'll try. If the man agrees, you'll be ahead of the competition. Isn't that what you boys are all about, Mister McNaught? Beating your rivals to the scoop?"

Again there was that pregnant pause then McNaught, realising he was getting nowhere with Downes, slowly said, "When can I expect to hear from you, Chief Inspector?"

"Give me your direct…no, make that your personal mobile number. I want this kept strictly between us both. Agreed?"

"Agreed," though it irritated McNaught that she inferred, but would not confirm he had the correct name.

He dictated his number and before ending the call, Downes said, "Now that we've reached an agreement, Mister McNaught, there's just one more, wee thing."

Her voice grew quiet as she said, "If you try to fuck me over with this, if you publish that name before I contact you, the 'Glasgow News' will be *persona non grata* for as long as I command this Department. Are we clear, Mister McNaught?"

"Yes, we're clear, Chief Inspector."

The call was ended just a minute or so when Downes flicked through her rolodex and then dialled the phone number she sought.

When the call was answered by Detective Superintendent Glennie, she said, "John? It's Harry

Downes. I think we might have a problem."

The Bute House meeting was held in the Cabinet Room; the room that to Cairney's certain knowledge was swept daily by a technician employed by the Scottish Government's security department for the express purpose of ensuring that no listening device was secreted within the room or indeed anywhere within Bute House.

Accompanying the First Minister was her Deputy and the Justice Minister who were seated at one side of the lengthy oak table. The Chief Constable, Martin Cairney and the officer in charge of the Counter Terrorism Unit, Detective Chief Superintendent Cathy Mulgrew, sat on the opposite side with a Parliamentary secretary seated at the bottom of the table, minuting the meeting.

Thanking the officers for their attendance, the First Minister requested that Mulgrew again recount her suspicions the attack in Glasgow, ostensibly perpetrated by Islamic Jihadists, might have been orchestrated by others meantime unknown.

As he listened, Cairney thought it significant that on the occasion she interrupted Mulgrew with a question or sought clarification of a point, the First Minister skilfully avoided mentioning the Security Service.

However, it came as no surprise to those present when she sat back bolt upright in her chair and shaking her head, said, "My God, Miss Mulgrew; what you are suggesting is a conspiracy that undoubtedly is with the knowledge and probable sanction of individuals at the highest level of the Westminster Government."

"Perhaps not *all* the Westminster Government, First Minister," Cairney interjected and leaned forward onto his forearms on the table, "but I am sure it will come as no surprise to you that undoubtedly there are individuals within the Government and likely the Security Service who either have their own agenda or who have no qualms about acting on behalf of what they believe to be the Defence of the Realm. While I have no desire to engage with you in a political discussion, Ma'am, it is no secret that one aim of your Government is to achieve independence for Scotland. You *must* know, First Minister, that the very idea of independence is abhorrent to many of those in the Westminster Government."

"And you believe or rather you and your officers assess that on what little evidence you have accrued," she pointedly stressed, "this terrorist attack is possibly the work of these individuals?"

"Without positive and court worthy evidence, Ma'am," Mulgrew interrupted and darting a glance at Cairney, replied, "I'm certain that you realise that all I have told you is purely conjecture on my part, or I should say mine and that of my colleagues."

"Other than Mister Cairney here I do not know your colleagues, Miss Mulgrew; however, your career is not unknown to us here at Bute House," the First Minister grimly smiled, "and conjecture or not, your opinion is highly valued and rest assured, trusted by me and my Government. I am also aware from previous conversations with Mister Cairney," she inclined her head towards him, "that he also trusts you implicitly in matters where judgement and experience can on occasion overrule supposed fact or analysis. However," she deeply inhaled and chewed at her lower lip for a brief second, "as you so correctly stated earlier this evening, what we the Scottish Government might suspect and you the police endeavour to prove might in the long run do us more harm than good. What I do *not* understand is that if indeed there is a conspiracy behind this, why arrange an attack of this nature?"

She slowly shook her head and snorting with derision, continued, "I am well aware as are many of my nationalist colleagues that the Security Service hold files on us all and in the past been known to conduct dirty campaigns against individuals they consider a danger to the political *status quo*. But," she paused, "why the attack and why now?"

She glanced around the table and added, "Opinions, please?"

"I have no answer to that question, Ma'am," Mulgrew pursed her lips and shook her head, "but consider this. The financial cost of the terrorist attack will likely be borne by the Scottish Government."

"How so?"

"Well, there is the huge cost of the police operation that continues to be ongoing, the likely loss in tourism if it is continually publicised by the media, some of whom are quite openly opposed to your goal of independence, that Glasgow is no longer safe from terrorist attack. It's no secret that in recent years the city of Glasgow has quickly established itself as a location popular for world seminars as well as the many hundreds of thousands of visitors attracted annually to the entertainment venues that sit on the Clydeside. All that revenue drawn in to the city hotels, shops, restaurants and other attractions will be at risk because of the terrorist attack. I suspect that a downturn in that revenue will in turn impact on the number of jobs employed to cater for those visitors."

She shook her head and added, "I'm no accountant, but I can only imagine over the period of even a year, the cost must run to many millions of pounds in revenue. Is it fair to say that the loss of those jobs will impact on the social services and the welfare system that

I'm sure must already be financially stretched? Services that are a large and costly part of your Governments budget?"

"You make a valid point, Miss Mulgrew, and in particular with regard to the media moguls who continue to harangue my Government in their newspapers," she slowly shook her head.

A silence hung over the room broken when the First Minister said, "I will share this with you, Mister Cairney and you Miss Mulgrew, though it is not yet in the public domain."

Cairney and Mulgrew stared curiously at the First Minister as she continued,

"I received a personal telephone call earlier today from the Chancellor of the Exchequer who after boring me with all sort of platitudes about the financial effect of the attack, informed me that he was instructed to 'very generously,' his expression I must add," and she could not help but scowl, "offer a massive influx of cash to the Scottish budget for some of the very reasons you have just outlined, Miss Mulgrew."

She paused as though the idea was repugnant to her and continued again, "If my Government were to accept the extra funding that the Westminster Government is currently and very publicly offering to bolster our Police Scotland service as well as the reopening of military bases that were previously closed due to," she waggled her forefingers in the air, "MoD budget cuts, it would be a clear and public admission that we as a Nation cannot independently exist without the support of our English neighbours and the Westminster Government."

She paused and drummed the fingers of her right hand on her desk pad before continuing. "Miss Mulgrew, I am acutely aware that as a police officer you act without fear or favour and I have no wish to involve you in politics. However, regardless of your political persuasion, as your elected First Minister I require the following from you."

She paused as if about to carefully choose her request. "I am to travel in three days for a meeting with the recently elected Prime Minister who I am certain will again offer all sort of public condolence on the murder of our citizens. I am also of the opinion that she will try to use this attack as a rallying point for the Union to remain as it is; the old cliché about together we are stronger. In short, it will be a subtle demand that my elected Government abandon our ultimate goal of independence."

She paused and then pale faced stared at Mulgrew when she forcefully said, "I am the elected leader of the Scottish people and I absolutely refuse to be bullied!"

She took a deep breath and said, "If at all you can provide even a small shred of evidence that the Westminster Government or individuals acting on their behalf had prior knowledge of the attack or even," she took a deep breath, "had some complicity in the organisation of the attack, then when I am in private discussion with the PM I can use that information to prevent a publicity campaign whose intention is to show us as a country to be weak against terrorist attack. Such a campaign might threaten the very existence of our Scottish Parliament, regardless what political party is in power at that time. In short, it is no surprise to anyone within the political spectrum that the Westminster Government make no secret of the fact they wish the Scottish Government to be subservient to their will."

Cairney permitted himself a small smile and quietly said, "If I didn't know otherwise, First Minister, I would think you want Miss Mulgrew to obtain some facts to enable you to black…"

"If you please, Chief Constable," the Justice Minister quickly interjected and raising a hand, continued. "This meeting is being minuted, Mister Cairney, and I cannot possibly permit the use of language that might infer any action by the First Minister or any of us here present, at some later time to be construed as illegal."

"I understand, sir," Cairney nodded and turning towards the First Minister, he added, "Forgive me, Ma'am."

"Nothing to forgive, Mister Cairney," she replied, then added with a mischievous grin, "but I like your way of thinking."

"What about the man who intervened in the attack, Chief Constable. Have your officers identified him?" asked the Deputy.

Cairney cast a brief glance at Mulgrew before replying, "Yes, sir, we have. His name is Ian Macleod, a former wounded soldier and decorated war veteran. We have not publicly disclosed his name for the following reason. Mister Macleod's actions in," he hesitated before continuing, "*dispatching* the wounded gunmen has, as likely you are aware, attracted the attention of the left wing press, some of whom advocate that he be prosecuted for murder under the terms of the Geneva Convention while others quote Scottish Law. Now, I am advised the Geneva Convention, sometimes referred to as the Law of War, applies to combatants engaged in, if there is such a thing, civilised war. However, therein lies the problem. The terrorists who attacked Glasgow city centre were not enemy combatants, but criminals; men engaged and intent upon murdering unarmed civilians. That said, under *Scottish* Law, Mister Macleod's actions could be construed as criminal if it were proved the three wounded men he shot in the head were alive, helpless and unable to defend themselves."

"Then I might be able to cast some light on his actions," interrupted the Deputy. All eyes turned towards him as he continued.

"Earlier today I spoke with a friend of mine, a retired Brigadier and discussed the media frenzy that currently surrounds Mister Macleod's action in shooting those men in the head. The Brigadier categorically assures me that Macleod did the correct thing, that if he suspected any of those men to be wearing one of those body things that explode..."

"An IED vest, sir," smiled Mulgrew.

"Yes, one of those," he agreed with a nod, "then Mister Macleod was within his rights under the rules of war. According to the Brigadier, if a soldier in the field advances past a wounded enemy combatant and believes a threat continues to exist from that enemy combatant to the soldier or any of his comrades, in this case I would suggest the civilians nearby, then the soldier is quite within his right to take what the Brigadier called punitive action; in essence, the soldier would be acting in defence of himself and his colleagues." Cairney turned to stare at Mulgrew and eyes narrowing, asked the Deputy, "Would the Brigadier be prepared to provide his expert opinion to the Crown Office, sir?"

"I'll certainly put it to him this evening, Mister Cairney and if so, I'll have him contact your inquiry team in Glasgow, first thing tomorrow morning."

"That, sir, would be a great relief to my Detective Superintendent Glennie who is at this moment preparing a report to Crown Office. My understanding is that Mister Glennie is in a bit of a quandary regarding Mister Macleod's status in this whole issue."

"Of course that is a decision to be made by the Crown Office, however, if Crown Office were to agree that by shooting those men in the head, Mister Macleod was acting in both his and the civilians hostages defence," the First Minister's brow creased, "it also solves another issue."

She stared at them in turn and continued, "My Government has for some time considered creating an award for our citizens, ordinary folk who act with gallantry, heroically or simply to help others in the face of adversity; something that would honour ordinary folk and not just those with money or who back political parties," her face paled. "Currently, the Scottish people and particularly the Glasgow folk are reeling from this attack. What we in Government need to do is to bolster their morale and one way would be to give them a hero. If he agrees," she smiled, "Mister Macleod *might* just be that man."

It was when they were returning to Glasgow in Cairney's official car that Mulgrew received the text message to phone John Glennie at her convenience.

"John, it's me," she began. "I'm in the car with Mister Cairney and putting you on speaker."

"Sir, Ma'am," Glennie greeted them, "I'm calling regarding the intense media interest in Ian Macleod. I've had a phone call from Chief Inspector Downes who tells me that the 'Glasgow News' have both Macleod's name and address. A reporter tried to visit him earlier this evening, but while I don't know the details yet, it seems two uniformed officers chased the reporter and his cameraman off. The news desk editor is threatening to complain that interviewing Macleod is in the public interest and that we're harassing his staff."

"Should have jailed them, not chased them off," Cairney quietly muttered, then guffawed, "Did I say that out loud?"

Mulgrew grinned at him as he added, "What does Chief Inspector Downes suggest, Mister Glennie?"

"She's persuaded the editor to hold off for now with the promise he'll get the first interview, sir. However, she is of the opinion that all the media will soon learn of Macleod's name and address and thinks we should pre-empt further harassment by suggesting that he consider attending a formal press conference."

"What about Crown Office? What if after the press conference they should decide to proceed with charges of murder against him?"

"It's too late this evening to speak with anyone at Crown Office, sir, but the final decision will likely lie with Mister Macleod. Currently in my inquiry he's neither a witness nor a suspect so legally we have no say what he decides nor are we in any position to offer him advice. That's down to his lawyer who of course will also need to be informed."

"Have you spoken with Macleod?"

"No, sir, I wanted to run it past Miss Mulgrew first."

Cairney turned to glance at her and said, "What do you think?"

She frowned as though deep in thought before replying, "Yes, I believe we should speak to Crown Office first and John, you might be getting a phone call tomorrow from a retired Brigadier whose name we don't yet have; however, the Brigadier might have some information for you before you speak with Crown Office, so if you can hang on till he calls. Once you've spoken with the Brigadier contact Crown Office and let them make the decision before we ask Mister Macleod to do anything."

Cairney asked, "When does Chief Inspector Downes need to inform the 'Glasgow News' of our decision?"

"She didn't say, sir, but I suspect tomorrow will do."

"Right then, Mister Glennie, for the time being we'll leave it in your capable hands. Good evening."

He glanced up at the rain filled sky and the drizzle that bounced off the windscreen.

With a shiver he pulled on the woollen ADIDAS hat and opened the door.

Standing at the car, he glanced about him, but there was nobody walking on the side road. In the near distance the sound of a siren filled the air and he presumed an ambulance was making its way to the nearby casualty department.

Lifting the boot of the car he opened the emergency tool kit and lifted out a flat bladed screwdriver that he shoved into the pocket of the tracksuit jacket, then placed the brown paper bag in the other pocket before securing the car.

Head down and hunching his shoulders against the rain he jogged across the road to the newly constructed building and with a final glance about him, slipped into the shadowed darkness at the side of the building and made his way to the rear.

The windows at the back were set almost a metre and a half high. One suitable window, he saw with a smile, was a few centimetres ajar. He looked about him and saw a discarded wooden crate that had once contained oxygen bottles and dragged it under the nearest window.

Testing that the crate would bear his weight, he reached up to the window sill and forced the blade of the screwdriver into the gap, then with a sharp, vicious jerk forced the lock. The window bounced free of its restraint and he breathed with relief before reaching up and slowly pulling himself through into the darkened room, then climbed down over a sink and sank quietly onto the tiled floor.

He stopped, held his breath and listened for any sound, but there was nothing.

The meagre moonlight from the window seemed to indicate the room was a wash room of some sort and he was pleased for it was unlikely the door of a washroom would be locked.

He was correct and made his way slowly into the corridor outside the wash room.

He startled when a sensor switched on the overhead lights, but the corridor had no windows and breathed a sigh of relief that the light would not be seen from outside. He had no way of knowing where she lay and realised that he had no option other than trying all the doors he came across.

It was the fifth door he tried that again was unlocked and led into the sudden chill of the cold chamber.

His throat felt tight and he knew he was breathing with difficulty, yet it had to be done.

Again, there were no windows in the room and believed it was safe to switch on the overhead lighting, yet still the sight of the stainless steel doors set into the far wall unnerved him.

In the decade since the Russian Federation attacked his country, Eldar Umarov had seen countless bodies and even himself been responsible for a great many deaths; the faces of men and some women who haunted him in his dreams.

He choked back a sob and stood motionless, unable to look away from those shiny, steel doors.

With a sigh he turned and saw the white board attached to the wall behind him. The names of those within the coffin like fridges were scrawled upon the board and to his dismay, saw that of his daughter, Malika Umarov.

He leaned towards the board and his eyes narrowed for the small card in the slot next to her name indicated that Malika's body was to be collected the next day for burial in the Muslim Section at a place called Cathcart Cemetery.

Unconsciously, he reached forward and touched at her name with his fingers and closing his eyes, slowly shook his head as he murmured, "That it should have come to this, my darling daughter. To meet again in this foreign land, this place so far from home; so far from me."

He walked across the room towards the far wall and bracing himself, pulled at the handle of the lower drawer marked with the number twelve.

The drawer slid easily open and taking a deep breath, he lowered his eyes to the figure that lay within.

He saw that Malika's body had been carefully bound with white cotton sheets and recognised the skilled handiwork of Muslim sisters and for that he was grateful.

His fingers, shaking slightly, gently touched at the serene face of his child and from his pocket he drew out the brown paper bag.

Opening the bag he withdrew the small Qur'an with the white leather dustcover and carefully slipped it under the sheet at her waist, then reached under the cloth to gently place her clod, lifeless hand upon the book.

Holding the side of the drawer, he sank to his knees and placing both hands flat on the floor, bowed his forehead to the cold tiled tiles.

Drawing in a breath, he began to slowly recite the Salat al-Janazah, the funeral prayer.

He finished with a long sigh, but for some strange reason, found it difficult to raise his head and stared curiously at the tears that had fallen to make small pools upon the tiled floor.

At last with a sigh, he pulled himself to his feet and slowly returned the drawer into the recess.

He was making his way back to the washroom and the forced window before he realised that he had never before in his life been so enraged.

CHAPTER THIRTEEN

As he stared at her he could see the bruising to her face where she had been struck with the rifle butt was already fading and the butterfly stitches would soon drop off.

They were sitting chatting quietly with the radio playing in the background when they heard the loud knocking.

Daisy grimaced and said, "Here comes trouble," then making her way to the front door opened it to a smiling Joan Crawford who held a steaming bag of chips in one hand and a plastic carrier bag of bottles in the other.

Behind Joan stood the diminutive Mickey Allison who like his neighbour wore a civilian jacket over his uniform polo shirt.

Grinning at Daisy, he asked, "Where is he, then?"

She stepped to one side to allow them to enter, then followed her two colleagues through to the lounge where Ian Macleod was standing to greet them.

"So, here's the hero," grinned Joan and handing the chips and plastic bag to Daisy, to Ian's astonishment the strongly built six foot tall woman grabbed and enveloped him in a bear crushing hug and planted a sloppy, lipstick kiss upon his cheek.

Releasing him, Joan grinned at his red face as Mickey stepped forward and vigorously pummelled his hand.

"Right," Joan rubbed her hands briskly together and nodding to Daisy, said, "I'll organise the bevy while you get plates for me and Mickey boy here. We've not had our break because we've been stuck down in Buchanan Street monitoring the crowds."

"The crowds?" Ian asked, rubbing at his cheek, his eyes betraying his curiosity.

"Oh, aye," Joan nodded. "It might be pissing down outside, Ian, but the rubber-neckers are there in their droves. Tell me," she smiled coyly at him as she gently took his arm in hers, "have you got a wife or a girlfriend?"

He stared dumbfounded at her, his mouth opening and closing as he fought to reply, but was saved by Mickey who flopping down onto the couch, told him, "Don't worry about her, Ian, she's all talk. I've been trying to get into her knickers for months, but she keeps avoiding me."

"Well, maybe that's because I want a real man and not a dwarf," she retorted, then grinning at Ian, said, "Don't you be worrying, Ian. I'm only joking. I think Daisy's got first call on you."

"First call on who," Daisy asked when she re-entered the lounge carrying a plate of chips in each hand.

"Right, I'll organise that bevy," Joan said with an exaggerated wink at the startled Ian.

"You okay, big guy?" Mickey asked from the couch, stuffing his mouth with chips.

"I'm not sure," Ian wide-eyed to Daisy. "Is she always like that?"

"Oh, aye, though sometimes she can be a bit outrageous," Daisy smiled at him.

Joan returned with a small round tin tray from which she handed Ian a chunky glass that was half full and asked, "I take it you like a dram?"

He stared with surprise at the three fingers of whisky before replying, "Occasionally."

Joan who held a glass with an equal amount, handed Mickey a can of lager and a glass of wine to Daisy.

"Here's to Ian, the man of the moment," she loudly declared and threw back her head to finish her whisky.

Glancing uneasily at Daisy who slyly winked, he sipped at his whisky then said, "I'm very grateful to you both for getting me out of that awkward situation, back at my flat."

Calm now, Joan eased herself down onto the couch beside Mickey and said, "No, Ian, it's us that are grateful for what *you* did."

Cocking her glass towards Daisy, she continued. "Our wee pal here means a lot to Mickey and me, as well as the rest of the station and we know that if it hadn't been for you, well…"

She didn't finish, but toasted her glass to Ian and said, "To friendship."

"To friendship," they all agreed.

A quietness descended upon the room, broken when Daisy's house phone rung.

"Hello," she answered the call and the other three watched as rubbing at her furrowed brow, she listened then replied, "Yes, I've got that and thanks again."

She replaced the handset and turning, her face betrayed her surprise when she said, "That was DS McInnes, one of the inquiry team. The detective that took my statement. She's just given me permission to attend the funeral tomorrow and the time I've to be there. The homeless girl," she glanced at them in turn. "She's told me her name. She was called Malika Umarov."

DS Mo McInnes knocked on John Glennie's door and popping her head in, asked, "Are you free, Boss?"

"Aye, come in," he waved her forward to the chair opposite.

"I've spoken with the Interpol representative at the International Court of Justice at The Hague, the man who deals with the inquiries relating to alleged war criminals and asked if he has any information about this man Eldar Umarov."

"And?"

"Officially, he tells me he has a file an inch thick on Umarov and that it's the Russian Federation who are seeking to extradite Umarov from Chechnya. However, the Chechnya Police are not members of Interpol and the Chechen Government have refused to hand him over. Unofficially, he tells me that it's the same old story; one man's hero is another man's war criminal and as far as he is aware, Umarov is unable to leave the safety of his home country because the FSB are keeping tabs on him. Privately he is of the opinion that if Umarov does leave Grozny then he's in danger of being snatched from wherever he is and thinks it's unlikely he will leave Chechnya."

"So in short, Interpol are of the opinion that Umarov is currently in Chechnya?"

"Yes, Boss."

"But they aren't definite."

"No," McInnes shook her head.

"Well," he exhaled, "wherever Umarov might be, let's not take any chances of him coming over here to exact revenge upon the families of the four terrorists, so request that a Ports Watch be issued and see if you can drum up a current photograph. I don't want our cousins down south having to deal with an enraged father killing innocent people because of this," his brow furrowed, "what is it called again?"

"I think when you briefed the team you called it an Adat, Boss."

"Aye, well, this bloody Adat thing."

She was about to rise from her chair when he said, "Did you make the call to the young policewoman, Daisy Cooper?"

"I did, sir. I told her about the funeral ceremony tomorrow morning at ten at Cathcart Cemetery."

"What's your thoughts, Mo?"

"Well, in the short time I spoke with her when I took her statement, I believe the lassie feels in some way guilty about the young woman getting killed, as though by being there and surviving, it's somehow her fault."

"Survivors guilt. Is that what it's called?"

"Yes, sir, it's something like that."

"Malika Umarov had no family here, or at least none that we know of, so I don't expect that apart from some reporters there will be many people there. However, I'll be attending tomorrow's ceremony. Are you up for it?"

"Yes, sir, I'll go with you," she nodded.

"Thanks, Mo. Right, anything else?"

"Just that DCI Sheridan said to tell you she spoke with the old guy from the Glasgow Mosque, Sheikh Abdul Muiz and based on what the interpreter Mister Drugov told us that as it's likely the Umarov girl was Muslim, he's agreed and willing to conduct the funeral service."

"Good. It's the very least we can do for the poor lass. If nothing else, if her father ever contacts us we can at least inform that we did as likely he would have wished."

Carrying a shopping bag in each hand, Rahib Chowdhury turned the corner into Anglesea Road and was walking towards his mid-terraced house when he saw the car parked outside. His eyes narrowed for he neither recognised the car nor was expecting visitors at this time of the evening. He slowed his pace, his mind in a whirl then stopped, for two women had stepped out of his door into the pavement and were walking to the car. He could see the taller of the women wore a hajib.

Head down, he quickly crossed the road and turned into Newson Street, then slowed down when from the corner of his eye he saw the car drive past the junction of Anglesea Street and out of sight.

He stopped and retracing his steps, hurried home where he pushed open the front door and loudly called to his wife.

Rabia nervously joined him in the kitchen where he dumped the shopping bags onto the worktop. Turning sharply, his nostrils flaring, he growled, "Who were those kafir women?" then before she could respond, took a menacing step towards the timid woman and demanded, "Why did you permit them to enter my home!"

"I...I..." she stuttered, before finding her voice and fearfully telling him, "They were police ladies. Both of them. The sister too."

"Sister?" he remembered the hajib. "One of them was of the Faith?"

"Yes, my husband, the older of the two, the tall one."

His stomach lurched and he said, "What did they want?"

"To speak with you, Rahib. They wanted to interview you about a friend of yours."

"What friend?"

"I do not know, they did not say his name."

"Did they say if they would return?"

"They left this," she handed him a business card and he read, 'Detective Inspector Aamira Khalifa, Metropolitan Police' with a phone number underneath.

"The sister asked if you could phone at your convenience," his wife added.

The police could not know, he thought and if they suspected anything at all they would not be leaving business cards. No, they would be kicking down his door and arresting him with their guns. He swallowed with difficulty, trying to decide whether or not to phone the number on the card.

"She said she would return if you did not contact her," his wife said.

That decided him.

Better to speak with the bitch on the phone than have her call again at his home.

"I'll be in my study," he brushed rudely past Rabia and headed upstairs.

In his luxury fourth floor apartment at Anchorage Point in the affluent Canary Wharf area of London, the Security Service Director of Operations, Barry Ashford, was seething. Stood peering through the window in the expensively furnished lounge, he stared with anger down to the docklands below.

His mind was in turmoil and all because that bitch in Scotland had made him look like a fool.

The DG, another bloody political appointment, was like a nervous old woman whose hand needed held. All he worried about was if questions would be asked by that idiot of a Home Secretary.

Afraid, that's what was wrong with them; anxious about getting their fucking hands dirty!

No, he unconsciously shook his head, leave the shitty work to men like him. Men who stuck their head above the parapet and were prepared to do what was needed, no matter the consequence; for King and Country, he unconsciously toasted his reflection in the window.

Those fucking bureaucrats were so wrapped up worrying about their pensions, they no longer represented the steel will of the Westminster Government.

They could not tolerate those Jock bastards crying out for independence and feared the thought that the Union might be divided, but would the cowards do something about it?

No, they were too afraid of questions being asked.

Scowling, he sipped at the brandy from the glass in his hand.

His thoughts turned to the near disaster that was the attack in Glasgow.

There was no way that anything could be traced back to him or any of the men he covertly employed to do his bidding. He was far too careful, far too long in the tooth to make such errors.

And yet there might be one small glitch and that glitch, he smiled at his own brilliance, would be taken care of within the next few days.

Nothing drastic, a simple accident and after all, he sipped again at the brandy; accidents were a daily occurrence of life, were they not?

The Service was going to shit, he angrily sniffed.

Gone were the days when the word accountability didn't figure in any of the operations in which he had been concerned.

Gone were the days when he was able to make decisions without seeking the nod of approval from senior management.

Senior management, he thought and his eyes narrowed.

It would be different when he assumed the position of Director General; the position that should so rightly be his.

The DG has at the most just two further years then the job will be mine, he confidently smiled.

And no matter what it took, no matter what he had to do, he would ensure that when he was Director General he would make sure it would be a Service that represented the United Kingdom and included those wayward Jocks.

Of that he was determined.

John Glennie was about to head for home when his door knocked and with a sigh was about to call out 'come in', but the door was pushed open by a grinning Lou Sheridan.

"Bit of an update for you," she breathlessly began. "The Octavia car that I had moved from Waverly station to Gartcosh for Forensic examination?"

His eyes narrowed and he stopped pulling on his coat. "Aye?"

"Well, it *is* a stolen vehicle and we've been in touch with the registered keeper who reported its theft to the Met cops over a week ago. The Scene of Crime got a fingerprint lift from the refuelling cap. They're running it through the Live Scan system as we speak and hopefully we should get a result anytime soon."

"Good," Glennie grinned at her. "Maybe this will be a real break."

She watched as he laid his coat on the desk and eyes frowning, asked, "What are you doing?"

"I'm waiting for the result."

"No," she firmly shook her head. "You've been here early doors; in fact, you were first in this morning and we both know the first in doesn't mean you have to be the last out. You not the captain of a bloody sinking ship, John. It's unlikely we'll be able to do anything at this time of night, so get yourself up the road. I'll phone you if there's any news."

He stared at her with a smile. "Are you ordering me home, Detective Chief Inspector?"

"Yes, sir, I am. Now get your arse in gear and tell Celia I send my love."

He began to laugh and shaking his head, replied, "Maybe you're right. I'm done in and I've the ceremony to attend tomorrow morning. Can't say I'm too keen. I've always hated attending victim's funerals. By the way, I'm taking Mo McInnes with me as my driver in case you're looking for her."

"I'm sure we'll cope, so safely home."

"Okay and thanks, Lou," he lifted his coat from the desk.

In the CTU office at New Scotland Yard, her shift almost ended, the young analyst Jenny Fielding heard her mobile phone beep and lifting it from her handbag, made her way to the ladies toilet in the corridor outside.

The room was empty and in a cubicle she opened the text message and read; *get adress for Chowdhury.*

She tightly closed her eyes, and gritted her teeth against the throbbing and shook her head.

Didn't he know how fucking difficult this is, she inwardly snarled. Her heart missed a beat when she heard the door to the washroom squeak open and then heard someone closing a cubicle door.

Taking a few seconds to compose herself, she flushed the toilet and made a pretence of washing her hands before returning to her office.

Ian Macleod lay on his back in the single bed, staring at the recently painted ceiling. A crack in the curtain permitted illumination from the lamppost in the road outside to create a lengthy, narrow sliver of light on the wall by the door.

He breathed easily and guessed the whisky he had drunk was keeping him awake. As a younger man, he did as young men did, drinking and having a good time with his mates, but in his early thirties, though he still enjoyed a pint and a dram, decided to ease up on his consumption of alcohol and amazed himself at the money he saved by not drinking; money that was now part of the nest egg safely banked towards his dream of opening his own place.

He heard the slightest of a sound within the house and stopped breathing, wondering what the noise was. Turning his head, he saw the digital clock read almost two in the morning and slipping out of the bed, made his way in his bare feet to the door. Yes, he was certain there was someone in the lounge, maybe the kitchen.

The door opened easily on its oiled hinges and he padded quietly though, then saw the light from the kitchen.

He breathed a little easier and not wishing to startle her, softly called out, "Daisy, it's me. Ian. I'm coming through."

In his shorts and tee shirt, he limped into the kitchen,

Standing by the worktop in her bare feet, he saw she wore a short length, maroon coloured silk dressing gown, her hair untidily falling to her shoulders and he could see she had been crying.

"Sorry, did I wake you?" she sniffed, using a tissue to wipe at her eyes. "Look at the state of me."

It occurred to him to say she never looked lovelier, but thought she might be offended and instead, said, "I couldn't half murder a cuppa. Is that the kettle boiling?"

She smiled and he saw the tears continue to roll down her cheeks.

Taking a deep breath, he continued, "If you don't take this the wrong way, do you want a reassuring cuddle?"

Not daring to speak, her lips trembling, she could only nod and fell into his arms.

He held her tightly as they stood there in the kitchen wrapped together while she silently wept and behind them, the kettle boiled.

At last, she pulled gently away from him, his arms falling to his sides, Dabbing at her eyes with the tissue, she mumbled, "Sorry."

"For what?" he pretended to be puzzled and added, "For being human? For demonstrating that you have emotions? For being kind in letting me stay here, for the time being? For…"

She surprised him by placing her forefinger against his lips to hush him and then reaching up, kissed him softly on the lips.

"Don't be getting the wrong idea," she took a deep breath and forced a smile. "That's for being thoughtful and kind…and brave."

He was tongue tied and didn't know how to respond, but continued to stare at her.

She reached up again and gently brushed a lock of hair from his forehead and said, "Will you come with me? To the funeral, I mean?"

His brow furrowed as he stared at her and slowly nodding, replied, "Yes, of course."

They sat together on the couch with the mugs in their hands.

"The guy in the photo," he asked. "Boyfriend?"

She sighed, "Ex-boyfriend. Billy. We were to be married, but common sense kicked in and the wedding was called off."

"Whose commons sense; his or yours," he teased her.

She turned to stare at him and he thought he had annoyed her, but she smiled and replied, "Mine. He wanted a domestic goddess running after him. I wanted a career in the polis. He wanted to control my life, I wanted a partner. It wasn't an affable split."

"I'm curious; then why keep his photograph?"

She didn't immediately respond, then replied, "To remind me that I almost gave up my own dreams for someone else's dream; someone else's ambition."

"What happens if a new guy comes into your life? Will you take the photograph down?"

It was her turn to tease him when she replied, "Are you applying for the job, Mister Macleod?"

He could feel himself blush and he stuttered, "I think you could do a lot better than me, Constable Daisy."

He hadn't called her 'Constable Daisy' since saving her life in the Precinct and for some peculiar reason, his name for her seemed to please her.

"Just for argument sake and purely hypothetical," she raised a hand, "why is that then?"

"Well," he shrugged and slowly drawled before replying, "For a start I'm unemployed."

"Not a valid reason," she shook her head. "You have an ambition to open your own café, yes?"

"Aye," he stared curiously at her.

"That means you have prospects."

"Oh, okay then." His brow furrowed and chewed at the inside of his mouth, a boyhood habit he had never quite got over. Patting at his left leg, he continued, "I'm disabled, the left side of my face would scare weans rigid and I'm slightly deaf in my left ear, or what's left of it."

"You think I'm the sort of woman that judges a man by his looks?"

"No, I'm not suggesting that…" he stopped when he saw her grin and pretending to scowl, continued, "You're taking the mickey, aren't you?"

"Yes and no."

To his surprise she slowly reached up and drew her fingers tenderly along the scars on his face towards his ear, then said, "It's obvious that you've suffered some horrific injury, Ian, but it's how *you* feel about it that matters, not anyone else. Do you believe it makes you any less of a man?"

"No," he was blushing again, "of course not."

"Then what were those reasons again?"

"I think you're too smart for me and I also think if we're attending the funeral later today, then it's time for bed."

"Is that a proposal," she coyly smiled at him.

"Dear God, woman," he growled and choked back laughter, "have you no shame?"

"You've still to convince me why you're not applying for the job of my boyfriend?"

"Because I like you," he slowly said. "I like you and you are very attractive. You're smart, you're kind and yes," he tried to control his breathing, "very desirable."

"But?"

He licked at his lips and laid his mug down onto the floor by the couch to give him a few seconds to compose himself, be sure about what he was going to say.

"But right now you are very vulnerable. You've been through a traumatic experience and having been there, believe me, Daisy, it sends your head haywire so you *think* you know what you're doing, what you're saying, but you're not really," he shook his head. "You look at me and you see the man that saved you, not the man I am. If this whole bloody affair had not happened and you and I were to meet, say in a pub; let's be honest, would you have approached me, spoken to me, considered me to be someone you'd want for your boyfriend?"

He knew he wasn't explaining himself properly and saw her nostrils angrily flare when she brusquely replied, "You're right of course. Not about how you look, but about me. Yes, I was scared shitless when that bastard pointed his rifle at me and yes, I'm finding it difficult to keep my emotions in check. I am so very grateful that you saved me, Ian."

She paused, her lips quivering with anger, then continued, "But you're wrong to judge me, to believe that I wouldn't consider you as a boyfriend on the basis of your looks. That's not me at all," she angrily shook her head. "There's a lot more to me than what *you* see, too."

Abruptly getting to her feet, she turned away and walking towards the door called over her shoulder, said, "I'll see you in the morning. Goodnight."

He took a deep breath and slowly exhaling, knew he had really fucked up.

Lifting his mug from the floor, he limped to the kitchen and placed it in the sink before quietly heading back to bed.

CHAPTER FOURTEEN

Eldar Umarov arose before dawn for Fajr prayers, but first glancing through the window saw it was setting out to be a bright, sunny day. Again he knelt by the window to face east and once prayers were completed, showered and dressed in the chinos and a light coloured polo shirt.

Fortunately, the navy blue Italian suit that Akhmad Soslanbek's organisation had acquired for him was so dark as to be almost as black as was the tie he had purchased at the ASDA retail store.

On his way to the hotel restaurant, he picked up two local newspapers from the cheery receptionist and read them both while enjoying his light breakfast.

Both papers again led with the terrorist attack, though seemed to be regurgitating the news for there was nothing that he read that was new. However, on page four of one of the papers, the 'Glasgow News', he read that two of the victims of the attack were to be buried that morning; a man who had been one of two shot down beside an underground station and a young woman, who was not named.

Umarov knew the woman to be his daughter Malika and his brow creased.

The authorities obviously knew her identity, but why wasn't she identified to the media, he wondered?

There could only be one reason…and alarmed, he almost leaped from this seat.

"Are you finished here, sir?" smiled the young waitress at his elbow who nervously added, "I'm sorry, I didn't mean to startle you, sir."

He forced a grin and lifting his hand to his heart, made the slightest of bows before telling her, "I was daydreaming, young lady. Forgive me."

The girl blushed and lifting his plate, moved on.

He slowly exhaled, inwardly grinning at his own fright, then thought again why the authorities did not release Malika's name.

There could only be one explanation.

They feared that he might learn of the burial ceremony and attempt to enter the country.

Too late, he smiled grimly at the thought; I'm already here.

John Glennie's wife Celia had prepared a light breakfast that she insisted he sit and eat, muttering, "You're not leaving this house with just a cup of coffee in you, my lad."

As he tucked into the small fry-up, she sat on the chair to his left and said, "Tell me about your day."

"Well," he swallowed, "I'll head into the office to find out if there's any news or developments, then Mo McInnes and I are attending the young woman's funeral. The young homeless lassie who killed in the Precinct."

She reached across to place her hand on his and with a shake of her head, said, "God forgive me, but I believe those men deserved what they got. Wantonly killing all those poor people. The news on the early morning breakfast show said there is to be two funerals today; the girl and a man from Glasgow."

"Aye, he was one of the two shot dead outside the subway. Cut down like a…"

He didn't finish, just shook his head at the sad and futile waste of life.

"Do you think you'll be late again? Alison is popping in and bringing the weans over to visit before she puts them down to their bed."

"I'm not certain, love," he sighed. "At the minute, there's still a number of inquiries to be made so I'm just playing it by ear. I'll phone you and Alison too if I get caught up."

He hurriedly finished the meal then slurping a mouthful of coffee, said, "I'd better be going."

She walked him to the door and kissed him on the cheek, admonishing that he be careful in the morning traffic and watched as he drove away.

Returning to the dining room, she collected the dirty dishes and for the rest of her day, worried about her husband.

Across the city, Cathy Mulgrew, dressed and moments from departing for work, was carefully filling her Costa travel mug with coffee when her partner Jo, wearing an ankle length dressing gown and looking disheveled, her long blonde hair lying unbound on her shoulders, slipped into the kitchen and yawned as she stepped towards Mulgrew.

"Sorry we didn't get much time together last night, love," Jo wrapped her arms about Mulgrew's waist and laid her head against Mulgrew's neck. "By the time that bloody taxi arrived at the airport…"

"I've told you before," Mulgrew cut in. "When you're away on these long haul business trips, you should consider parking up at the airport and then you don't need to wait on transport. Anyway," she turned and cupped Jo's chin in her hand, "if I hadn't been tied up with the Chief I could have collected you. Sorry about that," she smiled.

"No problem, honey. So, what's on the agenda today?"

"The first of the funerals, I'm sorry to say. John Glennie, one of my Superintendents will attend the homeless woman's service and I'll be going to the one at Dalnotter. One of the victims killed at the underground. Then it's the same old, same old."

"What time do you expect to get home," her hand at her mouth, Jo yawned again.

Mulgrew turned and taking Jo in her arms, replied, "Can't say, but do try to get some sleep. " She grinned, "We've missed a week together so we need to catch up."

"Well, that's me off for at least four days, so I'll be waiting for you with dinner, a bottle of chardonnay and a hot bath when you get in, no matter what time it is," she demurely smiled.

"I'll be sure to remember that," Mulgrew grinned and kissed her goodbye.

Daisy opened her eyes earlier than she anticipated and reached to switch off the alarm.

She hadn't slept well and swung her legs from the bed to sneak her feet into her slippers then reached for her dressing gown from the chair.

It had been silly arguing with Ian over such a stupid and trivial matter. He must think me a fool, she shook her head and standing, slipped on the dressing gown. She rubbed at her eyes with the heel of her hands and blushed at the memory of weeping in the kitchen. He had been kind to hug her like he did, but that's all it was. Kindness.

She thought about the funeral service, of asking him to accompany her and realised he probably like her, would her be embarrassed and no longer want to come. She would make an excuse, tell him the media would be there and he could end up being the focal point of their attention rather than the young woman who was being buried. Yes, that's what she would say and slowly turning the door handle, was about to quietly step into the hallway when she heard the slight rattle of cutlery from the kitchen.

She pushed open the door and saw Ian, dressed in dark coloured jeans, a cream coloured shirt and wearing a brightly coloured floral patterned apron as he stood over the cooker. The tempting smell of bacon sizzling in the pan assailed her nostrils.

"Good morning," he smiled warily at her. "I nipped out and bought some rolls and this," he pointed with the spatula at the frying pan. "Thought we might get something in our stomachs before we leave for the cemetery."

Her brow furrowed. "I didn't hear you get up or even leave the house," she muttered as she sat down at the small kitchen table.

Ian laid a mug of tea in front of her and with a soft grin, replied, "It was that all that covert army training I did, sneaking about the countryside. Made me quite an expert, even with a bum leg."

She knew she had to say something and was about to speak, but he held up a hand and forestalled her by saying, "Daisy, I was out of order last night. I wasn't deliberately trying to offend you. If anything," he shrugged, "I was trying to say that…" he laid the spatula down onto the worktop and turning, licked at his lips and spreading his hands wide, carefully said, "Look, I've only known you a few days and it's not your emotions that are all over the place; it's mine."

He took a deep breath.

"Like I told you the other day, I was briefly engaged and yes, I've known a few women in my day, but since I got blown up I've never had a relationship, never had the courage even to speak with any women because I was so wrapped up in what they might think, what they might see when they looked at me. I lacked confidence in myself and because I knew what it's like to suffer from PTSD, I realised that your head would be all over the place and that you probably feel guilty for surviving and these feelings manifested themselves in wanting to attach to me. I just didn't want you to feel so grateful to me that you might one day realise you're mistaken, that your gratefulness to me is really that you feel…well, feel…"

"Feel sorry for you?"

He didn't immediately respond, but staring at her, slowly nodded and softly replied, "Yes. Feel sorry for me."

She slowly nodded and stared at the mug of tea for a few seconds. He had taken her aback with his honesty and she realised she must be careful how she responded.

Choosing her words carefully, she lifted her head and staring thoughtfully at him, replied, "Ian, I lay awake most of last night, or rather I dozed now and then, so I'm feeling pretty shitty right now due to the lack of sleep. But let's get one thing clear. I really don't care what you might think about yourself. What other women see or think when they look at you is not my concern. What *I* think and see when *I* look at you is *my* concern and what I think and what I see is a man that I want to get to know better, someone I think I would like to spend time with. If you feel the same way about me as I currently feel about you, then perhaps spending that time together…"

She stopped when to her surprise, he stooped down and taking her face in both his hands, gently kissed her.

Releasing her, he grinned and said, "I agree. So, how do you like your bacon?"

John Glennie had just driven into the rear yard at Helen Street police office when his mobile phone activated. He glanced at the screen, but there was no name and the number was unknown to him.

"Hello?"

"Mister John Glennie is it," the male voice with a striking Scottish brogue crisply asked.

"Aye, it is. Who's calling?"

"Mister Glennie, my name is Hamish MacLachlan, lately retired Brigadier of the Royal Regiment of Scotland. You were expecting my call?"

"Ah," Glennie was taken aback, "Yes, sir, I was informed by my boss that you might be calling," he switched off he car engine.

"If you're happy not to stand on ceremony, I'm Hamish. Can I call you John?"

"Please do, Hamish," he grinned at MacLachlan's clipped, machinegun speech and if the voice was any indication, in his mind's eye imagined MacLachlan to be a barrel-chested, bearded, gimlet eyed, grim-faced, kilted former soldier.

"Right then, this young man who slotted those four bastards," MacLachlan said. "I understand it was that bloody rogue Ian Macleod, formerly of the RHF. Is that correct, John?"

"That's correct, yes," his eyes narrowed. "I'm sorry, slotted?"

"Slotted, John. Sent the bastards to their graves," he explained before continuing, "Well, Staff Sergeant Macleod is known to me. Good man. First class soldier. Cracking shot, as I recall. Bloody hero in anyone's book, that man. Sad loss to the Regiment when those bastards in Afghanistan blew him up. So, what can I do to help?"

Glennie couldn't help himself and grinned at the short, sharp sentences

"To be frank, Hamish, I've a bit of a quandary at the minute. It's to do with Macleod's shooting the terrorists in the head after he had already shot them down. It might be argued in Scottish Law…"

"Bugger the law!" interrupted MacLachlan. "We're talking about the safety of my soldiers and I believe in this particular case, the safety of the general public; am I correct or what?"

"Yes, Hamish," Glennie agreed.

"Then I will stand in any bloody court in the land and inform any bloody judge who is in damn doubt that when I commanded the Regiment, my instructions to my soldiers was clear and concise. When an enemy combatant and that includes those engaged in acts of terrorism, is shot down and wounded; if that combatant, wounded or not, continues to present a viable threat then my soldiers were and I know for a fact continue to be instructed to neutralise that threat. If that means shooting the bastards in the head, then so be it. I categorically refused to lose men to an enemy who either feigns surrender or being wounded, remains determined to inflict casualties. Staff Sergeant Macleod was completely correct in his actions and followed his training as he had been taught. Now, John," he snapped, "who the hell do I have to convince about that?"

Glennie sighed with relief and asked, "Where are you calling from, Hamish?"

"From my home, here in the outskirts of Dunblane. Why?"

"How do you feel, Hamish, about accompanying me this afternoon for a wee visit to the Crown Office at the Scottish Crime Campus in Gartcosh? I'd like them to have a wee chat with you about what you have just told me."

"Will it assist Staff Sergeant Macleod?"

"Oh yes, I believe it will."

"Give me the time and the map coordinates and I'll meet you there."

Rahib Chowdhury had not slept well.

Chasing his wife to the spare bedroom, he had comforted himself in his bed with photographs of naked children; photographs like those that had got him into this damn mess in the first place.

Ignoring Fajr prayers, he lay on and listened through the thin, plasterboard wall to his wife softly chanting.

It angered him that he must phone the woman, the detective. Muslim or not, she was kafir. Munafiq; a hypocrite who professed to be a true believer, yet according to his wife's description, dressed as a westerner and obeyed the laws of England when she should be obeying the law of Sharia.

Though he did not know Aamira Khalifa, Rahib had already made his mind up that she was an enemy and as such could not be trusted. He knew that the old Sheikh would have told her of his association with Abdul-hameed Muhammad and her questions would be about their relationship.

He must lie, deny everything.

His brow creased.

But how could he prepare himself to deny everything when he did not know what her questions would be?

He rubbed nervously at his chin. Should he phone and tell John that the police wished to interview him; ask him to intercede as he did when he was arrested with the photographs and the films?

But John did not intercede to help him.

John did so to use and to later manipulate him.

No, he shook his head. John would not help him. Why would he, for Rahib had little doubt that at the first opportunity, John would abandon him to his fate.

Nevertheless, he realised that not to inform John would be a great mistake for undoubtedly the man had his own informants within the police, for how else had he known about the arrest for child pornography?

With nervous hands he opened the phone and began to compose a text message.

That done he pressed the send button and glanced at the faint light coming through the thin curtains.

It was still early, but he arose with the determination that he must phone the kafir woman.

Calling to his wife to demand she make his breakfast, he made his way to the bathroom to complete his ablutions.

He had decided that after Malika was laid to rest, he would remain a further night in the hotel, before making his way south in readiness for his contact to provide the addresses for the relatives of the dead terrorists.

His Faith had been tested when he heard the men who murdered Malika described as Muslim, but in his heart knew that was not so. They were not true believers, for had they been they would not have indiscriminately cut down helpless, unarmed civilians. No, the four men were an abomination; animals who used Islam as a crutch to justify their twisted interpretation of a Faith that was based on peace, honour and a love for fellow man.

He sat on the edge of the bed and his thoughts again turned to the attack.

The men who had murdered Malika and the others were part of a disease that was rampaging throughout the Islamic world and as an educated man knew that murder and atrocity was not the prerogative of Islam.

No, throughout centuries of religious intolerance Christianity, Hinduism, Sikhism, Judaism and countless other religions had their shameful periods and many continued to do so. As recently as a couple of decades ago, even the United Kingdom reeled from the intolerance between two of their own Christian groups; the Irish Catholics and the Irish Protestants.

These days though, he grimly smiled, it's fashionable to blame all the Muslims for the act of a few individuals who twisted the teaching of the Holy Prophet, Muhammad, bless his name, to suit their own evil agenda.

He glanced at his watch and was reaching for his suit jacket when the mobile phone informed him a text had been received.

Opening the phone, he read; *rahib chowdhury suspcted by met plice adress to folow. phone at 6.*

Reading the text, it occurred to him the sender's first language was not English and suspected the sender was the same individual to whom he had spoken.

However, the important thing, was he now had a lead to follow, but first he had better destroy this phone and obtain another.

Collecting the BMW from the car park under the hotel, Umarov first visited the ASDA store where he purchased a new 'pay-as-you-go phone', though from a different assistant and in the car, went through the same procedure of transferring the unnamed contacts phone number to the new phone and destroying the current mobile phone.

Starting the engine, he smoothly pulled out of the car park and followed his car Satnav instructions as it directed him towards Cathcart Cemetery.

He had decided to arrive early and reconnoitre the area, fearful that though it was highly unlikely the FSB might be in contact with their British counterparts, the FSB might have learned that it was his daughter Malika who was to be buried. If so, there was no doubt they would take the opportunity to attend the ceremony to either abduct him or more likely, silence him for good.

Arriving at the imposing entrance with its wrought iron gates and dilapidated Victorian building just within the gates, he decided that it would be foolish to park in the grounds for to do so would leave him vulnerable should he require to get away in a hurry.

Instead, he drove around the area and choosing an exit route, parked in the nearby narrow road called Clarkston Avenue then walked towards the cemetery gates.

He spent twenty minutes walking around the overgrown graves, surprised that just within the entrance where the Commonwealth Graves were located, that they were so carefully tended while others lay in a sad state of disrepair.

A ramshackle sign informed him that the cemetery had been opened in 1875 and from the state of some of the older plots and headstones, he had little doubt that many of the families of the early interments no longer existed.

He glanced at his watch and saw the time of Malika's service was approaching and so stood discreetly to one side in an area of thick foliage, watching the entrance.

A police car with two officers, a man and a woman, arrived and parking their vehicle just inside the entrance he watched as they took up a position on either side of the gates. It was clear to Umarov they were positioned there as guards of some sort. He narrowed his eyes and as far as he was able to make out, neither of the two carried sidearms and he smiled at the curiosity of a police force that did not routinely arm its officers.

Shortly after the arrival of the police car, there followed a number of vehicles that when the drivers were spoken to, were waved through the gates by the officers and parked in the area near to the entrance.

To his surprise, he saw at least a dozen men and women, perhaps more and who were clearly brothers and sisters, exit some of the vehicles that included a large people carrier.

One aged man helped by two brothers seemed to be the Sheikh and he caught his breath.

Tears of joyful surprise sprung to his eyes and his heart gladdened when he realised that Malika was to have an Islamic funeral.

A number of other vehicles waved through the gates brought some non-believers who joined the group of Muslims as they quietly awaited the hearse.

He watched as a small, green coloured car, a Fiat he thought, discharged a young woman driver and a man who limped. They stood to one side of the crowd, though he did see the woman briefly speak with an older man and another woman that Umarov thought might also be plain clothed police officers.

The younger woman he saw had what looked like a darker patch of skin at her hairline, bruising he guessed, and a thought occurred; is this the policewoman who spoke with Malika and was injured when struck by a rifle and is this the man who saved her?

His eyes narrowed as he peered at the limping man. He grimly smiled and took a deep breath. He had seen such men before, recognising the tell-tale signs; the way he slowly glanced about himself, the manner in which he cautiously stepped.

He took a deep breath for he decided that this limping man was a warrior; a man who had witnessed much and his limp aside was not be someone who would be easily intimidated.

A few minutes before ten, the hearse transporting his daughter arrived and at the sight of it he bit at his closed fist and his body shook as he choked back a cry, but could not prevent the tears that fell.

The crowd watched silently as the undertakers removed the plain, brown wooden coffin and passed the burden to six of the Muslim men who solemnly carried the coffin along the wide though overgrown pathway.

The crowd followed and in the thick shrubbery at a distance, so did Umarov.

The man he believed to be the Sheikh conducted the funeral ceremony and though Umarov was too far off to hear, he followed the service that he knew from the memory of attending too many similar ceremonies. Watching the brothers and sisters raising their hands in prayer, he silently mouthed the Salat-al-Janazah with them, the tears continuing to roll down his cheeks as he did so.

He watched as his daughter was carefully lowered into the freshly dug grave and he turned away.

He had made his mind up.

The sight of the young woman and the limping man and the recollection of the articles he had read in the newspapers reminded him.

No matter that it was dangerous to him, he had a debt to repay; a debt for Malika that he could not ignore.

CHAPTER FIFTEEN

Aamira Khalifa was puzzled.

Following her instructions, DC Clare Ball had checked Rahib Chowdhury's name with the corresponding address they had for him on the Police National Computer and got one hit. Ball had hurried off duty after receiving word of a family bereavement and Mira believing it unnecessary to disturb her with questions about the PNC check at such a sensitive time, instead read through Ball's note again.

The information from the PNC, Ball had written, merely indicated that fourteen months earlier Rahib Chowdhury had been recorded as arrested and transported to the Suffolk Constabulary Headquarters at Martlesham Heath in Ipswich. Curiously, there was no mention of the charge nor any follow-up inquiry and the case was dropped with Chowdhury being discharged from custody the following day. What was helpful to Khalifa was that Ball had taken a note of the name of the Suffolk detective who arrested Chowdhury.

She consulted her Police Almanac and obtaining the phone number for Martlesham Heath, dialled and asked to speak with DC Peter Brompton, but learned he was on late shift and not due to resume till later that afternoon. Requesting a call-back, she had just replaced the receiver when the phone rang.

Before she could speak, a male voice said, "As-salāmu ʿalaykum. Is that Detective Inspector Aamira Khalifa that I speak with?"

"Waʿalaykumu s-salām," she courteously replied and asked, "Who is calling?"

"Brother Rahib Chowdhury, sister. I understand from my wife that you called at my home to speak with me. How can I help you?"

"I have information, Mister Chowdhury that…"

"Please, sister, I believe we are of the same Faith. Call me brother."

She was nobody's fool and recognised what he was doing, that he was trying to assert his male dominance and she softly smiled. She hadn't got this far in life and the Met Police without facing such men, regardless of their creed of belief and replied, "This is a formal interview, albeit by telephone, Mister Chowdhury, so I'm sure you will understand if I keep this conversation on a professional level."

"If you wish," he replied and she heard him heavily sigh as though disgruntled with her response.

"I am told that you were friendly with a man called Abdul-hameed Muhammad?"

Without hesitation, he smoothly replied, "I knew him of course, as did most if not all the brothers at the Bond Street Mosque. Friendly is perhaps too strong an adjective; I would describe our relationship as," he paused slightly, "more acquainted."

"Yet according to your Sheikh, he told me that you and Muhammad spent quite a lot of time together."

"We offered prayers together as good Muslim's are required to do, sister. Apart from that I had little knowledge of Muhammad's personal life."

"But you are aware that Muhammad was one of the men killed in the Glasgow attack?"

"Yes, of course," he replied, the irritation evident in his voice. "It is no great secret and is much discussed in the Mosque."

Doodling on her desk pad, she realised that she would get nowhere with Chowdhury on a telephone conversation, that she might need to either visit or detain him to get the answers she wanted and without details of his arrest in Ipswich, was not prepared to ask him about it either. Instead she decided for the time being to cut the conversation short and asked him, "Do you have any information about Muhammad's associates or his life outside the Mosque, anything at all?"

"No, sister, nothing at all," he said and in her mind's eye, Mira could almost see him smirking.

"Well, Mister Chowdhury, I believe that's all I need from you for the moment. You're not planning any holidays soon, are you?"

The question took him by surprise and before he had time to consider his response, replied, "No, why?"

"Well, I intend visiting you at some time in the near future, but I'll phone ahead to ensure that when I do call, you *will* be at home. Goodbye."

She ended the call before he could argue then tapping the pencil against her perfect white teeth and deep in thought, dialled the phone number for Paul Cowan in Glasgow.

"Mira," he greeted her, "don't tell me you've left your husband and decided to come and live with me after all?"

"Yes, in fact I have," she coyly replied, then giggled at his stunned silence before asking, "Anything new in your inquiry?"

"Bloody joker," he laughed with her and replied, "No, nothing, other than that's the funerals commencing this morning; the young homeless woman and one of the victims murdered at the underground exit. How did your inquiry go with…" he searched his desk for the slip of paper with the name, "Rahib Chowdhury?"

"Him," she snorted. "Yes, that's why I'm calling, Paul. I tried his house yesterday evening, but he wasn't at home. However, he phoned me this morning and," she paused, "you know that feeling you get when you just know that you're being lied to?"

"You're a woman, Mira. You've the advantage over us mere males because of your intuition; but yes, I think know what you mean."

"Well, Chowdhury tells me he's a three monkey man; see nothing, hear nothing and speak nothing. However," she slowly drawled, "you didn't happen to PNC him, did you?"

"No," he inwardly kicked himself, "I don't think we did."

"Well, it turns out he was arrested about fourteen months ago in Ipswich by our Suffolk colleagues, but there's nothing about any charge or details of why he was detained other than he was released from custody the following day."

"That's odd. Will you be able to find out what the reason for the arrest was?"

"Way ahead of you. I've arranged that the arresting detective call me this afternoon and once I've more details I'll get back to you."

"One thing before you go. I don't know if you are aware, but one of the victims, the homeless woman being buried today, turns out to be the daughter of a Chechen who is wanted by the Russian Federation for war crimes. By all account, her father, a man called Eldar Umarov, is a very, very bad man. My boss is of the opinion Umarov might try to exact some vengeance upon the relatives of the terrorists; something to do with an old custom of blood revenge. There is nothing definite, but just to be on the safe side, my boss authorised a Ports Watch for him. That and Mister Glennie has informed the local police offices where the relatives live to also be aware of a possible threat against the relatives."

"Is there a photograph?"

"An old photo that's with the Ports Watch. Maybe you can let your people know to keep an eye out if they have occasion to visit the relatives again. Just in case he's hanging about the area."

"Yes, I'll do that and again, if I hear from Suffolk this afternoon, I'll be in touch."

Replacing the phone into its cradle, she was unaware of the intense interest her phone call had provoked in the young analyst Jenny Fielding, seated at her desk twenty feet away.

The ceremony had concluded and as the mourners departed from the graveside towards their vehicles, they could not know that the man who had covertly watched from the thick foliage was already nodding with a grim smile to the bored officers stood at the entrance gates as he purposefully made his way to the BMW parked in Clarkston Avenue.

In the car, Umarov breathed a sigh of relief that Malika had been laid to rest with the proper observance of Islamic rites and was now with Allah in the glorious garden that is Jannah.

He waited patiently as the vehicles began to depart from the cemetery and watched for the bright green Fiat car. When he saw it at the gates with the young woman driving and the limping man beside her, he started his engine and drove off, determined that he would follow the car to where it travelled.

John Glennie decided that after the victim's ceremony at Cathcart, he would drop Mo McInnes at the office while he travelled to meet with Brigadier MacLachlan at the Gartcosh Crime Campus.

The worst of the early morning traffic had eased and after dropping McInnes off, the motorway journey to Gartcosh was made without getting caught up in traffic jams.

Turning into the security gate at Gartcosh car park, he swiped his card and parked in one of the visitors' bay. Another security gate permitted him through to the reception area where a uniformed security officer stood with not the barrel-chested, bearded, gimlet eyed, grim-faced, kilted former soldier that Glennie had imagined, but a small, slightly built dapper man wearing a dark brown, three piece herringbone tweed suit, heavy brogue shoes and a regimental tie with gelled hair swept back from a fresh face upon which rested heavy rimmed, bottle glass spectacles.

Thrusting a hand at Glennie, there was no mistaking the machinegun voice when Brigadier MacLachlan introduced himself and cocking his head to one side, said, "Slightly early, old chap, but better that than late, eh? Now, who do I have to see here to beat some sense into?"

Supressing a grin, Glennie shook the Brigadier's hand, a little surprised at the vicelike grip and nodding thanks to the bemused security officer, guided the smaller man through the toughened glass security doors and towards the elevator.

Exiting at the first floor, Glennie led the Brigadier into the suite of offices occupied the Crown Office personnel and informed the reception they were there to meet with Mister McCole.

He followed the small Fiat car the relatively short distance and passed a signpost that indicated he was on Castlemilk Drive, then at a row of shops busy with pedestrians, almost missed the smaller car turning right into a narrow street. He slowed and indicating right, followed the car that had raced ahead. The street signpost told him he was now traveling on Kingsheath Avenue, then caught his breath as he saw the cars brakes lights flash and it slowed before sharply turning right into a driveway.

Umarov reduced the BMW's speed as he passed by and glancing to his right, saw both the woman and the limping man exiting the car in front of a white door. Continuing on, he stopped and parked the BMW outside a house a further fifty metres on.

Cathy Mulgrew was becoming frustrated, for it seemed that John Glennie's inquiry was grinding to a halt.

Arriving at Helen Street office from the funeral service at Dalnotter, she was informed by DI Paul Cowan that Glennie had travelled to

Gartcosh to meet with a retired Brigadier and discuss with Crown Office the possibility of discharging Ian Macleod from the threat of a multiple murder charge.

The Forensics examination of the Skoda Octavia recovered from the Waverly car park in Edinburgh had not turned up any fresh evidence and the fingerprint lifted by the Scene of Crime from the refuelling cap did not match any held on the Live Scan National Database, though the report concluded the SOC were confident they would be able to match the lifted print with any suspect later arrested or detained.

"Great," she irritably shook her head. "We've a print, but no suspect and it begs the question; when was the stolen car last filled with fuel? Could it be that the registered keeper was the last person to fuel the car? Has anyone thought to have *his* prints checked against the one that was lifted?"

Cowan inwardly grimaced, for it had not occurred to him to send the print to the Metropolitan Police and reaching for his phone, dialled the number for the Scene of Crime at Gartcosh.

"What about Mickey Hughes at Stewart Street CCTV?" Mulgrew turned to Mo McInnes. "Any word from him about the DVD from the Waverly car park that he's viewing?"

"Nothing yet, Ma'am," McInnes replied then added, "I'll phone him and see how he's doing."

"Yes, do that," Mulgrew snapped, more crossly than she meant to.

"That's the fingerprint on its way to the local Scene of Crime at the Met office that covers the registered keepers address for the Octavia, Ma'am," said Cowan. "They'll compare it with the registered keeper's prints and get back to us.

"Good," Mulgrew nodded and loudly clapped her hands together. "Right, what are we missing? Come on people," she urged the staff in the room, "Think! What *should* we be doing?"

A weighty silence filled the room, broken when a young female detective hesitantly raised her hand and said, "The two-way radio that was recovered, Ma'am. The brief we were issued said that type of equipment is expensive and I was wondering; how difficult would it be to trace where it originated or even to whom that sort of equipment was sold? I mean, don't those sort of things have serial numbers and are they sold in pairs? If it was expensive, could it be that the purchaser might have taken out the manufacturers insurance for it or perhaps it's possible the manufacturer might be able to tell us where that particular one was retailed."

"Good," Mulgrew grinned as she nodded and added, "That's what I'm talking about. Get onto the Forensics and obtain what details you can, then chase up the origins of that radio. Now," her eyes swept the room, "anything else?"

Emboldened by their colleague's initiative, the room started muttering then a stoutly built detective raised his hand and called out, "Why Glasgow?"

Mulgrew's brow creased and she replied, "What do you mean, Angus?"

He shrugged and said, "Me being from the Islands, Ma'am, I mean no disrespect to my Weegie colleagues here, but why did those bastards…" that remark earned him a loud laugh, "gunmen I mean, attack Glasgow? What was the significance of attacking Glasgow? They must have known that being a major city and the largest in Scotland, there would be armed police patrolling, albeit maybe not with the same profile as say in London or Birmingham perhaps." He shrugged as he continued, "Mister Glennie has indicated in his briefings that this was not a suicide attack and the attackers were determined to escape. What I was wondering, Ma'am, these guys obviously didn't want to involve themselves in a gunfight with armed cops, so is there any indication the attackers might have had prior knowledge of armed police response times, that sort of thing?"

"Good question, Angus," Mulgrew, her arms folded across her breasts, but with one thumbnail tapping at her teeth as she strode back and forward across the front of the room, "but if the attackers *did* have that sort of knowledge, how would we go about researching that?"

She stared thoughtfully at him then said, "Just on the off chance they've had a call, contact the Firearms Department and ask if anyone, anyone at all and I mean police or whoever it might be so dismiss no one; if any individual or organisation have made inquiry about the armed response times in say, the last six months."

"Yes, Ma'am," Angus nodded to her.

"Miss Mulgrew," she turned as her name was called towards a flush faced McInnes. "I've spoken with Mickey Hughes at Stewart Street. He might have something for us and is on his way over with the recording."

He glanced at the houses and realised that they were four homes in each building, two upper and two lower with two doors to each end of the front of the building and a door at each side of the building. The question was though, what door did the limping man and the women enter and did the door at the front serve the lower or the upper home.

He turned as an elderly man opened a door in the front of a similar building across the road from the BMW and before the man closed the door, Umarov saw stairs that led upwards.

Ah, he slowly nodded. Then the side door must serve the ground house.

He glanced along at the building where the man and woman had entered, but remained uncertain what door they had used.

It was the sight of the two small boys, not more than ten or eleven years old, who were walking on the footway towards the car, bouncing a football between, them that gave him the idea.

Pulling a handful of coins from his trouser pocket, he stepped from the BMW and with an engaging smile, held out his hand with the money and said, "Can you help me, please. The lady who drives the green car along there; the small car in the driveway. What house does she live in?"

They stared greedily at the change that contained several pound coins before the lad who carried the ball in his arms, said, "That's Daisy, mister. She lives in the house with the red door. Why?"

"Oh, I've a delivery to make, but I'd forgotten the name. Silly me," he grinned widely and handed the boy the change.

The lads were too caught up with dividing the change he handed them to really wonder why the tall man wanted Daisy's address and hardly noticed him lock the BMW and walk purposefully towards her house.

They had been in heated discussion now for almost thirty minutes. Queens Counsel Richard McCole, a slightly built, fair haired man in his late forties with a stubbly beard and a nervous habit of touching his nose, was employed by the Crown Office to review criminal reports submitted for consideration of prosecution. Sat behind his desk, his fingers arched in front of his nose, he considered the appeal by the two men who sat facing him.

Detective Superintendent John Glennie he knew of old; a competent and highly experienced officer whose opinion McCole often regarded with favour. On the other hand Glennie's companion, Brigadier MacLachlan seemed to be a staunch and formidable individual who despite his diminutive appearance, McCole inwardly considered the Brigadier was a man would not wish to cross swords with.

"Yes," he admitted, "I understand that Mister Macleod is a decorated war hero and yes," he turned to the Brigadier, "I also understand that Mister Macleod's previous training was, in your own words, to neutralise anyone he considered a threat to his or others safety. But, sir," he stared at the Brigadier and spread his hands wide, "consider this. Can you imagine the outcry if Crown Office were to grant what would appear to be immunity to this man Macleod? The media would have a field day, accusing us of double standards when it comes to homicide; likely we would be accused of suiting ourselves as to who the law applies or not. If we *were* to decide that Mister Macleod acted in defence of both himself and those civilians who were about him, it might lead to individuals or even vigilantes deciding that they could with impunity attack minority groups or anyone simply because," he waggled his fingers in the air, "they *believed* the bulky sweater or jacket hid a bomb vest."

MacLachlan stared pointedly at McCole and sighed before replying, "Correct me if I'm wrong, Mister McCole, but does Crown Office judge each case presented to you on its own merit?"

"Yes, of course," then took a deep breath for he didn't like where this was going.

"Then it might be argued that Staff Sergeant Macleod, who does not deny shooting them in the head and undoubtedly admits killing those men, might reasonably have believed he acted in both his own defence and the defence of others. Agreed?"

McCole did not answer, but simply nodded.

"Then, does that not suggest to you that at the material time of the shooting, Staff Sergeant Macleod reacted as though in a combat situation and carried out his orders as he had been trained and need I remind you, sir, trained by the British Army. Would it then suggest to you, sir, that the British Army should also be on trial, that by training Staff Sergeant Macleod to carry out the drills as he was taught by the British Army then they are complicit in the killing of those three individuals?"

McCole was astonished at such a suggestion and stared aghast at MacLachlan. "Are you suggesting, Brigadier, that I recommend issuing a summons against the British Army!"

"Why not," he coolly replied, "for are they not as liable as is Staff Sergeant Macleod?"

Beside him, Glennie choked back his laughter. The old guy was a worthy adversary for McCole whom he privately considered to be an excellent Advocate.

McCole shook his head as though trying to clear it. Issue a summons against the British Army?

Preposterous!

Taking a deep breath, he slowly exhaled then said, "Brigadier, as it was explained to you it is my job to determine if there is sufficient evidence to warrant Crown Office pursuing a complaint at court against individuals whom the police believe have committed serious crime that would be called to trial at the High Court. In this case, the allegation of murder against Mister…I beg your pardon," he softly smiled, "Staff Sergeant Macleod. I am already aware of Mister Glennie's opinion in this issue and therefore, with some *reluctance*," he stressed, "I find that the argument for committing Staff Sergeant Macleod to trial is outweighed by the obvious evidence that at the material time of the incident and in continuance of his army training, he believed there to be a real and genuine threat that the wounded men might activate bomb vests and so I believe it is fair to conclude he acted in the defence of both himself and of others."

He stopped and reaching down, pulled open the bottom drawer of his desk. "On behalf of the Crown, I therefore determine that there is insufficient evidence to warrant such a motion and in due course will issue Mister Glennie with a memorandum indicating that this office do not intend pursuing any proceedings against Staff Sergeant Macleod."

Lifting a bottle of Grouse and three glasses from the drawer, he smiled as he added, "Shall we now conclude this debate with a small dram?"

He approached the red door, still a little uncertain how he would handle the situation, but decided that the truth would be far easier than a lie. Knocking on the door, it was opened by the limping man who staring curiously at him, said, "Yes?"

"I've come to visit Daisy," he said with a disarming smile.

Ian, his hand upon the side support of the door, began to turn away to call Daisy to the door, but Umarov took him by surprise when he bundled him through into the hallway and turning, closed the door behind him.

As Ian stumbled, he regained his footing and prepared himself to tackle Umarov, but was taken aback when the big man defensively raised his hands and quickly said, "Please, I only wish to speak with you and the woman called Daisy. Please! I mean you no harm!"

Daisy, her hair bound up into a bun and still wearing her white blouse and black skirt, was alerted by the scuffle and rushing into the hallway cried out, "What's going on? What's happening?" then staring from one man to the other, her eyes settled upon Umarov and she asked, "Who are you? What do you want?"

Ian, his hands bunched into fists was about to approach Umarov who with his hands still raised, quickly shook his head and backing against the closed door, again said, "I wish you no harm. I only want to speak with you," he turned to the snarling Ian and added, "both of you. I am not a reporter," he continued to shake his head, "it is about Malika, my daughter."

They both startled and glancing at each other, Ian lowered his fists and glanced towards Daisy for a decision.

"Your daughter?" she asked, her brow furrowed.

"Yes, Malika, my daughter. My…" he licked at his dry lips and swallowing with difficulty, added, "my child."

Still wary of the big man, Ian watched him carefully as Umarov slowly lowered his hands to his side.

"You'd better come through," said Daisy and turning, led the way into the lounge, followed by Umarov and then Ian.

She walked to the hearth and turning with her arms folded, indicated with a nod that he sit.

Behind him, Ian stood with his back to the wall and said, "You were at the cemetery earlier this morning; you were stood in the bushes."

Daisy sharply glanced at this revelation while Umarov softly smiled and replied, "I was correct. You are military, yes?"

"Once," Ian agreed with a nod, then touching lightly at his scarred face, added, "but no longer."

"You said Malika was your daughter, Mister, eh…" Daisy interrupted.

"My named is Elda Umarov. You have heard of me, yes?"

She slowly shook her head and said, "No, I'm sorry. Why would I have heard of you?"

He half smiled and waving a hand of dismissal, replied, "Perhaps I am mistaken. It is of no consequence."

"Why didn't *I* see you at the cemetery, Mister Umarov," she slowly repeated his surname.

"There are certain people who seek me," he simply replied, "and I am not truly welcome in your country, Miss Daisy."

She could not help but smile. Constable Daisy to Ian and now Miss Daisy to this charming man, the father of the dead homeless girl.

"And why is that, might I ask?"

"I am having," he paused and smiled, "certain difficulties with the Russian Federation, my dear young lady."

"So, I ask again. Why are you here, in my home I mean?"

He didn't immediately reply, but then said, "To repay a debt, Miss Daisy. I read in a news article that you were the last person to speak with my Malika; it was written by a reporter that were seen to give her something. Money perhaps?"

"Yes, but nothing of real value," she blushed. She neither understood why nor could explain, but some inner instinct told her that this strange man meant her no harm and slowly moving to the couch, she sat beside him.

Ian also instinctively decided that Umarov didn't seem to present a threat to either of them and sighing, said, "I'll stick the kettle on, then," and limped into the kitchen, but prudently left the door ajar.

"We had not spoken for some time, my Malika and I," he began. "An argument, a foolishness that drove her from me."

She sensed he wanted to unburden himself and decided not to respond, to let him continue with his story.

"We lived in an apartment in Grozny or," he smiled, "what remains of Grozny. I fought the Russians during the war. That is why they hunt me. My wife and my son and Malika's sister; they were killed in the fighting with the Russians. She was all I had left. We should have been close but," he shrugged.

She could see that his throat was tightening as he struggled to explain.

"Fathers and daughters. They do not always see eye to eye, no?"

"No, not all the time," she smiled at him.

"I was trapped there, in Grozny; nowhere that I could go for fear of being hunted. I could not permit Malika to leave for if she did, the FSB," he turned and saw her confusion and added, "The Russian security people, they would have found her and taken her and used her against me. To get to me. You understand, yes?"

"Yes."

"So, together we remained in Chechnya, because of my fear. But Malika, she wanted out, wanted to travel. I tried to tell her, persuade her that it was foolish, dangerous even, but one day I returned home from a friends flat and she is gone."

Ian stepped through from the kitchen carrying a tray with three mugs of coffee, milk and sugar and set the tray down onto a low table. Handing a mug to Daisy then Umarov, he said, "You were in the fighting? The battle of Grozny?"

"Both fights, yes," Umarov nodded to him.

Ian exhaled and sat down in the armchair as the older man continued.

"I tried to find her, but not myself you understand? I used contacts; Chechens who had fled the country into Europe, but she seemed to have disappeared. I knew the FSB did not have her else they would have tried to make a deal."

He drew breath and continued, "Then a few days ago I get a phone call from your police telling me that a young woman of Malika's description had my phone number. That is how I learned she is dead. Killed by people who say they are Muslim," his voice began to rise and angrily shook his head as he added, "but not like me. I am Muslim. I am a true believer. I do *not* kill innocent people."

They sat in silence for a few seconds then Ian asked, "Mister Umarov, if you are of such interest to the FSB, what in the world possessed you to come here to Scotland?"

"Would you not do the same for a child, Mister…"

"Sorry, my name is Ian Macleod. Ian, please."

"Do you have children, Ian?"

"No," he shook his head.

"Then Allah be praised there might come the day you have a child or children and you will learn as a parent that you give up your last breath for that child or children. I could not let my Malika be laid to rest without at least trying to say farewell; without bringing with me her sacred Qur'an. You understand?"

"I believe so, yes; I think I understand."

"But why here, to my home," Daisy asked again.

"The debt," he smiled at her. "I am what you call old fashioned and it is the custom of my people that a debt must be repaid. May I ask, what *did* you give to Malika?"

She shrugged, "You have to understand, Mister Umarov, I am a police officer. I had been sent to move her on, move her away I mean because she was begging in the street," then thought it might upset him to hear that and quickly added, "I'm sorry. I didn't mean to tell you that to upset you…"

"No, no," he gently laid his hand on her arm and said, "go on. Please."

"Well, I spoke briefly to her and I could see that she was wet and cold so…it was nothing, really. I gave her a five pound note to buy some hot food and a small card that had an address where she might find some shelter," she lamely finished and licked at her lips. "That's when the terrorists, the gunmen…they attacked us."

The memory brought tears that trickled down her cheeks and her voice trembled as she continued, "I couldn't do anything to stop them. We're not armed in this country and…I was really frightened. I'm sorry."

He stared thoughtfully at her and then turned his gaze towards Ian. "You are the man the newspapers and the television people are looking for, yes?"

He didn't reply, just nodded.

"You…killed the man who shot my daughter?"

Ian swallowed with difficulty, his whole being wanting to move to the couch and take the upset Daisy in his arms and assure her that everything would be all right, but he remained seated and again nodded.

"Then you have also placed me in your debt, Ian. There is nothing I can say, nothing I can do, but offer you both my thanks. I could not protect my child, but you," he turned to Daisy, "were kind to her and you," he turned to Ian, "acted as the vengeance that should have been mine. For that I will always be grateful."

Daisy, composed now but still dabbing at her eyes with her handkerchief, said, "You told us that you're not welcome in this country, Mister Umarov. Does that mean you're here illegally?"

He smiled at her. "You are police and it is perhaps better you do not know the answer to that question, Miss Daisy."

"Oh, right," her eyes widened then she asked, "What do you intend doing now? I mean, where are you going next?"

"That is at the wish of Allah, praise be his name, but part of the reason I am here is to thank you and also to speak with this young man," he nodded to Ian.

"About what?" Ian asked.

"You were military, so I have some questions, Ian. The men you killed. They were disciplined?"

"Ah," his face wrinkled and he slowly exhaled, "that's hard to say. They were certainly dressed in camouflage fatigues and carrying Kalashnikov's, but that didn't make them soldiers and for what it's worth, I wouldn't say they were particularly disciplined. They knew how to fire the weapons yes, but so do ten-year-old kids in Helmand. What I mean is in the few minutes of the firefight they didn't act like soldiers. The attack did not seem to be that of a trained unit. The first guy I killed…" he glanced sharply at Daisy and licking at his lips, continued. "The first guy was too caught up watching what his mates were doing instead of protecting their rear. That's why I was able to come upon him without him spotting me approach."

His brow furrowed, for the police had not yet formally interviewed him and he was uncertain if they would ask such questions, but the questions prompted him to think of the men's actions.

"The second two guys; both of them were grouped together when trained soldiers would have been spread apart to make less of a target and that's why I was able to slot them both so quickly. In fact," his eyes narrowed and he turned towards Daisy, "the man who dragged Daisy by the hair; he tried to shoot her but his magazine had run dry and when he changed it for a fresh magazine he forgot to cock a round into the breech. That to me smacks of someone not properly weapon trained. No," he decided with a shake of his head. "The men were not trained professionals."

"Ah," Umarov nodded as though in understanding. "Do you believe they were suicide terrorists?"

"Hard to say, but for what it's worth I don't think they were. The four men all wore balaclavas. That suggests to me that they didn't want to be identified. If they *were* intent on suicide, why would they hide their faces?"

"Yes," Umarov nodded, "I understand your logic and I agree. So, if not suicide killers it's possible that they expected to get away, yes? Perhaps to meet with another man, someone waiting to get them away from the area; someone who is the, how do you call them…"

"You mean a getaway driver?" Daisy interjected.

"Yes, a getaway driver. A man with a vehicle."

They fell silent while they considered this notion, then Ian said, "He would be difficult to find, if there is such a man…or maybe it might be a woman."

"Yes, he would," Umarov quietly agreed, "but I believe if he exists, it is a man. These type of people who call themselves Muslim do not recognise the worth of a woman," he scoffed. "They believe themselves to be superior to women and would never trust a woman with such a mission."

"But you would, Mister Umarov?" Daisy smiled at him.

"But I would," he returned her smile, then added, "You have courage, Miss Daisy. I would trust you."

Taken aback, she did not know how to respond, then Umarov surprised them both by quickly rising to his feet and saying, "It is time that I leave. I regret that I cannot remain longer, but I will request one thing of you both. It is a simple request, but very important to me."

"And that is?" Ian asked.

"I request that you tell no one of my visit. If your British authorities know of my presence in this country," he shrugged, "it might go badly for me for the Russian FSB have ears everywhere. Will you do that for me?"

He watched as they both nodded then turning to Daisy as she got to her feet, he reached for her hands and holding them both in his, raised them to his lips and kissed her fingers.

"Again, Miss Daisy, I thank you for being a friend to my Malika. I regret it is a debt I cannot hope to repay."

"You just have," she softly replied and then to his surprise, hugged him to her.

Taken aback, he smiled at her, surprised to find he had a lump in his throat then turning to Ian, said, "Walk me to the door, please?"

They left Daisy in the lounge and at the front door, Umarov turned and staring with narrowed eyes, said, "She is very pretty. I hope you will both be happy."

Ian was about to explain that no, they weren't a couple, but instead simply nodded and replied, "Thank you," then firmly shaking Umarov's hand, added, "You're going after him, aren't you? The getaway driver."

He didn't immediately respond, but simply returned Ian's stare and then smiling, replied, "May Allah keep you and Miss Daisy safe, Ian Macleod. Da-svidaniya, my friend," then turning, opened the door and left.

CHAPTER SIXTEEN

Seated at a computer console with Cathy Mulgrew, Paul Cowan, Lou Sheridan and Mo McInnes crowded together as they stared over his shoulder, Mickey Hughes inserted a USB stick into the machine then opened the files it contained. Selecting the most recent, he played the recording that showed a Transit van exiting a car park. The recording was dark, but he said, "I think the Forensic might be able to clean it up, Ma'am, and maybe provide you with a decent photograph of the driver."

"Tell me again why you think this is significant, Mickey?" asked Mulgrew.

"For a start, the time frame coincides with the Skoda Octavia haring into the car park a few minutes earlier. No vehicles enter or leave the car park in those few minutes other than the Transit van that you could see literally raced out of the exit. Then there's this," he closed down the recording and opened another file that was a slightly fuzzy photograph of the van's registration number.

"I took the liberty of checking the number on the PNC and the van is registered to a hire company in Ipswich."

From his shirt pocket, he handed Mo McInnes a slip of paper and continued, "That's the hire company details along with their telephone number. I didn't want to overstep the mark and call them; though I'd let you guys that earn the big bucks do that," he grinned at them.

Sheridan slapped a hand onto his shoulder and replied, "Well done, Mickey. That's good work. We owe you for this."

"And don't think for one minute I'll won't remind you of that," he smiled at her.

Mulgrew turned to McInnes, but she raised a hand and said, "I'm on it, Ma'am," and went hunting for a phone.

Detective Constable Peter Brompton slid into his desk and stared curiously at the slip of paper lying there.

Now, he wondered, why would a DI at the Met's Counter Terrorism Unit want me?

Dialling the number on the paper, the call was answered, "DI Khalifa."

"Eh, hello, Ma'am, it's a DC Peter Brompton from Suffolk CID here; I received word you wanted me to call you?"

"Yes that's correct; thanks for getting back to me. Can I call you Peter?"

"Yes, of course, Ma'am…"

"Then I'm Mira," she interrupted before continuing. "The reason I phoned, Peter, is I'm currently interviewing witnesses and collecting local statements on behalf of our Scottish colleagues following the terrorist attack a few days ago in Glasgow."

"Yes, I read about it," he replied then thought, what a stupid thing to say. The attack had been headline news since it happened.

"Indeed. Anyway, one of the witnesses I spoke with is a man called Rahib Chowdhury. I was doing a bit of background check on the PNC and saw that fourteen months ago, you were the arresting officer, but there were no details of any charge. The entry only said that the following day, Chowdhury was discharged from custody. Can you fill me in with any details that you might have of his detention?"

She sensed there was an obvious pause, but could not know that the mention of Chowdhury's name had caused nervous perspiration to trickle down Brompton's spine.

"Ah, yes, Rahib Chowdhury," he repeated, trying to think on his feet. "Let me think again. Fourteen months ago, you say?"

"That's correct," she drily replied, wondering why he was stalling.

"Let me see now. Hmm, Chowdhury. Yes, I remember now. There was an allegation made against him by a school janitor; a local primary school janitor as I recall."

"And what was the allegation," she asked, thinking this was like drawing teeth.

"Eh, apparently the janitor thought he was hanging about the school gates, watching the children when they were playing. The young ones, I mean."

"And was he? Hanging about the school gates, I mean?"

"No," he slowly drawled, gaining confidence with the lie. "It was just a mistake. We had nothing and permitted Mister Chowdhury to go."

"But not till the following day. Why was that? Why was he detained overnight, Peter?"

"Is that what the PNC entry said? Oh, I don't think he was detained overnight; not that I recall anyway," he gulped away the saliva that was threatening to choke him.

She knew he was lying and realised that she would get nothing more from him.

However, rather than deflect her interest in Chowdhury, he had instead unwittingly piqued her interest even more and so said,

"Thank you for calling back, Peter. Have a nice day," then angrily slammed the phone down.

At his desk, Brompton wiped his forehead with his handkerchief and took a deep breath.

The bastard had promised that nothing would ever come back to him, that burying the case was in the national interest, he had said. Well, Brompton shook his head, the fucking national interest wouldn't save his arse or his career if his bosses discovered he had deliberately supressed evidence; that he had destroyed the child pornography he had taken from Chowdhury's home then lied to get him released.

His hand shaking, he scrawled through his mobile phone, searching for the number of the spook who called himself John then pressing the green button, waited for the call to be answered.

Sitting in John Glennie's office with Lou Sheridan, Cathy Mulgrew asked her, "Now that we know Crown Office won't pursue a complaint of murder against him, has anyone contacted Ian Macleod to inquire if he would be willing to face a news conference?"

"Not to my knowledge, Ma'am. We have his home address, of course and a mobile number for him. Do you want me to phone him? Maybe set up a meeting?"

She thought briefly about it and then replied, "Maybe leave it for now, Lou. That's John's decision, but he'll probably want to do it officially and likely he'll contact Macleod's lawyer to inform her and have her break the news to him that Crown Office won't proceed with any charges. He can arrange with the lawyer to ask if Macleod is willing to face the press. However, in the interim can you contact Harry Downes at the Media Department and give her a heads up. If Macleod agrees, John might want to arrange a conference at short notice and if Harry has made an agreement with this man at the 'Glasgow News'…"

"Larry McNaught."

"That's him," she agreed, before adding, "We should give him first call. He's held up his end of the deal so there's no point in pissing off the press."

The door was knocked and when Sheridan called out, "Come in," Mulgrew saw it was the young detective who had suggested following up the one-way radio inquiry and holding a sheet of paper in her hand.

"Yes?" Sheridan asked.

"Ma'am," the detective glanced from one woman to the other before asking, "Can I relate the result of what I learned?"

"Go ahead, please," Mulgrew smiled encouragingly at her.

"I received the details from Forensic regarding the radios' serial number and manufacturing code numbers. In short, I contacted the manufacturer and learned that several hundreds of this type of two-way radio are sold commercially in sets of two or four throughout the UK each year, though primarily by companies such as security firms. The manufacturer was able to tell me from the serial number I provided," her voice grew more enthusiastic, "the numbers referred to a set of two radios that were provided to an electrical and computing store that operates from within," she glanced at her sheet of paper, "Sailmakers Shopping Centre in Ipswich."

"Ipswich?" Sheridan moodily interrupted. "That bloody town seems to crop up in several of the inquiries."

The young detective, glancing at Sheridan, nervously continued, "I contacted the store and spoke with the supervisor who told me that because of their cost the radios are not great sellers and that to her knowledge, they've sold just three sets this year. She remembers selling one set of two radio's to a man she said was either Middle Eastern or Pakistani and described him as shifty; her words, not mine," the detective smiled.

"Go on," said Mulgrew, pointedly ignoring Sheridan's impatient frown.

"Anyway, Ma'am, she told me that she had decided when the man was about to pay for the radio's that she was so wary of him because he kept glancing about him that if he'd tried to pay with a credit or debit card, she was so suspicious of him she would have refused the sale."

"So, I'm guessing he paid by cash?"

"Yes, Ma'am," the younger woman nodded. "Two-hundred and eighty-five pounds."

Mulgrew glanced sharply at Sheridan, her eyes narrowing and said, "In these days of debit cards, that's a lot of cash to be carrying about and suggests to me the purchaser must have known the cost of the sets prior to the purchase, if he carried that sum of money on him. It sounds promising. When he paid, did he take out the insurance for the radios?"

The detective frowned and shaking her head, replied, "No to the insurance, Ma'am. However, the supervisor told me that because of the high incidence of fraudulent transactions in the electronic industry, they have a CCTV camera mounted above the till that faces the customer. She will try to obtain a still photograph of the man and will forward it to me via e-mail."

Mulgrew slapped the desk and grinning, said, "Good work," before turning to Sheridan and telling her, "First thing first, we'll try to match the photographs with the dead terrorists and if there's no match, we might be looking at terrorist number five."

Leaving the office, the young detective stood to one side to admit John Glennie who asked, "What's all the excitement?"

"That young officer," Mulgrew smiled as she nodded towards the younger woman, "has a possible lead regarding the purchase of the two-way radio discovered in the van and Mickey Hughes tells us that there's a possibility the driver of the Skoda might have transferred into a Transit van. Mo McInnes is checking with the van hire company as we speak, that and…"

The door was knocked and opened by the portly detective called Angus stuck his head into the office and in his soft lilt voice, said, "Can I come in?"

"Got something for us, Angus?" asked Sheridan.

"No, not really, Ma'am," he replied then said, "I spoke with the Inspector in charge of the Firearms Department at the Police Training Centre in Jackton. He tells me that they've not had any inquiries regarding police response times in Glasgow; nothing out of the ordinary other than the usual one."

"The usual one?" Mulgrew's brow creased.

"Aye, Ma'am," Angus bowed his head to read his notebook. "Just the usual inquiry seeking an annual update on response times; about four weeks ago from the Anti-Terrorist Unit of the Operations Office at the Security Service."

Mulgrew felt her blood cool and glancing at Glennie and Sheridan in turn, read the same suspicion in their eyes.

Slamming down the mobile phone onto his desk, Barry Ashford rubbed furiously at the sudden ache in his head.

That fat, bottle-crashing wimp of a detective phoning him and panicking about *his* career!

Who the *fuck* does he think he is?

He glanced at the name he had written on his desk pad.

First Cathy Mulgrew and now this…this *bitch* DI Aamira Khalifa of the Met's CTU.

Another bloody woman causing him problems!

The text from Chowdhury had been worrying and patently clear that this woman Khalifa was panicking the useless bugger. What concerned him more though, was she scaring Chowdhury enough to throw himself at her mercy and disclose everything he knew, Ashford wondered?

Why those bitches just don't stay at home where they belong and let the men do the work!

He took a deep breathe to calm himself then calling his secretary on the intercom, simply said, "I have a headache."

The sleekly dressed and shapely blonde woman in her mid-thirties who answered his summons closed the door behind her. Gliding across the room to stand behind him, wordlessly she drew his head back onto her breasts and began to gently massage his forehead.

He smiled and with his right hand, reached down behind him to softly stroke at her nyloned leg. He heard her softly moan as his hand reached higher, his fingers probing at the soft skin at the top of the nylon.

She leaned down to whisper in his ear, "Shall I visit you this evening?"

"I think that would be delightful," he quietly replied, then reaching his left hand up to his forehead, tightly held her fingers and added, "But first things first. We have the number for our source in the Met's CTU. Contact the source and find out what you can about a Detective Inspector called Khalifa. She shouldn't be hard to find," he sneered. "She's probably wearing a fucking burqa."

DI Paul Cowan smiled when he realised that it was Mira on the phone.

"Just a small update for you," she said and from the abrupt tone of her voice he guessed she wasn't happy about something.

"I told you about this man Chowdhury having been arrested and had an overnighter in the Suffolk Constabulary nick? Well, I've spoken with the arresting officer, a DC Brompton and frankly, I strongly suspect he lied to me."

"About what?"

"He gave me some cock and bull story about Chowdhury mistakenly being suspected for watching children through a school fence or gate or something; that the janitor was suspicious. Even denied Chowdhury had spent a night in the cells, that the PNC entry was mistaken."

"But you didn't believe him?"

"Not at all, Paul, though for the life of me I have no idea why he would lie unless…"

"Unless?"

"Unless Brompton is on the take and took a bribe or more likely…" her voice faded.

"Okay," Cowan sighed. "I give up. Or more likely what?"

"That he was pressurised or coerced into dropping the case by a higher authority."

Cowan's eyes widened and he said, "Mira, can you hold on for a moment? I want to transfer this call to my boss and put you on speaker."

"Will do."

A minute later, Cowan lifted the phone and said, "Mira, I'm with my boss, Mister Glennie and also present is Detective Chief Superintendent Mulgrew and DCI Sheridan. Can you repeat what you just told me?"

Khalifa recounted her suspicions and then conscious she was speaking with senior management, formally added, "I am of the opinion that DC Brompton was nervous when he spoke with me and like I told DI Cowan, there is a possibility he has deliberately dropped the case against Rahib Chowdhury, but why, I'm not certain."

Mulgrew glanced knowingly at Glennie before speaking, then said, "DCS Mulgrew here, DI Khalifa. I understand that because this man Brompton is a member of the Suffolk Constabulary, there is no way you can, how can I put this, informally interview him?"

"No, Ma'am, not at all. If I do wish to interview DC Brompton, I must make a formal application through my management team here and disclose my suspicions and…"

Khalifa's hesitation didn't escape Mulgrew's notice and interrupting, she suggested, "They might not be sympathetic to your request?"

"Yes, Ma'am, something like that. I'm *certain*," she stressed the word, "that you will understand."

Mulgrew turned to stare at Sheridan and sighed, then into the speaker said, "I appreciate all that you have done for the inquiry, Detective Inspector Khalifa, but as likely you have already guessed, we have our own thoughts on the difficulties you face and who the real culprits for this atrocity might be. For now, I'll pass you to DI Cowan, but please be assured that under no circumstances do we wish you to come to the attention of your management team for anything other than our grateful thanks. I look forward to speaking with you again in the future."

"Ma'am," Khalifa simply replied.

Nodding that Cowan complete the call, Mulgrew shrugged and said quietly to Glennie and Sheridan, "I don't believe we can rely on our Met colleagues to act for us. I can only assume that they might be under a pressure that we can't deal with. It's obviously nothing to do with their commitment, but I suspect rather more to do with some sort of intervention by our cousins at Thames House."

Eldar Umarov decided that he would check out of the hotel in the morning and drive to the London area where he would be better placed to find the man who had got away; the getaway driver. He fervently hoped the contact would have news for him and the key to finding this man might be the name his contact gave him; this man Chowdhury.

He glanced at the dashboard clock and realised that he had time to purchase a new pay-as-you-go then return to the hotel for a shower and change of clothes before the six o'clock call to his contact. Making his way again to the ASDA store, he purchased the mobile phone and spent time selecting a change of clothing; two new casual shirts, sets of underwear and two pair of casual trousers. His soiled clothes were not worthy of retaining and he would simply dispose of them in one of the hotel bins.

Driving through the city, he thought of his visit with Miss Daisy and Ian Macleod.

They were good people and in any other situation, he might even had considered them as friends.

He was confident that both would respect his request of them that they did not disclose his visit or presence in the country. He smiled for he recognised that the young woman was a strong character and even though she had been through a terrible experience, she would survive and be the stronger for it.

Ian Macleod was a brave man; a man who without hesitation and at the risk of his own life had tackled the terrorists who took his beloved Malika.

He wondered how Ian had come by his terrible injuries, but had been too polite to even glance directly at them.

He smiled for it was obvious that Ian was…his brow knitted as he tried to find the English word in his vocabulary; infatuated, that was it. Infatuated with Daisy and he inwardly wished them well.

The young man had been correct, he decided. The four dead men were not a suicide squad; they must have expected to get away from the scene of their murders with impunity and that suggested to Umarov that there must have been what Miss Daisy had called a getaway driver.

He glanced again at the dashboard clock and with a sigh thought perhaps one final farewell to Malika then turned the car to retrace his route towards the Cathcart Cemetery.

The secretary knocked and without waiting for his permission, opened the door and wordlessly laid a sheet of paper on Ashford's desk.

He grunted his thanks and staring at the information, waited till she had left the room and closed the door before dialling the number in his mobile phone.

When the call was answered, he said, "I have a small job for you both. No," he shook his head, "not Chowdhury. He'll keep for the time being. Someone else. I'll text you the information and make sure it looks accidental, understand? I do not want any fuck-up or anything relative to your task crossing my desk. Are we crystal clear?"

The call was acknowledged and he carefully sent the text, then sat back and reaching into a desk drawer, withdrew a bottle of whisky and a cut glass.

DS Mo McInnes scribbled the information onto her pad and made her way to John Glennie's room where he was just about to see Cathy Mulgrew off.

"Sir, Ma'am, bit of bad luck regarding the hire van inquiry," she said. "It seems the van was hired by a man who used a stolen driving licence. Unusually, however, the van was left back at the van hire premises, though they were closed at the time and the keys were shoved through the letterbox. And before you ask, the van has been hired out a couple of times since it was returned."

"How did they know the licence was stolen?" Glennie asked.

"Ah, they don't sound like they're a professional mob, sir. The woman I spoke with could hardly speak English, but I managed to learn they hire out mainly to the building trade. I also spoke with a local community cop in the nearest police station who told me that he's forever receiving complaints about the hire company. Anyway," she shrugged, "the woman I spoke with said that *after* hiring the van out, they did a retrospective DVLA check and discovered the licence was stolen, so a dead end I'm afraid. All she could tell me about was the hirer seemed to be Pakistani or certainly of Middle East appearance. When I asked about the photograph on the licence she was shown, she told me that according to her," McInnes screwed her face, "that all those *types* looked the same to her."

"Sounds like a woman of tolerance," Mulgrew drily commented, then added, "But regarding it being a dead end, maybe not," she mused, tapping at her teeth with the nail of her thumb. "You said the hirer returned the van to the hire company and the place was closed?"

"Yes, Ma'am."

"Now, it's a long shot, but why did he return the van? It might suggest he had parked a vehicle nearby and that's why he went back there, to collect his own vehicle. Just on the off chance there *is* street CCTV in the area, Mo, can you contact the community cop again and ask? If there is CCTV what's the odds we might catch the driver going to his own vehicle."

"I'll get onto it, Ma'am," she replied and hurried off.

The CTU analyst Jenny Fieldling watched as DI Aamira Khalifa lifted her coat from the rack and carrying it over one arm and her handbag over the other, cheerfully smiled goodbye to the officers on duty and made her way to the elevator in the corridor outside. Exchanging some good natured banter in the lift with some fellow colleagues who were also departing for the evening, she exited the main door of New Scotland Yard and wound her way to Howick Place with the intention of walking to her car that was parked on the nearby Thirleby Road, then home where she promised herself a long soak in her bath.

As she strode along on the narrow footway, her thoughts turned to her husband and she smiled, keenly looking forward to the celebration of their third wedding anniversary.

The hooded man in the passenger seat of the stolen Ford Mondeo intensely stared through the binoculars at the woman wearing the brightly coloured hijab and checked the photograph on the screen of his mobile phone. The woman matched the face and the description of the clothes she wore was the same as those described in the text message.

The woman, now just thirty yard away, continued to walk towards the Mondeo.

Nudging the driver, he quietly confirmed, "That's her," and braced himself as the driver stamped suddenly on the accelerator, causing the idling engine to speedily screech into motion before racing off at breakneck speed.

The two witnesses later described seeing the woman look up but before she could even scream, was struck full on by the vehicle that had mounted the pavement.

The female witness broke down and sobbed when she told the Traffic officers that the woman was thrown not over the vehicle, but in front of the dark coloured car which then continued to bounce over the top of her.

"Yes," the male witness, his shirt covered with the victim's blood, numbly confirmed. "I held her hand and she was certainly alive for a few moments after being struck, but her injuries," he exhaled and sorrowfully shook his head.

"Really, I don't think anyone could have survived those kind of injuries," he added.

CHAPTER SEVENTEEN

The deliberate running down of a police officer by a vehicle that when it was later discovered burned out in waste ground in the Islington area of the city and confirmed to be stolen, provoked a media frenzy.

In immediate response to the eyewitness statements, the Metropolitan Police launched a murder inquiry.

The death of Detective Inspector Aamira Khalifa, the beautiful Muslim woman who had made such an impact in the predominantly Christian, male dominated world of police intelligence reverberated throughout the UK police service and not least with Police Scotland.

The inquiry team at Helen Street learned of the murder of their English colleague through the media when the report was broadcast on both of the TV news channels on the large screens fixed to the general office walls.

Shocked, Paul Cowan stared open mouthed from his desk as the anchor-woman reported the incident, his eyes dancing across the screen as he read the updated scroll at the bottom.

Quickly he made his way to John Glennie's office to break the sad news.

It immediately came to mind that the implication Khalifa might have been deliberately targeted for her actions in rendering assistance the Police Scotland inquiry hit the dumbstruck Glennie who in turn phoned both Cathy Mulgrew and Lou Sheridan.

Mulgrew was of a similar thought and instructed that all three directly travel to Tulliallan Police Training College and there meet with the Chief Constable, Martin Cairney.

Seated in the kitchen while he made their evening meal, Daisy Cooper and Ian reflected on the visit by Malika Umarov's father, Eldar.

"If like he said and I'd no reason to doubt him, that he's in this country illegally and the Russian security people, the FSB are hunting him, he took one hell of a risk coming to visit us," Ian said, turning the lamb chops in the pan and lowering the gas under the potatoes.

Daisy was puzzled and tapping the IPod screen in front of her, replied, "This article about him. It says he was a Professor of Languages at the Grozny University and spoke several languages; English, French, Italian and German among other Slavic languages. How can an apparently educated man be responsible for all these deaths and what he's being accused of? It just doesn't seem to fit with the man that sat on my couch a couple of hours ago."

He turned and shrugged. "History is filled with stories of educated men and women doing the most horrific things, committing all sort of atrocities for all sorts of reasons; racial or religious hatred, envy," he wagged fingers in the air, "and even that old chestnut, 'I was only obeying orders.' You know what I mean. Still," he twisted his mouth as he stared at her, "it does seem at odds to the man that was here." He pulled out a chair and sitting opposite her, said. "I did a couple of tours in Bosnia during the conflict there. Daisy, you wouldn't believe and I'd be reluctant to repeat what I saw. Neighbour murdering neighbour and all because of feuds that were decades old. People who lived with each other in the same villages and towns turning upon each other for no other reason than their religious faith. Heavens, we've only to look across the Irish Sea to see what the Prod's and the Tim's were doing to each other and *they* called themselves Christians."

"And another thing," he continued, "That's what the Internet tells us. Who's to say we're getting the full story? Remember too that history is written by the victors and in this case the victors were the Russian Federation. He told us that he lost his wife and a son and daughter in the fighting. Who knows what that kind of grief will do to a man?"

She smiled and reaching across, tenderly stroked at his cheek; his scarred cheek, he realised.

"So you think we should give him the benefit of the doubt?"

"Isn't that your job, Constable Daisy? To be objective?"

She smiled again and replied, "Yes, of course, you're right."

He was tempted to tell her what Umarov had said when he was leaving, but thought that could wait till the proper time.

It was when arose to tend to the cooker that his mobile rang in his trouser pocket. He stared curiously at the unknown number and pressed the green accept button.

"Mister Macleod, its Louise Hall," the lawyer said. "I've had a phone call from the police," she cheerfully told him, "and it's good news."

Staring with horror at the television screen, Rahib Chowdhury listened as the reporter stood in the rain at the bottom of Howick Place and pointed to the blue and white tape some fifty yards away where the detective had been murdered.

His mind racing, he reached for the phone and with nervous fingers, tapped into the sent message file then deleted the text to John.

He lowered his head into his hands and thought, one text message was all it took; one fearful plea and the man John had arranged for the detective to be murdered.

One *fucking* text and all because she had interviewed him.

If all it took for her to be murdered was a text message that she intended again interviewing him, then what he knew was even more dangerous to John.

He gulped as the realisation struck him like a thunderbolt; dangerous enough to have him murdered too.

His wife stood at the kitchen doorway and staring curiously at the television screen, turned to him and asked, "Husband, was that not the woman who visited you?"

He turned and forcing his voice to be calm, hissed, "Be silent and prepare my dinner."

The young detective checked her e-mail and almost with excitement, opened the message from the supervisor of the shop within the Sailmakers Shopping Centre in Ipswich.
To her dismay, when she opened the photograph attachment she saw it to be so dark that the man whose face was displayed was almost unrecognisable.
With a sigh she shoved back her chair and crossed the room to inform DI Cowan of the bad news.

He had just arrived back at his office after attending at an incident and walked through the rear door from the yard when he heard the murder being discussed by some of the uniformed officers stood at the charge bar.
"What's going on?" DC Brompton asked the sergeant.
"Some woman detective at the Met in London. Run down near to New Scotland Yard by a stolen car and killed," the sergeant sniffed. "Murdered they're saying."
"Yeah?" he reached for the crime reports stuffed into his pigeonhole. "That will mean a vacancy there then," he grinned.
"Maybe if you start wearing a burqa," the sergeant returned his grin. "She was one of that lot; a Mossie, apparently. A Detective Inspector."
Brompton felt a chill run through him and swallowing with difficulty, turned to the sergeant, his face pale and asked, "Her name. Did you get her name?"
"Probably couldn't fucking pronounce it if I did," the sergeant replied to hoots of laughter.
He stumbled through to the CID office and with relief saw it was empty.
With nervous hands, he searched for the television remote control, mentally cursing the idiots who left it lying about. At last he found it and switching on the small TV tuned into the twenty-four hour news channel.

He slumped into a chair when he read her name on the ribbon scrolling across at the bottom of the screen.

"Oh God, oh my God," he mumbled, his body unaccountably shivering.

"What the fuck have I done?"

His thought were everywhere at once; his mind racing with fear.

Murdered because she had phoned him?

Killed because he had complained about her to the man called John?

An icy fear grabbed at his heart and his balls shrunk into their sac.

If the man John or whoever he worked for were prepared to run down and kill a Detective Inspector simply for phoning him, what would they do to a guy like him who was party to perverting the course of justice on their behalf?

What would they do to shut *him* up?

He slumped forward, his head in his hands.

He had to protect himself, make sure that he was safe.

He turned to ensure there was paper in the printer then with shaking hands, reached for his keyboard and drew it towards him.

Showered, he sat at the desk and waited till the seconds counted off then precisely at six o'clock, dialled the number.

"Four minutes. You have news?" he asked, again curiously wondering why the man he spoke with was quite obviously Chechen, but insisted on speaking English.

"You have a pen and paper?"

"Go ahead."

"Rahib Chowdhury. House is number nineteen in a place called Anglesea Road in the town of Ipswich," the man carefully spelled out the word 'Anglesea.'

"Why is he of interest to the police?"

"He was friend of dead man, Abdul-hameed Muhammad. Police detective very interested in this man Chowdhury, but not know why. Watch TV news. Detective now dead, but also not know why."

Umarov glanced at his watch then said, "How reliable is your friend?"

There was a definite pause then the voice said, "We have someone close to dead woman detective."

"Will you have further information?"

"Not certain. Call again at same time tomorrow and," he heard the man softly laugh, "Udači!"

Ending the call, Umarov wryly smiled at the man switching to Russian to wish him good luck.

Rising from his chair, he turned on the television. Now the news programmes had obtained a photograph of the dead detective; a photograph of a very beautiful woman and to his surprise when he saw she wore a hijab, mused that she was of the Faith.

He decided it was too coincidental that the detective was murdered after speaking with the man he intended visiting.

Now, he wondered as he stared at her photograph, why were you so interested in this man Rahib Chowdhury? What did you know or suspect that caused you to die?

He switched off the television and moving to the window, knelt for Maghrib prayer and almost as an afterthought, decided that he would include the dead detective in those prayers.

His mobile phone chirruped from the dressing table across the room. Sliding from the bed, he turned to stare at the naked, sleeping blonde who lay face down and grinning, very gently pulled off the single silk sheet to expose her sculpted figure.

Lifting the phone, he glanced at the screen and his eyes narrowed, then pressing the green button, snapped, "Wait one," before making his way into the en-suite and closing the door behind him.

"Yes," he said and reached behind the door for his dressing gown.

"Your instructions have been carried out, sir," Ernie, the former Royal Marine crisply informed him. "Regretfully, due to the urgency of the issue, we were unable to ensure it looked like an accident, but there is nothing that will tie us to the incident."

"For your sake, I hope not," Ashford icily replied.

"The second issue, sir," Ernie ignored the inferred threat. "When do you wish us to proceed?"

Ashford hesitated.

Ordering his men to silence Chowdhury so soon after murdering the detective bitch might attract unwarranted attention.

"Leave that with me," he sighed. "I still have to make a decision regarding that issue."

"Sir. Anything else?"

"Not at the moment," Ashford replied then abruptly hung up. Returning to the bedroom, he saw the blonde had not stirred and feeling himself become aroused, slipped off the dressing gown and letting it fall to the floor, climbed onto the bed and straddled her sleeping body.

Detective Sergeant Mo McInnes took the call from the helpful community cop in Suffolk and with a happy grin, heard him say that yes, there was CCTV cameras in the streets surrounding the van hire premises. If she made a formal request to him via the Internet, he explained, something that he could show to his boss then he would arrange that the recordings for the approximate time on the date the van was returned could be researched, though he was unable to confirm how long this research would take.

"No matter," she told him, "I'll get the email down to you within the next ten minutes," she said and before ending the call, noted the constable's details.

Punching the air in delight, she informed DI Cowan that at last there might be something they could learn from the van hire.

"Sorry, Paul," she said, a little deflated. "The Met DI that was killed; she was your friend, wasn't she?"

"Aye, I really liked her," he nodded. "Mira was a good pal, a thoroughly nice person. She was smart, funny and civil to everyone regardless of their rank and importantly," he grinned, "she liked a good joke. Being a woman as well as being a practising Muslim woman didn't hold her back from anything. Not Mira."

He smiled. "I remember when we were on the course together there was a debate about a glass ceiling for woman progressing through the ranks in the police service. Mira argued for equality in all aspects of police work and let me tell you, Mo; she was some advocate for women's rights and absolutely wiped the floor with her male counterparts who were arguing for the return of the women's departments in the police."

He shook his head at the memory.

"Mira was going places. I reckon that in a few short years, she might even have achieved one of the top ranks in the Met." His face clouded as he went on, "Then to be fucking run over in the street like a dog! Bastard!"

"I understand from the media reporting she was married?"

"Yes, her husband is a doctor; well, a surgeon I think. I met him at the dining in night for the course before we broke up. Nice guy and if I wasn't happily married, I would have been as jealous as hell of him." He slowly exhaled. "Poor sod, I can't imagine what he's going through right now."

Her brow creased. "Where has the boss gone?"

"He's away with DCI Sheridan to meet with Mulgrew and the Chief at Tulliallan, but we can contact him on his mobile. Something on your mind?"

She pulled up a chair from a nearby empty desk and sitting down, drew closer to Cowan and said, "I was just wondering how far the inquiry is going to go, Paul; how much further we can take it. We've got four dead terrorists, a hero who stopped them killing anyone else and only the suspicion that there might have been a fifth getaway driver. But what if there isn't a fifth man? What if we're chasing a suspect who doesn't really exist?"

She glanced about her and lowering her voice, continued, "What if the bosses are wrong, that the supposition that it's some sort of conspiracy is just a load of shite? Is it possible that we're feeding our own imaginations with this nonsense about the Security Service being the bad guys? Look, you've worked with these guys on different operations through the years as I have and to be honest, I haven't had a problem with any of them. What if we're getting it wrong because of the obsession up here about independence?"

He stared at her before carefully replying, "You think that we might be overreacting, that up here in Bonnie Scotland," he smiled, "we're so sensitive about the independence issue that we're seeing bogeymen where there aren't any?"

He shrugged and continued, "I can't deny that I have some reservations about the theory that it is some sort of conspiracy to keep us in the Union, but there's also an itch at the back of my neck that tells me there's something just not right. I've met and mixed with some of the ruthless people who work in the Service and who believe they *are* beyond the rule of law. It's not the first time I've heard one of them tell me," he wagged his fingers in the air, "that what we do 'is for the greater good', whatever the fuck that's supposed to mean. Don't forget too, Mo, there's also the issue about the signature of the Semtex being previously recorded and was apparently in the possession of the Thames House people as well as that issue about the serial number for the Kalashnikov's being erased. We've both prepared cases for court and you know as I do that sometimes it's the small indicators that fit to make the larger picture. And now, just as she was acting on our behalf and trying to interview witnesses or suspects or whatever the hell they turn out to be, a good woman is murdered?" He slowly shook his head and added, "That to me is highly suspicious."

He leaned forward and continued, "Mo, you've been in the CID long enough to know that there is no such thing as coincidence. Whatever we dig up or discover is fact and circumstance and the facts and circumstances so far lead us to conclude that this is *not* a straight forward inquiry. There's deviousness here, Mo, and with a bit of hard work, not luck," he smiled at her, "we *will* get to the bottom of it."

"I can't truthfully admit I'm convinced, Paul, but you're right. The murder of your friend is suspicious unless of course," she stared at him "she was targeted for some other reason; perhaps by a right wing group who believed her to be a high profile Muslim?"

"Now *that's* guesswork," he grinned as she stood up, but inwardly admitted that without evidence to the contrary, Mo might not be far wrong.

Cathy Mulgrew arrived at Tulliallan Castle minutes before Glennie and Sheridan and when they arrived were conducted with her by a uniformed Inspector to the Chief Constables suite of offices.

To their surprise, Martin Cairney was not dressed in uniform, but an old sweater and a baggy pair of cargo pants.

Seeing them stare at him, he grumbled, "What? It's almost seven at night and I'm not allowed to wear civilian clothes?"

Suppressing their grins, they sat at his bidding and before the Inspector left, heard him order coffee for all four. Stood resting with his arms folded across his broad chest and his backside against the edge of his wide desk, he said, "Needless to say I've heard the news and already sent our Police Scotland commiserations to the Commissioner on the tragic loss of his officer. Now," he glanced curiously at them in turn, "why does this young woman's tragic murder cause three senior officers of my inquiry team to visit me at this time of the evening?"

"Sir, if I may," Mulgrew replied and at length related the investigation that DI Aamira Khalifa was conducting on behalf of the inquiry team.

"So, she was lied to by a couple of witnesses..." he shrugged.

"One of whom was a police detective, sir," Mulgrew interrupted to remind him.

"Perhaps so, but as operational police officers you must know that you are lied to every day of your working life," he pointedly reminded them. "Yet from the little conversation that you had with this unfortunate young woman, you suspect that there is something amiss about her murder in that it somehow connects with our ongoing terrorist inquiry?"

Mulgrew glanced quickly at Glennie and Sheridan before responding, "Yes, sir. We have this united belief that one way or another, the inquiry and DI Khalifa's murder are related."

"So, if you are correct, what's your next move?"

"That's where you come in, sir," she smiled at him.

He sighed and paused for a few seconds before replying, "Okay. What will you have me do?"

"What we request of you, sir, is that you have a personal discussion with the Commissioner at the Met. Preferably face to face because..."

"Please, Cathy," he raised a hand, "don't tell me you suspect that our communications might be compromised."

"Perhaps not ours, sir, but I can't speak for the Met. We both know the access the Security Service have to GCHQ and the facilities available to that organisation."

"Okay, so you want me to travel to London and say what?"

"That would depend how much you trust the Commissioner, sir."

"Well, we're not friends *per se*, but we have met and he strikes me as a good man."

"But a man subject to the whim of the Home Secretary, sir."

"Good God, woman. Now you're telling me that you don't trust the bloody Home Secretary either?"

"It's not a question of trust, sir. If as we suspect this is a conspiracy by individuals within the Westminster establishment, we just don't know who might be involved and I don't need to remind you that when Barry Ashford met with us at Dalmarnock office, he made a point of boasting that he has the ear of the Home Secretary, did he not?"

"Point taken, Miss Mulgrew," he formally addressed her. "So, assuming I agree that I travel to London and meet with the Commissioner, what *exactly* am I to tell him?"

"If I might," Glennie interrupted. "As the SIO in the inquiry, Mister Cairney, I would be grateful if you inform the Commissioner that no matter what other lines of investigation his officers conduct into the murder of DI Khalifa, he consider she might have been murdered because of the inquiries she was conducting on my behalf. I have no operational objection to you also disclosing her suspicions regarding Suffolk Constabulary's Detective Constable Brompton or this man, Rahib Chowdhury, who has come to the attention of my inquiry. Of course, I would be grateful if such inquiries might be conducted with…" he shrugged, before adding, "*complete* discretion."

Cairney rubbed thoughtfully at his chin, then suddenly grinned at Glennie and said, "It's been quite a while since I received instructions or been involved in a major inquiry, Mister Glennie."

He took a deep breath and addressing the three of them continued. "Chief Constable or not, I must remind myself, ladies and gentleman that at the end of the day, I am still a serving police officer and just as it is my officers duty, it's also my duty," he grinned, "to catch the bad guys. Okay then, I'll do as you ask. I've very little on tomorrow, so I'll arrange to travel to London and if he's available, meet with the Commissioner. Now, anything else while you are here?"

"You might be interested to know," said Glennie, "that Crown Office have agreed that there will be no proceedings against Ian Macleod, the man who…"

"Saved many of our citizens and dealt with the terrorists. Well, that is good news. And what about the press conference. Has he agreed to that yet?"

"We haven't yet had a response, sir," he diplomatically replied when in truth, he just didn't know.

"Right, then ladies and gentleman," Cairney glanced at his watch. "If that's all, I believe I *might* just get home in time for the glorious Partick Thistle's kick-off against Celtic."

Lou Sheridan, a devoted Celtic fan, stared bemusedly at him before replying, "Perhaps, sir, if you keep your fingers crossed and you're *really* lucky, there might be heavy traffic on the way home and save yourself a night of pain, anguish and utter disappointment."

CHAPTER EIGHTEEN

Eldar Umarov arose before dawn and after his ablutions and getting dressed, knelt by the window for Fajr prayers. He permitted himself a light breakfast before attending at the reception desk to settle his bill.

"Was everything to your satisfaction, Monsieur Marchand?" asked the pretty young receptionist who wide-eyed stared admiringly at the tall, strikingly handsome man.

"It would have been so much better had I such a delightful companion like you to share in my visit to your lovely city," he replied with a twinkle in his eye.

So charmed was she that she swiped his card through the machine without a second glance, completely unaware that he was a little tense while she did so.

However, true to his word, his Chechen friend Akhmad Soslanbek had provided Umarov with documents that seemed to be almost genuine and so far to his relief he had not encountered a problem with any of the cards or for that matter, the passport.

Taking his leave of the young lady he made his way to the underground car park and before driving off, set his Satnav with directions to the house at nineteen, Anglesea Road in Ipswich.

Ian Macleod was showering when he heard his mobile phone sound with a text message. Drying off, he reached for the phone and reading the text, read it a second time. "Bloody hell," he murmured. Pulling on a pair of dark coloured jogging pants and carrying a sweat vest and the phone in one hand while he rubbed at his hair with a towel, he made his way bare-chested and barefooted into the kitchen where Daisy, her hair tied back with a piece of ribbon and wearing her dressing gown over pink coloured cotton pyjamas, was already up and filling the electric kettle.

"Morning," she smiled at him then sensing something was amiss, asked, "What's up?"

He waved the phone at her and said, "Morning, I've just had a message from the police; Mister Glennie, the guy in charge of the inquiry. He's asking if I would call him regarding a press conference."

"Press conference," she repeated, a little flustered at the sight of his bare torso and caught her breath.

"Does that mean he wants you to be publicly identified?"

"I suppose so. I mean, it won't be long before they all know anyway," he shrugged. "Those guys that Joan and Mickey chased off. They know so I suppose the word will get out eventually. What do you think?"

She was flattered that he considered her opinion and replied, "Why don't we have a cuppa and sit and discuss it. There might be some advantage in getting it done and over with."

"Like what?"

"Well," she slowly drawled, "it would mean you wouldn't need to hide here anymore. You could get back home to your flat."

"So, what you mean is you're fed up with me and trying to get rid of me?"

She knew he was teasing, but wanted to clear the air and replied, "No, that's not what I'm suggesting. In fact, Mister Macleod," she moved closer to him and taking his hands in hers, said, "I'm getting rather used to having you around."

She stood so close he could feel her breath on his bare chest and to his surprise, she wrapped her arms about his waist and pulled him even closer.

He stared down at her and his mouth suddenly dry, said, "Moving back to the flat doesn't mean we won't see each other again, Constable Daisy. In fact, if you like you could visit me sometimes and even stay over; me returning your hospitality I mean."

"Is it a one or a two bedroom flat?"

"My flat? Eh," his eyes narrowed and he stared uncertainly at her, "it's a one bedroom flat."

"Then I quite like the idea of you giving me some hospitality, so that that sounds like a plan," she softly said and reaching up, kissed him softly on the lips before quietly adding, "but before you telephone Mister Glennie, why don't we go through to my room now and pretend we're in your one bedroom flat?"

True to his word, the Suffolk community constable caused a search of the recordings for the CCTV cameras that were located near the van hire premises in Ipswich. However, he told Mo McInnes in a return e-mail, the research might take several days if not longer.

At five minutes after nine that morning at Edinburgh Airport, the Police Scotland Chief Constable, Martin Cairney, and his aide, a Chief Inspector who like Cairney was attired in a business suit, boarded a British Airways plane for the short flight to London City Airport.

One hour and fifteen minutes later, they disembarked from the aircraft and were met by the Metropolitan Police Commissioner's private vehicle that conveyed them directly to New Scotland Yard.

By midday, Eldar Umarov was well into his journey south and decided to leave the motorway for a comfort break, fuel, coffee and a snack.

Seated at his desk, John Glennie was becoming frustrated.
The inquiry was dragging to a halt and it was becoming increasingly difficult to motivate the team.
"The problem is," he explained to Lou Sheridan, "that we've so few inquiries left. We've got the bad guys; well, what I mean is they're dead so we don't need to hunt them."
Sheridan, buoyed by her teams previous night gubbing of the unfortunate Partick Thistle, guffawed and spilled some coffee onto her skirt.
"What's so funny?" growled Glennie.
"You, John," she giggled as she wiped at the spill with a tissue.
"Your comment 'we've got the bad guys, they're dead.' Bloody hell, if that's not a result, what is?"
He grinned and replied, "Well, you know what I mean. Anyway, other than this admittedly strong suspicion that there's a fifth guy who is now returned to England, we've no real local inquires here."
"So, what do you propose?"
"I'm thinking we should begin to wind down the inquiry, release some of the team, Lou. Return the seconded detectives back to their divisions and thin out our own CTU people; get them to continue with their local inquiries that we've been forced to neglect because of this incident."
"When do you wish me commence?"
"There's no time like the present. I'll contact Cathy Mulgrew and as a courtesy, make her aware of my decision. I don't see her objecting for I suspect she will have been under some pressure by the divisions who provided resources to beef up our team; likely they'll be happy to have their people returned."
"Excuse me," he said, turning to lift his ringing phone, then with surprise smiled at Sheridan and said, "Mister Macleod, thanks for getting back to me."

She watched as he listened and saw him nod his head, then reply, "That's grand. Right then, I'll make the arrangements and text you with the time. Yes, it will be at Dalmarnock police office. Will you need a lift here or…? Okay, that's fine," he nodded. "If you can make it though, can you be there a little earlier today, say for half past twelve for an interview with the 'Glasgow News?' Right then, till later today. Goodbye," and returned the phone to its cradle.

"That was Ian Macleod," he confirmed. "He's agreed to a press conference, so can you inform Harry Downes to set it up and she can liaise with that guy from the 'Glasgow News.' He's kept up his end of the deal so it's only fair he gets first crack at an interview."

His brow creased as she stood up from her chair and staring at him, she asked, "What?"

"Nothing I can put my finger on," he quietly replied, then demurely smiled, "but I got the feeling that Macleod wasn't alone. I thought I heard someone giggling in the background."

He was striding along the carpeted corridor when his phone indicated receipt of a text message. He stopped, ignoring the staff who heads down or glancing away, nervously passed him by for it was commonly whispered the Director of Operations was a man who did not encourage curiosity.

Reading the message, he frowned.

Damn, he thought. His source at the Met's CTU demanding a meeting.

Demanding?

Who the fuck…but stopped and his eyes narrowed.

This was another problem he just didn't want to deal with, but if he had to then he would quickly quash that nonsense before it became a problem

Typing a response, he continued to his office where throwing open the door, he snapped his fingers at his blonde secretary, "Amend my schedule. I have a meeting at one this afternoon and will be out of the office for an hour…no, make that one and a half hours. Then get me the DG on the phone or if he's busy, request his secretary grant me an immediate meeting. If she asks, I need ten minutes of his time."

"Sir," the secretary nodded, the intimacy of the previous evening forgotten as she busied herself with his demands.

Closing his inner office door behind him, he slumped into his chair and dialled the number on his mobile phone for Ernie, his bodyguard.

"I have a meeting at one this afternoon," he began without preamble. "I will be walking there so pick me up when I depart from the office, say ten minutes before the meeting. A discreet tail, if you please and," suspicious as always, he added, "be sure that you and your Welsh associate confirm there are no observers. Any issues, the usual indication to alert me to abort the meeting. Also, please ensure you get a good look at the individual I meet. It might be that at some time in the near future, I will ask you to retire the individual."

"Sir," was the bland acknowledgement before he ended the call.

His intercom buzzed.

"Yes?"

"The meeting with the DG, sir; fifteen minutes, if you please."

"Thank you."

He glanced at the wall clock, his head beginning to throb and with the heel of his hand rubbed fiercely at his forehead.

The whole Scottish situation was getting out of hand.

The operational planning, the discreet acquisition of the equipment, the careful screening and recruitment of those…those incompetent idiots!

It had seemed so straight forward.

A rapid assault on their largest city; quickly in, kill some locals, then quickly out and gone.

All calculated to shock the Scots into realising that without the protection of the Westminster Government they were open to further terrorist attacks. An operation planned to circumvent the rise in nationalism and parallel a newspaper campaign orchestrated by some sympathetic media moguls to question the validity of a nationalist government that could not protect its citizens.

And while the police up there were running about like headless chickens trying to identify the Jihadists, the Westminster Government would be seen to render immediate and practical assistance.

The Government campaign had been intended to publicise the ploughing of money into Police Scotland, the re-opening of a number of derelict MoD bases to bolster the economy in rural areas; then the full resources of the Service, committed to identifying the attackers one week later and who of course would be lawfully killed when they resisted arrest by the Special Forces the Service controlled.

It should not have failed…but it did and all because of some lone, crippled, interfering bastard who wanted to be a fucking hero!

His head pounded, but he did not have time for a massage, not when he had to meet with the DG.

Now this. The killing of that Muslim bitch was not enough; now he had to hold the hand and deal with his CTU source and for her sake, she had better not be too demanding.

His thoughts turned to the Scottish bitch; that queer Mulgrew and her boss, that loathsome man Cairney. Another bloody problem, but one that he could deal with in due course for regardless of what they might think, they had nothing; no evidence to link him or the Service to the attack and if they made any kind of public accusation, the Service lawyers would ensure a D Notice was slapped onto them and quickly follow that with personal lawsuits.

No, for the moment Cairney and his bitch Mulgrew were the least of his worries.

Taking a deep breath, he slowly exhaled then stood and made his way into his private bathroom where he splashed cold water onto his face and drying himself, stared into the mirror.

He had little doubt the DG would be aware that the murder of the Met detective was his handiwork and prepared himself for the Pontius Pilate attitude; the fear that somehow or other the Met investigation would land at the door of the Service or more accurately, at the DG's door.

Gripping the enamel bowl, he continued to stare at his reflection.

He was sick of holding the old bastards hand; tired of having to continually assure him that his bloody pension was safe.

A thought came to him as he stared into the mirror.

Perhaps this might be the right time to subtly suggest to the DG that he consider retirement, that he had already done more for the Service than was required of him; that at his age the pressure was becoming too much when could quite easily step down and enjoy the obligatory knighthood and generous stipend that is commensurate with his exalted positon.

A position, Ashford was quite certain, that would soon be his.

Leaving his office he confidently strutted with self-importance to the DG's office where the secretary, a rapier thin, hawk nosed woman in her early sixties who clearly didn't like him and made no secret of it, kept him waiting while she announced his arrival.

She would be his first dismissal, he promised himself.

"Come in, Barry, come in," the DG waved him to sit in the chair opposite.

"You will have heard, Director," he began, "of the unfortunate demise of the Met's woman detective."

"Indeed I did," he glared at Ashford. "Are our hands dirty, dear boy?"

Carefully he replied, "Let us just say it was an ongoing issue that left us clean as a whistle, Director."

"I hope so, Barry. I really do. Now, explain to me," he leaned forward to peer at the younger man, "Why has the Chief Constable of the Scottish police arrived this morning here in London and why is he now meeting with the Met's Commissioner?"

Taken aback, Ashford rapidly blinked, his mind racing as he blustered, "Martin Cairney? Here in London? Really, Director, I have no idea."

"Can it possibly be connected to your little project up north?"

Ashford turned pale and did not fail to miss the reference to 'your little project.' Clearly, the DG had already washed his hands of the operation.

"Perhaps," he began to suggest, "the meeting is routine and has nothing whatsoever to do with the operation, Director. I'm certain that the meeting between the two Chief Constables of the country's major Forces is merely routine; a collaboration and exchange of intelligence, no doubt."

"Perhaps," the DG slowly nodded. "However, my source tells me that the meeting was hurriedly arranged late last night and by this man Cairney. Hardly a routine event then, eh?"

He decided to brazen it and said, "I am absolutely certain, Director, that the meeting you speak of has nothing to do with the operation that is now wound down. There will be no comeback to the Service. You have my personal assurance on that matter."

"Yet the murder of the detective yesterday evening, Barry. Am I assured that it was the final phase of what we can only describe as a foolish misadventure?"

He swallowed with difficulty, all thought of suggesting the DG's retirement gone from his mind and replaced by the politics of saving his arse.

"It was a necessary cleansing, Director. A final phase as you so succinctly put it."

"Thank you then, Barry, and please," the DG nodded tot him, "don't let me keep you from your office."

He arose from the chair, inwardly fuming at the curt dismissal, but more annoyed with himself for underestimating the bastard and walked from the room.

Ian Macleod turned in the bed and stared at Daisy, her hair falling over her brow.

"Will you come with me to the press conference?"

"Don't you think that might start tongues wagging," she smiled at him.

"I bloody hope so," he grinned. "An ugly guy like me pulling a good looking bird like you? Why, I'll be the envy of all the men there."

She reached behind her head and pulling at the pillow, lifted it and brought it down onto his head.

"Who are you calling a bird, you cheeky bugger.

He laughed and said, "Aye, but I did say a *good* looking bird, didn't I?"

"So, you think I'm good looking, then," she snuggled into his arms.

"I think you're just perfect for a guy like me."

"What about when I grow old and grey-haired?"

"Do you intend hanging about that long?"

She raised her head and stared meaningfully at him, her eyes narrowing. "Would you like me to?"

"Ask me again in ten years."

"Why ten years?"

"My God, woman, you don't half go on," he smiled at her. "Okay, make it twenty…no, thirty years."

"Hmm, thirty years, I'll consider," she again squeezed closer to him. "What time did Mister Glennie say for the conference at Dalmarnock?"

"One o'clock for the conference, but apparently he wants me there at half-twelve for an interview of some sorts. So, will you come?"

She stared into his eyes and slyly reaching under the bedsheet with her hand, grinned when Ian startled at her gentle touch and said, "Yes, I'll go with you, but I think we'll get a little more of that practise in first."

The Commissioner's driver dropped Martin Cairney and his aide off at the London City Airport entrance and making their way through to the almost empty departure lounge, he requested the Chief Inspector fetch them coffee while he sat alone and made a phone call.

When the call was answered, he said, "Cathy, Martin Cairney. I'm at the airport lounge waiting on my return flight."

"Yes sir," Mulgrew acknowledged, "How did the meeting go?"

"Well," he sighed, "needless to say I dropped a bombshell when I informed the Commissioner of our suspicions and quite frankly, he's already had some of his own people tell him that they are not happy, that they believe the murder of his DI was an assassination. He did disclose that he already has a detective working covertly *within* the investigation for the purpose of determining if DI Khalifa's murder was orchestrated by someone close to her. His detective, I don't know if it's a man or woman, apparently already suspects that whoever killed Khalifa likely had prior information about her and where she would be at the material time of her murder. That concluded him to agree with his aides that it was an assassination."

"Good God, sir, are you telling me it might have been a colleague who killed her or conspired in her murder?"

"Either that or someone colluding with the killer. Saying that, witness's statements place two individuals in the murder vehicle, but what gender they were is yet to be determined."

"How did the Commissioner react when you mentioned Barry Ashford?"

"He knows him, of course, having worked with him on operational matters here in London. Doesn't like him and doesn't trust him. That's it in a nutshell."

"What's his next move?"

"He's hindered for the moment and will need to await the outcome of the murder investigation to see what that turns up."

He saw the Chief Inspector returning, and held up his free hand to halt him from coming near while he spoke with Mulgrew. Taking the hint, the Chief Inspector sat down on an empty chair some fifteen feet away.

"Obviously," he continued, "he's not in any position to challenge the Security Service about what we discussed and to be frank, doesn't completely trust the people about him. And as you so rightly pointed out yesterday evening, he confided he doesn't even trust his office phones."

He sighed as he shook his head and continued, "You might recall, Cathy, he was appointed to the position of Commissioner from a rural Force, so he's never been a Met police officer and you might also recall there was some disparaging comments made by the media when he was appointed to the post."

"Yes, I remember," she replied.

"However, my trip hasn't been a complete waste of time. The Commissioner is aware of our suspicions and if we do need to exchange further information, he will instruct a trusted senior officer to visit me at Tulliallan. Now, what do you have for me?"

"We're no further forward, sir," she sighed. "The press conference is due to commence at one this afternoon at Dalmarnock and Mister

Macleod has agreed to attend. John Glennie has decided that with so few lines of inquiry he intends winding down the investigation and I'm pleased to say, sending some much needed CID officers back to their parent divisions. John is still considering whether or not to send a pair of detectives down to Ipswich to interview a man called Chowdhury; he's the man that DI Khalifa spoke with, but Glennie's office manager, DI Paul Cowan didn't receive a full statement from Khalifa for Chowdhury, though Cowan did learn that she was suspicious of him."

"Remind me again, Cathy. Chowdhury?"

"His name turned up as a close friend of one of the dead terrorists; the man called Abdul-hameed Muhammad."

"Ah, that name I do recognise. He's the bugger that tried to shoot my officer, the young lassie Daisy Cooper."

"That's him, sir. The only other viable line of inquiry regarding the possibility of a fifth man is being conducted by DS McInnes of John Glennie's mob who is continuing an inquiry about the van hired in Ipswich that was seen departing the Waverly car park shortly after the Skoda Octavia was dumped there. In light of the murder of DI Khalifa, I've instructed John Glennie that we do not pursue any further inquiry through the Met CTU, that if we need to speak with Chowdhury we will make our own arrangement."

"I'm guessing that you believe there might be possible a link between DI Khalifa's murder and this man Chowdhury?"

She didn't immediately respond, but then replied, "I find it too coincidental that the poor woman make an inquiry for us then is killed, sir, and you know the old adage in the CID about coincidence."

"Yes, there's no such thing," he solemnly replied, before asking, "What if the Met CTU come back to Glennie asking for information about Khalifa's inquiry with this man Chowdhury?"

"John will be wise to that, sir, and simply fob them off; tell them it was one of a large number of inquiries regarding associates that went nowhere."

"The Met won't be pleased if they think you're holding back on them, Cathy."

"Frankly, sir, I don't really care. It's our inquiry and it's also a question of trust. My Detective Inspector, Paul Cowan, knew Khalifa and that's why he asked her to act locally for us. Now she's dead. To me, that says a lot."

"I can't argue with your logic," he sighed, "but tread carefully, Cathy. I don't want any kind of fallout with the Metropolitan Police. We have too many areas of mutual interest.

Now, anything else for me?"

"No, that's it for now, sir."

"What about the rest of the Force areas this morning? Anything I should know?"

"There was a murder last night in Coatbridge and the body was discovered this morning, but it's being investigate by the local CID as a domestic. A husband whose wife took an axe to him when he was sleeping. Apparently the couple were known locally as a pair of alkies, always on the bevy."

"Ouch!" Cairney shivered.

"Also, an attempted robbery at a bank in Inverness when it opened this morning. A man with what was thought to be a handgun. No mask and no one hurt, but the dye pack in the bag the staff gave the culprit exploded, so the local boys are hunting a man with a bright red face."

He grinned and said, "Maybe they should try Ibrox on a Saturday. They'll find quite a few there. Is that it?"

"Pretty much. If there's anything else, I'll contact your driver and he'll apprise you when you land at Edinburgh."

"Thank you, Cathy," he said and ending the call, smiled and waved his Chief Inspector to sit with him.

Harry Benson, the community constable in Suffolk had been at it for over an hour and was becoming bored and the more bored Harry became, the faster he wound forward the CCTV recordings.

Yawning, he decided another brew was called for and pausing the footage, was about to leave his seat when he stopped, his attention taken by the Transit van on the screen that had just turned into South Street.

The tea for the moment forgotten, he slowly wound the footage back one minute and running the film at normal speed, watched as the white coloured van arrived on the screen, then turning from Orford Street into South Street and stopping outside the van hire premises. Harry's excitement increased when he saw the man exit the driver's door and in the officer's opinion, furtively glance about him before making his way to the door of the van hire premises and though he didn't see the man *at* the door, presumed that the man was dropping the van keys through the door's letterbox.

He watched as the man then turned and head down, began to walk away from the premises in the direction of Orford Street, but frustratingly out of the cameras arc of vision.

"Bugger," he muttered and scrambling among the DVD covers on the desk, located the DVD for the CCTV camera that he knew was mounted in Orford Street, though first checking the time of arrival for the Transit van, then inserting the DVD.

Winding the recording to the correct time, Harry saw the man appear on the screen and continuing to glance about him, make his way to a vehicle that…

"Shit!" the constable cried out and beat in frustration at the desk with his fist.

"Problem, Harry?" asked the young, dark haired woman from behind him who was responsible for the storage of the CCTV recordings and who wore the uniform white blouse and navy blue skirt that denoted her position as a station assistant.

"I was hoping to see what vehicle this guy went into," he pointed to the screen, "but the camera doesn't cover that stretch of the road."

"No, it doesn't she agreed," shaking her head and bending over his shoulder to manipulate the controls. He caught a whiff of perfume and sat perfectly still, trying with difficulty to avoid nudging her firm breasts that hung over his shoulder and tickled at his ear.

"Now," she whispered with a husky voice, one hand lying gently on his opposite shoulder as she bent over him, "if you consider the time and distance," she screwed her face in thought as she inserted a third disc into the machine, "we might catch him on the cameras when he turns from Orford Street onto the Norwich Road, but of course that depends what way he turns; left or right."

Blushing, Harry was too preoccupied by the sudden weight of her breast against his cheek and his neck to worry what way the bugger turned his vehicle and squirmed uncomfortably in his seat as nature took control of his manhood.

"Ah, I *think* that's the car there," she pressed the pause button, then turning to him pretended to frown and asked, "You're looking a bit flushed there, Harry. Are you feeling okay?"

"Fine, thanks," he squeaked and with nervous fingers concerned himself searching among the DVD's for the scrap of paper with the Scottish detective's phone number written on it.

"I can print you a photograph of the car, if you like," offered the young woman and without waiting for a reply, again leaned across Harry to push at a button, deliberately teasing him and with an inward, but knowing smile at his obvious discomfort.

Before turning the Fiat into the entrance at Dalmarnock office, Daisy Cooper was surprised to see the number of vehicles in the car park that displayed media logos as well as the dozen or more men and women who hung about the front door, some smoking while others clearly awaiting the arrive of the man they had come to interview.

"Quick, get your head down," she reached across and to his surprise, literally dragged Ian Macleod's head down onto her lap.

Grinning from the awkward angle he now found himself in, he said, "This is definitely the weirdest sexual offer I've ever had, Constable Daisy. Now, how exactly do we…"

"Shut up, you idiot. If that lot over there see you, we'll never get into the office. Stay down, I'm going to drive to the staff car park at the rear. I don't have a pass, but hopefully there should be an intercom connected to the reception desk."

She drove past the crowd at the entrance, some of who gave her a cursory glance while the majority ignored what seemed to be a woman driving alone in the small car.

As she correctly guessed, at the rear of the office she saw the metal security gate beside which was a wooden post with an intercom.

Explaining who she was and who accompanied her the gate was buzzed open and she drove through into a spacious car park.

She and Ian were walking from the car towards a rear door when it opened and a pleasant looking woman with shoulder length fair hair and wearing a dark grey business suit stood waiting for them, her hand on the door handle and a smile of welcome on her face.

"Mister Macleod," she said, "I'm Chief Inspector Downes of the Media Department," and extended her hand. Staring inquiringly at Daisy, she asked, "And you are?"

"Constable Daisy Cooper, Ma'am, from Stewart Street."

"Daisy Cooper," Downes slowly repeated as she stared at the younger officer and noticing the healing wound on the left side of her head, nodded and added, "Ah, yes. I know who you are now." Her eyes narrowed. "Why are you here, Daisy? Were you asked to come along for the interview?"

"No, Ma'am. Ian...Mister Macleod," she blushed, "Well, he's been kind of hiding out at my place since the reporters tracked him down to his flat."

"Oh, indeed," Downes fought the grin that threatened to overtake her smile and clamping her teeth together, instead said, "Well, you're both very welcome, so come through and we'll discuss what's to happen today."

Downes led them through corridors to a stairway, up to the first floor and then to her office where she offered them coffee or tea.

"Tea, please," they both agreed.

Turning to her secretary, Downes smiled as the woman acknowledged the request and left the room.

Inviting them to sit, Downes sat behind her desk and said, "Mister Macleod, with your permission and before the conference commences, the reporter from the 'Glasgow News' would like to meet with you and if you agree, he'll interview you and take notes for an article about you. Does that present any issues?"

"Will I be able to vet..." his eyes narrowed, "is that the word? I mean, see what he's going to write before it's printed."

The secretary arrived through the door carrying the coffee and watching her place it upon the desk, Downes replied, "Let's just say,

Mister Macleod…can I call you Ian?"

"Yes, of course."

"Well, Ian, let's just say there should be no need for you to edit what is written about you. You won't be alone on the podium either, I'll be there as will Detective Superintendent Glennie and your own lawyer, Miss Hall, who will be looking after your interest."

She glanced at her watch. "Miss Hall phoned in about half an hour ago and intimated she will be a couple of minutes late, but don't worry; we won't commence the press conference without her."

She smiled and continued, "You must be aware that the general public and particularly here in Glasgow see you as a *bona fide* hero. Trust me, no newspaper or television station is going to upset their readers or viewers by making you look anything other than that. You have my word; you need not worry about that."

He still didn't seem convinced and turning to Daisy, comically grimaced.

Watching them, Downes smiled and asked, "I take it since the incident you two have…" she searched for the word before settling on, "bonded?"

Daisy blushed and nodding, with forced cheerfulness replied, "What other woman has her own superhero these days, Ma'am? Yes," she turned and rubbed at Ian's arm. "We've bonded."

She could not have made a wiser statement and her open declaration cheered him more than he could have imagined.

Suddenly bursting with confidence, he smiled at Downes then said, "When do we begin?"

Turning into the motorway Cambridge Services located at Junction 27 on the A14, Eldar Umarov switched off the engine and stepping out of the vehicle, stretched to ease the ache in his arms and legs. The cafeteria did not seem too be too crowded and lifting his jacket from the rear seat he made his way across the car park, smiling at the young children in the rear seat of the camper van who cheekily pulled faces at him. When he finished using the men's toilet, he decided that a short break wouldn't do him any harm and after purchasing 'The Times' newspaper from the shop, went into the small café. Fetching some loose change from his pocket, he ordered coffee and a pastry from the tall and heavyset, cheerful black woman aged about thirty who wore a broad smile and colourful dread locks and whose eyes opened wide at the sight of the tall, handsome man with the cute accent.

Seating himself at a table against the wall, he unfolded the paper and read the again about the murder of the woman detective in London that continued to be headline news. According to a press release the Metropolitan Police he read, believed the driver of the stolen vehicle recognised the police officer and panicking, lost control of the vehicle when he tried to make off.

His eyes narrowed, for he did not for one moment believe the article. No, he thought; according to his Chechen contact the dead woman had interviewed this man Rahib Chowdhury.

That she was now dead was beyond suspicious.

His eyes flickered as he contemplated why she was killed. It seemed apparent that the police were covering up the true nature of the murder, but the worry was; were the police aware of her interest in Chowdhury and did they suspect that was the reason she was killed? He realised that he would need to proceed with extreme caution, that perhaps if indeed this man Chowdhury was of interest to the police, they must surely be watching him.

His eyes narrowed.

What if Chowdhury was already in police custody being questioned about the woman's murder?

He decided to break protocol and fetching the mobile phone from his trouser pocket, called the Chechen contacts number.

"Yes?"

"Four minutes," he warned the man. "The dead detective. You said she interviewed the man Chowdhury."

"Yes, that is correct."

"Is Chowdhury in custody or being watched?"

"Five minutes," the man replied then abruptly ended the call.

He laid the phone down onto the table and glanced up. The cheery black woman laid his coffee and pastry down onto the table and said, "On your way south, are you love?"

"Touring," he smiled at her.

"Well," she touched lightly at her brightly coloured hair and with a coy smile, run her tongue over her top lip before replying, "If you're stopping local, love, and you need someone to show you around, you know where to find me."

With that, she turned and exaggerated the swing of her massive hips as she made her way back to the counter.

Speechless and taken aback at the very open invitation, Umarov could not but grin and slowly shaking his head, opened the newspaper and waited for the return phone call.

The two bodyguards, one twenty metres ahead of Barry Ashford and one trailing twenty metres behind him, tensely watched for any sign of covert surveillance as they walked on the Victoria Embankment. Confident of the two men's ability to both identify any interlopers and protect him, Ashford made his way to the seat that faced the Thames where the young fair haired woman sat alone.

Seating himself beside her, Ashford crossed one leg over the other then tugged at the trouser material to straighten the crease before asking, "Now my dear, what is it that seems to be troubling you and so important that I brings me to this wet and windy embankment?"

She didn't turn, but voice quivering, hissed, "You killed her. Murdered her. And you did it because of the information I gave you, you bastard!"

"My dear, I think you're rather overreacting."

"Overreacting!" she quickly turned, the vehemence obvious on her face. "Don't you care? Don't you realise what you've done? You've fucking involved me in a murder! It was my text and the photograph I sent that makes me as complicit and as guilty as the bastard that run her over!"

He didn't immediately respond, but glancing about him saw that Ernie and the Welsh bugger had taken up positions twenty yards on either side of the bench where he sat; Taff hanging over the embankment and the former Marine idly standing against a lamppost reading a partially folded newspaper; a newspaper that he would quickly rap against his arm to indicate any compromise of the meeting

"Now listen here," he sharply replied, his eyes blazing. "You know nothing about the death of Khalifa! All you need to know, my dear girl, is that you did as you were told and thus kept yourself safe. What I do, I do for the defence of the realm! That woman involved herself in matters that did not concern her and certainly need not concern you!"

His voice became scornful as he continued, "In future, you do not contact me to whine and seek sympathy or hold your fucking hand because of what you did! Must I remind you that *I* am the man responsible for settling your excessive gambling debts and dealing with the man who threatened you expose you? I need not remind you again, my dear girl that you are mine and as such you will continue to serve me and my Service for as long as I require you to do so. However, there are benefits in working for me," he softly smiled then frowning, picked at a loose thread on his sleeve. "The unfortunate demise of your boss will leave an opening in your Department. As in all professions with a rank structure, it is likely that at least two individuals in your Department will be advanced in rank to compensate for the tragic loss of the Detective Inspector, so let's hope that my office can influence your management to consider you for advancement. I must assume that an advancement will be both financially and career advantageous, will it not?"

She did not respond, but lowered her head and fought her tears. She had never queried how Ashford had dealt with the man who was blackmailing her; never wanted to know when she heard that he had disappeared. All she had really done was swap one blackmailing bastard for another.

He sat for a moment, permitting her to compose herself before firmly instructing, "If you have anything relevant, then contact me, but otherwise you will not do so until I call you.

Do…you…understand?"

She swallowed with difficulty, her lips tightly together and hatred in her eyes before slowly nodding.

He smiled and reaching across, patted at her clenched hands and added, "I'm so glad that we understand each other, my dear. Now," he arose and taking a deep breath, smiled down at the troubled young woman and said, "I'll let you return to work for I'm certain that there must be issues in your office with which you might wish to keep me apprised; isn't that correct, DC Ball?"

He had finished the coffee and eaten just half of the pastry when his phone rang.

Accepting the call, Umarov was about to speak, but smiled when the voice jokingly said, "Four minutes," before continuing, "My friend tell me nobody as far as she know," so it's a woman, smiled Umarov, "that police not go near Chowdhury for now. But friend not certain if this continue and that police might visit Chowdhury soon."

"But your friend is not certain?"

"No, not certain."

"Nothing about surveillance on Chowdhury?"

"Surv…what is this word?"

"The police, they are not watching Chowdhury?"

"Friend not certain," sighed the man, "but if any more information comes to me, I call you, okey dokey?"

"I understand," replied Umarov and concluded with, "expect a text with a new number."

Ending the call he folded his newspaper and rising from his seat, saw the waitress was watching him and before exiting the café, gave her a saucy wink.

On his way his way to the self-service WH Smith store, he dropped the newspaper into a bin then in the store purchased a new pay-as-you-go phone and suitable car charger.

Returning to the car, he unlocked the boot and glancing about to ensure he wasn't being watched, lifted the carpet and ignoring the black leather shoulder holster for the moment, removed the brown envelope containing the handgun and ammunition that he took with him into the driver's seat.

Within the car he locked the doors and removed the handgun and ammunition that he shoved under his seat before dismantling the current phone and snapping the SIM card. The phone and the broken card he placed into the envelope. Breaking open the packaging of the new phone and charger, he assembled it and plugged it into the car to charge the phone.

Again ensuring no one was nearby, he doubled over and with his head almost touching the bottom of the steering wheel, lifted out the Berretta to ensure it was still loaded. The spare magazines he left under the seat.

He was about to raise his head and startling in fright, almost had a heart attack when the driver's window was loudly tapped.

Snapping his head around, he quickly shoved the handgun under his leg when he saw the black waitress standing by the door, a scrap of paper in her hand that she waved at him.

He slowly exhaled, his heart beating wildly and lowering his window, forced a smile.

"You weren't going without my number, were you?" she pouted, leaning down into the window with her hands on the car roof and her heavy breasts swinging almost through the window into the car.

"No, of course not, you foxy woman," he grinned at her and accepted the scrap of paper.

"I get off in an hour if you're still hanging about," she smiled at him, "and we could have some fun."

He gulped, but whether with relief the woman apparently had not seen the Berretta or the anxiety of becoming entangled with her, he wasn't certain. As diplomatically as he could, he waved the phone number back at her and said, "Let me fill up with fuel and...what door do you leave from when you finish work?"

She turned and pointing to a door at the side of the building, replied, "Just over there in oh, say fifty-five minutes?" and to his amazement, she reached in and with surprisingly soft fingers, gently stroked his cheek before turning and walking off.

He watched her return towards the building and with a smile, raised both hands palms upwards then clasping them to his chest, quietly muttered, "Oh, Allah, praise your name. Forgive me my lies, but the taqqiya was meant to save the woman embarrassment and despair if she were to become involved with a sinner such as I."

Seeing her approach the building, he bent over to place the Beretta in the glovebox and as she turned at the door, a little guiltily returned her wave before carefully driving off towards the garage to refuel the car and resuming his journey on the A14.

CHAPTER NINETEEN

DS Mo McInnes took the phone call from the Suffolk constable and thanking him, turned to her desktop PC and tapped in her password. There it was, his e-mail with the attachment and opening the attachment, saw the photograph of the rear of a dark coloured Nissan Qashqai with the registration number clearly visible.

She read the e-mail and saw that the constable, Harry Benson, had quite clearly indicated that that his CCTV inquiry led him to believe this might be the vehicle used by the van hirer, but stressed he was not absolutely certain.

However, he believed in all probability it *was* the vehicle used to convey the van hirer from the premises and listed his reasons for suspecting the Qashqai was used by the van hirer.

Benson had PNC'd the registration number of the Qashqai and discovered it was registered to a garage in Ipswich. Contacting the garage, he learned the car had been sold eight weeks earlier for cash to an Asian man in his late twenties or early thirties, but the details the man provided to the garage later proved to be false for when the garage tried to contact the man both by phone and letter to remind the purchaser to register the vehicle in his own name, the phone number was not known and the correspondence returned marked 'not at this address.'

However, suspecting the man to be local to Ipswich, Benson had caused the vehicle to be on a traffic watch list, both locally with his Force and also inserted an entry on the PNC, requesting officers stopping the vehicle determine the drivers identity and if necessary, seizing the vehicle, detaining the driver and contacting the Police Scotland terrorist incident room.

"Smart guy," McInnes nodded at the e-mail and printing it off, took the copy through to Lou Sheridan.

Reading the e-mail Sheridan nodded at the Suffolk constable's diligence and instructed McInnes that when the inquiry was finally concluded, she did not forget to phone Benson's divisional boss to commend his action on behalf of the inquiry.

"So," she laid the e-mail printout on his desk, "it's a waiting game to see when and if the driver of this Qashqai turns up."

"If nothing else, Ma'am, it suggests that the man who drove the van from the Waverly car park seems to be hiding something; trying to evade his identity being established. That seems suspicious to me."

"And to me, Mo," she agreed and wearily scratching her head, asked, "Anything else doing?"

"No. I'm aware that the press conference is ongoing. Any word back from Mister Glennie?"

"Not yet. He's there with Cathy Mulgrew and likely they'll give us a briefing when they come back to Helen Street this afternoon. How are the lads and lasses that are returning to their divisions taking it?"

"They're fine with it. Most of them have their own work to be getting on with anyway and I think they all realise that we've taken the inquiry as far as we can with a big team. It's now down to the nitty gritty bits, so we don't need everyone for that."

"Good. I know the boss wants to have a word before they leave and thank them for their efforts. For now though, let's hope that one of our Suffolk colleagues happens upon this bloody Qashqai."

Stopping at the outskirts of Ipswich, Eldar Umarov used the phone to Google local hotels and decided on a Travelodge in Duke Street that had on-site parking, but more importantly was less than three kilometres from Anglesea Road where his target Rahib Chowdhury lived.

Setting the Satnav, he made his way to the Travelodge and manoeuvring the car into a bay, ensured no one was watching as he slipped the Beretta and the magazines into his jacket pocket.

Opening the boot, he stuffed the shoulder holster into the suitcase and then made his way to the reception desk where he booked in with the pleasant young man who considerately provided him with a town map and recommended the Italian restaurant a little way down the road.

"I have some paperwork to complete, but have no stationary with me," Umarov smiled. "Where can I find somewhere that would sell such items, please?"

Eager to help, the receptionist suggested the convenience store that was located on Duke Street, two hundred metres away just past the traffic lights.

Thanking the young man, he made his way to his room where he stowed his suitcase, but decided to keep the handgun and ammunition with him. Taking the usual precaution with a strand of hair after locking the door, he visited the convenience store where he purchased a cheap, plastic folder, an A4 pad of lined paper, a pair of cheap, heavy framed reading glasses, a brightly coloured lanyard that was attached to a blank ID card holder.

Returning to the Travelodge with his purchases, he nodded to the receptionist and made his way to his room where he decided to have a rest before visiting the Italian restaurant.

Once fed, he would then plan his evening excursion.

Cathy Mulgrew accompanied John Glennie to the Helen Street office where gathering the team about them in the general office, Glennie reported that the press conference had been a success, though Ian Macleod had seemed a little surprised and confused at the attention he was getting.

"No problems regarding his, eh…" Paul Cowan pointed a forefinger at his own head and grinned.

"Shooting the gunmen in the head you mean," Glennie shook his head. "No, not really, though there was one guy, a Welsh reporter, but I didn't get what paper he was from," he turned quizzically towards Mulgrew, but she also shook her head. "Anyway, he asked if Mister Macleod had any regrets about killing those four men."

"What did he say, Boss?" someone called out from the back.

"He didn't get a chance to respond," Glennie smiled. "The rest of the reporters didn't sound to be too happy with the question and directed some of their own comments at the guy that to be frank, were less than kind. In fact," he grinned "I thought there was going to be an impromptu lynching. I didn't see the guy leave, but Harry Downes at the Media Department said he slunk away before the conference ended."

Mulgrew reached a hand to Glennie's arm to interrupt him and turning to the assembled team, said, "When the conference concluded, I spoke with Chief Inspector Downes. She thinks the guy was a plant; apparently it's not an uncommon ploy by extreme left wing journalists to ask provocative questions and provoke responses that can create a headline that derides not just the subject being interviewed, but the authorities in general. Harry Downes checked the invited journalists list after the conference and the man who asked the question seemingly provided genuine documents, but he's not known to the Media Department and had never before attended an interview at Dalmarnock. Anyway, he's on the Department's watch list from now on."

"But in general, Ma'am," Cowan continued, "Mister Macleod presented himself well at the interview?"

"Very well," she smiled.

"Right, ladies and gentlemen," Glennie slapped his hands loudly together, "as DCI Sheridan has already informed most of you, our investigation is now running down. Most of the inquiries have been completed and to a very high degree, ladies and gentlemen, and for that I thank you. I will continue to keep a small team here for now as there are some loose ends to tie up, but the majority of you will return either to your parent divisions or back to the CTU. Miss Mulgrew?" he turned to her and took a step back.

"To those of you who are winding up today, as Mister Glennie just said, we owe you all a vote of thanks for the hard work and effort you all put in. This inquiry is perhaps one of the largest inquiries the recently formed Police Scotland has investigated and while I accept there are still lines of inquiry that are open, most of the hard work is completed."

Behind her, DS Mo McInnes answered a ringing phone and spoke quietly into it as Mulgrew continued to thank the staff who were leaving.

"To those of you who have been seconded from CID units in the divisions, you have had an insight into the work that the CTU perform. If you have such an interest in that type of work," she smiled, "you can add this major inquiry to your CV."

McInnes scribbled details of the phone call onto a scrap of paper and catching DCI Lou Sheridan's eye, nodded towards the door that led to the corridor.

While the farewell continued in the general office, McInnes and Sheridan huddled together in the corridor where the DS said, "That was the controller of a police office in Ipswich, Ma'am. He was calling about an entry our Suffolk cop, Constable Benson, put on the PNC about the Qashqai."

"And?"

"One of the local beat cops has found the vehicle parked in a street called," she glanced at the scrap of paper, "Berners Street in Ipswich."

"Nobody with the vehicle?"

"No, apparently it's locked and parked on the roadway in that street. I asked what kind of area Berners Street is and he told me it's mostly private housing with quite a lot of rented properties, a few B and B's, narrow roads and a couple of local corner shops. Describes it as a quiet neighbourhood and they don't get too many calls there. Oh, and the cop's marked the vehicle," she grinned.

"Marked the vehicle?"

"The cop that found the car must be an old hand. The controller says that she's shoved something under one of the rear wheels so when she's back in that street and checks the car again, if it's been moved, she'll know."

"Smart woman," Sheridan nodded. "Right, get onto the local CID. Ask if they have the resources to assist with a surveillance on the vehicle and that we'll get the request on paper to their Chief Constable as soon as possible." She shrugged and then stood to one side as the general office began to empty as the officers began crowding out into the corridor. "Our priority is identifying and if it comes down to it, detaining the driver of that vehicle. Good work, Mo. I'll brief Ma'am and John Glennie."

They had been back in Daisy's house just a few minutes when Ian Macleod said, "You know at some point I'll need to return to my flat."

"Yes, of course," stood at the sink with her back to him as she filled the kettle, she smiled, but was a little uncertain how she felt about that. In the few short days she had known him, he had quite literally turned her life upside down.

"It doesn't mean we can't continue to see each other," he continued. "In fact, I *want* to continue to see you, Daisy."

She switched on the kettle and turning towards him replied, "How do you feel about me?"

"How do I feel about you?" his eyes widened. "Well, there's what, some years between us; I'm forty-one and you're what, thirtyish?"

"Thirty-five…almost."

"So, I'm an older guy," he grinned. "I'm unemployed and you have a career. I have some savings, but not enough to open my own place yet." He was about to raise a hand to his face when she cried out,

"Stop! Don't you dare give me any of that guff, Ian, about you being scarred and lame! I don't want to hear it! You proved to me that you are as much a man as anybody. In fact, in more ways than one," she couldn't help but smile, "so your physical appearance isn't an issue, okay?"

He raised both hand in surrender and agreed, "Okay."

"Back to my original question. How do you feel about me?"

He swallowed hard and slowly said, "You are the most exciting thing that has happened to me in a very long time. I just don't want to *see* you," he wagged his fingers in the air, "I want to be with you. Every day, in fact."

Ignoring the boiled kettle, she sat in the chair opposite him and reaching across the table, clasped his fingers in hers and decided that if she didn't speak now, tell him about her idea, she might never again have the nerve. Licking at her lips, she said, "This morning, when we, eh…"

"We were in bed together," he smiled at her.

"Yes, and very nice too, it was," she shyly returned his smile. "Well, when we were lying together, you told me again about your dream of opening your own place, but what you lacked is the capital, yes?"

"Yes. Like I told you, I have some savings, but just not enough and the bank would require a substantial deposit before they would grant me the money I needed to purchase a property."

"What if you had that kind of money, though?"

He stared at her and his eyes narrowed. Then crossing his hands back and forth, he firmly said, "No, Daisy, no way am I taking your money. Thank you and I love…" he stopped and swallowing with difficulty, said instead, "Thank you for it, but no. End of argument."

"It's not an argument, you idiot," she grinned at him, "it's a proposal."

"Proposal?" he suddenly smiled at her as though surprised, before adding, "Shouldn't you be down on one knee, Constable Daisy?"

"Aye, very good, smart arse," she retorted, then more seriously, continued, "What I'm *suggesting* is use your flat as the deposit."

"What, you mean try for a mortgage on the flat?" he frowned. "No, that wouldn't work. I'd then have a mortgage on the flat and possibly a mortgage on the property I purchase. I'd never get clear of that kind of financial commitment. Any profit from the café would be used to pay the mortgages."

"No, I mean sell your flat. You told me you own it outright, don't you?"

"Yes," he slowly drawled.

"Well, if the money you make on the sale of the flat isn't enough to buy the property outright and refit it as you need, then it will at least be enough for the deposit if you should require to take out a bank loan or a mortgage."

"Aye, I see where you're going with this, Daisy, and it's a good idea, but you're forgetting one thing. If I sell the flat, where will I live?"

Their fingers were still entwined and gently squeezing them tighter, she smiled and replied, "Here with me, of course."

Back in his office, Barry Ashford sat on the couch in front of the small flat screen mounted on the wall and expressionlessly watching the recorded news interview of the man called Ian Macleod, the veteran soldier who had so dramatically, yet unknowingly ruined his plan to undermine the Scottish Government.

"Bastard," he hissed at the scarred face on the screen.

Much as he so dearly wished to send Ernie and the Welshman after Macleod to exact a bloody revenge upon the man, it would be irrational and a complete waste of time and only succeed in further enhancing Macleod's hero status.

He used the remote to switch off the set and arched his aching back, briefly considering sending for his secretary whose nimble-fingered dexterity at massage was as competent as her proficiency on the keyboard. She had been a lucky find when he trawled the Service for an appropriate secretary; beautiful, discreet and most of all, willing to visit him at his flat and do that much more for her master.

But alas no, for he had things to do and rising from the couch, thought more of the loose ends he had to tie together.

The policeman Brompton worried him. The Suffolk detective was a definite weak link and one that he must deal with before the nervous fool developed a crisis of conscience and opened his mouth to the wrong person.

Seated behind his desk, he arched his fingers in front of his nose and considered the problem.

The botched murder of Khalifa had created too much interest and while he was angry with his bodyguards for the slack way they had dealt with the situation, he had to admit they had little time to make proper preparation and in fairness, they *did* get the job done.

Rahib Chowdhury crossed his mind and he hissed, for Chowdhury was another concern that must also be retired.

Ernie had suggested retiring him sooner than later, but he had overruled the former Marine's anxiety for in the back of his mind, he believed that Chowdhury might still have a usefulness.

That's when the beginning of an idea began to take shape and he smiled.

He was absolutely certain there was nothing to connect either the Service or him personally with the detective Brompton and while the dead woman Khalifa had not apparently discovered a link between him and Chowdhury, she represented a real and possible threat to the security of his operation and thus not just to him personally, but also to the Service.

Presumably when she discovered Brompton's arrest and release of Chowdhury she had grown suspicious and if her reputation as a tenacious and bright detective had been correct, it would not have taken her too long to discover Chowdhury's addiction to child pornography. Brompton's almost naive enthusiasm to assist the Security Service had been pathetic and procuring his assistance with Chowdhury had been so very easy. Regretfully, it had been his instruction to Brompton to release the paedophile without charge that had obviously piqued Khalifa's interest and tenacious though she quite obviously been, he could not permit her to continue her inquiry.

Her death had simply been an expedient necessity, but such a pity that she died before confirming her suspicions with DC Ball.

He smiled at his own brilliance then rolled the new idea about his mind.

What if Brompton is discovered murdered and with an envelope full of cash, he wondered?

There was little doubt that the investigating officers would delve into Brompton's case file and if they were doing their job properly, likely discover what Khalifa had discovered. He could even have Clare Ball drop a hint that before she died, Khalifa mentioned some kind of connection between the two men.

Yes, he nodded, that sounded more plausible.

Then let's say Mister Chowdhury finds the guilt of is perversions too overwhelming and decides to end it all.

Yes, he again unconsciously nodded, that definitely sounds like the beginning of a plan.

The Chief Constable of Police Scotland was at his desk, watching a recording of the news conference on the television bolted to the small, wheeled table when his intercom rang.

"Yes?"

"Sir, that's a call from the Commissioner at the Metropolitan Police. Are you agreeable to receive the call?"

He smiled at his secretary's fortitude and believed no matter that it might be Her Majesty herself calling, she would not get through to him without the prim and humourless woman first screening the call.

"Yes, please put him through," he replied.

Almost immediately, the phone rung and he greeted the Commissioner who replied, "That matter we spoke of when you visited me, Chief Constable…"

Instantly alert, Cairney realised that the Commissioner's observance of formality must mean that either he was with someone he didn't trust or more likely as they had discussed during Cairney's visit, the Commissioner did not trust the telephone.

"Yes, Commissioner, I do recall," he replied.

"The officer I spoke of is currently assessing the situation," he spoke slowly, "and displeased with some aspects of his current post. I await further information and when that information is received by me I will advise you as per our agreement."

Cairney realised he must soon expect a visitor, a senior ranking officer trusted by the Commissioner.

"That's very kind of you to contact me, Commissioner," he carefully replied, "and I await your next contact."

They concluded the call with some pleasantries and replacing the handset, Cairney was thoughtful. The Commissioner's man inside the team investigating the murder of DI Khalifa was apparently unhappy with how the investigation was proceeding and wondered was it to do with the actual method of the investigators or something more sinister within the Counter Terrorist Unit?

Well, he sighed, there was one person he needed to tell of the call and lifting his mobile phone, dialled the number for Cathy Mulgrew.

He awoke as the sun was setting, the hotel room bathed in a dull shadow that cast across the bed.

He shivered slightly in the coolness of the dimly lit room and calculated from the shadow which direction was east before settling himself onto his knees for Maghrib.

His prayers finished and while the kettle boiled for coffee, he fetched the blank card holder from the plastic bag. Seated at the desk sipping at the coffee, he carefully and painstakingly printed the passport name 'Fernand Marchand' in bold letters and underneath, the word 'Representative.'

Attaching the card holder to the lanyard, he knew it would not pass a close examination, but in the dim light guessed not many people would give it a second glance.

He used his phone to access the Google Instant Street View to determine where number nineteen Anglesea Road was located and marked the house location on the town street map the young receptionist had provided him with.

That done, he decided to take the young receptionists advice and visit the Italian restaurant to dine before venturing out later that evening to visit the man called Rahib Chowdhury.

CHAPTER TWENTY

After much discussion and a few heated moments of disagreement, Ian Macleod had at last gracefully decided to accept Daisy's proposal and said, "Well, if we're going to be partners in more than the biblical sense of the word," he coyly grinned at her, "I think we should celebrate with dinner, but only if you agree that I'm on the bell and I choose where we dine."

"Yes, please," she returned his grin. "To be honest, the day just seems to have dragged on and I'm feeling worn out. That and the number of calls I've had to field from everyone who wants to know about you and congratulate you."

"Right, are you ready to go then?"

Bemused, she stared at him. "What, you mean right now? Without getting dressed up or anything?"

"You're fine as you are, believe me," he smiled.

Her brow wrinkled and glancing down at her grey sweater and blue jeans, she replied, "I take it we're not off to anywhere swanky then?"

"Believe me, you'll love it," he teased her.

"Yeah," she stared suspiciously at him, "do I drive or how do we get there?"

"It's not too far," he brightly smiled. "We can take your car unless that's a problem."

"So, I won't be having wine with my diner, then?"

"Eh, no. No alcohol for either of us. We can save that for when we return home."

"Home? You mean here? So you consider this your home now?"

"Anywhere you are is home," he reached across and took her in his arms, "so grab your jacket and let's go."

Sitting in her parked car at Helen Street, Cathy Mulgrew listened on the car speaker as Martin Cairney related his brief conversation with the Metropolitan Commissioner.

"I assume, sir, that you believe the Commissioner's inside man has discovered something, but he was worried that to disclose it on the phone might compromise his officer."

"That's exactly how I read it."

"Okay, sir."

"Any other news for me?"

"You recall the Transit van that was seen to quickly depart from the Waverly car park in Edinburgh?"

"The Skoda Octavia you believe might have been used as a getaway vehicle by your mysterious fifth man and then the van that you assess was used by the driver of the Octavia?"

"That's correct, sir. Well, we were fortunate to obtain a registration number for the Transit van that identified it as a hire vehicle from a premises in Ipswich. As a result of that identification, one of John Glennie's people, a DS McInnes, was in touch over the last day or so with a constable of the Suffolk Constabulary and I'm pleased to report that the constable came up trumps with what seems to be a definite lead for the driver of the hired van. Unfortunately, we don't have a name or address yet, however, we have what seems to be a vehicle that we believe is the van driver's current vehicle; a Nissan Qashqai."

"And this Qashqai currently is where?"

"As of an hour ago the vehicle is parked in a side street in Ipswich. The driver didn't re-register the vehicle that he bought for cash…"

"That's suspicious right away," mused Cairney.

"Aye, well, McInnes's man, this Constable Benson, put the Qashqai registration number on the PNC and requested a local lookout too and that's how we got onto it. McInnes has contacted the local CID and asked them to monitor the Qashqai and identify or detain the driver when he arrives at the vehicle."

"Another bloody waiting game," he growled.

"Regretfully, yes sir, but hopefully this time with a positive result."

"Well, good work anyway by both DS McInnes and this the Suffolk officer. Keep me apprised, Cathy, of any developments."

"Sir," she acknowledge before ending the call.

At Ian Macleod's instruction, Daisy Cooper drove through the city towards the West End and at last, her curiosity killing her, parked in an empty space in Great George Street thirty yards from its junction with Byres Road.

"Come on, Ian, tell me," she insisted. "Where the heck are we going?"

He grinned and trying with difficulty to contain his excitement, replied, "It's a surprise, but I'm certain you'll like it."

She locked the car and reaching, took his hand as he led her towards Byres Road.

Grinning widely, she shook her head and said, "God, you're like a wean on a sugar rush. I'm starving, Macleod! Where the hell are you taking me?"

Almost pulling her, they crossed the road at the pedestrian crossing and then his hand on her waist, he spun her quickly round and with his free hand pointed across the road to the boarded windows of the premises on the corner.

"What am I looking at?" she asked, confused.

"Our new café," he beamed.

Her eyes opened wide, his enthusiasm infectious and she could not but help grin with him.

"So, *that's* my dinner date?"

He turned and a little uncertainly, stared at her. "You don't like it!"

"No, that's not it at all," she smiled and oblivious to the curious stares of the passers-by, wrapped her arms about his neck as she stared up at him. "You love it and because of that, so do I."

"Really?"

"Yes, Ian, really. Now, will I have to wait for it to open as a café or do you intend feeding me?"

Walking with her arm in arm to the restaurant in the nearby Ashton Lane, he excitedly told her of the plans he had for the café, recounting his meetings with the vendor and of being crushed when he learned that the price sought was beyond his means.

"But now, well," he shrugged, "if we move in together we can afford our own place. Me and you, Daisy. Together. Or own business."

She was inwardly thrilled that when he spoke of the café, of the plans he had for the premises, it was as a couple, a partner; an equal.

After a quick meal, Eldar Umarov returned to his room where deciding to remain in his shirt and tie, he slid the Berretta into the shoulder holster and tried it on. Checking his reflection in the long wall mounted mirror, he adjusted the shoulder holster for comfort then shrugged into his suit jacket and examined his profile, pleased that the weapon did not appear unduly bulky.

Collecting his lightweight, dark coloured raincoat from the wardrobe, he lifted the card holder with its lanyard, the heavy rimmed reading glasses and the plastic folder.

With a final glance around the room, he locked the door behind him and again used his spit to place a strand of hair across the door jamb.

He ignored the BMW, for the route to Anglesea Road was already memorised and at a quick pace began to make his way there.

As he walked he thought about the man he was hunting.

Rahib Chowdhury.

The name suggested Pakistani origin and more than likely, Muslim. If his assessment was correct, that Chowdhury was associated with those murdering pariah who had professed to be believers, then may Allah, praise His name, deal in the afterlife with them as He sees fit. Of course, he could be wrong; Chowdhury might have had nothing to do with the attack in the city of Glasgow and might even be as innocent as was his Malika.

Thoughts of his daughter brought a knot to his stomach.

That his beloved Malika should be killed so far from home…so far from her father and everything that she loved.

His throat tightened as visions of his daughter flashed before his eyes; Malika as a child, Malika's first day attending school with her hand tightly held in his and yet it was the image of Malika as a rebellious teenager that caused him to smile.

He was unaware he was smiling and shaking his head as he recalled the many quarrels they had during those teen years; conscious that he would gladly now give his very life for one more opportunity to argue with her, to hold her and to tell her that no matter what occurred between them he never stopped loving her.

Just under fifteen minutes later, Umarov arrived in Graham Road and walked to the junction that connected the road with the nearby Anglesea Road.

Pulling on the dark coloured raincoat, he tugged the name badge and the lanyard out from under his suit jacket to hang outside his coat and slipping on the heavy framed reading glasses, held the folder prominently against his chest with his right arm

It was a disguise that would not stand up to any close scrutiny, but he believed that in the twilight and from a distance, to the casual observer he would present the appearance of a door caller.

Turning the corner from Graham Road into Anglesea Road he hesitated for almost immediately he saw the darkened car with the silhouette of two men sitting in the front seats. To confirm his suspicion, he watched as the faint glow of a lighter or a match was struck for a cigarette.

He faltered and glancing about him could not see any other vehicle with any persons aboard, but knew that did not mean they were not there.

He had memorised the layout of the area around Anglesea Road and turned quickly to walk off in the opposite direction of the watchers. Five minutes later, a lengthy circular route found him approaching Anglesea Road from Berners Street, but to his frustration saw a second darkened car with two persons inside the car that faced away from his direction of approach.

He stopped and found a position in the shadow of a hedgerow where he could stand and consider his next move.

His brow furrowed.

It was odd that the second car was not also watching the address in Anglesea Road and stood under a dim street lamp, Umarov opened the folder and checked the street map.

His fingers traced where he had marked the location of Chowdhury's house at number nineteen with an X and he frowned.

According to the map he scanned, if Chowdhury were to leave his house then the watchers in the second car in Berners Street would not necessarily have a clear indication of his departure. He was in no doubt the watchers were there for Chowdhury, but what did this mean, he wondered?

Did the watchers have some other means that would alert them to Chowdhury's movements or, it suddenly crossed his mind, they were not *actually* watching Chowdhury, but something else; something connected with Chowdhury?

He startled when out of the darkness an elderly woman walking a small white dog approached from behind him.

Warily, she cast an eye at the tall man who smiled and said, "Good evening, Madam." He waved the map at her and still smiling, continued, "I'm a bit lost. My company told me that Anglesea Road is around here somewhere, but I have become a little disorientated with all these streets."

The dog stared curiously at Umarov as the woman uncertainly replied, "It can be a little confusing and especially at this time of the evening in the dark. You are in Berners Street and," she waved with her hand, "Anglesea Road is just a little further on."

"I am *so* grateful," he gushed at her and the now growling dog. "I am sorry that your dog does not seem to like me."

"Oh, she's just a bit nervous of strangers," the woman answered, now reassured by the tall man's politeness and smiling, nodded as she continued on her way.

He breathed a sigh of relief and quickly dismissed the woman and her dog from his mind while again he studied him map.

He tried to recall his training from all those years ago when he had been recruited by the Moscow FSB.

If not the house at number nineteen, what else would the watchers be interested in?

He glanced about him and closing his eyes, inwardly cursed himself for his stupidity.

The street was full of vehicles and it was obvious.

One of the two watching cars was possibly surveilling a vehicle with the other vehicle acting as a cut off car if the vehicle moved.

But whether that vehicle was in Anglesea Road or here in Berners Street, he could not know nor what vehicle.

Unconsciously shaking his head, he decided it did not matter what vehicle the watching cars were interested in.

But it also posed the question. Was there some sort of watch being conducted on Chowdhury's house, perhaps from a static observation point located in a nearby house?

Were the two vehicles he saw merely cut-off vehicles waiting for word of Chowdhury departing from his house?

He could not know and it was useless to speculate, deciding that he had come too far now to not call at nineteen Anglesea Road.

It was Chowdhury that he needed to interrogate, but realised that if he had discovered two watching vehicles there might possibly be more and that brought on a further question.

Who were the watchers?

Were they police or more likely because the attack in Glasgow was terrorism, were they the secret police; the British MI5?

No matter who they were, he would need to move with extreme caution and ensure he clean himself of any tail when he returned to the hotel.

Licking at his lips, he made sure his badge and brightly coloured lanyard were visible and with his folder clasped against his chest, decided to brazenly walk towards the address at number nineteen.

If the watchers saw or paid any attention to him, he mentally crossed fingers they would simply see what appeared to be a door caller; or so he hoped.

Detective Sergeant Mo McInnes glanced at the wall clock.

She was well past her time for home and yawned. It had been a long day and now this, but she had no right to complain.

It was her due to her good fortune the Qashqai vehicle had been identified and so as the direct contact for the Suffolk CID who had agreed to monitor the Qashqai, it was down to her to remain on duty.

"Penny for them," said the voice at her back.

She turned and seeing Cathy Mulgrew was about to respectfully rise to her feet, but was waved back down by Mulgrew who pulled over a chair to sit beside her.

"Evening, Ma'am," she nodded towards the older woman.

"I take it apart from the nightshift guy over there manning the phone," Mulgrew nodded to the young civilian analyst reading a newspaper, "that you're the last man standing?"

"Something like that," McInnes grinned. "I volunteered to stay on just in case the Suffolk CID identify our driver. Mister Glennie instructed that if there is no word by midnight, to get myself home and leave the nightshift to take any calls."

"Where's home?"

"Oh, my husband and me and our toddler son have a three bedroom detached over in Baillieston. We're in a wee housing estate. Jagger Gardens just off Mount Vernon Avenue."

"I know Mount Vernon Avenue, but I'm not that familiar with the estate," sighed Mulgrew and arched her back, then rubbed at her aching neck. "It's been a long day," she smiled.

"Aye, I was just thinking that myself," replied McInnes.

"What does your man do? Is he in the job?"

"He's a Traffic constable working out of Motherwell office."

"Can't be easy, the two of you working different shifts."

"Between the two of us and my mother-in-law acting as a childminder, we get by," she smiled, then commented, "I understand the press conference went well, that Mister Macleod presented himself well."

"Indeed he did," agreed Mulgrew who then smiled knowingly and added, "I admit to being a little surprised to see the young constable, Daisy Cooper, there with him."

"What," McInnes stare wide-eyed at Mulgrew, the hint of a bit of gossip appealing to her feminine instinct, "the young cop from Stewart Street that he saved?"

"Yes. I think there's the beginning of a romance there," Mulgrew grinned.

"Good for him," nodded McInnes. "There's a real feeling among the team, Ma'am, that the threat that was hanging over him was unnecessary."

"We must go where the law dictates though, Mo, and that's just the way of it," shrugged Mulgrew, who continued, "However, the real reason I popped in before I go home is to say that was good work with the Qashqai. If we identify the driver and he *does* prove to be an associate of the four, the fifth man as it were, then it might be the only real lead we have left."

"Thank you and fingers crossed, Ma'am," agreed McInnes who twisted her mouth and asked, "What if the driver of the Qashqai does prove to be a dead end. Is that the inquiry completed?"

"I would think so," sighed Mulgrew who then added, "apart from the interview that's still to be conducted with Mister Chowdhury."

McInnes brow creased. "DI Cowan. He took the death of the Met woman, DI Khalifa, pretty bad, Ma'am. We're hearing rumours in the office that her murder might be associated with her inquiry about this guy Chowdhury."

Mulgrew's hesitation was enough for McInnes who watched as her boss grimaced before replying, "Let's just say the poor woman's murder was too coincidental to *be* a coincidence, if you take my point."

Pressing her luck, McInnes asked, "Do you have any suspicions who might be responsible?"

"What," Mulgrew softly smiled, "you don't believe the Met press release that it might have been a random homicide?"

"Not for a second, Ma'am," McInnes solemnly shook her head.

"Well, without evidence Detective Sergeant McInnes," she formerly replied before rising to her feet and lifting her handbag from the floor, "there's not much I can say. However, what we might believe or might think and …"

"What we can prove. Yes, Ma'am," McInnes interrupted and nodded, "I think I understand."

Mulgrew smiled. "Again, good work on the Qashqai, Mo, and safely home tonight," she said before turning and making her way from the room.

Leaving the Ashton Lane restaurant, both her arms gripping his left arm, she snuggled into Ian Macleod and said, "Let's have another look at those premises before we return home."

"Okay, Constable Daisy," he grinned at her.

Caught up in Ian's excitement, she was now firmly with him in his plans to renovate and open the corner premises as a café.

Initially, she had her doubts and had pointed out the number of food outlets in the area, but he reminded her of the number of people who used the Byres Road area both during the week and at weekends.

"There's plenty of opportunity for a hospitable café," he had said.

"A place where Ma, Pa and the weans and students from Glasgow Uni over there," he nodded backwards to where the ancient university was located, "living on a tight budget can obtain good, wholesome food. Nothing too fancy," he had shaken his head, "and certainly not fancy prices. A common folk's café," he had grinned.

As they walked, she thought again of their meal in the busy restaurant. Finished eating, they had sat on for almost another twenty minutes, sipping at the coffees and discussing a theme for their project.

Ian favoured a Glasgow theme with prints of old Byres Road and the surrounding area while Daisy suggested one or perhaps two walls be decorated with the work of local artists and on behalf of the artists, offering the art for sale. "What I mean," she explained, "is we not only involve the local community, but it would attract customers who might be interested in purchasing the artwork too."

It was when they called the young waitress across to settle the bill that she shyly smiled and raising her hand, said, "Can you hold on for a minute, please," before disappearing towards the rear kitchen.

To their surprise, a moment later an elderly grey haired and bearded man hobbling on a stick and wearing spotless whites approached the table, followed deferentially by a woman of similar age, the waitress and three young male's, two of whom were also wearing immaculate white chef uniforms.

The other diners, curious at the assembly of the staff at Ian and Daisy's table, watched in silence as bowing slightly, the old man greeted them with, "As-salāmu ʿalaykum."

Taken aback, Ian nodded and replied, "Waʿalaykumu s-salām."

Turning to the older of the young men, the man spoke rapidly in what Ian thought was Urdu.

The young man nodded and smiled and in a broad Glasgow accent, interpreted, "My grandfather recognises you from the tele, Mister Macleod, and wishes you to know that your money is no good here, that you and your lady will always be welcome."

The old man again spoke at length and was interpreted by his grandson, who continued, "He says that your bravery and courage in dealing with the men who killed our Christian friends will be celebrated in all the mosques in the land by the true believers in Islam."

Speechless, Ian could only nod as the old man reached out to grasp his hands and pat him upon the shoulder before turning away.

Then to his acute embarrassment and with his face burning bright red, the other diners and the staff all broke into a spontaneous applause.

One middle-aged man, his camera phone in his hand, left his table with the intention of asking for a 'selfie' with Ian, but was courteously and firmly intercepted by a waiter who sensing Ian's discomfort at the attention, with a smile persuaded the man to return to his table.

Taking a deep breath, Ian stood and nodded at the applause then with Daisy almost rushed from the restaurant.

Now still a bit dumbstruck with Daisy grinning at him, they stood staring at the corner premises that they hoped would be their new café.

After a last inspection of the boarded up premises, they headed towards her car and home.

The two detectives sitting in the unmarked car in Anglesea Road were bored. The last radio check from their colleagues sitting in the unmarked car Berners Street had indicated nothing was happening there either, that the Qashqai their colleagues watched had neither moved nor had anyone approached it.

"This is a lot of crap," whined the younger of the two who slumped in the passenger seat was annoyed at missing the party at his girlfriend's house.

The older detective's eyes narrowed and he idly glanced at the tall man wearing a raincoat who though still over a hundred yards away, was walking purposefully in the narrow road on the opposite footway towards the car.

Ignoring his colleague's complaining, he mumbled, "Who's this then?"

As they watched, the man stopped and head down, appeared to be checking something on a clipboard or folder, his head bobbing up and down as he glanced about him. Something brightly coloured was hanging around his neck.

"Bravo Two to Bravo One," the driver spoke into the microphone. "We've a guy walking towards us. Looks like he's checking doors or something. Tall, wearing a dark coat."

"Yeah, Bravo Two," replied the bored female voice. "He passed us by a few minutes ago. Some kind of rep I think. He's got an ID card on a lanyard round his neck. Likely double glazing sales or something."

"Oh, okay then, Bravo One. If he offers a police discount, get his business card," the driver replied to laughter and yawning widely, replaced the microphone into its bracket.

Nerves stretched tensely and tempted through he was, Eldar Umarov ignored the watchers in the vehicle no more than thirty metres away and counted down the door numbers till at last he was outside number nineteen.

He made a pretence of checking the folder then subtly unbuttoned his coat and suit jacket.

The wooden door, its red coat of paint now flaked and peeling, had no bell nor name on it though a plastic sign screwed a little lopsidedly to one panel indicated that hawkers and unsolicited callers were unwelcome. Leaning forward, the folder covering his hand, he gently tried the door handle only to find as he expected, it was locked.

He clutched the folder firmly in his left hand against his chest for if it became necessary it would leave his right hand free to retrieve the Berretta from the shoulder holster for he did not know what awaited him behind the locked door.

His stomach knotting, he forced a broad smile and knocked loudly. A moment passed and he thought that perhaps nobody was at home. Anxious and apprehensive, he dare not turn his head, but worried that his ruse had failed and the watchers in the car were now fast approaching when to his relief, the door opened a crack. A young woman's face stared curiously out at him and seeing she wore a white coloured hijab, grey blouse and full length dark coloured skirt he greeted her with, "As-salāmu ʿalaykum, sister. I have been asked to come and visit with Mister Chowdhury?"

She did not respond and he asked, "Do you speak English, sister?" She nodded, but guessed she was fearful of making eye contact.

He could see the uncertainty in her face and realising that she was unlikely to open the door to a strange man, he added, "It is of vital importance that I speak with him, sister. Is he at home?"

He watched as her face full of doubt, she turned her head inwards to the house and taking the opportunity he pushed through the door, but not so quickly as to hurt the slightly built woman, though she did stumble back, her eyes betraying her alarm.

Before she could scream Umarov had dropped the folder and using his heel, kicked the door closed then clamping a hand over her mouth and his arm about her waist, held her slight body close and whispered, "I will not hurt you, sister, but I *must* speak with Rahib." He could sense her fear and then a man's voice called out from upstairs, "Rabia! Who was at the door? Rabia!"

Umarov twisted the frightened and compliant woman around, his eyes staring at the stairs that led to the first floor. Holding her arm behind her back and with his hand still clasped at her mouth, he leaned forward and whispered, "Call him downstairs and do not be foolish, sister. Please, do as I say and you will not be harmed." He slowly released his hand from her mouth, but her terror had choked her and without spit, she could not reply.

"Rabia! Answer me you foolish woman!"

He could hear the sound of a chair being scraped back and footsteps as Chowdhury impatiently began to descend the stairs.

His right hand free, Umarov carefully withdrew the Berretta from the shoulder holster and holding the handgun by his side, awaited his first glimpse of Chowdhury.

He watched as the first the legs, torso, then the head and shoulders descended the stairs.

Chowdhury's eyes widened and turned from alarm to fear when he saw the tall man who tightly held Rabia against him.

"What the…who are you?" he almost screamed at Umarov and was about to advance upon the tall man who slowly raised the Berretta and pointed it at the shocked Chowdhury's head.

"As-salāmu ʿalaykum, brother. My name is Eldar Umarov," he softly replied, his face expressionless, "and I have a number of questions for you. Now," he waved the gun at Chowdhury, "why don't we go through to your lounge where we can sit and talk and you can tell me all that you know about the attack in Glasgow."

CHAPTER TWENTY-ONE

The bar within the exclusive Special Forces Club in Knightsbridge was quiet for that time of the evening.

Seated with his back to the wall at a table in the corner, Barry Ashford awaited the arrival of his bodyguards; Ernie, the former Royal Marine and Taff, Ernie's Welsh colleague who had once served with the Airborne Brigade.

He didn't particularly enjoy meeting in the Special Forces Club, but the one thing that the place guaranteed was anonymity. Even though most of the individuals who used the club were familiar to each other, there was always the possibility that the occasional invited guest would eavesdrop or that a member would discuss who he had overheard or whom he might have seen within the club.

As for his bodyguards, he neither liked nor disliked either man and even though they had served him for almost ten years, considered them to be no more than a resource that he would and on many unrecorded occasions did utilise for what the Americans had come to term, 'black bag operations.'

It did not concern Ashford that the two men disliked him; their sentiments were irrelevant as long as they did what he instructed and without question. Their official function on the Service payroll was as janitorial staff; a cover that masked their true occupation as hired muscle who at the beck and call of Ashford, were often tasked to perform clandestine operations such as burglary, theft or retiring individuals deemed by the Service or Ashford in particular, as a threat to national security. In this role they were above the law and even Ashford had to admit, damned good at what they did.

He sipped at his fifteen year old Glengoyne single malt and thought of the salary each man drew that was commensurate with their employment; a salary that he knew provided them comfortably though he had no interest in their private lives.

Over the preceding month he had thought long and hard about the two men and with a little reluctance, formed plans for the bodyguards own retirement. He was acutely aware that while he kept an extremely private record of the murders they had committed on behalf of the Service, but of course with no noted connection to himself, they were *also* privy to his part in authorising and condoning those murders.

Thus, with some regret for they had been faithful servants, when he assumed his rightful place as the Director General of the Security Service he would as a matter of urgency necessitate the recruitment of two replacements; for after all, he couldn't have Ernie and the Welshman holding any kind of influence over the newly appointed DG.

However, for the time being both men would continue to serve him hence this evenings meeting.

He glanced up and saw that they had arrived, both stood at the bar and ordering their drinks; ale for the Welshman and coffee for the teetotal Ernie.

He watched as they made their way to take up seats facing him.

"Good evening, gentlemen," he greeted them.

"Sir," they acknowledged him in unison.

"The issue we recently discussed," he spoke quietly, "about our reluctant organiser of the Glasgow attack, Mister Chowdhury. I believe it is time that he be retired, however, there is one more little favour we must ask of him."

Ernie glanced briefly at Taff, his eyes narrowing and said, "Don't you think it might be a little too soon, sir?"

He sighed and replied, "How so?"

"Well, after retiring the police woman, what if her colleagues investigating her murder realise that she was onto Chowdhury. Won't that lead them back to us?"

He swallowed deeply, wondering why the fool believed that he could question someone like him and replied, "For one, my dear fellow, there *is* no direct connection between the Service and Chowdhury, so pray tell me; how exactly can those dolts at Scotland Yard backtrack to us?"

Ernie didn't answer, but simply bowed his head. His overriding wish was to take Ashford's head and bounce it several times off the laminated table then tear his fucking arm off and beat him to death with the soggy end, but he kept his cool and said nothing.

"Now, perhaps you might indulge me and permit me to relate my plan, yes?"

"Sir," Ernie replied.

"The detective, this man Brompton in Ipswich. I want you to monitor his movements over a period of forty-eight hours. However, do not commence the surveillance until such times I have met with Chowdhury. I still have to persuade him to…" he smiled, "to retire DC Brompton and after he has done so, you gentlemen will arrange that Mister Chowdhury will meet his own, dear Allah."

The detectives in the unmarked CID parked in Anglesea Road were not just bored, but the younger man needed to piss and besides that, he was starving too.

"I told you to bring a sandwich with you," his partner reminded him.

"Yeah, well I didn't think we'd be here all bleeding night," he whined.

"Look, it's really dark now," the driver said, "Nip out to a bush if you need to take a pee. The place is dead quiet. Nobody will see you."

"That's all very well, but what about getting something to eat?"

"Well," the driver slowly drawled, "there's a Tesco Express on Norwich Road across from the junction at Sherrington Road and a there's a couple of takeaways there too; a chippy and a Chinese."

"Okay," the younger man sighed. "Take me there, then."

"What," the driver laughed. "Drive you? No way, I'm not leaving here. What if someone approaches the Qashqai and we're off getting grub? If you want food, me old son, you'll need to hoof it there."

"You mean I need to walk there?"

The driver grinned and shook his head. "Fuck me, you *are* a detective after all."

In the dimly lit lounge of the mid-terraced house along the road at number nineteen, Eldar Umarov, his raincoat lying neatly folded on the floor beside him with the folder on top, sat comfortably in the armchair while Rahib and Rabia Chowdhury sat together on the couch, facing him. He darted a curious glance at the fading bruise below the young woman's left eye, but made no comment.

Umarov's hand retained a hold of the Berretta that lay in his lap. The young woman had stopped crying and was now suffering a spell of hiccups brought on by her weeping and her fear.

"Sister," Umarov softly addressed her, "I will not harm you if you give me your word that you will not try to escape and you swear this upon the holy name of Allah, praise His name."

She stared curiously at him as though doubting him, then lowered her gaze and slowly nodding hiccupped, "I swear upon the holy name of Allah."

"Then perhaps you might consider getting yourself a glass of water for your hiccups and making some tea while I speak with your husband?"

Through narrowed eyes, she stared curiously at Umarov before nodding and watched by her husband, rose slowly from the couch, her eyes now settled upon the handgun resting in Umarov's lap. Stumbling towards the kitchen door, she stopped when he called out to her, "Please, sister, leave the door open."

She did as she was asked and he turned towards Chowdhury, but before he could speak, the mobile phone in his pocket activated. Before he retrieved the phone from his suit jacket pocket, he lifted the handgun so that the barrel pointed towards Chowdhury then answered the call, but without the usual four minute warning.

"You can speak?" asked the voice.

"Yes."

"My friend tell me there is no further news yet. My friend also tell me that detectives investigating woman's murder not happy it was...word, not sure. Random?"

"The murder was not random," he slowly repeated as he digested the information, then said, "Yes, I understand."

"My friend think detectives think woman killed because woman work for Scottish police people."

Umarov's eyes narrowed and he deliberately asked. "The dead woman was acting for the Scottish police about the man Chowdhury?"

At the mention of his name, Chowdhury's face turned pale and he gulped, an action that did not go unnoticed by Umarov who inwardly smiled.

Rabia Chowdhury, carrying a tray upon which sat two mugs of tea and a glass of water, returned to the lounge and placed the tray onto a low table then her hands clasped in front of her, stood quietly while Umarov continued his phone call.

Adding nothing to what Umarov already knew, the caller concluded with, "Do you have a new number for me?"

Umarov sighed and said, "Not yet. I will contact you tomorrow," then glancing at Chowdhury, added, "I am about to speak with my new friend."

Rabia Chowdhury, standing nervously by the small table, stared at Umarov as he turned to her and quietly said, "Sister, I have no issues with you. Do you have a mobile phone?"

She shook her head and her voice almost a whisper, replied, "No, my husband does not believe women should have such things."

"I believe you," he smiled to reassure her and added, "If you will, please go to your bedroom and tightly close the door. I wish to speak with Rahib and please Allah, praise His name, if Rahib answers me truthfully I will not harm him and then I will go and leave you in peace. Do you believe me, sister?"

Her back to her husband, her eyes narrowed and he thought that behind them was the hint of a smile.

"I believe you, brother," she replied, then with a slight nod of her head added, "Ma`a as-salāma."

She nodded and lifting the glass of water from the tray, demurely bowed to Umarov and left the room.

When she had left he glanced about the room, at the gaudy wallpaper, the tacky prints hung upon the walls, the cheap furnishing and the scuffed and worn carpet. Even the armchair upon which he sat was threadbare. No, he inwardly thought, this is not the home of a man who had orchestrated the attack in Glasgow. However, his connection with the dead men and his interest to the Scottish police and in particular the dead detective; *that* made Chowdhury of interest to Umarov.

Turning to the frightened man, he said, "Now that we are together, brother, perhaps you might explain to me exactly what it is that you know of the attack in Glasgow?"

"I know nothing of such an attack," he almost choked the response out.

"Then let me explain," Umarov softly said, leaning forward with the gun still lying loosely in his lap. "I do not believe you brother, so here is what I intend to do. You heard me tell your dear wife that I will not harm either of you if you tell me the truth and what I wish to know. That is correct, but only if you are truthful. First, you need to know I have killed many men. Some women too," he added with a shrug and calmly added, "But mostly men. I have no compunction about killing those I believe have or might hurt me or mine. You might also wish to know that the reason I am here is not for the Scottish police or for any police, but for revenge. You see, brother, one of the victims in Glasgow…was my daughter."

The simple admission was what broke the terrified man.

Chowdhury's blood run cold and he almost fainted for he knew then that the tall man was not acting in the name of any law, but for intiqām; revenge for his daughter's death.

"If you are untruthful," Umarov lifted the Berretta and pointed it between Chowdhury's legs and said, "I will place this handgun into your groin and blow your balls off. It will be a little noisy, but the pain, I assure you, is excruciating. There will be lots of blood too," he added almost as a matter of fact, "but you will not die. That done, I will shoot off both your hands so that you might never again feed or cleanse yourself."

He tilted the barrel of the Berretta upwards to his own face as he stared at it and added, "The ammunition I have loaded the weapon with is quite capable of this, should you have any doubt."

"I know nothing…" Chowdhury weakly said, his mouth dry and his tongue feeling as though it had expanded to twice its size.

He shrieked in terror as without warning, Umarov snarled and leapt from his armchair, lifting a cushion as he did so and shoving it against Chowdhury's groin with the weapon forced into the cushion.

Staring into the tall man's cold, impassive eyes, he realised he had wet himself and tears broke from him.

"Please," he begged, "I will tell you! Please!"

For almost ten seconds, Umarov did not move, his teeth gritted as though in disappointment, then taking a deep breath, slowly slumped back into the armchair.

"What was your part in the attack?"

"My part?" he slowly shook his head, sobbing now and broken; resigned to giving out all that he knew, everything if it stopped this tall man from hurting him.

"I was told to recruit four men, four brothers and supply them with the weapons that I was given. Train them and drive them to the hills in Wales to practise with the weapons and the explosives. I was to take them to Glasgow for the attack then bring them back south. When they were killed, I fled."

"Who was behind the attack?"

Chowdhury's eyes narrowed. "Who…?"

"Who were you working for?"

He stared at Umarov, his eyes narrowing and considered there might be a way out of this nightmare. "I do not know."

Umarov's eyes flashed, but Chowdhury raised a hand to stall any further threat and squirming backwards into the couch, added, "He said his name was John, but I do not know who he is other than he is a kafir."

"A kafir? Why were you working for a kafir?"

Chowdhury bit at his lip. "He knew things about me; was blackmailing me."

The blackmail did not interest Umarov; it was John who interested him.

"Tell me about the kafir?"

The elderly former Coldstream Guardsman employed as the doorman at the Kensington club hailed a black hackney cab for Mister Ashford, grateful for the nod of thanks that the gentleman gave him.

Nice man, Mister Ashford, he thought; always appreciative of his service.

Inside the privacy of the cab Ashford scrolled down his mobile phone directory till he found the number he wanted and typed a quick text message.

When the message was sent, he sat back, smiling when the whisky and the urge overtook him. Scrolling down the directory again, he selected a number that was answered almost immediately by his secretary.

"My dear, please attend in thirty minutes at my flat," he smiled, "and bring a change of clothing. I want you to arrive wearing something light and flimsy, something that can easily be ripped off."

With a satisfied sigh, he slumped back into the horsehair seat and then grinned widely.

Arriving home, Daisy Cooper checked her phone messages on the answer machine while Ian put the kettle on.

"Bloody hell," she murmured, glancing at the fifteen messages that awaited her attention. With a sigh she pressed the play button and listened as friends and family all wanted to let her know that they had watched the press conference, but the most interesting message was from Ian's lawyer, Louise Hall, who failing to get him on his mobile phone, requested that Daisy tell Ian to contact her at Hall's office the following morning.

In the kitchen she asked, "Did you give your lawyer my home phone number?"

"Yes, was that okay? My mobile was dead," he handed her a coffee and replied with a grin. "I'm pretty slack when it comes to charging it."

"No bother, but she left a message asking if you would contact her tomorrow morning at her office."

"Oh," his eyes narrowed, "I wonder what that's about?"

"So, this man you call John. You meet him when he texts messages to you?"

"Yes. He gave me a mobile phone with just his number on it. If I have any problems or need to contact him, I text a message to the only number on the phone. He has given me four locations and each location is known by a different number. When I attend any of the locations, I always take a varied route and I am instructed to beware of being followed."

Umarov recalled his FSB training and recognised that Chowdhury was talking about tradecraft. This man John was obviously some kind of spy, but why he wondered, would a kafir be interested in mounting a Jihadist attack in Glasgow?

He indicated with the Berretta that Chowdhury lift his mug from the tray and watched as the thirsty man slurped at the cooling tea suppressing a laugh when he noticed Chowdhury squirmed in his seat because of his wet trousers.

"Describe John to me."

Eager to please, Chowdhury shrugged and said, "Perhaps late forties, once dark hair now greying, always wears expensive tailored suits and always accompanied by two bodyguards who I am certain are armed. The last time I met with John at a restaurant he told me that even though I changed my route and took several different forms of transport, his men followed me, but it was not the bodyguards for they were already in the restaurant; it must have been other men," he reasoned.

Umarov's face wrinkled as he considered this information. If Chowdhury was to be believed, the man John seemed to have a great number of resources at his disposal.

His FSB surveillance training had taught him that when following a target through a major city, unlike the follows portrayed upon television, real surveillance required a great number of footmen and if the target used public transport, would include the deployment of a number of vehicles.

"What occurred when you met with John?"

"He provided me with information about the men I was to recruit. Also information about the weapons and the explosives and where to collect them; where to obtain vehicles," he shrugged. "The times, dates and where I was to take the recruits to train them in the use of the weapons and the explosives. He also gives me money so that I need not work. Always cash in an unmarked envelope."

His head bowed as shamefully he added, "I am his to use as he wishes."

It was then that the phone in Chowdhury's pocket activated with the arrival of a text message and hesitant about making any movement, he stared questioningly at Umarov who nodded.

Removing the phone from his pocket, Chowdhury's eyes widened and he said, "It's him."

"Read it to me,"

"It says; *midday at number three*."

"Where is number three?"

"Eh," Chowdhury screwed his eyes as he recalled, "number three is a small Chinese restaurant in Finchley Road in London."

"You have previously met with John at this location?"

"Twice," he nodded.

"Tell me about this location."

"It's just a small restaurant, nothing particularly fancy about it."

"How many doors is there?"

"Just the main door off the street. Oh, and a door in the back wall that leads into a small corridor where the toilet cubicle is and continues through I think, to the kitchen area."

"Where does John sit when you meet with him?"

"He is always first to arrive; always before me. He sits at the rear of the restaurant, usually next to the door I speak of, the door waiters use to bring out the food. The door at the rear wall," he added.

"The bodyguards; where do they sit?"

Chowdhury's eyes narrowed.

"You cannot get to him. He is too well protected."

"Where do the bodyguards sit?" he patiently asked again.

Chowdhury swallowed and replied, "Usually to my right when I go through the door. The table perhaps," he screwed his eyes tightly shut as he tried to recall, "second in from the front windows. They watch me all the time."

Umarov's eyes narrowed as a thought struck him. "Do you own a vehicle?"

"I have a car, a Qashqai. It is parked round the corner. I bought it with the money John gave me. He told me to get a car, a large vehicle to drive the brothers back and forth to Wales and for collecting the weapons…the brothers who were killed," he explained. "John instructed that I was not to register the car in my name, but I was to always obey the law and not come to the attention again," he hesitated and licking at his lips, continued, "not to come to the attention of the police. He said I was to stay below the police radar, not to bring attention to myself; you understand?"

"I understand," Umarov nodded, then thoughtfully asked, "Do you wish to live, brother, and be free of this kafir John?"

"Of course, brother," his eyes widened as a spark of hope raced through Chowdhury's body.

"Then you must do exactly as I tell you."

CHAPTER TWENTY-TWO

It was still dark outside when Barry Ashford awoke.

Lying on her side beside him, her face turned towards the bedroom door, the creamy white, naked body of his secretary quietly snored. He glanced up and saw the seamed nylon stockings he had used when tying her hands were still attached to the bedposts and the tattered remains of her torn clothing and undergarments lay about the floor.

Rising quietly from the bed, he made his way to the en-suite where he completed his toilet then shaved and showered. When fifteen minutes later he opened the bathroom door, he saw the bed was not only empty, but had been re-made and that the nylons were gone from the bedposts and the secretary's clothing removed from the floor.

He smiled when he heard the distant click of the front door closing, appreciative that the woman knew her place and decided when he was promoted to Director General, he would dispense with the DG's frosty-faced bitch and promote his secretary to be with him.

Glancing at the digital clock, he hurriedly dressed and in the kitchen, prepared a light breakfast.

While his eggs boiled, he used his mobile phone to contact Ernie the bodyguard and curtly instructed that Ernie and Taff accompany him to a midday meeting with their friend, Mister Chowdhury.

"Where? The Chinese restaurant in Finchley Road," he replied. "Please arrange for the surveillance team to pick Chowdhury before he boards the train at Ipswich railway station."

"Yes, sir, and the operational objective for the team leader?"

"Continue the cover brief. Inform the team leader Mister Chowdhury is of interest and drop the hint that we intend signing him on as our source in the Bond Street mosque. Once he has arrived at the venue, the team can stand down."

"With respect, sir, we've used the same team on a number of occasions now. I'm of the opinion that reason will no longer serve as an operational objective. I'm a little concerned they may be suspicious."

"Neither your suspicions nor theirs interest me," he abruptly replied, "and let us not forget, my dear fellow, this *will* be the last time we need officially meet with Chowdhury."

"Sir," Ernie acknowledged.

"One final thing. Chowdhury will require a tool to complete the mission I intend setting him. I suggest something small, but effective and most certainly, untraceable."

"Yes, sir," Ernie replied as Ashford concluded the call.

It was DI Paul Cowan who answered the early morning call from the Suffolk police officer.

Teeth gritted, he took note of what he was told and slamming the phone down, hurried into John Glennie's office.

"Morning, Boss," he greeted the older man who was in the act of hanging up his coat.

Turning, Glennie's eyes narrowed at the anger in Cowan's face. "What's up?"

"I've just had the Chief Inspector from the Suffolk office who provided the guys that were watching the Qashqai. He told me that because of a lack of resources he has stood down the surveillance and who the fuck did we think we were to demand his men participate in a Scottish operation!"

Bemused, Glennie stared and replied, "My understanding is that Mo McInnes requested the local CID assistance and that they agreed. We didn't *demand* anything."

"I was sitting across from her when she telephoned the request to the CID, Boss, and she couldn't have been more pleasant about it. Anyway," he shrugged, "the Chief Inspector pulled his men off first thing this morning when he heard about the surveillance. Said it should have been routed through him."

"Bloody politics," Glennie shook his head. "Right, have they completely abandoned the vehicle then?"

"No, as it happens. He said that as a *courtesy*," he almost spat the word out, "he will arrange to have the Qashqai put onto a low loader and examined by their Forensic people, but wants some paperwork sent down to confirm the job. If there is anything of value or any fingerprints seized, he said the Forensics will let us know, but," Cowan took a deep breath, "he also said that without the paperwork being there at this time, the job is not a priority."

"Oh, did he indeed," snorted Glennie. "Right, leave it with me, Paul, along with the Chief Inspectors name and his phone number."

Fajr prayers completed and now washed and shaved, Eldar Umarov carefully dressed in a black coloured polo shirt, dark cargo pants and laid the dark raincoat on the bed next to the shoulder holster and the Berretta. The remainder of his clothes he packed in the suit carrier. While he waited for the kettle to boil for coffee, he sat at the writing table and reflected on his visit to Rahib Chowdhury.

The man was an out and out, cowardly weasel and if his wife's face was anything to go by, an abuser too.

He had no doubt that to save himself, Chowdhury had spoken the truth and was as he had said, desperately keen to rid himself of the man who he knew as John.

His thoughts turned to the mysterious John.

He had already decided that John was a member of the intelligence community and if the resources he could command was an indication, likely a senior member. His access to weapons and explosives and the monies he provided to Chowdhury seemed to indicate the influence he was able to exert.

But to what intelligence department did he belong?

He was not police, of that Umarov was certain. Neither was he MI6, for to Umarov's certain knowledge that Department only operated abroad.

That left MI5, the British Security Service.

Yes, his eyes narrowed; John must be MI5 or at least some associated department.

But if he was correct, that opened up a myriad of questions.

Why would MI5 orchestrate and finance a Jihadist operation against one of their own cities? What possible motive would they have for killing their own citizens?

What reason would an attack in Glasgow…he stopped and took a deep breath, unconsciously drumming the fingers of his right hand on the table.

Glasgow was a Scottish city and throughout his years of solitude in his Grozny apartment, he had become an avid scholar of world politics and recalled that in recent years the Scottish people were seeking independence from the United Kingdom, or more correctly from British Government rule.

Might that be the reason, he wondered?

Is it possible that just as the nations of the former Soviet Union sought and on occasion fought for autonomy from Moscow rule, the British Government fear that the Scottish people might achieve the independence they also seek?

He remembered from his studies that in 1968, the Soviet Union led Warsaw Pact troops in an invasion of Czechoslovakia to crack down on reformist trends in Prague. The invasion successfully halted the Czechoslovakians ultimate goal of independence, but the invasion had unintended consequences for the unity of the communist bloc and led to later problems for the Soviet's such as the Polish Solidarity movement of the late 1980's.

The kettle clicked off and carefully pouring the boiling water into the mug and over the two sachets of coffee, idly stirring the liquid as his mind turned over.

Though he could not possibly envision a democratic country like the United Kingdom sending troops to subdue Scotland, he recalled his FSB training that taught undermining a country's will could be achieved by spontaneous acts of terror. Such acts would demonstrate that the country's leadership and police, incapable of dealing with the violence, would have little option but to seek assistance from a stronger nation, that nation being the Russian Federation; or if he is correct, in this case the British Government based in London.

But is the fear of Scottish independence enough reason to launch an attack on a Scottish city?

No, even he with his knowledge of the machinations of government agencies he could not believe the British Government capable of such a monstrous act.

However, just as in the FSB, he also knew there were always individuals who *were* capable of organising and carrying out such atrocities; individuals who must at the very least have the tacit agreement of those in power to carry out such operations.

Without evidence to the contrary and only his own assessment of the limited information he had to hand, Umarov theorised the attack by the Jihadists in Glasgow that killed his beloved Malika was conducted to either remind or persuade the people of Scotland into believing that without the support of the British Government, they were at risk of further attacks.

He now posed himself the question; was the man called John acting alone or under the orders of another?

He knew that was a question he would never find the answer to, that any accountability for such an atrocious act would terminate with John. No matter that he might suspect some senior figure or figures in John's intelligence background were probably aware or even might have authorised the attack, just as in the FSB, Umarov would never be able to trace who was ultimately responsible for giving the final orders.

There would be no written evidence, no documentation and he had neither the resources nor the will to abduct and question the man John.

Like it or not, his teeth gritted, the ancient custom of Adat must be settled with the death of the man called John who he intended would settle the account for Malika's murder.

Ian Macleod phoned his lawyer, Louise Hall's office and being put through to the young woman, thought she sounded breathless.

With a wink to Daisy seated in the armchair, he pressed the loudspeaker button.

"Are you all right, Miss Hall?"

"Fine, just running about like a headless chicken, Mister Macleod and thanks for returning my call. I couldn't get through on your mobile."

"No, I was out of battery," he replied then asked, "You need to speak with me?"

"Ah, yes. Bit of good news for you. Yesterday at the press conference, I handed out a few business cards to some of the reporters who expressed a wish to speak with you again. Well, yesterday afternoon, one of them got in touch and informed me his editor is keen to gain exclusive rights to your story with photographs and is willing to pay an excessive amount of money."

When she told him what the sum was, his eyes widened.

"Mister Macleod? You still there?"

"Eh, yes, I am. Sorry, I was a bit taken aback, Miss Hall. You mean they are willing to give me all that money just for an interview and taking some photographs?"

Open-mouthed, Daisy stared at him and began to vigorously nod.

He closed his eyes against the sudden throb in his forehead and taking a deep breath, replied, "Thanks, Miss Hall, but no thanks. I won't be giving any interviews."

There was a few seconds silence before she said, "May I inquire why?"

He paused before replying, "Miss Hall, innocent people died that day. Men and women who were going about their regular business.

A young lassie sitting in Buchanan Street, cold and hungry and begging for money. A pregnant woman on the bus looking forward to the birth of her child. No," he shook his head. "I won't accept any money for what I did. It would make me seem like some sort of…of…some sort of parasite, benefiting from their deaths. No, thank you for contacting me and I am grateful, believe me, but I couldn't take that kind of blood money."

"I see. Well, I *think* I understand and if there's anything else or if you change your mind, Mister Macleod…"

He smiled and replied, "I won't be changing my mind, Miss Hall, but I *will* be in touch with you regarding some conveyancing and hopefully in the very near future."

"Then I look forward to speaking with you again, Mister Macleod. Goodbye," she ended the call.

He turned to see Daisy staring at him, her face expressionless.

"You think I'm an idiot for refusing that kind of money, don't you," he gulped.

She stood up from the armchair and moved towards him.

She stared blankly at him for what seemed like an eternity, then slowly smiled and wrapped her arms about his neck.

"No, I don't think you're an idiot, Ian. I think you're my hero and definitely the man I want to be with. Right, now, how do we go about selling your flat and buying that shop?"

Rahib Chowdhury had experienced intestinal panic three times that morning, his bowels now drained and leaving him feeling weak. Rabia had offered to make him breakfast, but he rudely declined and such was his fear that he directed it as anger against her, taking pleasure from watching her flinch as he raised his hand and threatened to strike her.

Seated again in his toilet, he thought of the tall man, Eldar Umarov, whose instructions last night had been quite explicit.

He was to meet the man John as instructed, but not to drive his car to the railway station and he was to avoid his usual route.

"I believe your car is being watched," Umarov had shocked him, "but I am uncertain by whom. If as you say the car is not registered to you, I would suggest you do not approach the car or consider ever again going near it."

"Then how am I to get to London?" he had asked.

He was to depart the house earlier than planned, Umarov told him, adding he was to leave via the rear door and make his way through neighbour's gardens to exit onto the street some distance from his house. He was to travel to London by bus, then make his way by underground to Finchley and walk from the tube station to the rendeavous.

"Under no circumstances attempt to contact John before the meeting," Umarov warned him. "To do so will alert him that something is wrong. If you do try to contact him I will know," Umarov had bluffed, then surprised him by asking, "Are you aware of the ancient Chechen custom of Adat?"

He had nodded, his throat suddenly tight.

"Then you are aware that if you fail me, Rahib Chowdhury," Umarov had stared with grey eyes at him, "you know that I will kill you and kill your wife and anyone who is related to you. Do you understand?"

He did understand and had little doubt that the fear-provoking man spoke the truth.

Now, here he was dressed in his best business suit and ready to make the trip to London.

Gathering his thoughts, he prepared to leave the house and inwardly prayed that if Umarov was successful and kept his promise, then today he would finally be free of the man John.

Commencing early shift, Detective Constable Peter Brompton had experienced yet another sleepless night.

Parking his car in the rear of the police station, he glanced nervously about him before quickly making his way across the yard.

He still couldn't believe how stupid he was to land himself in this situation, but knew it was the excitement of being part of a Security Service operation and the vague promise that his actions would be brought to the attention of his Chief Constable.

What a fucking idiot he had been!

Reaching the rear door without incident, he breathed a sigh of relief and again wondered was he imagining that the man called John was intent on hurting him? Would John see him as a threat as he obviously did the Met DI?

If John did intend hurting or…he involuntarily shivered, killing him, then he had every right to protect himself.

Seated at his desk, he ignored his colleagues early morning banter and with a shaking hand, reached into the desk and retrieved the two sealed envelopes; one that contained his typed and signed confession, his admittance that acting upon the instruction of a member of the Security Service he had falsified a police report and destroyed evidence that permitted a paedophile called Rahib Chowdhury to escape justice.

That and a full description of John.

He glanced at the envelope upon which he had written; *In the event of my death, this envelope is to be delivered to the Crown Prosecution Service.*

The second envelope was not yet addressed, for who exactly was John?

He cursed himself that apart from a mobile telephone number, he had no other means of contacting John. All the previous day he had pondered how to get the letter to John and finally decided that a face to face meeting was the only way.

He would hand the envelope to John and firmly tell him that if anything untoward happened to him, a signed copy would be delivered to the CPS.

That would settle the bastard's hash, he confidently thought, but then grimaced. He still had the unsettling feeling that it was not enough, that John would somehow intercept or steal the copy.

His brow furrowed. Perhaps he should address the letter to the local newspaper, but sighed. He knew about D Notices and besides, no editor in his right mind would print such an accusation; not if he wished to continue in the media profession.

He lowered his face into his hands and thought of his wife and children.

Jesus, he squeezed his eyes tightly shut, what have I done?

He came to the decision that he had no option and accepting that his career was probably over, reached for his desk phone.

The eight man surveillance team plotted up in their designated locations about and inside the Ipswich railway station, already bored with the predictable target.

The team leader checked his watch. The operational brief said the target was meeting with the principal at midday in Finchley Road, a location they knew well and had already taken the target to twice before. He frowned. If the sod didn't hurry, he'd miss the train.

He tapped the button in his trouser pocket and called for a radio check.

Call sign by call sign, his team responded.

Checking his watch a few minutes later, he realised the target had less than three minutes to appear.

He tapped the button again and in a quiet voice, spoke into his jacket collar and asked his team, "Anyone got eyes on Tango One yet?"

Call sign by call sign, the team replied "Negative."

From his position near to the platform gate, he could see the train guard impatiently checking his watch, then raising a brightly coloured paddle to the driver at the front of the train, she stepped aboard and the train.

"Shit!" the team leader spat and closing his eyes in frustration, reluctantly reached into his pocket for his mobile phone.

Ernie the bodyguard kissed his wife goodbye and headed out the front gate of the modest mid-terraced house to join Taff in the two-year old, gleaming black coloured Jaguar XE the Welshman had drawn from the Service pool of vehicles.

"He wants picked up at the main entrance," Ernie said, belting himself into the front seat.

"Right," Taff drily replied, then asked, "What about the tool for the Paki?"

Ernie squirmed in his seat as he reached into his suit pocket and withdrew a small handgun.

"My mate at the Met's Firearms Department came across this during a raid on a drug dealer's house in Southall, last week." He held the handgun up for Taff to glance at, but discreetly below the level of the windscreen. "A Ruger SR22P. Small enough for an amateur to use, but does the damage at close range. Full mag of ten rounds. All that prick Ashford has to do is ensure he tells the Paki to be within five feet and go for a head shot."

"Serial number?"

"Chiselled off," Ernie replied then leaning forward to tap at the dashboard clock, added, "We'd better get a move on because you know…"

He was interrupted by his phone ringing and eyes narrowing when he glanced at the screen, muttered, "It's the surveillance."

"Hello?"

"Team leader. Your Tango didn't use the usual route. It's a loss."

"Fuck! Can you recover?"

"No way. We're dead in the water here. No wheels because we thought…"

"That the Paki was catching the fucking train! See what thought did, you wanker!" Ernie abruptly ended the call. Shaking his head, he said, "I'd better let him know," and dialled the mobile phone number for Barry Ashford.

When the call was answered, he said, "Sir. Surveillance has failed to pick up the target. Do you wish to go ahead or abort the meeting?"

"Failed? What do you mean failed?"

"The target did not travel by the usual route. Surveillance are dead in the water without transport. Respectfully, I recommend that you abandon the meeting. This change of routine…"

"No," Ashford snapped at him. "The meeting goes ahead. I can't afford Chowdhury to be active for much longer and besides, as we are both aware, my dear chap, we have plans for him. Pick me up and while I recognise you are being security conscious, I trust that you and the Welshman will be adequate cover."

"Sir," Ernie replied.

"So, it goes ahead?" Taff asked.

"It goes ahead," Ernie confirmed with a nod.

Chowdhury sat in the window seat in the middle of the bus on the driver's side, relieved that Eldar Umarov was not on the bus. His wary observation of his fellow passengers failed to detect any who appeared to have an undue interest in him and twenty minutes into the journey, he began to relax.

He thought about John's comment that his tradecraft needed work and that on the occasion they had last met, John's men had spotted him when he arrived at Liverpool Street station. Well, he inwardly grinned, if the bastards were there today they were going to be extremely disappointed.

He could no know that on each occasion he met with Ashford, he had in fact been followed on the train from Ipswich railway station to each venue.

He glanced down at his hands, surprised to see they were shaking and forced himself to make fists.

It was then he remembered; in the anxiety of worrying about the midday meeting and what he expected to occur and the constant running to the bathroom, he had forgotten this morning to pray. Bowing his head, he closed his eyes and mindful of those passengers sitting close by, began to softly praise Allah and beg forgiveness for all he had done.

After signing out of the Travelodge, he made his way to a local ASDA and purchased yet another phone, then after destroying the old phone sent a text message to his contact with the new number. En route to London, he readied himself for the confrontation that he knew was inevitable.

The new phones Satnav directed him to Finchley Road where he located the Chinese restaurant. His eyes narrowed when he saw that the bottom half of the restaurant front windows were glazed a light grey colour preventing anyone inside the premises seeing out and similarly preventing passers-by from staring at the diners within. He drove about the area for ten minutes and finally decided on an escape route if for any reason he was pursued by vehicles.

Passing the premises, he glanced again at the small Chinese restaurant that was situated in a row of shops with parking bays outside. He considered perhaps maybe he would park the BMW in one of the bays, but almost immediately excluded this idea for he was certain if the bodyguards were on the ball, they would be immediately suspicious of a man sitting alone in a car outside the restaurant and instead parked the car in Ridge Road, a distance of less than one hundred metres from the restaurant. He grinned for though no longer a young man, he thought if he was pursued on foot he would make the run to his car without too much trouble.

He needed somewhere to wait for the man John to arrive, but on the opposite side of the road from the Chinese restaurant there were mid terraced houses and no suitable shops.

With inner reluctance, he finally decided on the bus stop that was almost directly opposite the restaurant front door and glancing at his watch, saw the meeting was due to take place in just less than thirty minutes.

According to Chowdhury, John was always first in attendance at each of their meetings while Chowdhury made a point of always arriving within a minute or two of the meeting time.

From his description of John, Umarov thought the intelligence operative did not sound to be a man who liked to wait about and guessed John would likely arrive within ten minutes of the meet time to permit his bodyguards to secure the location or cancel if they believed there was anything amiss.

Gambling his assessment was correct, he decided to take up his position at the bus stop roughly fifteen minutes early and inwardly prayed to Allah, praise His name, that he would be neither too early nor too late.

He smiled and in the privacy of the BMW removed the Berretta from the shoulder holster under his coat and wondered at his calmness while he removed the magazine, checked it was full and with the magazine still removed, dry fired the handgun and heard the satisfying click.

Sliding the magazine into the pistol grip, he cocked the weapon and listened as the working parts smoothly inserted a round into the beech then returned the weapon to the shoulder holster.

He glanced again at his watch. Less than twenty-five minutes now. He started breathing exercises and cleared his mind of all thoughts bar his mission; for that's what it was.

He had no qualms, no second thoughts about what he intended.

He had no time to question the man John; no time to force answers from him.

This was to be a straight forward assassination, nothing more.

The custom of Adat had to be observed and the debt paid for the murder of his daughter Malika.

The four men responsible for slaying her had been accounted for by the Scottish man, the former soldier Ian Macleod and for that he would be eternally grateful.

However, the man who was responsible for recruiting and arming them for their task was now close at hand and the Adat would end with him.

Umarov fully accepted that he might himself be killed, that the bodyguards might exact their own revenge, but that was the nature of the beast.

Less than twenty minutes now and reaching into the rear seat, he lifted the newspaper and smiled as he recalled the words of his FSB surveillance instructor who all those years before, had taught the class they must never be without a newspaper, for it is the best cover for any static observation.

He locked the car and his coat unbuttoned, began to walk swiftly and purposefully towards the bus stop.

Seated in the rear seat of the Jaguar, Barry Ashford had his briefcase opened on his lap as he perused some papers then almost absent-mindedly called out to Ernie in the front passenger seat, "The weapon for Chowdhury. I trust you did procure one?"

"Sir," Ernie leaned over and butt first, handed him the Ruger SR22P. "Ten rounds in the mag, sir. Untraceable," he added.

"Nice," Ashford weighed the weapon in his hand then brow knitted, asked, "But why a two-two? Why not a nine mil?"

"I didn't think Chowdhury would have much experience with heavier handguns, sir, so thought something light and manageable might be preferable. If you will, when you give him the weapon you might suggest he gets in close and goes for a head shot, maybe tell him to fire three or four rounds. I've no doubt a two-two will do the business at close range."

"Right," Ashford sighed then almost absent-mindedly shoving the handgun into his suit jacket pocket, returned to his paperwork.

Two women, mother and daughter Umarov guessed, stood at the bus stop in earnest conversation when he arrived there and barely glanced at him. Positioning himself behind them, he leaned back against a garden wooden fence and opened his newspaper.

So far his observations had not spotted anyone hanging about who might be surveillance operatives, but glancing at the windows opposite, wondered if there might be a static watch on the Chinese restaurant. Almost immediately he dismissed the idea. Chowdhury mentioned a number of venues where he met with John. If the MI5 budget was anything like the FSB then it was unlikely they would own or hire properties to watch locations that were infrequently used.

He glanced up as a number eighty-two bus trundled along the road and to his disappointment, saw the older woman raise a hand to the driver. The bus pulled up with a hiss of brakes and both women got on.

When it pulled away he realised how exposed he was, but with no other vantage point available, he had little alternative than to use the bus stop.

DS Mo McInnes glanced round at the now depleted inquiry team. The officers about her were concluding their reports that would now find their way to the desk of DCI Lou Sheridan who would collate all the reports for a final submission to Detective Superintendent John Glennie.

Glennie in turn and acting upon instruction from the Crown Office, would submit his final report that would be the basis for the Crown Office to establish a Fatal Accident Inquiry. With no accused to stand trial, the FAI that would publicly and judicially hear the circumstances that occurred when the four gunmen initiated the slaughter in Glasgow city centre and in consequence of the evidence presented, attribute blame.

In this way the Crown Office hoped that the FAI's findings would help the bereaved families of the murdered victims find some closure, if not justice.

McInnes, suffering the effects of a toddler's bad dreams and thus a sleepless night, irritably rose from her desk to answer the phone on the empty desk opposite.

To her surprise it was the deputy manager of the Forensic department in Gartcosh who said, "DS McInnes? Mo, is that you?"

"Aye, Charlie, it's me. Well, some of me," she yawned. "That wee bugger had me up again last night and his lordship slept through the whole bloody wailing and greeting and everything."

"The joys of parenthood," she could almost hear him grin. "Right, did you guys have some sort of arrangement with the Suffolk cops, something about a vehicle being examined?"

Her ears perked up and she replied, "Yes. We had them watching a Nissan Qashqai, but I'm told they called the surveillance off. However, they low loaded the Qashqai back to their Forensics and told us they'd get in touch if there was anything of value in the vehicle."

"I don't know what you might be hoping to find from the vehicle," his voice grew a little excited, "but their mob lifted a number of prints that they Live Scanned to us here at Gartcosh. I'm pleased to say we matched the prints from the...a Qashqai you said?"

"Yes," she could almost feel her heart pounding.

"Anyway, there was a large number of prints they lifted from the inside of the Qashqai, but I'm pleased to report that one set of prints matched the single print that was lifted from the refuelling cap of the Skoda Octavia. Is that any use to your guys?"

"Yes," she slowly drawled, "for if nothing else it tells us that the driver of the Skoda and the guy using the Qashqai was part of the team. The fifth man. However, we don't have his prints on file, but it's a start. Thanks, Charlie, I'm off to tell the boss the good news."
"One thing before you go that I suppose is also good news for you guys, Mo. Of the other prints that were sent up, we matched four sets to the dead guys, the gunmen I mean."
"Oh, well that is good news, Charlie."
Well, partial good news, she thought as she replaced the phone and made her way to Glennie's office. If that bloody Chief Inspector hadn't pulled his guys off the surveillance, we might have made an arrest for the fifth man.

Taff turned the Jaguar onto Finchley Road and could almost feel Ernie beside him tense. He slowed the Jaguar to just under thirty miles an hour; not to comply with the speed limit but to permit both he and Ernie to study the area around the restaurant before he parked there. Passing by the restaurant on his right side, he spotted the empty bay directly outside the restaurant, but could see nothing else untoward while Ernie, monitoring the left side of the road, muttered, "Tall guy reading a paper at the bus stop. Seems okay."
Taff continued and at the busy junction, turned the car left into the slip road that led to Cricklewood Lane, a wide road with shops on either side.

Umarov had seen the black coloured Jaguar and head down as though reading the newspaper, covertly watched as the front seat passenger got a good look at him while the rear seat passenger, his head bent, seemed to be looking at something on his lap.

Taff found a safe place to do a U turn and driving back to the junction, waited at the red light till it changed to green before safely turning right into Finchley Road.

Umarov could feel his heart beating widely and from the peripheral of his eye, saw the Jaguar returning and slyly watched it park outside the restaurant.

He did not react to the vehicle stopping, conscious the driver was staring at him.

While Taff remained in the driver's seat to watch for any threat, Ernie sprang from the car onto the footway and made his way into the restaurant.

Pushing open the door, the surprised waiter stepped back, before grinning in greeting and gesturing towards a table.

Seeing the restaurant to be empty and apparently free from any threat, Ernie ignored the young man and quickly returned to the car where he snatched open the rear door to permit Ashford to step from the Jaguar.

Almost on top of him, he shepherded his boss to the door then when Ashford was safely inside, nodded at Taff and stood holding the door open while the Welshman locked the car and hurriedly joined him inside.

Across the road, Umarov glanced up at the approach of a number thirteen bus and tightly smiling at the female driver as she slowed the vehicle, waved it away before returning to read the newspaper. John had arrived.

Now all he had to do was wait for Chowdhury to get here.

Rahib Chowdhury exited the Finchley Central underground railway station and making his way outside, caught a taxi for the short trip to the restaurant in Finchley Road.

In the rear of the cab, his nerves were taught as he replayed in his mind the dozen scenarios he believed that could occur at the restaurant, all that ended with Eldar Umarov getting himself killed by John's bodyguards; scenarios that would mean he was forever under the control of John.

He glanced at his watch. It was about to be five minutes to midday as the taxi drew up outside the restaurant.

Paying off the Polish driver, he climbed from the cab and staring at the door, took a deep breath before pushing his way into the restaurant.

Across the road, Umarov folded his newspaper and placing it in the black, kerbside bin at the bus stop, glanced both ways for a break in the traffic before quickly making his way across the road.

The bodyguards, seated at the table to the right of the door, watched Chowdhury as he entered the restaurant, their eyes following him as he made his way to the table at the rear to join the man he knew as John who sat with his back to the rear wall.

"Mister Chowdhury," Ashford greeted him with a smile, "how are you, my dear fellow? Please," he indicated with his hand towards the chair opposite and then as Chowdhury sat down, turned to the waiter who hovered nearby and said, "A coffee for my friend."

At their table no more than twenty-five feet away, Ernie and Taff continued to watch Chowdhury, ever alert for any threatening move he might make and that was their undoing.

The door burst open to admit the tall man they had earlier seen standing at the bus stop across the road; the tall man they had without conversing both dismissed as of no threat to their principal. However, on this occasion the tall man was not holding a newspaper, but a black handgun that he held in both hands and was raising to point in their direction.

Simultaneously, their training kicked in and both men reached for the Glock pistols in the holsters under their jackets, each acutely aware they were a heartbeat too late as Eldar Umarov levelled the Berretta and fired.

His first shot caught Ernie full in the face, entering beneath his left eye and ricocheting off his cheekbone to travel upwards into his brain before exiting the back of his head. The shock of the bullet striking him forced his head backwards to strike the wall causing the blood splatter to create a magnificent pattern of crimson across the white wall.

Ernie's partner Taff fared no better that his partner, though he actually got his hand onto the butt of his handgun and was in the act of rising to his feet, but stared death in the face when Umarov's second bullet took him in the throat. Again, the force of the bullet slammed him back and he spun against the table as he collided with the falling Ernie. Though critically wounded and with his left hand held at his throat in a vain attempt to stem the flow of blood, he tried to draw breath through his shattered trachea while crawling under the table and was reaching for his weapon when Umarov fired again, this time the bullet striking Taff in the back of the head, instantly killing him and collapsing his body to lie awkwardly on the floor. With both bodyguards neutralised and no longer presenting a threat, Umarov advanced towards the two startled men seated at the table at the rear of the restaurant, the Berretta held out in front of him and saw the panicked young waiter prudently run for the kitchen door. Continuing to hold the Berretta in both hands, he stopped at the table and pointing the handgun at Ashford, said, "John, I presume." Swallowing with difficulty, Ashford forced a smile and his left hand on the table with the fingers splayed, stared into Umarov's eyes as he slowly reached for the Ruger in his jacket pocket.

"My dear chap," he forced a smile, "I don't believe it's too late to come to some sort of arrangement; perhaps even a short discussion as to who you are?"

His fingers felt the cold metal and slowly, very slowly, clasped the butt of the handgun.

"This is not a Hollywood film, John. We do not discuss anything," replied Umarov and calmly shot him in the forehead.

The bullet passed through Ashford's head and spun him from his chair to fall untidily upon the floor.

Rahib Chowdhury stared with horror at the fallen body and slowly turned his head to stare wide-eyed at Umarov.

"It is as you promised, brother. I am free of him. Now, you let me go, yes?"

Umarov sighed and his eyes narrowed and almost sorrowfully, he muttered in his native tongue, "Forgive me, Allah, for I am a sinner and I have lied," then shot Chowdhury between his eyes.

CHAPTER TWENTY-THREE

Waving a hand that she stand where she was, Mo McInnes remained in the office when her boss John Glennie called Suffolk CID on the number Paul Cowan had given him and spoke with the Chief Inspector.

"That's right, you fucking idiot!" Glennie thundered down the phone. "I don't give a shit who you want to complain to! Your bad decision has permitted a terrorist to remain free and by God I'll see to it that your Chief Constable is made aware of that decision!" he ended, slamming the phone down.

Red-faced, he turned to McInnes and said, "Pardon my bad language, Mo, but in this case I believe it was necessary."

"Apology accepted, sir," she grinned at him then added, "as for the fingerprints for the unknown man, I've requested that they be flagged up on the Live Scan system so if they turn up anywhere at all for any reason, we'll be contacted."

"Good work, Mo, and thanks," he replied and slumped down onto his chair.

Pulling through the entrance gates of Tulliallan Police Training College, Cathy Mulgrew wondered at the sudden instruction to report to the Chief Constable, Martin Cairney.

Making her way through the ornate entrance she was met by a uniformed Chief Inspector who conducted her through the building then opening the door to Cairney's inner office, closed it behind her.

"Good morning, sir," she greeted Cairney and eyes narrowing, added, "Ma'am," to the uniformed Assistant Commissioner who sat in one of the easy chairs beside him at the coffee table.

"Detective Chief Superintendent Mulgrew," Cairney rose to formally introduce her, "this is Assistant Commissioner Angela Redditch from the Met."

Shaking hands with the willow thin grey haired woman who stood to greet her, Mulgrew smiled when Redditch added, "Please, Angela, and it's Cathy, right?"

"Cathy, yes," she nodded.

"I wanted to wait till you arrived before hearing Angela's full report," Cairney told Mulgrew as he poured her a coffee then bid her and Redditch to sit.

Resuming her seat, Redditch began, "You are aware the Commissioner has certain reservations about the inquiry being conducted into DI Khalifa's murder and in consequence, instructed his own detective officer to make discreet inquiry inside the investigation. Well, the officer reported that a PNC investigation was conducted into all recent name checks made by officers and civilian personnel working within the CTU. You are also aware that to access the PNC it requires a logon name and individual password. That investigation disclosed that the name Rahib Chowdhury had been accessed by two individuals in the office; one was a Detective Constable Clare Ball who apparently legitimately carried out the inquiry on behalf of DI Khalifa. I am aware that this man Chowdhury is of interest to your terrorist attack, Cathy."

"Yes, he most certainly is," she agreed, then asked, "and the second check?"

"The second check was carried out by a civilian analyst called Jennifer Fielding who was *not* part of DI Khalifa's inquiry team. How Fielding came to know of Khalifa's interest in Chowdhury has not yet been determined."

"She hasn't been interviewed?" Cairney interrupted.

"No, Chief Constable, she has not and for the following reason. When it was discovered that Fielding had made what is now assessed to be an unauthorised PNC inquiry about Chowdhury, suspicion fell upon her for the murder of DI Khalifa. In pursuance of that suspicion, the Commissioner instructed the National Crime Squad, not our own people," she raised a hand to stress, "conduct surveillance upon Fielding. That same night she was seen to meet with a Chechen asylum seeker called Abdulbek Basayev who is known to Criminal Intelligence and the Drug Enforcement Agency as a member of a newly formed drug cartel operating in the Home Counties. From the nature of what the surveillance team recorded, it is assessed that Fielding is linked to this man and," she shrugged, "though whether romantically or otherwise that has not been determined, but it is assessed she is likely providing him with Intel."

"So, you intend arresting Fielding?"

"Ah, no," she grimaced, then added, "at least not yet. The Commissioner is of the opinion that leaving Fielding in situ might be more beneficial than arresting her for if we limit her access to operational matters, we can feed her what we need her to know and thus learn more about this cartel and how they operate. If the need arises, we can arrest Fielding and turn her to our advantage."

Mulgrew glanced quickly at Cairney and saw it in his eyes; it was exactly the thing he himself and she would do.

"But do you think that this man…"

"Abdulbek Basayev."

"Basayev was complicit in DI Khalifa's murder? "Cairney asked.

"No, sir, and there's the rub," replied Redditch. "In the short time that we've known of Fielding's association with Basayev, we've had technical surveillance on him…"

"You mean, you tapped his phone?" Mulgrew interjected.

"Yes, Cathy," she smiled, "but all we can discover from a retrospective billing check is that Basayev has on a number of occasions contacted what seem to be pay-as-you-go phones; no subscriber listed, but assessed to be the same individual who is changing his numbers on a frequent basis. In short, one contact with Basayev then a new number. What we *have* determined from the billing check is that Basayev sent a text of Rahib Chowdhury's details to one of the numbers and that was recorded after Fielding made the inquiry on the PNC."

"So," Cairney thoughtfully rubbed at his nose with a stubby forefinger, "Fielding somehow learned of Khalifa's interest in Chowdhury, informed this man Basayev who in turn sent the information to another individual via a text message?"

"Yes, sir," Redditch nodded.

"But you *don't* believe Basayev is involved in the DI's murder?"

"No, sir."

"What a bloody bag of worms," he shook his head, then turned as his intercom activated on the desk.

Rising from his chair, he said, "Yes?" to be informed by his secretary the Metropolitan Police Commissioner was on the line.

"Put him through, please," he turned to stare curiously at the two women.

"Good afternoon, Commissioner," Cairney greeted him.

"Martin," the Commissioner replied then asked, "Is Angela Redditch with you?"

"Yes, she's here with my Detective Chief Superintendent, Cathy Mulgrew; the head of my own CTU."

"Good. Can you put me on speaker, please?"

Puzzled, Cairney pressed the button and said, "Go ahead."

"Good afternoon, ladies. Martin, I am informed just ten minutes ago that a multiple shooting occurred within a restaurant in the Finchley area of the city. Information is somewhat scant, however, it seems from the identification the dead men carried that three of the four male victims who died are members of the Security Service. The fourth man, according to a bank card on his person, was identified as Rahib Chowdhury."

Stunned, Cairney glanced at the women who equally shocked, stared back.

"Do you have any names of the Security Service personnel involved?" asked Cairney.

There was a definite pause before the Commissioner replied, "It seems that one was Barry Ashford, who of course is known to us both and the other two were his bodyguards. I have no further information at this time, Martin, but I will no doubt be hearing from the Director General in the very near future."

When Cairney had hung up, he turned to Mulgrew and said, "Well, Cathy, what's your thoughts on that?"

Her mind racing, Mulgrew glanced at Cairney then turned to Redditch before responding, "Maybe I'm adding two and two and coming up with five, Angela, but it seems to me from the very little we know that whoever committed the murders might quite possibly be the man that Abdulbek Basayev has been contacting. What I'm suggesting is perhaps Rahib Chowdhury was the target."

But privately, she thought; perhaps not.

Arriving at the car park at Terminal Four, Eldar Umarov parked the BMW and fetching his suit carrier from the boot, glanced at the carpet to ensure it was neatly patted down. The shoulder holster, Berretta and spare magazines remained in the hollow beneath. Locking the car he quickly bent to replace the keys beneath the nearside rear wheel and then strode towards the Airport Terminal.

In the debating chamber of the Scottish Parliament in Edinburgh and while the leader of the opposition droned on at the Scottish Government's alleged failings in Social Housing, the First Minister of Scotland glanced at her wristwatch and frowned.
She was due later that evening to travel from Edinburgh Airport to London for a supper meeting with the Prime Minister, but had heard nothing from Detective Chief Superintendent Mulgrew. She considered having her secretary call the officer, but trusting her own judgement believed if Miss Mulgrew had any information she would contact the First Minister.
Raising her head she politely smiled in a vain attempt to appear interested in the opposition leader's monotone and mind-numbing rhetoric.

As the afternoon continued, John Glennie worked at his report to Crown Office while his team engaged themselves in completing their own paperwork.
The news of the murders in London of the Security Service personnel and the man called Rahib Chowdhury had sent shockwaves through the inquiry, but in reality made little difference to the outcome of Glennie's report.
Chowdhury had been a man of interest, but now that interest was terminated, for his murder was the business of a Metropolitan Police investigation and because of his apparent involvement with the Security Service, likely the investigation would be conducted under the Official Secrets Act.
Or so he thought.

His door was knocked and as he glanced up, DCI Lou Sheridan burst in with both DI Paul Cowan and DS Mo McInnes trailing behind her.

All three were grinning widely.

"Okay," he threw down his pen, "please tell me the office lottery has come up."

"Better than that, John," Sheridan slumped down into a chair opposite. "We've just had a call from the Met Scenes of Crime. The officer who made the check obviously informed us before the spooks got to know what he'd found…"

"Know what?" he interrupted.

"Well," she slowly teased him, drawing out the good news, "the Met guy who fingerprinted the deceased in the restaurant shooting identified Rahib Chowdhury…"

"But we know their names," Glennie interrupted.

"Ah, but Chowdhury's prints weren't previously on the Live Scan system, John. However, when the Met guy submitted the prints he took from Chowdhury's corpse they flashed up on the Live Scan screen that we were to be contacted. It seems that Chowdhury's prints match those from the Skoda fuel cap and the Qashqai down in Suffolk!"

"Bloody hell! So, he's the…"

"The fifth man, yes. Confirmed," replied a gleeful Sheridan.

He slowly shook his head and smiling, said, "Seems I'll need to start this bloody report again."

The Director General was in a high state of anxiety and when his door was knocked, screamed in a high pitched voice, 'Come!"

The balding, bespectacled, nervous man wearing the three piece ill-fitting suit who entered swallowed with difficulty.

"Well," the DG growled. "You were his fucking Deputy in Operations, Clive! What the hell happened!"

"Sir, you know what Barry was like. He told me what he believed I needed to know. At this time all I can tell you is he was apparently meeting with prospective source in the restaurant in Finchley when an unidentified man entered, killed both bodyguards then shot Barry and the man Barry was trying to recruit. According to the surveillance team leader I spoke with, Barry was trying to recruit this man as a source within an Ipswich Mosque."

He paused to lick at his suddenly dry lips.

"I've learned the Metropolitan Police obtained a statement from a waiter who simply says he saw a tall man wearing a dark coat enter the restaurant, shoot both bodyguards then the waiter fled into the rear kitchen to hide. He then heard two further shots, but did not see Barry or the prospective source being killed."

"And do we know who this *fucking* tall man is!"

"We…we don't yet know, sir."

"Do we know *anything* about him?"

"No, sir," Clive miserably shook his head.

"Christ, what a fucking disaster!" He pressed the button on his intercom and instructed, "Fetch me Barry Ashford's secretary. Now!"

He ignored Clive who stood there, uncertain whether to sit, leave or even speak.

A few minutes later, Ashford's stunning blonde secretary arrived and was shown into the DGF's office by the sullen faced older woman. Taken aback, the DG smiled at the fashionably dressed young woman, acutely aware of her attractiveness as she dabbed at her eyes with a lace handkerchief in an attempt to compose herself.

"Sit down, my dear, sit down," he indicated the chair in front of his desk. "Now, what can you tell me about Mister Ashford's engagements for today?"

She could tell him nothing that he did not already know and staring at her, wondered again about the rumours of Ashford's liaison with his secretary; rumours he had previously dismissed it as office gossip.

However, with a glance at his own secretary who stood behind the striking and much younger woman, it occurred to him that as Ashford had no further use for the blonde, he might perhaps permit himself a little of her professional time before he retired.

With a tight smile and a nod, he watched as the shapely woman left his office then clearing his throat, said to Clive, "Contact the

Metropolitan Commissioner and request that this investigation be carried out not by the local CID, but by their CTU. We *must* put a lid on this event as quickly as possible and inform our lawyers to prepare a D Notice for the media."

Relieved to be dismissed, Clive nodded and left.

Rubbing at his head, the DG's first thought was self-preservation and reaching for his phone, dialled the private and direct number for Downing Street.

Stood in the footway outside St Vincent House in Cutler Street, Detective Constable Peter Brompton stared morosely at the entrance to the building.

"Are you absolutely certain about this, Peter?" asked his lawyer.

"I've no other option, have I?" he quietly replied. "As long as that bastard John knows that I know he probably killed that Met woman detective, then he has me by the short and curlies and *my* life is at risk."

Then, oblivious to the murders that had occurred just a few hours previously in the restaurant in Finchley, Brompton accompanied his lawyer into the offices of the Crown Prosecution Service to bare his soul and inwardly prayed his confession might enable him to bargain his way out of a possible custodial sentence.

A little over two hours after her husband's murder, Rabia Chowdhury answered a loud knock at her door to find heavily armed, black uniformed Special Forces soldiers wearing balaclavas, Kevlar helmets and bulletproof vests and who burst into her home. Unaware of Rahib's death, the terrified woman was quickly hooded, her wrists restrained with plastic ties and removed from the house to a nearby van. Forty minutes later she arrived for questioning at a Security Service safe house where after a few hours of intensive interrogation, it was decided she knew nothing of her husband's activities or association with the Security Service.

What the weeping woman did admit was her knowledge of Rahib's fondness for child pornography and disclosed that though he had been unaware, she knew he kept evil magazines and photographs hidden in his desk drawer.

When the frightened Rabia related that the previous evening a tall man armed with a black handgun visited her husband, the interrogators became most interested, but other than relating the man was a slight accented English speaker and probably a Muslim, she knew nothing more and offered the vaguest of descriptions that was of little use.

With shaking hands, Rabia was required to sign an Official Secrets Act form and threatened with dire consequence if she dare inform anyone of what had happened to her.

Almost six hours after her abduction from her home and again hooded, though not on this occasion restrained, Rabia was returned to the van then forty minutes later released at her front door.

Her first act upon returning home was to breathe a sigh of relief and after a cup of hot tea, celebrate the fact that Rahib her molester was dead and would never again would abuse her.

Fully updated with the new information from John Glennie, Cathy Mulgrew arrived at Edinburgh Airport and met with the First Minister in a private lounge forty minutes before she was due to board her London flight.

The two women formerly shook hands and seated opposite each, Mulgrew said, "You must know, Ma'am, that what I am about to disclose is not on record and as I said previously, is conjecture on my part from the evidence that has been obtained to date."

"I understand, Miss Mulgrew. Please, continue."

"The attack in Glasgow was, in my opinion, orchestrated by a Security Service operative, in fact a senior figure in the Department called Barry Ashford. I suspect that Ashford employed a man called Rahib Chowdhury to act as a middleman, probably to recruit and train the four attackers who were provided with weapons and explosives by Ashford. However, he could not be seen to be involved and as far as the attackers were concerned, they believed they were Jihadists and unaware they were being manipulated by Ashford through their recruiter, Rahib Chowdhury."

She paused, then continued, "We now know from fingerprint evidence that Chowdhury was the fifth man; the man who was to facilitate the escape of the four attackers. Unfortunately for them, they encountered a determined former soldier…"

"Mister Macleod."

"Yes," Mulgrew nodded in agreement, "Ian Macleod who thwarted their attack else there might have been many, many more victims. Chowdhury himself escaped, but as you might be aware he was one of the four victims in the London shooting that is being broadcast on the media."

"Oh, the murders in the restaurant?"

"Yes, Ma'am. The victims also include the man I speak of, Barry Ashford."

"So, who do you think is responsible for their murders, Miss Mulgrew? Surely not the Security Service cleansing themselves of liability in this affair?"

"No," she shook her head. "There is another possibility that the murder of Chowdhury and possibly that of Ashford can be attributed to a revenge killing. You might recall that one of the Glasgow victim was a homeless woman who was later identified as an illegal Chechen immigrant, Malika Umarov?"

"Yes, I remember; the homeless woman who was shot in Buchanan Street."

"It transpires that Malika Umarov is the daughter of a former Chechen freedom fighter, currently wanted by the Russian Federation as a war criminal; a man called Eldar Umarov."

"And you think this man Umarov might be responsible for Chowdhury and Ashford's murders in revenge for what happened to his daughter?"

"Again it's speculation, Ma'am, but there is evidence that a source in the Metropolitan Police Counter Terrorism Unit provided a London based member of the Chechen Mafia with information about Chowdhury and we now know that man has been forwarding Chowdhury's address to another unnamed individual."

"And you believe the information provided to this unnamed

individual was this man Umarov or someone acting for him?"

"It's a strong possibility, yes, Ma'am."

"But what I do not understand is, how could Umarov have come to know of and suspect Chowdhury?"

"Probably because of our interest in him when the murdered woman, DI Khalifa made inquiry about him as an associate of one of the dead terrorists and *that's* why the source in the CTU informed the Chechen Mafia man."

"Who in turn informed Umarov," sighed the First Minister.

She stared quizzically at Mulgrew and asked, "And who do you surmise might have been responsible for that poor woman's murder, the Metropolitan police detective I mean?"

Mulgrew didn't immediately respond, but tactfully replied, "Perhaps some individual or some *organisation* that believed DI Khalifa was getting too close to Chowdhury and that individual or organisation feared DI Khalifa might in turn connect Chowdhury to..." she paused, but did not go on, permitting the First Minister to draw her own conclusion.

The First Minister slowly exhaled and shaking her head, said, "My God, what lengths some people will go to. Well, Miss Mulgrew, you've certainly given me a lot to think about, though I'm uncertain how I might use this in my meeting with the Prime Minister."

"Added to what I have just told you, Ma'am, you might wish to also consider that the weapons and explosives we recovered from the dead terrorists were once in the custody of the Security Service."

"But that's an assumption; you're not one hundred per cent certain of that, are you, Miss Mulgrew?"

Mulgrew smiled and replied, "But if the Prime Minister was aware of the plot, for that's what it is, then *she* will be certain, Ma'am."

The First Minister grinned and nodding, stood and offering her hand, said, "Thank you, Miss Mulgrew. That's *exactly* what I'm looking for. You have tied the Glasgow attack to a fifth man who we now know for certain was associated with a senior ranking member of the British Security Service. Besides that, the weapons and explosives used in the attack were once in the custody of the Security Service…or so the PM will be told. I have little doubt she will deny any knowledge of the whole ghastly affair, but it gives me enough leeway to broker a deal without having to publicly acknowledge both the extra funding and reopening of the defence bases in Scotland." She sighed and added, "Regretful though the attack was, it could mean hundreds of jobs at the bases and better funding for our police without my Government having to beg with cap in hand."

"Ma'am," Mulgrew acknowledged.

Seated in the business class section of the British Airways flight to Frankfurt, Eldar Umarov, travelling again as French national Fernand Marchand, politely declined the offer of champagne from the smiling young woman and instead ordered a black coffee. Staring out of the window into the evening sky, he silently offered a prayer for the repose of the soul of his beloved Malika and begged Allah, praise His name, to welcome her into Paradise.

Seven weeks after the sale of his flat, Ian Macleod stood proudly on the corner at Great George Street and Byres Road outside the newly decorated and refurbished café.

His arm about the shoulder of his new fiancée, he lifted his head to gaze at the bright red sign above that read, 'Daisy's Café.'

"Well," he grinned at her, "what do you think?"

"What I think," she slowly replied, "is that I'm due to return to duty in just over an hour, so you have time to whisk me up a bowl of soup and a baked potato, Mister Macleod."

"Yes, Constable Daisy," he gently placed his hand under her chin and reached down to kiss her.

****

Needless to say, this story is a work of fiction. As readers of my previous books may already know, I am an amateur writer and therefore accept that all grammar and punctuation errors are mine alone. I hope that any such errors do not detract from the story.

If you have enjoyed the story, you may wish to visit my website at: www.glasgowcrimefiction.co.uk

The author also welcomes feedback and can be contacted at: george.donald.books@hotmail.co.uk

Printed in Great Britain
by Amazon

26405992R00185